CHAMELEON PEOPLE

HANS OLAV LAHLUM is a Norwegian crime author, historian, chess player and politician. The books that make up his crime series featuring Detective Inspector Kolbjørn Kristiansen (known as K2) and his precocious young assistant, Patricia, are bestsellers in Norway. *The Human Flies* was the first and was followed by *Satellite People* and *The Catalyst Killing*. *Chameleon People* is the fourth book in the series.

Hans Olav Lahlum

CHAMELEON PEOPLE

Translated from the Norwegian by
Kari Dickson

PAN BOOKS

First published in the UK 2016 by Mantle

This paperback edition published 2017 by Pan Books
an imprint of Pan Macmillan
20 New Wharf Road, London N1 9RR
Associated companies throughout the world
www.panmacmillan.com

ISBN 978-1-5098-0950-9

Originally published in Norwegian in 2013 as *Kameleonmenneskene*
by Cappelen Damm, Oslo

This translation has been published with the financial support of NORLA.

1 3 5 7 9 8 6 4 2

A CIP catalogue record for this book is available from the British Library.

Printed and bound by CPI Group (UK) Ltd, Croydon, CR0 4YY

Visit www.panmacmillan.com to read more about all our books
and to buy them. You will also find features, author interviews and
news of any author events, and you can sign up for e-newsletters
so that you're always first to hear about our new releases.

Dedicated to Ross Macdonald,

the last of the great classic crime writers and the last of

my sources of literary inspiration for this series . . .

The Boy with the Red Bicycle

I

It was the year that the referendum on Norway's potential membership of the EEC nearly caused my parents to divorce after forty-two years of happily married life. On Saturday, 18 March 1972, the day's talking point was the demonstration that took place in the centre of Oslo, drawing several thousand protestors who were against membership of the EEC. As many as thirty extra policemen had been drafted in, in case of disturbances which, in the end, never happened. The demonstration broke up peacefully around eight o'clock in the evening.

As a detective inspector, I was exempt from demonstration duties, which was a particular relief now, as my private life had changed.

My fiancée, Miriam Filtvedt Bentsen, had agreed to come by for an early meal at around half past four. She arrived with sparkling eyes and flushed cheeks, having come straight from tobogganing with her much younger niece, and it has to be said, it was not easy to tell who had enjoyed it most. I had gently but firmly declined her cheerful invitation to join them. I found it embarrassing enough that someone I knew might meet the young, female master's student whizzing by on a sledge, let alone if she then had me, a detective inspector, in tow. Her childlike joy at the arrival of winter was a side of Miriam's complex nature that still perplexed me, although I did find it refreshing and charming.

As usual, we had a couple of very pleasant hours together. Of course, neither of us mentioned the fact that she was going to the evening's demonstration and that I could not go with her.

Instead we talked about the injuries to her arms and shoulders, which were, fortunately, getting better. She could now write for several hours at a time and was increasingly optimistic about her prospects for achieving a master's degree in Nordic Studies. She had done even better than expected in her bachelor's degree and very well with her first essay on the new course. She'd sounded even happier than usual when she rang to tell me earlier in the day. So the atmosphere was very jolly when we raised our glasses to her success, to each other and to our future together.

Afterwards, we talked a bit about the approaching football season and then Norway's hopes for gold at the Olympic Games in Munich in the summer. And finally, about our wedding plans. She thought that it would be practical to have it all sorted before the Christmas holidays. I suggested that it might be both good and practical if we could have an autumn break. So we drank to that, without specifying the dates or any other details.

At exactly half past six, Miriam got up and said with a little smile that unfortunately she had to go now. I said that I could not go with her this time either, adding an 'unfortunately'. Despite my father's protests, I had allied myself with my mother in the EEC debate. This was largely due to my fiancée. Miriam seemed to be relieved the day I told her, but nodded with understanding when I said I had to keep a low profile all the same, because of my position. We smiled fondly at each other, and kissed fleetingly by the door.

I stood alone by the window and watched my Miriam go. It struck me that her movements were softer and more relaxed now than when she first came to visit. As always, she walked at a fast and determined pace, reading a book at the same time, and did not look back. And in a strange way, this conveyed a certain trust. It felt as though I did not need to stand here, but I did so all the same just to see her for a few moments more. She didn't look back because she knew that I would be standing here, watching her for as long as I could.

On that particular day, I remained standing there for some time even after she had disappeared down the hill in front of the house. I knew that she would under no circumstances return before the demonstration was over. But I was equally certain that she would come back as agreed for Sunday lunch the following day.

From time to time, I was still woken by a nightmare that Miriam was once again lying in a coma at Ullevål Hospital and the senior doctor had told me that she would not live through the night. And sometimes, when awake, I shuddered at the thought of how close I had been to losing her.

Fortunately, both happened less and less frequently these days. Miriam herself was remarkably untouched. She would to a greater or lesser extent always be affected by the injuries to her shoulders, the doctor said. But Miriam's attitude was that she was far less bothered by them now, and it could have been so much worse. If she did ever shed a tear over her chronic injuries, I certainly never saw it.

In fact, my fiancée had an impressive ability to see the bigger picture and to think constructively, without allowing her life to be blighted by the accident in which she had so innocently and undeservedly been caught up. She also possessed a remarkable blend of clear-sighted realism and irrepressible optimism that never ceased to fascinate me.

Now, as I had on my thirty-seventh birthday three days earlier, I reflected on how immeasurably my life had improved since that great drama in the summer of 1970. I was an exceptionally lucky man. Thanks to Miriam, my private life felt more settled and yet more exciting than it had ever felt before. And at work, it had been a quiet year with only routine work. My status as hero in both the police force and with the general public, arising from several widely reported murder cases in the past four years, remained intact, and I had had no reason to defend it in the face of new challenges thus far in 1972.

In brief, life felt good and secure in every way, and I was almost without a care in the world.

As I turned away from the window at a quarter to seven, ready to sit down on the sofa with my book for the week and the day's news on the radio, I still had no idea as to just how eventful the evening would turn out to be. Nor did I know how swiftly and dramatically my life would change over the following seven days.

II

At eight o'clock, I put down Johan Borgen's novel, *The Red Mist*, and turned my attention to the news. The mass demonstration against EEC membership was, as expected, the first item. At ten past nine, however, the programme was interrupted by a news flash to say that the well-known Centre Party politician, landlord and businessman, Per Johan Fredriksen, had been stabbed on a street by Majorstuen station barely half an hour before. The presumed attacker had been seen running away from the scene of the crime and the victim's condition was as yet unknown. There was little else to be said at this point, but the newsreader promised there would be more information in later bulletins.

As I listened, I got up and wandered over to the living-room window, my eyes focusing on the only movement on the street below.

The movement turned into a red bicycle of the simplest and cheapest type, previously sold by the Coop. It was approaching at alarming speed, given that the bike looked rather rickety and the cyclist rather small. At first I thought it was a woman, but then realized that it was a thin, dark-haired boy of around fifteen. He was definitely neither strong nor big for his age, and he was clearly out of puff.

However, he hung doggedly on to the handlebars and pedalled furiously up the last part of the slope.

There were no teenagers living in the building that I knew of and I was sure that I had never seen the cyclist before. So I stayed where I was and watched him slow down and then lurch, rather than leap, from the bike only a few metres from the apartments. The bicycle lay abandoned in the middle of the path, as the cyclist ran on towards the door.

Even though my mind was not working at full capacity, I did notice that the young cyclist had a terrible limp in his right leg as he struggled with the final stretch, and that he was exhausted and disoriented. I wondered for a moment which of the residents this apparently desperate and rather dubious character might know, and was very thankful that it was not me.

Then the doorbell rang.

It echoed around the flat – then rang three more times with only a few seconds' interval in between.

I went to the door, but stopped and hesitated. The idea of pretending I was not there was very tempting indeed.

While I dithered, the bell rung for a fourth and fifth time. And the fifth ring sounded to my ear like a long cry of anguish.

Suddenly this brought to mind the very unpleasant incident on the Lijord Line two years before, when I had seen the carriage doors close in front of a terrified young woman, who was then found dead on the tracks later that evening. It was an awful experience that I did not wish to repeat, so I swiftly picked up the intercom and asked who it was.

'Let me in! They're after me! I have to talk to you before they get me!'

His voice was ragged, gasping and shrill with fear, but did not mask the fact that the boy had a speech impediment.

I hesitated again for a fraction of a second. Then I looked out of the window and saw the car.

It was a big car with no lights, and it sped up the hill through the dark in an almost aggressive manner towards the abandoned bike.

The sight of the car made me spontaneously press the door-opener, and over the intercom system I heard my unexpected guest tumbling in downstairs.

Seconds later, I had opened the door to my flat. The boy on the red bicycle was by then clattering up the stairs towards me. He tripped on the last step and ended up prostrate and panting on the landing. I as good as dragged him into the flat and slammed the door shut.

It never occurred to me that my uninvited visitor might be dangerous. The boy was empty-handed, thin, just over five foot, and on top of that, completely done in by his frantic flight. He lay on the floor by my doormat for a few seconds, gasping for breath.

'Who is after you?' I asked.

Just then there was another ring on the bell.

I looked down at him and hastily repeated my question. His answer was a shock.

'The police.'

I asked him if he knew that I was a policeman.

He gave a feeble nod and a sheepish smile.

There was yet another ring on the doorbell. It was longer and louder this time.

I kept my eyes trained on my young guest, as I picked up the intercom.

This time I recognized the familiar voice of a constable. He said that a suspect had disappeared into my building and asked if everything was under control inside.

I answered yes and once again pressed the door-opener.

My guest remained seated on the floor, but had now managed to catch his breath again.

'I had to speak to you before they caught me,' he said.

His voice was almost a whisper and was drowned out by heavy steps on the stairs.

'And what did you want to tell me?' I asked.

'That I'm innocent,' he whispered.

And then it was as if he had said all he wanted to say. He sat there quietly on the floor by the doormat, without another word.

I opened the door when they knocked and assured them that everything was under control. 'They' being three slightly puffed policemen, who briefly shook my hand.

I watched them put handcuffs around my guest's skinny wrists. He did not resist in any way, and suddenly seemed utterly disinterested in what was going on.

The young man had one striking physical feature: a reddish-brown birthmark that covered the greater part of the right-hand side of his neck. Of course, that could not help us identity him there and then. And there was nothing in the boy's pockets that could tell us who he was. In fact, we found very little of interest. But the one thing we did find was both damning and alarming.

The boy on the red bicycle had a sharp kitchen knife in the left pocket of his jacket and both the handle and the blade were sticky with blood.

I realized then that the situation was serious indeed, but still did not join up the dots until one of the policemen heaved a sigh of relief and remarked: 'You've truly outdone yourself this time, DI Kolbjørn Kristiansen. You have single-handedly caught Fredriksen's murderer without even leaving your flat!'

I spun round and asked the policeman if Per Johan Fredriksen had died. He looked at me gravely and replied that the politician had been declared dead at the scene. He had been stabbed straight through the heart. It was done efficiently and apparently with a good deal of hate.

Given this information, I looked at the boy on my floor with some scepticism. He did not avert his eyes or blink.

'I didn't kill him. He was dead when I went back,' was the only thing he said.

And he then repeated this three times.

After the third, one of the policemen commented laconically that they could categorically dismiss his statement that Fredriksen had been dead when he got there. Two witnesses who were passing had seen the young man standing at a street corner in Majorstuen as the politician walked by. The young man had been visibly agitated, whereas Fredriksen had calmly exchanged a few words with him, and then carried on.

A few minutes later, the young man had been seen bending over Fredriksen further down the same block, with the knife in his hand. He then fled when three further witnesses rounded the corner. It had taken them a few minutes to contact the police and alert any patrol cars in the area. However, one of them had then spotted the fleeing cyclist in the quieter roads around Hegdehaugen.

We all looked sharply at the young arrestee.

'I didn't kill him. He was already dead when I went back,' he said yet again in a staccato voice.

He fixed me with a remarkably steady and piercing look when he said this.

Then he closed his lips tight and turned his dark eyes to stare pointedly at the wall.

It occurred to me that I had never come across such a clear-cut murder case. And yet the adrenalin was pumping given the evening's unexpected and dramatic turn in my own home, and the case was not closed yet, as the murderer's identity and motive were unknown. It struck me as rather odd that the young man had known where I lived. And it was quite simply mystifying that he had chosen to flee here, having murdered a top politician. Consequently, I accompanied them in the car down to the main police station.

III

It did not take long to drive there. The arrestee sat squashed between myself and a constable in the back seat, small and silent. In contrast to the explosive energy and will he had demonstrated only half an hour earlier, he now seemed not only resigned, but as good as disinterested in everything. As we drove past his bicycle, he asked if someone would look after it, then gave a curt nod when I said that it would of course be taken down to the police station. After that, he said nothing more.

I sat and looked at our prisoner for the first part of the journey. The conspicuous birthmark on his neck was close to my shoulder and drew my attention again. I had a strong intuition that this birthmark would in some way be significant to the case, without having a clue of how, what or why.

Just as we stopped outside the police station, I turned to the arrestee and again asked why he had come to my door. A glimmer of interest sparked in his eyes.

'You were the only person in the world I hoped might believe me,' he stammered in a quiet voice.

Then he seemed to lose both his voice and interest again. He had nothing more to say about the case. All the questions he was asked later that evening remained unanswered, including any about his name. And he shook his head feebly when asked if he would like a lawyer or to contact his family.

The suspect's identity was not confirmed that first evening. It was perfectly clear that he came from a very different background from the multi-millionaire Per Johan Fredriksen. But where the mysterious boy actually came from was not established. He did not say a single word more and no one called in to say that their teenage son was missing.

Once the arrestee had been locked up in a cell, I stood for a couple of minutes and looked at the red Coop bike, marked 'Item of Evidence 2'. The bicycle, like its owner, was not a particularly impressive sight. Several spokes were broken, the seat was loose and the tyres were worn down. If I had a teenage son, I would certainly not let him out on the streets of Oslo on such a rickety old thing.

One could hardly expect a murderer to have ID with him. But my curiosity regarding the boy's name, background and motive was further piqued by the fact that he did not have so much as a penny in his pocket, or anything else other than a bloody kitchen knife.

I called my boss, and was immediately given the necessary authorization to continue investigating the case. He expressed his relief that the culprit had already been caught.

I wrote a press release to confirm that the politician Per Johan Fredriksen had been stabbed and killed on the street, and that the case was as good as solved now, following the arrest of a young man with a knife who had fled the scene of the crime. I chose to say 'as good as' as something felt awry, but for want of more information, I could not put my finger on what exactly it was.

At a quarter to eleven, I ventured back out into the night. I took with me the young suspect's puzzling statement that I was the only one in the world he hoped might believe him.

I was at home in my flat again by five past eleven. I got hold of Miriam, thanks to the newly installed telephone at the student halls of residence, and quickly updated her on my unexpected visitor. She was naturally very curious and asked about the boy on the bicycle, but did not know him either. For a moment it almost sounded as though she regretted going to the demonstration, as it meant that she had missed the evening's drama.

'That does not sound good for the poor young boy. And his explanation "when I went back" is linguistically rather odd, as well,' she remarked pensively.

It was by no means the first time I had heard Miriam comment on a linguistic detail. This time, however, I understood what she meant, and was immediately interested.

The young arrestee's use of the word 'back' meant that he had, in fact, left the spot after an earlier meeting with Fredriksen, only to then return and find the body. There was nothing at present to disprove that this was what had happened, and that he had then taken the knife with him in his confusion when he left the scene of the crime. If this was the case and Fredriksen had passed the young cyclist there and carried on, then it was odd that, only minutes later, he was lying in almost precisely the same place.

I wished Miriam a good night and put down the phone, then stood there deep in thought, my hand still on the receiver.

I had remembered by heart the number of the telephone on the desk of Patricia Louise I. E. Borchmann, my invaluable advisor. I seriously considered ringing to tell her about what had happened, but then decided that it was a little too late in the evening and the case was more or less concluded.

But underlying this was also the fear of how she might react if I called. At the end of our third murder investigation together in the summer of 1970, the drama of Miriam's near-death experience had coincided most unfortunately with the death of Patricia's father. She had only helped me by phone during my fourth murder investigation, and we had met a few times in the course of my fifth and sixth investigations over Christmas 1971. As I understood it, Patricia had then hoped to hear very different news about my relationship with Miriam, and certainly not the announcement of our engagement on New Year's Eve. I had not spoken to Patricia since then.

The uncertainty as to where Patricia and I now stood had hung over my otherwise charmed existence like a dark cloud. But a situation had not yet arisen that made it necessary to find out – I had had no good reason to contact her again.

However, now that a good reason had, quite literally, come knocking at my door, I chose to delay the matter. I still felt not only deeply uncertain, but also alarmed at the thought of what Patricia's reaction might be. I could not imagine that she would in any way wish to be more public about anything. But it had struck me more than once that the consequences for my career would be catastrophic, should anything unintentionally provoke Patricia to say just how much I had told her about my murder cases, and the extent to which she was responsible for solving them.

I would have ample opportunity over the course of the next eight days to regret the fact that I had not immediately phoned Patricia following the events of Saturday, 18 March 1972. But I was as yet unaware of this. I fell asleep around midnight, having pondered some more on the boy with the red bicycle and his almost manic wish to talk to me, and somewhat odd use of the word 'back'.

DAY TWO

A Puzzling Suspect – and an Old Mystery

I

It was ten past nine on Sunday, 19 March 1972. Following an early breakfast, I was now sitting in an interview room at the main police station, opposite the young lad we all presumed was the murderer.

I asked for a third time if he wanted a lawyer or to talk to someone from social services.

Again, he dismissed my question with a flap of his thin hand, which otherwise remained flat on the table between us.

The first two times I asked what he was called, he just gave me a condescending look and did not answer. The third time he replied with a heavy lisp: 'You'll find out soon enough.'

We still had no idea who the mysterious boy was. He had nothing with him to give any indication of his identity. No parents, or anyone else, had called to enquire after him. His fingerprints had not been recognized in any records.

It was clear that the boy on the red bicycle heard my questions and could make himself understood, despite his speech impediment. His attitude to me seemed to be positive. And yet he just sat there and stared at me, his face completely blank. And he continued to do this when I asked, yet again, where he lived and what his parents' names were.

I went a step further and asked: 'You said yesterday that he was dead when you came back. Does that mean that you spoke to him, then went away, only to return and find him dying with a knife in his chest?'

The boy nodded. There was a faint glow in his eyes.

'In which case, why did you take the knife with you? And why did you then come to me?' I asked.

The glow in his eyes went out. He looked at me with a resigned, almost patronizing expression. There was something reprimanding in his look, but I could not understand why. I started to wonder whether I was dealing with an imbecile, or if this was an intelligent person who, for some unknown reason, did not want to say anything.

I told him that if he was innocent, being so uncooperative and unforthcoming was not making it any easier for us to help him.

'You'll work it out anyway,' was his curt reply.

Then he demonstratively averted his gaze and looked out of the barred window. He nodded almost imperceptibly when I told him that he would be taken back to his cell now, but that he should reckon on more questioning in the course of the day. He did not even flinch when I said that his situation was very serious indeed, and that it would be in his own interest to be more cooperative next time we met.

II

As promised, I went to my boss's office when I had finished questioning him. I was mildly irritated to discover that Detective Inspector Vegard Danielsen was also there. I greeted him curtly, then sat down and turned towards my boss and reported on the case.

My boss listened attentively.

'A most remarkable tale indeed. We can take it as a positive thing that you are now so well known that he came to you to give himself up.'

My boss gave me a bright smile and shook my hand in congratulations. I glanced over at Danielsen, who was fidgeting restlessly. He spoke as soon as he had the chance.

'The pressing question here, somewhat originally, seems to be the identity of the murderer, rather than who committed the crime. Though I am sure the mystery will be solved as soon as someone calls to report him missing. It would, however, be preferable if we could have it cleared up before tomorrow's papers. If you like, I could try questioning him to see if I have any more luck than you.'

I certainly did not want Danielsen to get involved in any way, but I found it hard to think of an argument to counter his suggestion. However, I had little belief that it would lead to anything.

So I gave a brief nod and a forced smile, then looked at my boss with raised eyebrows.

He seemed to have read my mind.

'Let's not worry too much about the newspapers, especially as the culprit has to all intents and purposes already been arrested. But we still do not know his identity or his motive. If you, Danielsen, try questioning the suspect again, and you, Kristiansen, go to talk to the victim's family and take a photograph of the young man with you, then, hopefully, we can start to unpick both matters.'

It was a compromise that both Danielsen and I could live with. Rather unusually, we nodded in agreement, then stood up and left the office without exchanging a word.

III

The address given for Per Johan Fredriksen in the National Registry was in Bygdøy. He was sixty-five years old when he died, and he had been married since 1933 to Oda Fredriksen, who was two years his junior. It said in the registry that they had three children: Johan, who was thirty-five, Ane Line, who was thirty, and Vera, who was twenty-six. Vera was recorded as still living in Bygdøy, whereas Ane Line had moved to Høvik, and Johan to Sognsvann.

I made a note that the youngest child resided at home and that the two eldest lived alone. Then I picked up the phone and dialled the number given for the address in Bygdøy.

The call was answered on the third ring by a woman

who said: 'Per Johan Fredriksen and family.' Then there was silence. And then a quiet sob on the other end.

I introduced myself and gave my condolences. Then I explained that the suspected killer had been arrested, but that the police still needed to talk briefly to the deceased's closest family.

The voice on the other end of the receiver was hushed and tearful, but clear all the same. The woman said that she was Per Johan Fredriksen's wife, Oda. Unfortunately, she had not been able to contact her eldest daughter by telephone yet, but was currently at home with her two other children. They would, of course, help the police as much as they could with regard to the investigation, but nothing would bring her husband back. It might be best if I could come to see them straightaway, she said.

I promised to come immediately and make my visit as brief as possible. She thanked me rather vaguely and then we both put down the phone.

On the way out, I checked whether there was any news on the arrestee's identity. But there were still no answers. I took a few photographs of him with me, as well as a growing concern about the lack of developments.

IV

I knew that Per Johan Fredriksen had been a successful businessman and was reputed to be one of the richest politicians in the Storting. But I still had not expected his home to be anything like the property in Bygdøy.

The given address turned out to be a big farm, though I neither saw nor heard any animals. With the exception of two very modern cars parked just inside the gates, the big lush garden and main house, with surrounding outhouses, were not dissimilar to a painting by Tidemand and Gude in the nineteenth century. The driveway from the gates to the main house was more than fifty yards and felt even longer. As I walked up to the door, I wondered what on earth the connection between the boy on the rickety red bicycle and the lord of this manor could be.

The door was opened by a blond man of around my age and height. His handshake was firm. He was to the point: 'I am Johan Fredriksen. And my mother and youngest sister are waiting in the drawing room.'

I searched his face for signs of emotion at his father's death, but found none. My first impression of Johan Fredriksen was that he was a sensible and controlled man. We walked in silence down the unusually long hall and up the unusually wide stairs to the first floor.

The room that we entered was very definitely a drawing room. I quickly counted seven tables dotted around it and reckoned that it could easily hold about a hundred guests. But today there were only four of us here, and none of us were in a party mood. The gravity of the situation was underlined by the fact that we sat under a large portrait of the now late Per Johan Fredriksen. The painting was signed by a well-known artist and was a very good, full-size portrait. Per Johan Fredriksen had been a broad-shouldered, slightly portly, tall man, who now towered majestically above us on the wall.

Oda Fredriksen was a straight-backed woman who carried her sixty-three years with dignity. She got up from the velvet sofa and briefly shook my hand. I could feel her shaking as she did so and she quickly sank back down into the sofa. My first impression was of a very composed and fairly robust person, who was visibly shaken all the same. I found nothing surprising about that, given that she had lost her husband of many years very suddenly and brutally the day before. I then held out my hand to the third person in the room. Instantly, I got the impression that she was even more affected by the death.

Vera Fredriksen was very different from her mother. She was about a head shorter and had an almost graceful lightness to her movement. If she had been wearing a nineteenth-century ball gown, I might have mistaken her for a fairy-tale princess, given the surroundings, and described her as very beautiful. As it was, she was wearing a rather plain green dress, her face was white as chalk, her hands were shaking and she was chewing mechanically on some gum. She appeared to be more of a neurotic than a princess. And she seemed to get even more nervous when I looked at her for more than a few seconds.

I swiftly turned my attention to her brother. In contrast to his family he was, apparently, unaffected by his father's death.

'So, here we all are, at your disposal. As I am sure you understand, we are still somewhat shaken by my father's passing,' Johan Fredriksen said.

The effect was almost comical, as he said this in a steady voice and neither his face nor his body language showed any sign of upset. But his mother's expression helped me to remain serious, so I focused on the widow when I spoke.

I once again expressed my condolences and told them, without mentioning the episode in my flat, that the suspected murderer had been arrested with a bloody knife in his pocket as he fled the scene of the crime. We believed that the suspect was a minor, but had so far been unable to establish his age or identity. Any motive for the killing was therefore also unclear. It was thus very important for us to find out if there was any kind of connection between the family and the arrestee.

I handed the police photographs to Oda Fredriksen. She studied the pictures, but then shook her head and handed them on to her son.

Johan Fredriksen looked at the picture with the same blank expression and said: 'Completely unknown to me too,' then handed them across the table to his sister.

The young Vera's hands were shaking so much that she dropped two of the photographs on the floor. She picked them up, then shook her head firmly. 'Never seen him before,' she said, and handed them back to me across the table.

We sat in silence for a few seconds. It was Fredriksen's widow who spoke first.

'As you have gathered, the young man in the photograph is completely unknown to us. I can guarantee that he has never been here. However, you should know that my husband led a very busy life, and we only knew a fraction of the people he met. The fact that we don't know the young man does not mean that he did not know my husband in some way or other. For us, Per Johan was always a good and kind family man. He wanted to spare us all his work-related worries. The boy could be a tenant in one of his properties for all we know, or an aspiring politician from one of the youth organizations. Though he does look rather young. Could he simply be disturbed, or perhaps it was a case of a robbery gone wrong?'

I told them the truth. It was unlikely to have been a robbery, as Per Johan Fredriksen's wallet, complete with notes and coins, had been found in his pocket. However, the culprit had provided very little information, so the possibility that he was a disturbed individual could not be ruled out. And the option that the murder had been carried out in sheer desperation could not be ruled out either.

Once again, there was silence in the big room. It felt as though we were all thinking the same thing: that it was highly unlikely that Per Johan Fredriksen had been the victim of a random killing, no matter how disturbed the murderer might be.

I said that as a matter of procedure, I had to ask about the contents of the deceased's will.

His widow replied that she had last seen it only a few months ago and that there was no possible explanation there. The will was simple and straightforward: she herself would receive two million kroner and the right to stay in the house for the rest of her life, and the rest of his wealth would be divided equally between the three children. There were no small allowances for anyone else that might give them a motive for murder.

In response to my question regarding the value of the

will, the widow said in short that in the course of her nearly thirty-nine years of marriage she had never discussed the business with her husband and that she had no idea of the current or earlier value of anything.

She looked at her son as she spoke. So I then turned to him as well.

'I'm afraid I don't know the details of my father's business operations either, but we did talk about it earlier this year. He estimated then that the total value of his assets, property and companies was somewhere between fifty and sixty million kroner,' he said, in the same steady voice. He might have talked about a fifty- or sixty-kroner Christmas present in much the same way.

It seemed that this information came as a surprise to the other two.

'I thought it was a lot, but I had no idea that it was that much,' his mother said. Her daughter nodded quickly and chewed even more frantically on her gum.

I noted first of all that the deceased's family seemed to keep secrets from each other, about things that other people might deem to be important. And, secondly, that the unexpected death would in no way benefit the presumed suspect, but the deceased's children each stood to gain at least 15 million kroner. This was a large enough figure to give them all a motive – but, as yet, I could not see anything connecting them to the murder.

I said to Johan Fredriksen that I presumed it was he who now had the job of documenting all the assets and dividing them.

'Yes, I will start on it first thing tomorrow morning, with the help of my father's accountant and office manager.'

I asked him to inform me immediately if anything cropped up that might be relevant to his father's death.

He replied: 'Of course.'

His mother asked me to contact her as soon as there was any news regarding the young man's identity and motive.

I replied: 'Of course.'

Then we sat in silence again. This four-way conversation felt rather fruitless. I thought that I would far rather speak to them one by one, but did not want to suggest that right now and had not prepared any questions. So I went no further than asking the children what they did.

The son's reply was succinct: 'I am a qualified lawyer and work as an associate in a law firm.'

The daughter's reply was even shorter: 'I've studied a bit of chemistry and a bit of history of art.'

This was a most unusual combination, but I saw no reason to pursue it now. So I had one final question, which was why Per Johan Fredriksen, who had his home in Bygdøy and his office in the Storting, had been at Majorstuen the night before?

I did not expect the question to cause any tension or drama. After all, as a politician and businessman, Per Johan Fredriksen might have been in the area for any number of reasons.

However, my query was met with absolute silence. Vera Fredriksen looked even paler and chewed even more frenetically and her mother sank even deeper into the cushions and sofa. It was certainly not my intention to upset any of them. So I turned to the still unruffled Johan Fredriksen.

'Strictly speaking, we are not sure why my father was at Majorstuen yesterday evening,' he said, in the same voice, but with more deliberation.

'But you have an idea?' I guessed.

Johan Fredriksen did not answer. He looked questioningly at his mother. I turned to her too. As, I saw out of the corner of my eye, did Vera Fredriksen.

The widow gave in to the pressure of our combined attention. She let out a quiet sigh, and sank a little more into the sofa, then said: 'No, we don't know. But she lives there, so it's reasonable to assume that he was either on his way to or from his mistress.'

These hushed words blasted into the otherwise still room like cannon fire. The picture that had been painted of Per Johan Fredriksen as a kind family man exploded in front of my eyes, though his smile in the portrait on the wall was just as friendly and reassuring. His wife's mask fell at the same time.

'You mustn't think badly of my husband. We all have our weaknesses. And his only weakness that we knew of was this, his physical attraction to younger women and consequent breaches of the wedding vow. He had so many other good qualities that we forgave him this.'

The son and daughter both nodded. Suddenly the family appeared to be united.

I found the situation vaguely uncomfortable, but also increasingly interesting. And I heard myself ask whether that meant he had had several mistresses.

Oda Fredriksen sighed, but she sat up when she answered. 'My greatest failure as a wife is that I did not keep my looks well enough to stop him from falling into the arms of younger women. But my greatest triumph is that he always came back to me, and remained my husband until death parted us. Yes, he did have more than one mistress. But for the past few years, there has only been the one in Majorstuen – as far as we know. Surely there is no reason to believe it has anything to do with my husband's murder, and I hope that as I am grieving, I will not need to spend a lot of time and energy thinking over this. Most of all, I hope that the papers will not get wind of it.'

The latter was said in a choked voice.

I realized that the topic was very difficult for Mrs Fredriksen on a day like today and I did not want to bother her with any more questions. However, I was increasingly intrigued by the clearly complex man in the painting above me and was not as certain that his mistress had nothing to do with the case. There could well be a link, for example, if his mistress happened to have a teenage son with a speech impediment.

So I said I would leave them in peace to mourn and that there was no reason why this aspect of the deceased's private life need reach the press. I was, however, obliged to ask for the mistress's name so that I could rule her out of the case.

'I have chosen not to know her name or anything else about her. But it is quite possible that my children can help you there,' the widow replied with another sigh.

I looked questioningly at her son. He took a visiting card

from his wallet and wrote down a name and address on the back of it.

'I have never been there or seen the woman. My father wanted me to know who she was in case anything unexpected should happen,' he explained curtly, and handed me the card.

I took it and read: Harriet Henriksen, 53B Jacob Aall's Street. The name was completely unknown, but the street was familiar to me and was undeniably in Majorstuen.

I found it interesting that not only did Per Johan Fredriksen have a mistress, but he also had had reason to think that the unexpected might happen. So, having said goodbye to his family and walked back down the long drive, I drove directly to his last known mistress.

V

In sharp contrast to Per Johan Fredriksen's green and pleasant home in Bygdøy, 53B Jacob Aall's Street was a grey, tired building in Majorstuen. I quickly found H. Henriksen on the list of inhabitants and rang the bell three times without getting any response. But then, as I turned to leave, the intercom crackled to life. 'Who's there?' asked a quiet, tense woman's voice.

I found the situation awkward, but had a murder investigation to follow up. So I looked around quickly, then whispered that I was from the police and that I had some routine questions to ask her in connection with a death.

There was a few moments' silence. Then the voice said:

'Please come up.' She did not sound entirely convincing, but I could understand that she might not be in the best frame of mind today and that the last thing she wanted was a visit from the police.

There was another little surprise waiting for me when the door to the flat on the second floor opened. I had obviously underestimated Per Johan Fredriksen and had assumed that his current mistress would be at least forty-five. But I was wrong. It was not easy to guess Harriet Henriksen's age, but I would not have protested if someone said that she was thirty. Her movements were soft as a cat and there was not a wrinkle on her smooth face, which gave her an almost doll-like appearance.

We shook hands briefly in the doorway. Her hand was small, but it was supple and firm. And from what I could see, given her plain black dress, the rest of her body was much the same. When I looked more closely, I could see red blotchy patches under her eyes. I caught myself thinking that Per Johan Fredriksen had either been very charming or very lucky to find himself such an attractive young lover at his age.

Harriet Henriksen put the security chain back on the door behind us and showed me into the living room. I could see that she lived in a simple and tidy flat that was modern and equipped with a TV and washing machine. There was no sign of anyone else living there.

On the other hand, there was plenty of evidence that Per Johan Fredriksen was there rather a lot. A large photograph of him hung alone on the hallway wall, and another photograph of the two of them was up in the living room. Seeing him again was unsettling, especially as these were the only photographs adorning the walls. One wall was hidden by an upright piano and the others were covered by bookshelves, landscape paintings and a couple of tapestries. The door to the bedroom was open and through it I could see a double bed made up for two. The most striking thing that caught my attention in the living room, however, was a large, framed photograph of the two of them, which was standing on the table beside an almost burnt-down candle. Per Johan Fredriksen had his arm lovingly around her shoulder. They were both smiling at the camera.

'That was in Paris,' she said suddenly. As if that explained everything. 'We could never show our love publicly here in Oslo. He was too well known. But we had two days together in Paris last summer and there we could walk around and be lovers without any worries. They were two of the happiest days of my life. And now they are all I have to live off for the rest of my days.'

She had not asked me to sit down, but I had done so all the same. We were sitting on either side of the coffee table, with the photograph and candle between us. And we looked straight at each other. She had the darkest brown eyes I had ever seen.

'I first heard about it on the news last night,' she said, without prompting.

Just as I had. I could suddenly picture it. He had been here, kissed her goodbye and left. She had, perhaps, like me, stood by the window and watched her beloved go. Then she had sat down alone and switched on the radio to listen to the news, only to collapse suddenly when she heard the announcement that he had been stabbed. I was oddly convinced that that was how it had been.

'So, he was here with you yesterday?' I asked, to the point.

She nodded. She looked away for a moment, out of the window. Her eyes almost accusing the world.

'Per was a very complex man and often appeared different in different settings. Politically, he was more conservative than me. I still thought that he was credible on TV and in debates, if somewhat boring and reserved, but he was completely different when he was here with me: open, humorous and even passionate. We could talk about anything, even that. And he always said that I was the only one who could see him for what he really was, the only person he could really be himself with. He said I brought out the best in him in a way that no one else could. He often came here on Saturday afternoons, between work and the family. And yesterday, he once again left the world behind and sought refuge with me for a few happy hours. We had both been looking forward to it all week. And as usual we experienced complete happiness and joy. I asked if he could stay a bit longer. And he said that he had to go back to his office at the Storting to check some important news about something he was working on before going home to his family. I accepted it, as I always did. I watched him walk away down the street and I was alone when the news that he had been stabbed was announced on the radio. It felt like the ground opened beneath my feet. In a split second, I fell into a cold, dark cellar I didn't even know existed. I, who have never believed in a God before, was prostrate and prayed that Per

Johan would survive, until it was then announced on the late-night news that he had died. I have been here alone at my table weeping ever since, not even so much as a phone call, until you rang at the door.'

As soon as she started to speak, the words just came tumbling out. There was a strange, almost compelling intimacy and intensity about this woman and her voice, which made me inclined to believe every word she said. I felt no physical attraction to her, but, all the same, I could well understand why Per Johan Fredriksen had.

I was still not entirely convinced that she had no connection to the murder. So I asked Harriet Henriksen if she had any children.

She shook her head vaguely and I noticed the light catch a tear in her left eye.

'No, no. I don't have any children and I guess I never will now. In fact, I don't have any family at all. I never had brothers or sisters, and my parents are no longer alive. I only had Per Johan, and we never had the children I hoped we might. That was my fault. Last night I went over it a thousand times. If I had just done as he suggested, I would still have a part of him. But now I'm thirty-seven and completely on my own with nothing to live for.'

She stood up abruptly, wringing her hands. Then she took two turns around the table before sitting down opposite me again.

'So, what you are saying is that he was willing to have children with you, but you said no?'

'Yes and no. The biggest question of all was the only thing we disagreed on. I wanted to have children and to

32

marry him. He was willing to give me a child and to look after both of us, but he was not willing to get divorced. It was less out of consideration for his wife than for his children, especially his youngest daughter, who suffers from nerves. He feared that a divorce might drive her completely mad or even to suicide. But she's grown-up and, what's more, intelligent and well educated. Personally, I thought she would cope. I truly wanted us to have our own children, but I did not want them to grow up without a father. It was the only snake in our paradise.'

'Yesterday as well?' I asked.

She nodded. There were tears in her eyes.

'Yesterday as well. It was the last thing we talked about before he left. And we couldn't agree yesterday either, and it will haunt me now for the rest of my life. But I thought when he left yesterday . . .'

Her voice broke. She turned towards the table. A tear spilled over from her left eye to leave a small dark patch on the light-wood table.

'When Per Johan left yesterday, it seemed he was closer than ever to taking that final plunge. I had renewed hope that everything would work out and we would actually have our own love child. I felt light as a balloon – but then it all popped when I heard the news on the radio that he had been stabbed. I hoped for the best for as long as I could, but really I knew that Per Johan was dead before I heard it on the last bulletin. I suppose you just feel it when you love someone as much as I did.'

She spoke in a quiet, intense voice. As if by magic, the

candle between us went out when she stopped talking. We sat spellbound in the silent gloom.

Then I hurried to ask some routine questions. Her answers were clear and prompt. She was born in 1934 to a Norwegian father and French mother and had grown up in Oslo and Paris. She came from a family of musicians and had studied music and art in Norway and France, without having ever made a breakthrough as an artist or a pianist. She had met Per Johan Fredriksen at an exhibition he had opened in the autumn of 1966, and despite the difference in age had quickly realized that he was the love of her life.

He had called the next day to ask if they could meet again, and she had said yes immediately. They had started a relationship 'only a few days later' and had been meeting once or twice a week ever since – nearly always at her flat and often on a Saturday. She had lived on money inherited from her parents, but largely on presents from him. She had never asked him for money. But he had paid the rent for her, and she always found a few hundred-kroner notes when he had gone.

I knew that she would not receive so much as a krone in her dead lover's will. So I asked, with as much tact as I could, how his death would affect her life financially.

She turned up her palms and shrugged indifferently, then replied: 'It won't be easy, but it doesn't feel that important. I am going to give myself a week to grieve and then start to think about what I can, and have to, do for the rest of my life. I certainly can't continue to live here now – alone in what was our universe . . . alone in what was our universe.' She repeated the short sentence thoughtfully.

The words echoed in my head for a while afterwards. I found myself wondering if I would still be able to live in my flat if I had heard on the radio that the love of my life had been killed. It was not a pleasant thought. But, fortunately, it was interrupted when Harriet Henriksen started to speak again.

'Something that feels more important here and now . . . What actually happened when he was killed? Do you know who did it and why?'

I told her the truth: that we had arrested a young man whom we were fairly certain had committed the crime, but, as yet, we did not know what he was called or what his motive might be.

I took out the photographs of the boy on the red bicycle and put them down on the table between us. I feared they might produce an emotional response, but there was no visible reaction.

Harriet Henriksen sat quietly and looked at the pictures. She narrowed her eyes, but said nothing. Then she shook her head. 'I've never seen him before. But it's strange, I feel no hatred when I look at those photographs. And I would, if he killed my darling.'

We sat and looked at each other. She suddenly seemed more relaxed, but her gaze did not waver.

'I can't be sure. I am not a religious person, but I am a people person. I think I would feel hatred if he had killed Per Johan, and I feel nothing. You can see that he is not happy, but he doesn't look evil enough or strong enough to commit murder. No, I really don't think it was him who killed Per Johan. Did anyone see him do it?'

I said nothing and thought for a moment or two. Then I replied slowly that no one had witnessed the actual murder, but the young man had first been seen in conversation with Per Johan Fredriksen, and then been caught running away from the scene of the crime with the murder weapon in his pocket. It would most certainly be a strange tale if he was not guilty.

'You are absolutely right. But there is still a considerable difference between being strange and being guilty, even though they are often confused. So no one actually saw him killing Per Johan. I don't think he did it. And I would be grateful if you could tell me who did, if you manage to find out one day.'

I had a growing appreciation of why Per Johan Fredriksen had been fascinated by this remarkable woman. But I also realized that, for the moment, she was not able to help me any further with the mysterious circumstances surrounding her lover's death.

So I offered my condolences once again, assured her that the investigation would keep all possibilities open, promised to contact her as soon as there was any news, and asked her to stay in town for the next few days in case we needed to question her further.

Harriet Henriksen's reply was short: that until her beloved had been buried, she had nowhere to go, nor any reason to do so. And as if to illustrate this, she remained seated by the coffee table and the burnt-out candle as I got up and left.

VI

I was back at the main police station by half past twelve. Danielsen was nowhere to be seen, but my boss was sitting in his office with the door open. He waved me in as soon as he saw me.

'Danielsen has questioned the suspect again. And despite applying considerable pressure, he got nowhere. The boy adamantly refused to answer any questions. Danielsen found this extremely provoking and is even more convinced of his guilt. He believes that the only question of any real interest is whether the murderer should be sent to prison or a mental hospital. And I am inclined to agree. So we decided that Danielsen could go home at the end of his shift. The lack of identity and motive remains a problem and I would like you to focus on that for the rest of the day.'

I immediately agreed to this. My impressions from the meeting with Harriet Henriksen were being diluted by the light of day and her conclusion now felt like no more than unqualified speculation, so I did not bother to mention it to my boss. However, I was less convinced than Danielsen about the boy's guilt. But I was quite happy to be allowed to carry on working on the case without Danielsen interfering – and without being asked to divulge my thoughts on the case.

The switchboard was remarkably still, but there was a growing number of journalists calling in from different papers. No one had as yet called to report anyone missing or to leave any other message that might help to identify the boy on the red bicycle. It was more and more mysterious. The boy was, as far as anyone could tell, Norwegian and he was a minor. Despite a speech impediment, it was clear that he spoke with an Oslo accent. If he had parents, it seemed very odd indeed that they had not reported him missing. If he lived with other relatives or in a children's home of some sort, it was equally odd that no one had contacted the police.

I guessed it was only a matter of time before someone would enquire about him. If nothing else, someone might recognize him if we published the photographs in the papers. But like the boss, I wanted the question of his identity to be solved before they went to print. I was finding it increasingly difficult to believe that the young man did not have some kind of connection with Per Johan Fredriksen. It seemed too incredible to be true that such a well-known politician should be randomly stabbed on the street.

I was sitting in my office pondering on the identity and motive of the killer when my phone rang. I heard the familiar and annoyingly slow voice of one of the switchboard operators. She said that I was about to be transferred to a lady who had asked to speak to the person in charge of the Per Johan Fredriksen investigation immediately. I was, of course, curious as to who it might be and why she had called. It was not long before I knew.

'Good afternoon. My name is Ane Line Fredriksen and I am the eldest daughter of the late Per Johan Fredriksen. My mother has only now been able to tell me that you wanted to talk to me as soon as possible. So, here I am,' she said.

I was slightly taken aback by her briskness. I expressed

my condolences and said that it would certainly be good to talk, if it was not too much of an inconvenience for her.

'Not at all. My daughter is with my ex-husband in Hamar and I have to pick her up around seven o'clock this evening. So it would be best if we could meet as soon as possible. Would you like to come here or should I come there?'

Her tempo left me breathless, but it was also refreshing to meet such a dynamic and outspoken member of the family. So I said that I was currently in my office at the main police station and perhaps it would be most practical if we could meet here.

'Of course. I'll be there in a quarter of an hour,' Ane Line Fredriksen said, and put down the phone.

I sat with the receiver in my hand, wondering what she looked like. And how many more people this investigation would involve.

VII

Exactly sixteen minutes later, Ane Line Fredriksen was shown into my office, as she looked around with obvious curiosity. I could not see much resemblance to her mother or siblings, but I knew it was the woman from the telephone call even before I heard her voice.

Ane Line Fredriksen was just over five foot six, and one of those modern women who was solid without being fat. The most striking thing about her was her mane of red hair, and the second most striking thing was the alertness of her distinctive blue-green eyes. She also differed from the rest of her family in clothes and style, in that she was wearing jeans and a denim jacket, and her blouse was unbuttoned at the top. My initial impression was that I would like her best of all.

This theory was not weakened in any way by her unusually firm handshake. She barely took the time to sit down before she leaned towards my desk and said impatiently: 'So, what is it you would like to know?'

I briefly told her about events the evening before and the arrest of the boy on the red bicycle, and that that was all we knew about her father's murder so far.

Ane Line Fredriksen continued to lean forwards and listened intently as I spoke. She had a bad habit of taking in the room, which annoyed me slightly, but otherwise my impression was very positive.

She gave a quick nod a couple of times, but still said nothing when I had finished my account. I therefore took out the photographs of the arrestee and put them down on the desk. She immediately studied them with interest, but then shook her head in visible disappointment.

'I have never seen him before. I would have remembered, because it does not look like he has had an easy life. Are you sure it was he who killed Father? Why on earth would he do that?'

So I told her straight: we could not be certain that it was the boy who killed her father, and if it was, we did not know why he had done it. There was much to indicate that it was him, but he had not confessed and we had no eyewitnesses to the murder itself.

'How intriguing,' she said.

I did not detect any great sorrow at the loss of her father in the otherwise very nice Ane Line Fredriksen. And apparently she saw my surprise.

'I understand that it might seem a bit strange that I am not more upset. I am actually easily moved at funerals and the like. But we come from very practical farming stock, my father was an elderly man, and we were not particularly close any more. Though I have to say he was a very good father when we were little. We got whatever we pointed at and had more time with him than many other children had with their fathers. But once we grew up he became busy with his politics and business. I never really knew him as anything other than a family man. When I saw him on the television I always thought he was too conservative in his politics and didn't show enough sympathy for people less well off. He was also conservative in his values. First, he didn't like the man I married, and then he didn't like the fact that I got divorced.'

'He had just left his mistress when he was killed yesterday,' I said.

'That never really bothered me. Father's women are something we have had to live with since nursery and this one was very discreet. So we knew about her, but never saw her. Have you met her? What is she like?'

Her boldness took me by surprise. I managed to blurt out that she was a thirty-seven-year-old pianist who made quite an impression, before I saved the situation and said that at present there was nothing to indicate any connection between her and his murder. His mistress stood to gain nothing from his death. On the contrary, she would, in fact, be worse off.

'I thought about that on the way here. His mistress has no rights and won't be left a penny, whereas my brother and sister and I will inherit all the money. It's unfair, really.'

That was the first time I could ever remember hearing an heir say that they were getting too much. And it was also the first time that I had heard anyone express any sympathy for a woman their father had betrayed their mother with.

I was struck by an unfamiliar thought, that I was now sitting talking to a multi-millionairess. So I remarked that the purely financial aspect of the case did not play much of a role here.

Ane Line Fredriksen stretched in the chair with slow, deliberate movements, like a gigantic ginger cat. For a moment I was worried that she might start moulting. Instead she leaned forward again.

'Well, that is not strictly the case. My siblings and I have never been poor. But as you may have heard, it suits us all rather well to get our inheritance now.'

I had not heard any such thing and immediately asked her to elaborate. She did not need to be asked twice.

'Well, Johan has always been aware that he is the eldest and also the only son. So he has always been the one with the greatest ambition with regards to money and the like. Since he graduated, he has wanted to start his own law firm and invest in property himself. Father never entirely trusted him and did not want to pay out the inheritance early. The atmosphere at Sunday lunch two weeks ago was tense, to say the least.'

I noted this down and asked why her younger sister needed the money now.

'Vera is another story altogether. My father's constant concern and care for her is perhaps the best illustration of what a good father he was. Vera has undoubtedly the best head of us all, but is also the one with the weakest nerves. She gets frightened if the wind blows, faints whenever she's startled. She has excellent qualifications, but no one really believes she'll ever be able to work. I've said to her so many times that she just needs to believe in herself and get out there. But she doesn't dare to. So she has a master's degree in chemistry, but just mopes around at home and doesn't even try to find work. And as far as I know, she'd never kissed a man before she was twenty-three. You can imagine the rest.'

I had to admit that I actually could not imagine the rest. She sighed with forced exasperation.

'Well, when Vera turned twenty-three, she met a man with whom she fell in love and is now in a rather disagreeable relationship. He's a very liberal Dutchman who was studying in Norway, although he did not do as well as her. He has an almost obsessive ambition to start an art gallery in Amsterdam where he can sell his own paintings and those of his bohemian friends. He wants a million or four in start capital, and my father was not, of course, willing to lend it him. The Dutchman is a bit suspect and Vera is terribly inexperienced and naive when it comes to love. It could end very badly. So, it would suit her very well to get some money right now.'

'And you? What about yourself?'

'I struggled more with books than Vera, so I stopped studying. I started to work in politics and in a shop when I was twenty-one. But at the moment I can't work because our society doesn't offer childcare to single mothers who want to work, and I had to pay my former husband a small fortune to get him out of the house. Father simply refused to pay for his only grandchild to lose one of her parents. He also felt he could not give me any of my inheritance without doing the same for Vera, and he certainly did not want to do that. So my only option was a bank loan which I'm paying interest on. I can get by, but a few million wouldn't go amiss right now.'

'And what about Johan's family situation?'

'Johan is more of a businessman than a charmer. He has always been well off, but never any good at going out and spending his money. Since he turned thirty, he has made it very obvious that he wants a family, but any attempts to get one have not ended particularly well. Although, we have not heard mention of it for a couple of years now. He is still unmarried and childless, but I think he might have something on the go at the moment. I have always had a good relationship with him – even though we are very different and he is rather boring – and last time we met at our parents', he told me that he might have a good deal in the offing, as he put it. I realized there was something he did not particularly want to talk about, so now I am waiting with bated breath to hear what the problem is this time. It's just as interesting every time.'

She stretched unabashed in the chair again – and managed to surprise me once more.

'So, how little have the unsociable people in my family actually told you? Don't tell me they said nothing about the murder mystery from Father's youth?'

At first I thought she might be joking. Then we exchanged looks and immediately became serious again.

I said that no one had mentioned any earlier murder mystery in Per Johan Fredriksen's life. I hastily added that I should, of course, be told about it now that he himself had been killed.

Ane Line Fredriksen sighed and rolled her eyes, then lay her arms heavily on the desk as she leaned forwards.

She leaned so far over that I could see the top of her unusually large breasts. However, the story that she told was so sensational that it quickly took all of my attention.

VIII

'When I was eleven and then again when I was sixteen, I noticed a certain tension at home both before and after my parents went out for a mysterious meal. It was just a few weeks after the second meal that I first heard the story about the murder in 1932. It was Father who started to tell me about it, one Saturday when he had had a few too many drinks. The case had always plagued him and he had been thinking about it even more in recent years. He said he would happily give ten million kroner to know what had happened. It was obviously a story that he and Mother both knew very well, but that they had never told us children. My brother and sister had never heard about it either until I told them.'

There was a short, dramatic pause. I waved for her to continue. She flashed me a coquettish smile and then carried on eagerly.

'Father was the MP for Vestfold. He was born there and was heir to a large estate with half a forest. There were big class differences in Vestfold back then. Our Labour prime minister was born around the same time only a couple of miles away, but grew up in poverty. Anyway, in March 1932, Father and five other friends from Vestfold went to Oslo for the spring break. They all came from very wealthy families at a time when there was widespread poverty and need. They had each booked a room at a hotel out by Ullern, which was one of the most desirable parts of town, and presumed to be a safe area. And yet, something very dramatic happened there. On their second evening at the hotel, the youngest, a twenty-one-year-old woman, called Eva Bjølhaugen, was found dead in her room. She was found lying on the sofa and there was no visible sign of violence. She suffered from epilepsy and it was assumed that she died as a result of a seizure. But there was no autopsy. Father was not convinced that that was what had happened at all. There were several things he felt did not fit.'

She stopped and looked at me with teasing eyes, but hurried on obediently when I asked if she could remember what it was her father had doubted. It crossed my mind that we had hit it off remarkably well, despite being so different.

'Yes, but unfortunately, he was more secretive about that. The strangest thing was the key, he said. The door to the hotel room was locked, but the key was lying on the floor out in the corridor. And apparently the woman only suffered from petit mal. But there were a few other things that were odd about the whole affair. Father, who was otherwise not prone to being abstract, became remarkably vague when he talked about it. It could as easily be suicide or murder, as epilepsy, he said.'

The story had piqued my interest now. I hastened to ask if she knew who else had been there.

'Apart from my father and the young Eva Bjølhaugen, her boyfriend and sister were there. There was also the young woman whom Father was engaged to at the time, and another friend. So there were three young men and three young women, two couples and one set of siblings. Plenty of opportunity for romance and jealousy there, I reckon. From what I understood, Father and his fiancée broke up soon afterwards.'

'How strange that there was no autopsy,' I said.

She nodded eagerly. 'That is what I thought. Father simply said that there was no autopsy.'

'And the restaurant visits – where do they fit in?'

Just then, the phone on my desk started to ring. I hoped that it might be information about the suspect's identity, and answered immediately. I was becoming so focused on the case that it was almost a disappointment to hear Miriam's voice at the other end.

'Hi. I just wondered if half past four was still a realistic time to meet, or if we should make it later? I'm sure you're having a busy day, and I should probably study a little more to prepare for the exam,' she said.

Miriam still had two and a half months left until the exam. However, her ambitious perfectionism meant that she pretended to have only two weeks left when, in fact, there were two months, and that she only had two days left when it was actually two weeks. I saw no reason to discuss this here and now, and was without a doubt having a busy day. So I gave it five seconds' thought and suggested that we meet at the Theatre Cafe for supper at half past six.

'Deal,' she said, and put the phone down.

'Apologies, I had to arrange supper with my fiancée,' I said.

To my disappointment, I saw no disappointment in Ane Line's eyes, only greater curiosity. She opened her mouth to say something, almost certainly to ask about my fiancée, but I just managed to pip her to the post.

'Now, where were we? Yes, the meals that the group from 1932 had are more relevant to the case than my own dinner plans.'

'Yes, they really are quite something, which only underlines how serious the situation was. The other five from the group who were in Oslo in 1932 continued to meet every five years to mark the day that Eva Bjølhaugen died, at the restaurant of the same hotel. They all hoped that someone might say something that would throw light on the tragedy, Father said, but that never happened.'

'But, if they met every five years and that was in March 1932 . . .'

Ane Line nodded eagerly again. 'The date was the fifth of March 1932. So the five last met just a couple of weeks ago. It is rather odd, isn't it?'

She looked up at me from under her red fringe with bright enthusiastic eyes. I nodded with equal enthusiasm. I still could not see any connection between the forty-year-old mystery and the stabbing of Per Johan Fredriksen on a street in Oslo yesterday. My gut feeling told me that there was some kind of link, but my head could not work out what.

'Very interesting. I will see what I can find about the case in our archives. Do you know if your father had any contact with the four others from 1932 in between these restaurant visits?'

Ane Line smiled again. 'Well, I know that he certainly had regular contact with one of them. I don't even know the names of the other three, so I couldn't say whether he had contact with them or not. But if you find their names in the archives, I'd be more than happy to answer that.'

Ane Line Fredriksen was clearly more curious than most. And her eagerness and openness were contagious. I picked up my pen to write down the name of the one person that her father had had regular contact with. And then promptly dropped it in shock when the redhead exclaimed: 'Oda Fredriksen! Eva Bjølhaugen was my mother's little sister.'

We sat and stared at each other for a few seconds. It seemed to me that she was almost teasing me, and enjoying it, despite her father's death and the gravity of the situation.

'So let me get this straight: three young men and three young women went to Oslo together in 1932. The young Eva Bjølhaugen, who was the girlfriend of one of the men, was found dead in her locked hotel room in circumstances that have never been clarified. Your father was engaged to one of the other women, but later married Eva Bjølhaugen's sister?'

She nodded energetically. 'Exactly. And it didn't take long either – Mother and Father got married just eighteen months later. And the five from the group who are still alive have met every five years since, most recently a couple of weeks before my father was killed. Surely that can't be a coincidence?'

I was open about what I thought: that it could, of course, be a coincidence, but that I very much doubted that it was.

'Exactly,' she said, her eyes shining.

As things seemed to be going so well, I took the chance to ask what else her father and mother had told them about this strange old story.

'Not very much, unfortunately. My father was a kind man, but was quick to put things off. Even when we've argued about money in recent years, he has never been mean or harsh with us, just evasive. This old story bothered him a great deal and he did not want to talk about it. I pushed him a couple of times, but he just said that we could perhaps talk about it later. That never happened, of course. Mother was more cagey than Father and completely clammed up when I tried to talk to her about it. She just said that both she and my father had been there, and that they both still wondered what had actually happened, and that it had been extremely painful to lose her only sister like that. I could never get any more out of her. You should ask her about it, she has to tell you now, even if she didn't want to tell me before.'

I nodded thoughtfully. Then I thanked her for the interesting conversation and asked if I could contact her again once I had looked up the case in the archives. She immediately offered to wait in my office while I looked through the file. We compromised, and she waited outside while I read through the case.

IX

The file from 1932 was disappointingly thin. Initially, it had been marked 'suspicious death' and then changed to 'no case to answer'. My attention was immediately drawn to a couple of photographs of the young woman on a dark velvet sofa. As far as I could see, the woman showed no physical signs of violence or illness of any sort, and was just lying there peacefully, as though asleep. She was slightly shorter than the sofa and had long blonde hair and pale skin. Her body was well shaped, almost like a statue. The photographs made me think of Sleeping Beauty. But Eva Bjølhaugen, born in Sande on 7 January 1911, had never woken up from her deep sleep.

I sat there with the forty-year-old photographs and mused on what secrets she had taken with her to the grave, and what significance they might have for yesterday's murder.

The reports and statements told me in short that Eva Bjølhaugen had been last seen alive by her boyfriend and four other friends at around five o'clock in the afternoon of 5 March 1932, when she had let herself into her room following a trip into town. And she was found dead in Room 111 at Haraldsen's Hotel in Ullern at a quarter past eight that very evening. She had arranged to meet the others for dinner at eight o'clock. They had all met in the lobby at the agreed time, and realized that something was wrong when she failed to show up by ten past eight.

Her boyfriend, Hauk Rebne Westgaard, had gone to look for her. Then at twelve minutes past eight he had come back to the others in the lobby. He had told them that the door to her room was locked and he had heard no sign of life when he knocked. Her boyfriend's concern only increased when he found the key to her door lying on the floor in the corridor, outside his own room.

In his statement, Hauk Rebne Westgaard said that he had been extremely worried about his girlfriend and did not want to enter her room alone. So he ran down to the others and they all entered the room at precisely a quarter past eight to find Eva Bjølhaugen dead on the sofa.

Eva Bjølhaugen's bed had obviously been used after it had been made up in the morning. But her five companions agreed that there was no sign that anyone else had been there. And the police found no evidence of this either, though they did find fingerprints of all five young people in the room. This was not seen to be suspicious, of course, as they had all been there after she had died, and had also been in there together the evening before. None of them had noticed anything different about Eva Bjølhaugen. She had been in a good mood earlier in the day and generally had an optimistic outlook on life. She had finished school with good grades and had talked about studying languages at the

University of Oslo. It was clearly stated in the report that there was 'no history of depression'.

The rest of the group had stayed in rooms on the same corridor. A certified transcript of the reception book documented the following:

Room 112: Solveig Thaulow, 22, Sande.
Room 113: Oda Bjølhaugen, 23, Sande.
Room 114: Hauk Rebne Westgaard, 25, Holmestrand.
Room 115: Per Johan Fredriksen, 25, Holmestrand.
Room 116: Kjell Arne Ramdal, 25, Tønsberg.

The bed in Room 111 had been used after it had been made up in the morning, but according to the police there was no technical evidence of sexual activity.

The deceased's suitcase was in a corner of the room, but only contained two extra sets of clothes, a pair of shoes and three women's magazines. There was a glass, a toothbrush and a tube of toothpaste in the bathroom, as well as a dressing gown, two used towels from the hotel, and some make-up. It appeared that nothing had been stolen from the room, and Eva's purse with almost one hundred kroner in cash was still in her coat pocket. The only thing one might expect to find in the room that was not there was the key. The police report confirmed, without any further speculation, that it had been found on the floor outside Room 114.

None of the deceased's friends said they had heard anything from her room or any of the other rooms in the few hours before she was found dead. The only exception was that Solveig Thaulow said she heard a muffled bang or thump at around half past seven. However, she was not able to say where it came from or what kind of noise it could have been. The deceased's boyfriend suspected that she might have been strangled or suffocated, possibly with the help of a pillow. However, there were no marks on her neck and there was no saliva or other bodily fluid on any pillow.

The assumed cause of death was given in the end as 'epileptic fit'. There was a short statement to say that, according to the deceased's sister and parents, she suffered from epilepsy, and from the doctor's initial findings, it seemed that she had had an epileptic fit that afternoon. Her sister Oda Bjølhaugen was very shaken and immediately demanded an autopsy. But when their parents arrived later that night, they asked if it would be possible not to have an autopsy, as it would only cause more distress for the family in a situation where everything indicated natural causes. Their daughter had 'very reluctantly' agreed to this in the end, and the police had done as the family requested. Thus there was no confirmation of the time and cause of death.

The group had visited the capital out of season. There were a total of eighteen rooms in the hotel, over two floors, and all the other rooms had been empty that night. The receptionist had been alone on duty that evening, and had seen no one other than the six guests. The window in the room was closed from the inside and the door was locked. I could understand perfectly well why this had been deemed to be a natural death, the strange detail of the key aside.

I called Ane Line Fredriksen in again. It did not take her long as she was standing waiting impatiently no more than a few feet from my door.

'Is there anything new about the lack of an autopsy?' she asked, before I managed to get a word out.

I replied that there had been no autopsy at the request of Eva's parents, even though her mother had very clearly wanted one. Ane Line Fredriksen said that she thought it was odd, and I said I agreed. Then I quickly moved on to the names of the other members of the party.

She shook her red mane when I said Solveig Thaulow, and then again when I said Hauk Rebne Westgaard. However, she gave a firm nod when I said Kjell Arne Ramdal.

'I've never heard the first two names, but I have heard Kjell Arne Ramdal mentioned a few times. Father almost never spoke about business at home, but judging by some of the telephone messages I overheard, I think Kjell Arne Ramdal was some kind of business associate. When I was a teenager and later, I always wondered what he looked like, as it was not often that I heard the names of any of Father's business contacts. In fact, I would be very grateful if you could tell me a bit about my father's life outside the family home at some point after the investigation. I never really knew him other than as a father.'

I nodded, half to myself, half to her. There was clearly a thread running from 1932 to 1972, which was becoming more and more interesting. But I was as yet unable to see any connection whatsoever to the still-nameless boy on the red bicycle.

I therefore decided to make another attempt to find out more about him. I managed to leave the office on the second try, having twice assured Ane Line Fredriksen that I would let her know as soon as there was any news about her father's murder and that I would not hesitate to call her if I had any further questions. I resisted the temptation, for the moment, to ask her how the three siblings could be so very different in both colouring and personality.

X

After my surprisingly interesting meetings with the victim's mistress and daughter, my meeting with the suspected murderer was yet again a disappointment. The press were ringing for details, but no new information about the mysterious young man had come in. I could not remember it ever having taken so long to confirm the identity of someone being held in custody. But not only that, I could not think of another arrestee who would be so easily recognizable.

To begin with, I tried to be pedagogical, and asked if he had any questions. His response was succinct: 'The bicycle?' He nodded when I told him it was being kept in a safe place and said no more.

I started by asking about his name. To which he did not respond.

I went on to explain that we would appoint a lawyer for him tomorrow morning, even though he had not asked for one, to ensure that he was treated fairly. His nod was almost imperceptible, and there was no other reaction.

I could see that there might be a connection, if the boy on the red bicycle was the son or grandson of one of the parties from 1932. I therefore decided to confront him with the names and give no further explanation. He looked at me with a glimmer of interest in his eyes when I said what I was going to do. But as far as I could judge, he did not react to any of the names I read out.

Again I tried to ask why he had killed Per Johan Fredriksen. Again, he replied almost mechanically: 'I didn't kill him. He was dead when I went back.'

I asked why he was not willing to help me, or himself, by telling me what he had seen.

He said nothing, and looked at me as if he had not understood.

'Well, then I am going to go home to my fiancée. And what are you going to do?' I asked, eventually giving up.

'Wait,' he replied.

His answer was solemn and concise, but he said no more when I asked him what on earth he was waiting for.

I stood up. I still felt some sympathy for the young boy, and did have my doubts that he was the murderer. But I could not work him out and his demonstrative silence was starting to irritate me.

Then just as I turned to leave, to my great surprise, he spoke.

'You can call me Marinus.'

It did not make the case any less complex. I had never heard the name Marinus before. I turned back, looked down at him and asked: 'Marinus what?'

His response was to raise his hands in a gesture that was at once defensive and condescending.

I left, closing the door behind me a little harder than planned. The boy seemed to be playing with me for reasons

I could not understand. Rather reluctantly, I had to admit that perhaps Danielsen was right, and the only question of any interest in this case was whether the murderer should be sent to prison or a mental hospital.

XI

I got to the Theatre Cafe at twenty-eight minutes past six. The air was cold, but I felt the warmth spread through my body as I approached.

She was right where I hoped she would be standing, where she always stood: leaning discreetly against the wall with a book in her hand. From what I could see it was a thick blue book about the history of Nordic literature in the nineteenth century. She had only read the introduction when she left yesterday, but was now almost a third of the way in. I was impressed – and happy when she snapped the book shut as soon as I put my hand on her arm. We gave each other a quick hug and then moved towards the door.

We had been there before, but not many times. Miriam thought that the Theatre Cafe was too expensive for normal Sunday suppers, and I did not want to protest. So we came here about once every two months or so. And then, whenever possible, we sat at a table for two in the middle by the window. Our favourite table was available, and there was no one else within earshot. It was perfect.

I started romantically by asking her if she had had a good day, and if there was anything more we needed to discuss about the wedding.

This, of course, did not work at all. She swiftly replied: 'My day was good. I studied all day. And of course there's more to talk about regarding the wedding, but there's no rush. So, how is the investigation going?' she asked in a hushed voice, as soon as the waiter left us. Then we sat there more or less whispering to each other for the rest of the meal. The staff clearly thought it was terribly romantic and gave us friendly smiles as they passed. Whereas what we were actually talking about was the stabbing of a politician and an underage murder suspect.

I knew that this was in part down to Miriam's inherent curiosity, but was still touched by the interest she showed in my work. Just how interested she was dawned on me when she said no to dessert. That had never happened before, certainly not at the Theatre Cafe.

Once we were back in the car, we returned to our normal voices.

'The story from 1932 is a strange and incredible coincidence,' I remarked.

'I agree. It's almost too incredible not to be connected in some way. But there is not much to be gleaned from details of the crime scene, and we know too little about the others to conclude anything more,' she said.

I had to concede to this and promised to talk as soon as possible to the four friends from the 1932 drama who were still alive.

'And the current case is no less mysterious. With a mysterious suspect, to boot,' I said.

Miriam nodded quickly. 'Yes, both things are very odd

indeed. It's so strange that he won't say anything even to you, when you are so good at talking to people.'

She said it in a way that was so characteristic of her, just as a passing comment. But it still made me so happy that I leaned over and kissed her quickly on the cheek once we were over the junction.

We were soon at Hegdehaugen. We walked in silence to the front door, as though we were suddenly scared that someone might hear us even if we whispered.

Once we were installed on the sofa with a cup of coffee in one hand and holding each other's hand in the other, we carried on discussing the case.

'Per Johan Fredriksen was also a bit of a mystery in terms of his politics,' she said.

I squeezed her hand and asked her to elaborate.

'He is part of the richest and most conservative group in the Centre Party, and is sometimes said to be right of even the Conservatives. Which is not a compliment in my circles. But he would take completely different stances on different issues, so he has also been called left of Labour. He was deemed to be a very important man for the no campaign, tactically, because he could potentially influence a number of the rich Conservatives.'

'But all that has nothing to do with the murder case, surely,' I joked.

Miriam was suddenly very still. She looked out of the window and her hand trembled faintly in mine.

'Surely it can't? People in Norway do not kill each other for their political persuasions,' I said, trying to reassure her.

Miriam carried on looking out of the window when she

finally answered. 'Three months ago, I would have said no and laughed. But now I am not so sure. There are a lot of powerful and frightening emotions out there in the dark at the moment. I have been called the most incredible things by men in suits, and the day before yesterday an old woman spat at me when I was manning the stand. Parents and children have stopped speaking to each other and a lot of people are worried about their partners and their jobs. I don't think anyone would kill in connection with an election in Norway, but I'm not so sure any more that some fanatic or other might not kill in connection with the referendum.'

We sat in silence and pondered this over our cups of coffee. I had assumed that the young murderer might be disturbed, but I hadn't even considered that the killing could have been politically motivated.

I said that it was food for thought. Then I went out into the hall and got the photographs of the suspect which I put down on the table in front of us.

Miriam leaned forwards and stared at them intensely, but then shook her head. 'He must be a very lonely boy, if no one has reported him missing. It all seems like a terrible tragedy. He's not active in any of the political parties' youth wings in Oslo, otherwise I would have known him. If his limp and speech impediment are so striking, I'm sure I would have known about him if he was active in any of the neighbouring constituencies.' She fell silent, sat there and stared at the photographs. 'I have never seen his face before. And yet, when I look at his pictures, I get the strange feeling that I've seen him in passing somewhere.'

I put my arm round her, kissed her on the cheek and asked her to think hard. She sat in deep concentration for about a minute before she said anything else.

'I might be wrong, but do you remember the cyclist we saw a couple of times outside here at a distance last autumn?'

I had to think for a while myself before answering. It was not something I had given much thought to. But now that she mentioned it, it gradually came back to me that we had noticed a cyclist outside here a couple of times. He had just been standing with his bike further down the road. Close enough for us to see him and his bike, but too far away for us to see any details.

The first time we saw him, he cycled off after about thirty seconds. The second time, he stood there for longer, and Miriam had wondered as we went in whether we should ask if he needed help. Maybe he was lost or was having problems with his bike, she said. I turned back somewhat reluctantly, and walked towards the cyclist with her, but when we were only a matter of yards away, he hopped on his bike and disappeared down the hill.

'It could certainly have been him. But that only makes things more bizarre, slightly crazy, in fact, if he was watching the flat already last autumn, only then to cycle all the way up here after he had murdered someone in Majorstuen.'

Miriam nodded. 'It's all very odd, no matter what. The strangest thing really is that he so purposefully sought you out after the murder.'

I took a couple of deep breaths, then I said: 'Do you think I should ring the Genius of Frogner?'

'The Genius of Frogner' was Miriam's nickname for

Patricia. Not only had Miriam been the first to suggest that I should call Patricia in connection with my last murder investigation, she had actually phoned Patricia and persuaded her to help me. But now, when I suggested it myself, she seemed far less keen on the idea.

'You can, of course, do as you wish and whatever you think will be best for the investigation. But I don't think you should call her, not yet anyway. At the moment it seems most likely that there won't be a major murder investigation, as the solution lies in the sad life of a disturbed young man. And in any case—' She stopped mid-sentence and did not continue until I asked her to.

'And in any case, she is a genius, of course, but you are much smarter than you appear to be when all you do is follow her instructions. You would have solved your last murder cases without her, it would just have taken a bit more time and you might have needed a bit more help from me. So I don't think you should call her just yet, I think you should talk to me a bit more first.'

Miriam smiled her lopsided, mischievous smile as she said this. I smiled back, kissed her and said that I would definitely rather talk to her than Patricia in her luxury palace in Frogner.

'Have you by any chance ever heard the name Marinus here in Norway? I don't think he is actually called that, but there must be a reason for him telling me that he was.'

Miriam straightened up and shook her head. 'No. It's an ancient Roman name that I've never heard used here. In fact, the only Marinus I have heard of since the Middle Ages, is the man who was beheaded after the Reichstag fire in

Germany. I can't remember his surname – Lubbe, or something like that? That was also a very strange story and a sad fate, if I remember rightly. It must have been sometime in 1933, or 1934 at the latest.'

Miriam and bookshelves are a story unto themselves. The first time she came to my flat, she went straight to my bookshelves and stood there for about ten minutes. Now, she was sitting beside me one minute, behaving like a perfectly normal fiancée, the next she was over by the bookshelves at the other end of the room, holding one of her favourite books: a five hundred-page history of the twentieth century in Europe. She flicked through it as fast as she could, then suddenly her face lit up with an almost childishly smug smile.

'He was called Marinus van der Lubbe – and it was December 1933! A rather disturbed, and almost blind, young man who was made into a scapegoat, even though it would seem that there were far stronger and more wilful parties behind it.'

I jumped up and went over to the bookshelves. Miriam held the book out and looked at me with a triumphant smile. I congratulated her on her excellent memory and immediately took the book.

There was a photograph of Marinus van der Lubbe standing between two prison guards with the Nazi emblem sewn on their uniforms. In purely physical terms, he bore no resemblance to our arrestee in Oslo in 1972. The 1933 Marinus van der Lubbe was a tall, broad-shouldered man in his early twenties, with short curly hair and surprisingly intense eyes. According to the text under the photograph, he had fallen asleep during the trial and had shown many signs of mental distress. However, the similarities in his case and the current situation were striking and thought-provoking.

'Not everyone who read about Marinus van der Lubbe would be able to see the parallels, to be fair,' I said slowly. I handed the book back to her, without thinking that it was, in fact, mine.

Miriam smiled, closed the book and put it back in its place, once again with a slightly triumphant air. 'You can certainly say that. And based on that we can ascertain that the suspect is an unusually well-read boy. But that, of course, does not mean that he is not in some way mentally disturbed. My books on the history of literature are full of examples of people who are well read and totally mad!' She let out one of her slightly morbid little laughs as she said this, but was soon serious again. 'Well, we have certainly made a step forwards and you now have a couple of new questions to ask of your mysterious arrestee. Perhaps you should drive down to the station now and see if you can get some answers.'

She looked at me questioningly. I glanced at my watch. As always, the hours had slipped by in Miriam's inspiring company. It was already a quarter past ten. I had certainly not planned to go out again this evening and did not want to now, either. So I shared my thoughts on the matter. In other words, that I could just as well ask him the questions first thing tomorrow morning rather than late on Sunday night, and that I had some slightly different plans for the rest of the evening.

'Good,' Miriam replied. She smiled when she said this. And I smiled back.

XII

Miriam was better than me when it came to falling asleep. Particularly when she had lectures the following morning. She said goodnight at half past eleven and was fast asleep three minutes later.

I lay there and looked at her peaceful face. I would never say it to Miriam, as I wanted her image of me as a hero to remain, as far as possible, intact, but on evenings like this I felt I was not only an incredibly lucky man, but also an undeservingly lucky one. With Patricia's help, I had gained a reputation and position in the police force that I could never have imagined was possible only five years ago. And thanks to having met Miriam, my private life was better than ever before.

Despite the unsolved case, my life as I knew it still felt good and secure. I found myself hoping that the remaining questions would be answered tomorrow and that we could confirm that the arrestee was indeed guilty, whether he was mentally disturbed or not. However, I still had a sneaking feeling that things would not be that simple. The story from 1932 was so striking that it seemed highly unlikely that it was sheer coincidence that one of the others in the group had now been killed forty years later.

I lay there thinking about it for nearly a quarter of an hour. And then I pondered for a further ten minutes about the boy on the red bicycle and why on earth he had come to my flat. Almost against my will, I found myself wondering what Patricia would have to say about the whole thing.

And so eventually I fell asleep just before midnight on Sunday, 19 March 1972, with my eyes on Miriam and my mind on Patricia.

DAY THREE

Another Death and an Old Eyewitness

I

I heard the alarm clock ring, but felt incredibly tired. I was relieved to discover that for some reason it was only ten past six – and so I went back to sleep.

I then slept very heavily until the alarm clock rang for a second time at ten to seven. At which point I woke with a start and sat bolt upright when I realized that I was alone in bed.

Fortunately, I remembered within seconds that Miriam had said that she had to go into the People Against the EEC office to sort out some post before her morning lecture.

I was still tired at ten to seven, so once again I was impressed by my fiancée's irrepressible energy and efficiency. On my way to the bathroom, I mused on the possibility of a no vote in the autumn referendum, despite the hard sell by Labour and the Conservatives.

The flat felt very quiet and almost gloomy without Miriam's bright voice, so I turned on the radio as I sat down to breakfast. The latest developments in the EEC debate were the second item in the morning news on Monday, 20 March 1972. The first was a minor sensation, and that was that Norway and the Soviet Union were close to reaching an agreement on rights in connection with any findings of oil and gas in the Barents Sea. Negotiations had progressed unexpectedly and it was hoped that a draft agreement would be ready for endorsement by next Monday. The acting leader of the Storting's Standing Committee on Foreign Affairs considered this to be excellent news which could be of great importance to the future of the country. He expressed his hope that the draft agreement would be passed by the Storting as early as the end of the week.

For a few minutes, I forgot the murder investigation and listened to the news with keen interest. It was no more than a few years since one of the foreign engineers involved in exploratory drilling in the North Sea had stated that he could personally drink all the oil to be found there. But now oil was being extracted with such success that there was talk of establishing a government-owned oil company in Norway. In my discussions with my father last year, I had always maintained that the oil industry could be a possible solution to the increasingly obvious problems in traditional industry. He did not agree. Whereas I believed that the oil industry could provide an income of up to several hundred million a year, he believed that it would never be more than tens of millions at the most.

It was only once the report was finished that it struck me that Per Johan Fredriksen had been chairman of the Standing Committee on Foreign Affairs. If he had not been stabbed to death the day before yesterday, it would have been his voice that I heard on the radio just now.

The newspapers carried a couple of obituaries and matter-of-fact reports on the death of Per Johan Fredriksen, in between the headlines about the EEC and negotiations with the Soviet Union. They reported that he had been murdered and where he had been murdered, and that a suspect had been arrested fleeing the scene of the crime. *Aftenposten* had picked up on the fact that he was on a bicycle and that the suspect was young, but they had no further details.

The sparse newspaper coverage suited me very well. But I was fully aware that pressure was mounting. If we did not manage to identify the young suspect in the course of the day, we would have to consider publishing a request for information along with his photograph in tomorrow's papers. This would not give a good impression and would no doubt lead to speculation and criticism of the police. Following my previous successes, the media and police force had precariously high expectations of me. And I was not at all certain that I could meet them in this investigation – certainly not without Patricia.

II

I was back at the station by eight o'clock. I met DI Danielsen in the doorway, as, of course, he had come a few minutes earlier in the hope that he would be there before me. His early rise had been to no avail. There were still no enquiries about anyone who could be the suspect. In fact, there had been no enquiries at all about the case, other than a growing number of calls from the press.

At a quarter past eight, I once again sat down opposite the arrestee. I did not expect to make any real progress and was not disappointed.

With a degree of irritation, I repeated my questions as to what he was called and who his parents were. He looked at me with raised eyebrows, but sat in silence.

I then confronted him with the fact that he had been spying on me outside my flat the previous autumn.

This did not appear to surprise him. He hesitated for a moment, then gave a quick but definite nod. A small smile slipped over his lips, but disappeared just as quickly. Once more, he sat there and did not say a word, his face almost devoid of expression when I asked why he had spied on me.

I played my final card and said: 'When you told me yesterday that your name was Marinus, you were referring to Marinus van der Lubbe, weren't you? You were trying to tell me that you are being made a scapegoat, just as he was, for a greater crime involving more powerful parties?'

I leaned forwards and tried to catch his eye. There was a sudden brief spark. He nodded – quickly and almost vigorously. Then he sank back into apathy without saying anything.

'Van der Lubbe was at the scene of the crime, but claimed he had not seen who set fire to the Reichstag building. Did you see Per Johan Fredriksen being murdered on Saturday?'

He did not look at me, but shook his head almost imperceptibly in response.

I interpreted this to mean that he had not seen the

murder, or who did it. But it could as easily mean that for some reason or other, he did not want to tell me what he had seen. Whatever the case, it felt more and more pointless to sit here questioning him.

He remained silent when I stood up and walked towards the door. But then, just as I put my hand on the door handle, he unexpectedly piped up: 'If you don't find out who the murderer is soon, my fate will be the same as Hauptmann's.'

Then nothing more. He didn't move a muscle when I asked who Hauptmann was, what had happened to Hauptmann and what he meant by all these riddles.

I left without getting an answer, and more confused than ever.

III

'Well, there is some progress, at least he is saying something, even if it is still not a lot.'

I gave a brief nod to my boss's first statement, and Danielsen gave a quick nod to the second.

Neither of them knew or remembered anything about any Hauptmann. We had just been informed that the unusually annoying lawyer, Edvard Rønning Junior, had been appointed as the defence, and that he found it 'highly unsatisfactory' that the police could not tell him his client's name. The atmosphere in my boss's office was somewhat strained, to say the least.

'This is just a waste of time. The boy is clearly guilty, and the court will just have to decide whether he is too disturbed to go to prison or not. Let's release his picture in the papers tomorrow if no one gets in touch, and in the meantime, we can get on with more meaningful work,' Danielsen said, opening his hands in suggestion.

The boss looked at me questioningly. I answered diplomatically that that might well be true and that we should perhaps not use too many resources on the case. I was not opposed to Danielsen taking on more exciting tasks, but would myself prefer to keep working on this one. Until we knew the identity of the suspect, the motive would remain unclear and could well be significant in terms of whether he was of sound mind or not.

It was my turn to look questioningly at my boss. He dithered for a moment or two, before nodding gravely.

'Let's do as you both wish. Danielsen can move on to other jobs and Kristiansen, you can continue to work on possible motives in the hope of solving the question of the suspect's identity. We will not make anything public yet.'

It was not a solution that any of us were entirely happy with, but it was one that we could all live with. Danielsen and I left the office together, but did not exchange a word or look.

I dutifully checked that no new information had come in that might help to identify the suspect. Then I left behind the growing pile of press enquiries to the switchboard and returned to my office. From there I rang Oda Fredriksen and asked if I could come and see her again.

IV

The drawing room in Bygdøy felt even larger when there were only two of us there. Oda Fredriksen and I sat alone at a huge mahogany table full of flowers.

The youngest daughter, Vera, was at home, and her son Johan was on his way. I had said to Oda Fredriksen that it would be best if we could first speak alone about things that she might not want her children to hear. She had pointed to the drawing room without saying a word. I was not entirely sure that she had understood what I meant.

I said that the flowers were beautiful. She flapped her hand with disinterest.

'I have always liked flowers so much, but I can barely look at them now. It is only a week since his birthday. The drawing room was full of happy people. Now it feels so empty.'

Fredriksen's widow appeared to be genuinely shocked by the news of her husband's death, even now, a day and a half later. I felt a surge of sympathy and did not want to add to her burden in any way. So I assured her that I would do my best to solve her husband's murder.

'In the meantime, however, I have heard a very strange story about a different death altogether; it's a very old case, but I am now obliged to investigate whether it might have any significance to our current case.'

I need wonder no longer how much Oda Fredriksen was taking in. She sat up on the sofa and sighed, then spoke.

'You mean, of course, the tragic case from 1932, and you

no doubt heard it from my eldest daughter. She called here yesterday evening to let me know in no uncertain terms that I should have told you myself. And I have to admit that this time she is right. It is just that the story of my sister's death, even though it was a long time ago now, is still so painful that I quite simply could not face talking about it so soon after my husband had died, and when the children were there.'

I said that I understood and that she had done nothing wrong, but that she should now tell me about the case so that I could determine whether there were any links. It was hard to imagine there wouldn't be some relevance, when the case had made such an impression on all those present that they continued to meet forty years later.

I hastened to add that I had read the police report and so knew the basic facts. I had noticed that there had been no autopsy, even though she had asked for one.

She sighed again, and swallowed a couple of times before starting to speak. 'It is one of my greatest regrets that I was not more persistent in my demands for an autopsy during those desperate and bewildering days in the spring of 1932. Eva did not die of an epileptic fit, both my parents and I knew that perfectly well. She did have epilepsy, it's true, and did sometimes faint after a fit. But she mostly suffered from petit mal, and two doctors had confirmed that her fits were not dangerous. I have always believed that Eva committed suicide. The problem was that my parents did too, and they were such religious and proud people. I wanted to know, rather than live with the doubt. But they preferred to live with the doubt than the scandal. And they got their way.

My father was a man of authority with lots of contacts, and the police did not manage to find a motive or a suspect. So twenty-three years after my father's death, I still have questions that will never be answered. The only positive thing that can be said really, is that now, after my husband's death, I will perhaps think less about my sister's.'

I took the hint and assured her that I would not ask more than was necessary, but that I would like to hear what she thought about the key in the corridor.

'Not a lot. I couldn't explain it in 1932 and I can't explain it now. Eva may have thrown it out of the room, or someone who paid her a visit may have taken it by accident and dropped it. Both alternatives sound slightly bizarre, granted. And yes, I guess it is possible that one of the others killed my sister.'

We looked at each other in suspense. I heard myself saying that if that was the case, might she be able to tell me a little about the three other people who were there. She nodded.

'I guessed you might ask about that and have given some thought as to what I should say. Solveig Thaulow was my best friend at the time. More recently, I have met her for dinner every five years or so. It was as though a great mountain sprang up between us the day my sister died. We were from the same town, and Solveig was in the school year between Eva and me. When asked who was her best friend, she would often reply that she knew Eva and me equally well, and knew both of us better than anyone else. We never had a bad word to say about each other, but we could not help but think of Eva whenever we saw one another and wonder about what had happened. It is strange how a tragedy like that can bring some people closer together and drive others apart . . .'

'Yes. And at the time, Per Johan was her fiancé, but soon afterwards became yours.'

She nodded. 'Yes. But you will have to ask her about what happened and why she and Per Johan split up, because I was never told. Per Johan never talked about it to me. The only time I asked, he said it was a sad story and he wanted to put it behind him, and now he wanted to focus on me and think as little as possible about former girlfriends. I liked his answer. And I also worried what his reaction might be if I asked again. So I never did. I had the impression that things were already deteriorating between him and Solveig, and that Eva's death was the push they both needed to break off the engagement. I had been jealous of Solveig because, to be honest, I had been in love with Per Johan for a long time. And then more than ever, I needed a supporting arm and a comforting voice. So she was not on my mind when he contacted me a few weeks later.'

I could not help but ask if that was before or after the engagement had been broken off. She gave a fleeting and crooked smile before speaking.

'Before. But only a matter of days. And when he came to my door, I soon got the impression that his engagement to Solveig was now more of a formality than a reality. And Solveig found someone else too, not long after.'

I asked if she knew Solveig Thaulow's married name and current address. She nodded.

'Goodness, of course I do. I thought you knew. She is

called Solveig Ramdal and lives together with her husband down at Frognerkilen. She and Kjell Arne got married six months after Per Johan and I, and we have lived barely a mile apart since the war. And yet, the four of us only meet every five years for dinner to mark the day my sister died.'

I asked whether I had understood correctly that Kjell Arne Ramdal had also been her husband's business associate. Then I asked what more she could tell me about him.

'He was definitely the one I knew least before that fateful trip. Kjell Arne Ramdal was a townie, unlike the rest of us. He was the son of a rich pharmacist in Tønsberg. He had been to Oslo more times than the rest of us put together and seemed very worldly. He was studying economics, had inherited a large sum at a young age and later went on to become a successful businessman. Believe it or not, I have very little idea of what kind of business involvement he and my husband had. Per Johan never wanted to bother me with his work and I never asked about it. The few times that I asked how business was going in the early years, he just gave me his most charming smile and said fine. I had no need to know any more.'

'And then there was your sister's boyfriend, Hauk Rebne Westgaard.'

'Ah, Hauk, yes. He's a chapter unto himself. The unusual name suits him. He even looks a bit like a bird of prey – a tall, thin, dark man with a sharp profile and even sharper eyes. Five years ago, on the way home from one of the dinners, my husband remarked that Hauk had scarcely changed in all these years. And that was more or less true three weeks ago too. He looked mature when he was young and so looked young for his age when we last saw him. He and Per Johan grew up together in Holmestrand, and were both in line to inherit big farms. Hauk's father was an alcoholic and naturally he was affected by it. As a young man, he was, as I said, more mature and serious than the rest of us. He was a man of few words, but obviously well read and very compelling when he did have something to say. I was a little frightened of him when my sister first took him home, but then became increasingly impressed. Hauk stayed behind when the rest of us moved into Oslo. He still lives on the family farm out by Holmestrand. He's been the mayor there several times and is reputedly a good shot. Hauk never says much when we meet, but as far as I know, he has never married and does not have any children.'

I jotted all this down. The gallery of people involved in the unsolved case from 1932 was more and more fascinating.

'This tradition of meeting every five years seems rather odd, given that it's now forty years since Eva's death. How did it start?'

She sighed again. 'It was Per Johan's idea. He suggested it shortly before the fifth anniversary of my sister's death. I did not want to go to that first reunion in 1937, nor to the second in 1942, but felt that I couldn't say no when he asked. I'm assuming it was the same for the others. He rang them all and said that we were a family of fate, bound by our shared experience of the tragedy and unsolved mystery in 1932, and that we therefore had to keep in touch. It felt a little as though if you said no, the finger of suspicion would point at you. So we continued to meet on that date, and everyone has always been there. Officially it's to honour my sister's memory.'

I reflected that the members from the group who were still alive had to a certain extent become what Patricia had referred to in a previous case as human flies: people who continue to circle round a dramatic event and are not able to move on with their lives. I, of course, saw no reason to complicate the situation further by mentioning this concept. So instead, I asked sharply: 'And unofficially?'

She gave an insipid smile. 'Unofficially, for reasons I have never understood, my husband was even more obsessed with finding out what happened than I was. He once said that he suspected that one of the others was responsible for my sister's death. But whoever he thought it was, he kept it to himself. It felt like we all wondered about the same thing and were always listening to hear if one of us said something that might throw light on the mystery. So the atmosphere was tense. Despite all the good food and vintage wines, the meals were never jolly affairs. I have not met Hauk, Kjell Arne or Solveig other than at these family-of-fate gatherings, as I still like to call them, since 1932. Our siblings of fate have become more and more estranged over the years. My husband never invited them to birthdays or any other kind of celebration here at home.'

'And you last met three weeks ago – did anything in particular happen that night that might be relevant to your husband's death?'

Oda Fredriksen did not answer at first. She sat in silence for a few seconds. Then she sighed twice before continuing. 'I wish I could answer no to that. As things stand, with the arrest of a possibly mentally deranged young man, it is probably not relevant. But yes, I had thought of telling you about something quite striking that happened. My husband was very sociable and was generally the one who talked most at these dinners. This year, however, he barely said a word for almost the entire meal. He only spoke once, in fact. And that was just after the dessert had been served. He said two sentences. And the rest of the meal was finished in absolute silence.'

Oda Fredriksen stopped, took a couple of deep breaths. She was obviously prepared for my question and answered as soon as I asked her what those two sentences had been.

'I now know exactly what happened the evening Eva died. And one of you knows too and must soon face the consequences.'

The two sentences made quite an impression now as well. Oda Fredriksen and I sat there and looked at each other for what felt like minutes.

I noticed that her hands were trembling and was almost surprised to see that mine were not. The tension around this old story continued to grow. I found it increasingly hard to believe that there was no connection to the murder of Per Johan Fredriksen.

However, our meeting did not end in silence. I still had two questions that had to be answered before I could leave. My first question was whether she had asked her husband for an explanation afterwards.

'Of course. It was a strange and almost unreal evening. We barely said a word in the car on the way home. But about halfway through the journey, I asked him what he meant and whom he suspected of what. He replied that I would hopefully understand soon enough. He didn't say any more and I didn't ask. I was used to my husband being right when he spoke about the future. So I expected to hear something dramatic about one of the others over the next few days. But as far as I know, nothing happened to any of them.'

Once again we sat caught in our own thoughts. I imagined that something very dramatic had happened to Per Johan Fredriksen. And I felt certain that his widow was thinking the same, and now we were sat wondering who was responsible for his death.

Then I asked my final question. In other words, what she believed had happened that day in 1932 when her sister died.

'As I said, I have always believed that my sister committed suicide. She was an impulsive young woman who had her ups and downs. It is most likely she did it with pills, although we never found any. It would be pure speculation for me now, forty years later, to say anything about what or who pushed her over the edge. Even though my husband's death now overshadows everything, I would be very grateful to know should you find anything that might cast light on my sister's death.'

I promised to let her know and thanked her for the information. I then added that I could speak to her children in another room if she wished to be left in peace. She replied that she felt she needed a bit of air now, so she would send the children in.

V

My conversations with her children were shorter. Young Vera was just as pale and seemed just as nervous as when we first met, but this subsided when we sat down. It appeared to be easier for her to talk when there were no other family members present.

I started by saying that as a formality, I had to ask the different members of the family about their civil status and future plans.

She gave a timid smile and said that she had a boyfriend, but hoped that he would soon be her fiancé. He was a 'very handsome and exceptionally talented' Dutch painter whom she had met while studying at Oslo University.

When it came to future plans, she let out a little sigh, and for a moment suddenly resembled her mother.

'To me, my father was the kindest man in all the world. I don't remember him ever saying no to anything I asked for. So it's very sad that the last months we had together were clouded by our only disagreement. It was an unavoidable conflict of generations, I guess. My father was a conservative man and never really understood the trends and possibilities of our time. He liked typical, classical art, portraits and landscape watercolours, and had nothing but contempt for modern and more abstract cubism, which is where my boyfriend's talents lie.'

She looked up at the portrait of her father. She gave him a sweet little smile, but then became serious again as soon as she lowered her eyes.

'And now you finally have the opportunity to live your own life,' I prompted, gently.

She nodded. 'Yes. I would so much rather it had been because Father had changed his mind than because he had died. But I have to say, it is a great help to have a boyfriend who can support me in my grief, and that we now can realize our art project and live our dream.'

Vera Fredriksen was suddenly even more like her mother, it seemed to me. She spoke in a slightly poetic language, which, combined with the surroundings, made her appear somewhat dreamy. However, it was difficult not to be charmed by the deceased's youngest daughter. There was something incredibly naive, graceful and almost angelic about her as she sat there in a simple black dress.

'I have now heard the story about your aunt's death in 1932, and that your father was still very preoccupied with it. Did you ever discuss it with him?'

She chewed a little harder on her gum, and waggled her head a couple of times before answering. 'No, well – that is, yes. Once I'd heard the story from my sister, I took it up with both Mother and Father. You can't help but be curious and I have always liked crime novels and other mysteries. Both were rather uncommunicative. Mother said that her sister's death had been the cause of such grief that she did not want to talk about it, which was perfectly understandable. Father, however, told the bare facts about what happened and when I pushed him a bit, he gave me the names of the others who were there. Which made the whole thing even more interesting, as I actually knew two of them.'

She chewed her gum and looked at me expectantly, then carried on as soon as I asked whom she knew and how.

'Solveig Ramdal is very interested in art, and I started to speak to her and her husband at some exhibition. They seemed nice, but as soon as I said whose daughter I was, they stiffened and moved quickly on. I only really understood why when my sister told me the bizarre story from 1932. Then I thought it wasn't so strange that they jumped a little, as my father had previously been engaged to the woman I was talking to. I have thought more about the case since then, especially in the past twenty-four hours, but I'm afraid I have not yet been able to solve the mystery from 1932 or think of anything else I know that might be of use to you.'

We ended there on a friendly note. She asked for my telephone number, in case she thought of anything that could help the investigation. I wrote down the number to the police station and my home number. I said that she could ring at any time, be it early or late, if she thought of something that could throw light on the deaths of her aunt in 1932 or her father in 1972. She promised she would and wished me good luck with the ongoing investigation.

Vera Fredriksen, just like her mother, was very light on her feet and she almost flew over the large floor.

Her older brother, Johan Fredriksen, had a heavier step, but was all the more steady and secure for it, when he entered the room shortly after.

We shook each other rather formally by the hand. And it struck me that in appearance, he was rather like me: the same height, hair colour, stature and build. And that, for some unknown reason, I did not particularly like him. I could not say why. There was something about his formality and reserve that was unappealing, even though I felt great sympathy for his situation following his father's death.

He sat down on a chair opposite me without saying a word.

I asked whether there was any news in relation to the family fortune and his father's estate.

He replied that it would take some time before they had a full overview, as his father had had quite an empire, including several tenement buildings that were valued at less than the market rate. The estimate of fifty to sixty million from the day before was possibly going to be too low rather than too high.

I then asked him, in as friendly a manner as I could, if he had any plans for his share of the inheritance. He told me that he would eventually like to start his own law firm and would therefore prefer the business to be sold and the profit to be divided up between them. It was something he still had to discuss with his mother and sisters, of course, but he thought his sisters would agree. Otherwise, the business could easily pay out a few million to each of the heirs.

Without further ado, I asked outright whether he knew what kind of business relationship there had been between Per Johan Fredriksen and Kjell Arne Ramdal.

Johan Fredriksen nodded pensively. 'I also wondered about that. And according to the accountant, they made a number of investments and ran a couple of companies together about ten to twenty years ago. However, Ramdal sold his share in the early 1960s and they did not appear to have had any joint ventures after that. Ramdal has been far more successful on his own and has become a property magnate in Oslo. He had put in an offer to buy all Father's real estate companies, in fact. Father had discussed it with his accountant and, rather unusually, with me as well. The offer was for forty-five million, which was, as far as we could see, above the market value. I said that I thought it would be a sensible move for the family. Father was getting older and still had political ambitions, and none of his children were interested in carrying on the property business. The feeling I had, and which I have had confirmed by the accountant, who felt the same, was that Father had focused more on politics in recent years and had been less successful in his business dealings. But Father was still hesitant, for reasons he kept to himself. He would have had to make a decision soon though, as Ramdal had set the deadline for his offer as 24 March.'

I noted down the date, and thought to myself that the timing of Per Johan Fredriksen's death seemed to be becoming increasingly significant.

Out loud, I asked if Ramdal's offer still stood, regardless of his father's death, and if so, if it was now likely to be accepted.

'The offer still stands, and I think it will probably be accepted. Though having said that, I would, of course, not want to jump the gun with regard to the reactions of my mother and sisters.'

Johan Fredriksen had become more communicative and I started to warm to him a little more. A feeling that was further strengthened when he continued of his own accord.

'In all confidence, I must say that in what is already a very difficult situation, the fact that my father discussed his business so little with us is proving very challenging. After all, we only knew him as this kind and loving family man. In my conversations with the office manager and accountant I have come to realize that there were other sides to him that we did not see, but which were evident in his business dealings. It would perhaps be best if you asked them directly about this, if it's of interest to you and the case.'

I said that I would and thanked him for his openness so far. Then I added that, as a matter of routine, I had to build a file on the people closest to the victim, and so had to ask about the civil status of his son.

Our conversation suddenly took a bit of a downturn. Johan Fredriksen furrowed his brow and paused before he started to speak again slowly.

'To tell you the truth, I am not entirely sure what to say. I live alone, and I am unmarried and have no children. Nor am I engaged. But—'

He broke off and sat in thought.

'But it would seem that you are now in a relationship or at the very start of one?' I prompted.

Johan Fredriksen said nothing for a few more seconds, then he continued. 'Yes, well, I certainly hope so. However, it was not entirely clear before all this happened, and does not feel any less complicated now. There are certain things about the lady in question's private circumstances which make me reluctant to make her name known or to give it to the police. And for the moment I do not want the relationship to be made public. More importantly, I know that she doesn't want it to be either. I could possibly ask her if I can give her name to the police, should that be necessary in connection with the ongoing investigation. But it doesn't seem very likely, so in the meantime, you will just have to take my word for it that she has absolutely nothing to do with the case.'

In murder investigations, I tend to like the people who put their cards on the table best, and, as he spoke, I became rather curious about Johan Fredriksen's secret girlfriend. However, I had to agree with his reasoning and felt a growing respect for him.

So I said that it was not optimal, but was acceptable for the present. We shook hands and walked out together.

VI

It was a quarter past twelve by the time I got back to the office. There were still no messages of any significance waiting for me. However, the phone did ring at twenty-five past twelve, when I was halfway through my packed lunch.

I heard the voice of the same annoyingly slow switchboard operator that I had heard the day before. She said there was another lady on the telephone who said she had some information that might be of importance to the Fredriksen investigation.

Naturally, I asked for her to be transferred immediately. A rather tense middle-aged woman came on the line, with a detectable east-end accent, accompanied by a clicking sound that told me she was calling from a telephone box.

'Good afternoon, this is Mrs Lene Johansen. I was away visiting my sister at the weekend and just got back this morning. I was surprised not to find any sign of my son, Tor Johansen, who is just fifteen. And then I discovered that his school satchel was still here, and when I went to the school, they said that he hadn't been there today. His bike is not here either. So I'm afraid that something serious might have happened to him over the weekend. I've told him so many times that he has to be careful when he's cycling around on the wet streets. I shouldn't have gone away.'

I heard an undertone of desperation in his mother's voice. And I heard the suspense in my own when I asked her if she could perhaps describe her son in more detail.

'Dark hair, thin, about five foot three. He should be easy to recognize as he has a limp in his right foot and a large birthmark on his neck.'

All the pieces fell into place as she spoke. I felt enormous relief, for my part, and great sympathy for the mother.

I told her, as calmly and reassuringly as I could, that her son was alive and unharmed, but that he had been remanded on suspicion of a very serious crime.

His mother gasped. It sounded as though she might faint right there in the telephone box. 'Goodness! What on earth has Tor done now?' she almost whispered.

I asked if she had heard that the politician Per Johan Fredriksen had been stabbed and killed. Her first answer was simply another gasp, then there was a sob and the clatter of the receiver falling.

I feared that the line would be broken, but her voice came back a few seconds later, even weaker than before.

'Yes, I saw on the front page that he'd been killed and that a young suspect had been arrested. And I hoped that it wasn't my Tor, but feared the worst. What a terribly, terribly sad story.'

Just then the pips started indicating that her time was up. So she spoke very quickly. 'The line will be cut any minute, and I don't have any more money. We live in a basement flat in thirty-six Tøyenbekken down in Grønland. Come here and I can tell you everything.'

The line was cut before I had the chance to ask her to come here instead.

I sat at my desk for a few seconds and mused on what possible connection there could be between a family from the east end and Per Johan Fredriksen. Judging by the mother's reaction, there clearly was a connection, and just as we thought, it would be a tragic story.

It took me a couple of minutes to decide whether I should go to see the mother directly or have another talk with her son first. I came to the conclusion that as he was a minor, it was my duty to tell him that his mother would be coming soon and to inform him that we now knew his identity.

VII

The prison guard and I both instinctively took a couple of steps back as the door to the cell swung open.

My first thought was that there had been an earthquake.

My second was that the prisoner had somehow managed to escape.

But there had been no earthquake – only a stool that had been pushed over and a bed that had been pulled apart, with the pillow and mattress left lying on the floor.

Tor Johansen was still in the room. He was hanging perfectly still and lifeless against the wall. The bedsheet had been torn into strips and plaited together to make a rope. One end of which was now firmly knotted to the bars on the window, and the other around his neck.

I felt a brief glimmer of hope when I took hold of him, as his body was still warm. But I had come too late. There was no sign of a pulse or breath.

I shouted to the prison guard that he should call a doctor, and heard his running steps disappear down the corridor as I stood there with the lifeless boy in my arms. I had seen death close at hand several times before in the course of my work, but standing here with a dead child in my arms was a horrible experience, all the same. To begin with I thought that I could not let him go until the doctor came. However, no matter how thin he was, he soon became heavy and I realized all hope was gone. So I slowly laid him down on the mattress on the floor.

I stood there and looked at the dead boy's body for a small eternity before I eventually started to cast my eyes around the room. There was not much to see. His shoes stood neatly just inside the door and he was wearing all his clothes. The only things on the table were a pencil and notebook. And on it, he had written in large, simple capital letters:

*BECAUSE EITHER IT IS THE WORLD THAT
IS TURNED TO SLAVERY, OR ME . . . AND
IT IS MORE LIKELY TO BE THE LATTER.*

I read the note containing Tor Johansen's last words to
the world over and over again, until an out-of-breath doctor
arrived and immediately declared the patient dead.

I had no idea where the words on the note came from –
or whether indeed it was something he had read or come up
with himself. Whatever the case, his note only increased
my puzzlement as to who Tor Johansen had been and what
he had been thinking.

VIII

Number 36 Tøyenbekken was at the very end of the street.
The Grønland neighbourhood was far from one of the best
in town, the street was far from one of the best in the neighbourhood and the building was far from one of the best in
the street. The paint was flaking from the walls, the steps
were worn down and what had once been a medium-sized
basement flat was now divided into two much smaller
homes.

The woman who was waiting for me in the basement
also seemed a little worn down. Her dark hair had started to
grey, and her cheeks were wet with tears. I guessed that she
was closer to fifty than sixty, but it did strike me that not so
many decades ago she could well have been an attractive
young woman. She was around five foot six and her body
appeared slim yet shapely even under her old threadbare

dress. The skin on her hands was creased and she was trembling with emotion.

'Come in,' she said quickly, and then closed the door behind us.

We went in and sat down in a room that was barely 150 square feet and appeared to be a combined kitchen, living room and bedroom. There was a table and a couple of chairs in the middle of the room, a made-up bed along one wall and a kitchen counter and cooker along the other.

It was half past two. The priest had been there before me. Lene Johansen knew why I was there. I, on the other hand, could still not see a connection.

The room gave me no clues whatsoever. The flat was clean and tidy, if incredibly small. The things I could see were somehow less striking than the things I could not see. I had not expected there to be a television in a basement flat in Grønland, but nor was there a radio or even any newspapers. There was no telephone or wall clock of any kind.

Above the bed, there was a simple old photograph of a couple in their thirties with a small child. The child was too young to be recognizable as Tor Johansen, but the woman was definitely his mother and she had indeed once been beautiful. The man beside her did not make much of an impression. He was just a clean-shaven, thin, dark-haired man. There was no striking resemblance to Tor Johansen, but nor were there any great differences. His smile was unusually broad, and he had his hand on the baby's head.

The woman followed my eyes to the picture. 'That was in 1957,' she said quietly. 'I was thirty-five, but felt younger and more optimistic than I had done for a long time. We had been married for twelve years without any children, and then all of a sudden, I was going to have one. It was a difficult pregnancy and a complicated birth. We never had any more children. So everything was focused on Tor. In the early days, when he was first born, we thought that everything was fine. But when he started to crawl, we noticed that he dragged one foot behind, and he struggled with words when finally he started to talk. So I had to give all my time to a child who would never learn to walk or talk properly. They were happy days all the same, while my husband was still healthy and alive. He had a good job at the steel works and spent practically everything he earned on the family. But then he fell ill and that same day lost any control over the bottle. Things went downhill with frightening speed. When my husband died three years ago, he left us seventy kroner in cash and twenty-three thousand, two hundred in debt. Since then, Tor and I have moved every year to smaller and smaller flats. And we can't even manage to stay here now the rent has gone up.'

She pulled from her pocket a folded sheet of paper and placed it on the table in front of me.

The letter was short, formal and brutal. The tenancy agreement had been terminated as the rent had not been paid. If they did not move out voluntarily within ten days from the date on the letter, they would be evicted. It was signed by Odd Jørgensen, office manager at Per Johan Fredriksen Ltd.

I immediately thought that here was the link I should have seen. And then I thought that Patricia would have seen it.

Lene Johansen seemed to have aged even more during this conversation, and she buried her head in her hands before carrying on.

'Tor was sitting here with the letter when I came home on Thursday, and was beside himself. He couldn't bear the thought of moving yet again and asked where we were going to go now. I told him the truth, which was that I had no idea. Tor wanted to go and talk to Per Johan Fredriksen personally. I said that he must never do anything of the kind. Then I went down to the office myself the next morning. I begged on behalf of my sick child, I cried and even got down on my knees in front of them. But there was no sympathy and no hope. I left when they threatened to call the police if I stayed on their floor any longer. So I went to visit my sister in Ski to see if she could perhaps find a corner for us in the meantime. The evening before I went, Tor said again that he would go and see Fredriksen himself. I told him it would only make things worse. And that seemed to make him change his mind. So it's not such a surprise that he might have tried to find Fredriksen. But I would never have thought that he would kill him. No matter how much Tor has suffered, he has never broken the law before. He was always kind and good like that.'

I took out a sealed bag with the murder weapon inside and put it down on the table. She quickly understood what it was, but looked at it with little interest.

'That's not from this kitchen, but there are plenty of other ways he could have got hold of it.'

I nodded thoughtfully. It was a piece that did not quite fit the puzzle, but it was in no way decisive.

'There is still one thing I don't quite understand . . . It is perhaps not so strange that he wanted to talk to Fredriksen. But it seems rather odd that he knew how to find Fredriksen in Majorstuen, and also knew the way from there to my flat.'

She let out a heavy sigh. 'Sadly, it is perhaps not as strange as it might seem. Tor never had any money, still couldn't walk properly or talk clearly. So there wasn't much he could do with the others after school. I had to work a lot in the evenings and he didn't like it here on his own. So he'd normally go to the library after school and sit there until it closed. Then he would cycle around in town for a few hours. He liked cycling more than walking, as then people couldn't see his limp. He called his bike Andreas, and used to say that it was his best friend. When I asked him where he'd been he'd say "I've been out with Andreas". They went all over Oslo, the two of them. Tor had a map of practically the whole town in his head. He never dared to talk to famous people, but could always remember where he'd seen them. He sometimes called himself a little spy. So Tor might have followed Fredriksen, if he'd come from the Storting, or waited for him at Majorstuen, if he'd seen him there several Saturdays before.'

That made sense. According to his mistress, Fredriksen had often been there on Saturdays.

I no longer doubted that Tor Johansen had killed Per Johan Fredriksen, but asked his mother all the same if she thought her son was capable of committing such a serious crime.

'To be honest, I don't know what to believe any more.

Tor was my only child. I loved him, but I never really understood him. He was clever with books and things like that. He often understood much more than I did, and sometimes I just had no idea what was going on in his head. He's never done anything wrong before, but I just don't know what he might be capable of any more.'

We sat in silence briefly, before she gave a sombre nod and continued. 'If he has, it's because we're so poor. If my son really has killed someone, it's another tragic example of what poverty can do to a good person.'

Her voice had an edge of bitterness and accusation against society. It soon disappeared, though, when she carried on speaking.

'It's my fault as well, of course. I grew up in a poor family myself, but was quite smart when I was young. Got the best grades in middle school. A rich uncle of my father was impressed and wanted to lend me the money to carry on with school. And I have bitterly regretted every day for the past ten years not taking it. Instead, I got married young, to the wrong man. And stayed with him for as long as he was alive. Despite knowing that he drank a lot and even though for many years we didn't have children. So it was partly poverty and partly the fact that I made the wrong choices that ruined the life of the only child I eventually managed to have.'

There was another silence. I racked my brains for something to say. Fortunately, she got there first.

'If you want to talk to someone other than me about Tor . . . None of the other boys at school knew him well, which is a shame. But he really liked his teacher; Eveline Kolberg, I think she was called. It's possible she might be able to help you, if you need someone smarter than me who might understand how my son thought.'

I wrote down the name. She asked me to take a note of her sister's address in Ski as well. 'In case you come back here and I've been thrown out, that's where you'll find me. Either there or at one of the schools where I'm a cleaner,' she said, her voice breaking.

The atmosphere was heavy and I suddenly longed to get out of the flat, away from this street. I felt a great deal of sympathy for the poor cleaning lady, who had now, along with everything else, lost her only son, but I was unable to see what on earth I could do to help her. It seemed inevitable that her son's story would sooner or later find its way into the press. And he would only ever be remembered as the person who murdered Fredriksen, the politician.

I took great care to assure her that it was never easy to see what the consequences of our choices might be in years to come, and that her son's tragedy was mostly due to poverty rather than her choices.

She brightened a little when I said this and gave a fleeting smile as she stood up and insisted that I see her son's room before I leave.

All I really wanted to do was get away as quickly as I could, but I realized that I should look at his room, now that I was here.

The late Tor Johansen's room was like the rest of the flat: tidy, small and sparse. For a boy who had enjoyed reading so much, he had no bookshelves. There was a shelf's worth of books lined up on the floor against the wall. None of them looked like they had been published after the war, and they all seemed well-thumbed.

There was not a single picture of the boy who had lived here on any of the walls. There were, however, some other pictures of a person I had not expected to see here. Namely, myself. Three newspaper clippings and photographs about my previous investigations were hanging on the wall. It was an unexpected and almost moving sight.

His mother's voice sounded brighter when she spoke. 'It's so strange to have you standing here now, and such a shame that Tor is not here to see it. He read a lot about criminal cases in newspapers and books. He read everything he could about your cases. When you were investigating, he was outside the library first thing Saturday morning to read about the latest developments. It's not so strange really that he'd found out where you lived.'

She was right about this and no doubt meant well in saying it. But it felt rather uncomfortable all the same. The boy on the red bicycle had almost instinctively sought me out in his hour of need and trusted that I would solve the case. Now he was dead and if he was innocent, I had not been able to help him in time.

I tried to push the thought to one side. I now had the answers I had needed from his mother. The boy had a connection to Per Johan Fredriksen and a motive, and the reason why he had known where I lived was obvious. It all added up with a double line under the name of the murderer.

Tor Johansen had slept on a mattress on the floor. The only furniture in his room was a small, old desk and a wooden chair. The desk was empty. A worn brown satchel stood by the chair.

I quickly looked through the satchel, but found no more than the usual schoolbooks. The only surprise was when I leafed through the one titled 'Introduction to Science'. His writing was clear and succinct, and his knowledge was evidently not far behind my own. Tor Johansen had obviously had a good head on him, despite his problems with his tongue and foot.

I shared my thoughts with his mother. That her son had been extremely unlucky and had had a difficult life, but that he had been very intelligent in many ways. However, as the case stood now and based on what she had told me, there was little reason to doubt that he had in fact killed Fredriksen.

She wrung her hands, looked down and said that she saw no grounds to contradict me. To the extent that it could make any difference, she asked me to convey her condolences and apologies to the family. I had been extremely understanding, but unless there was anything else I wanted to know, she would now like to be left in peace to grieve.

When she said this, I feared that she might be harbouring thoughts of suicide. However, I had no more questions to ask and nothing more to say. So once again I expressed my condolences and wished her all the best.

Our eyes met briefly as I turned to go, and I was impressed by the steadiness of her gaze and her firm handshake.

I left without looking back. But all the while I saw the boy's bare room in my mind's eye, the satchel on the floor and the pictures of me on the wall.

IX

Outside the building in Tøyenbekken, only a few yards from my car, my thoughts were interrupted by an unexpected little incident.

As I glanced over my shoulder, I saw a man around my age, who I at first mistook for someone I had gone to school with. He was around five foot nine and of slim build, with the same oval-shaped face and brown hair as one of my old classmates. He was also wearing the same kind of wide-brimmed hat that my friend often did.

I spontaneously lifted up my hand to wave, only to realize that the man was not my classmate at all. This man had broader shoulders and a brisker, more determined step.

The man with the hat, somewhat bewildered, raised his hand in response, only to see it was a misunderstanding. He lowered his hand again in embarrassment. The stranger then continued on his way and did not stop as he passed me where I stood by my car. I could not help but notice that the upper joint of the little finger on his right hand was missing.

I stood by the car for a few seconds and wondered who the man in the suit and hat with the missing joint on his finger might be. And what he was doing here in Tøyenbekken. He and I both stood out in relation to the others walking on the street, and I had no doubt that I would have to stand there for some time before I saw another man in a hat and tie.

It made me wonder if the strange murder case had started to affect my nerves and make me slightly paranoid. So I got into the car and drove back to the main police station, without giving the man in the hat another thought.

X

It was half past three. I had given my boss and Danielsen a report of the latest developments in the case.

I had feared that Danielsen might claim that he had been right, but he was remarkably quiet and seemed almost uninterested. The explanation came when my boss asked a question that I had not considered.

'How did he get hold of the paper and pencil?' he asked.

I immediately replied that it was not from me. Danielsen squirmed uncomfortably and said that he had given the prisoner the paper and pencil yesterday, in case he found it easier to write down his statement. This was a reasonable gesture, given that the boy had a speech impediment, but Danielsen apologized profusely and said that perhaps he should have mentioned it before.

Neither my boss nor I put too much importance on this. I, for my part, was happy as long as no one asked any critical questions as to whether I might have contributed in some way to his suicide. And no one did. Danielsen seemed uninterested in the case, and my boss almost content.

Danielsen said hastily that it was what we had thought, then, and that the death had actually made our work easier.

Our boss nodded and asked that I use the rest of the week to tie up any necessary loose ends and inform the Fredriksen family, as well as write a press release and some internal reports – in that order. I said that I was more than happy to do this.

The atmosphere when we parted at a quarter to four was light and almost friendly. Danielsen and I wished each other a good evening before heading off in our separate directions. At times like this, I almost liked him. But the feeling usually passed very quickly.

XI

I telephoned Mrs Oda Fredriksen and informed the victim's family of the latest developments. I heard considerable relief in her voice when I finished my account. She thanked me for letting her know, offered straightaway to tell her children, and had no objection to the details being released in the morning papers. She added that it had been of great comfort to the family that the person in charge of the investigation had shown so much understanding.

I thanked her, and asked her to convey my greetings and best wishes to her children. We finished the phone call in good spirits at a quarter past four.

I then sat down to write a press release, and had just formulated the first few sentences when the telephone rang at twenty past four. The switchboard operator's voice was like a snake slithering into paradise; she said that there was an elderly lady from Majorstuen on the telephone who insisted on speaking to me as soon as possible.

The voice at the other end certainly sounded like a woman well past retirement age. So what she said was all the more surprising.

'Good afternoon, inspector. This is Randi Krogh Hansen calling you from Kirk Road in Majorstuen. I apologize if I'm interrupting, but my old mother claims that she saw something through the window here the day before yesterday that you absolutely need to know.'

It was unexpected. Before I had even thought, I remarked that her mother must be very old. Fortunately, she took it well.

'You can certainly say that. My mother has been on this earth for over a hundred years now. But her eyesight is still good and after reading today's newspapers she is convinced that she saw something that you must know, today. Unfortunately, her legs are not what they used to be, so it would be difficult to get her to the police station. Would you be able to come and see us here as soon as possible?'

I had had time to gather my thoughts now and was curious as to what the witness might have seen. So I said I would come immediately.

XII

The address that Randi Krogh Hansen had rung from was a three-storey building on the corner of Bogstad Road and

Kirk Road, a couple of blocks down from the station. Once I had parked the car, I quickly checked that there was a clear view from the windows to where Per Johan Fredriksen had been attacked. Then I made my way to the main entrance.

Randi Krogh Hansen was standing ready to greet me just inside the door. Her face was wrinkled and she could easily have been in her eighties, but she was a slim lady who was still light of foot. Her thin hand shook slightly in mine. There was no one else in the hall, but she still lowered her voice and leaned forwards when she spoke.

'Welcome to our humble abode. I do hope we haven't called you here unnecessarily. It's my doing that you were not contacted before. My mother said yesterday morning that she had seen a man being stabbed on the street opposite the evening before. She sometimes dozes off in her chair and starts dreaming, so I thought that was probably what had happened. She eventually gave in with some reluctance. Then, about an hour ago, she read in the newspaper that a politician had been stabbed here and, let me tell you, she gave me a piece of her mind. So I had to ring the police immediately and now only hope that what she has to tell you will be of interest.'

My first thought was that we could perhaps have been spared a lot of work if we had got the message yesterday. But it had not been withheld with malice, so I forced myself to smile at the elderly lady in front of me and assured her that her reaction was perfectly understandable.

She smiled back, relieved, and repeated in a hushed voice that her mother had bad legs and weak lungs, but that her mind was clear and her eyes were still sharp as a pin, despite her great age.

We went up to the second floor and somewhat formally knocked on the door of a room that looked out over the street below. 'Come in,' said a high, sharp woman's voice from within. The daughter promptly opened the door and showed me through, but stayed standing outside herself.

A wall of heat hit me as soon as the door opened. A fan heater hummed merrily and the only person in the room was puffing on a good old-fashioned pipe. She was sitting in a rocking chair in front of the stove, looking straight at me. The tiny old lady looked as though she could not weigh much more than six stone, all wrapped up in her blanket. Her arms were skin and bone, her face wrinkled as a raisin, and some white wisps were all that was left of her hair. But her lips were still red and her blue eyes were piercing, with almost a twinkle, as she focused them on me. She nodded in acknowledgement when I held out my hand, and then shook it with an unexpectedly firm grasp.

'Welcome, young man. I do apologize that my daughter's neurotic objections prevented me from contacting the police yesterday, and also that it is so warm in here.'

Whether it was intentional or not, she was then racked by a coughing fit that lasted some thirty seconds, only to be replaced by a smile and the pipe moments later.

'As you can hear, my lungs are about to pack up on me. The cold seeps into my marrow and there is no reason to be frugal with the electricity or the tobacco. I celebrated my hundred and fourth birthday last week, and know perfectly well that it will be my last. I smoked my first pipe here in

1880. I gave birth to my first child here in 1884, while the great men in the Storting were fighting for independence. I was standing down on the harbour with my first grandchild on my arm when the new king and young crown prince came sailing to an independent Norway in the autumn of 1905. So I have been here a long time and seen many things. I got my first pension from the Nygaardsvold government, and have cost the state coffers dear. So I thought that this might be my final chance to do something useful for the country, and I should use it.'

I said that I was very impressed and that her daughter also looked remarkably well for her age if she was born in 1884.

She shook her head disapprovingly. 'My eldest children died a long time ago. She was an afterthought, and was not born until 1898. Unfortunately, she is not the brightest of the bunch. What nonsense it was not to call the police yesterday. But she is kind and does her best, and she is the only one of my children who is still alive. So I really shouldn't complain.'

I nodded politely to this and looked at the shrunken, ancient woman in the rocking chair with something akin to awe. All of a sudden, she reminded me of an eighty-year-old Patricia. I said, out loud, that she was absolutely right and what she had seen could be of great interest to the police.

She nodded and took a couple of puffs on her pipe before continuing. 'My eyes and brain are about the only things that work any more. So, I was sitting here resting on Saturday evening. My thoughts were wandering in the past, but snapped back to the present when I saw something very unexpected on the street out here. Unfortunately, it had started to get dark, so I could really only see shadows and silhouettes, not faces. However, what I saw, clearly enough, was a tall, rather stout chap, who must have been the right honourable Fredriksen, walking towards the station. There was a shorter, slimmer person waiting for him at the corner. Fredriksen stopped when he saw this person and they exchanged a few words. Then suddenly the person drew a knife and stabbed him. He fell to the ground. The attacker ran off down the street, away from the station. Fredriksen was left lying on the pavement. Then another person came along who knelt down and leaned over him. And then some more people came.'

Thus far, it all seemed to tally with what we knew had happened – and with what the newspapers had reported. I asked if Fredriksen had been stabbed once or several times. We had not released this information to the press.

She replied without hesitation, and without blowing any smoke in my direction.

'Twice. The person pulled out the knife, but Fredriksen remained standing. So he or she stabbed him again, and then he fell to the ground with the knife still in him.'

It felt as though the room was heating up around me. It was true that Fredriksen had been stabbed twice in the chest, just as she described.

I asked whether she had seen a bicycle. She shook her head.

'No, there was no bicycle when it happened. They were both on foot.'

Which did not necessarily prove anything, I told myself.

Tor Johansen may have left the bike somewhere close by and run back to get it afterwards. But if she had seen him running, she should have been able to see if he limped.

'Even though it was dark, did you notice anything more about the attacker? Could you tell me, for example, if the person ran in an unusual way?'

The old woman blew out another cloud of smoke and looked at me fiercely. 'Yes, I could, and there was nothing unusual about him or her. The person who stabbed Fredriksen was perfectly normal.'

I started to feel slightly hot around the collar. And I thought to myself that something was not right. Then I heard my own voice asking if she was sure there was nothing special about the way the attacker ran off.

'No, as I said. The person who stabbed Fredriksen walked perfectly normally and easily. But the first person to the scene afterwards limped heavily on the right foot. It was quite obvious when he came and when he ran away. And I was very surprised when the limping shadow ran off with the knife.'

The words hit me like snow falling from the roof. Suddenly my body felt ice cold, despite the heat of the room.

I sat there, unable to utter a word. The shock must have been apparent on my face, because the old lady in the rocking chair looked at me with increasing concern.

'I do hope I have not said anything wrong. I only wanted to help, not create more problems. I am too close to the grave to lie and I am absolutely certain that that is what I saw. The person who stabbed Fredriksen moved without any difficulty. But the person who came after, pulled out the knife and took it away. That person limped so heavily on the right foot that I thought he must have a club foot or something.'

I heard myself saying that she had absolutely done the right thing and that this could be very important and I believed every word she said. Then I asked if she had seen any other people down on the street before the second person came.

'Yes. There was one other person. He stood without moving on the other side of the road and watched the whole incident, the stabbing and then the person with the limp coming along and pulling out the knife. I was rather taken aback, but then thought that perhaps he was either looking the other way or was in a state of shock. The onlooker left at the same time as the person with the limp, only in the opposite direction. I say he, but it could equally have been a woman. It was not much more than a shadow I saw, but he was wearing a man's hat.'

The hat may have been a coincidence, but I was not convinced that it was. I felt as though I had been winded. The ancient woman in the rocking chair had turned everything upside down in the space of five minutes. Here she was sitting with a vital piece of the puzzle that only proved I had put it together completely wrong.

I had an overwhelming feeling of paralysis, but could also feel the adrenalin starting to surge. There was a strange sense of relief for the boy on the red bicycle and his mother, too, and mounting curiosity as to what had actually happened when Per Johan Fredriksen was killed.

I said that she had been of great help and asked if it

would be possible to send a written version of her statement for her to verify and sign.

We looked at each other for a brief moment. Then she started to cough again and said that if it was important, perhaps I should take a written statement straightaway.

'My cough is getting worse and worse,' she said. 'This past week I have been surprised to wake up every morning and realize that I am still alive.' She chuckled and then lit her pipe again, but it was clearly serious.

I wrote down her statement by hand on a plain sheet of white paper. She read it through, gave a brief nod and then signed her name, Henriette Krogh Hansen, underneath. Her ornate handwriting would not have looked out of place on a scroll from another century. Her gnarled little hand reminded me of an eagle's claw and it burned like a red-hot poker when I shook it, her eyes unblinking when I said goodbye. Henriette Krogh Hansen was in no doubt as to what she had seen, and I was in no doubt that what she had seen was what happened.

XIII

My boss was supposed to go home at half past five, but at a quarter to six he was still sitting opposite me. Danielsen's shift had finished at five, which was an enormous relief.

The boss listened in silence to my account of the most recent development. His expression was inscrutable, but it seemed to me that there was something disapproving about him.

'You are, as usual, to be praised for following up every lead, Kristiansen. How old did you say this new witness was?'

I took a deep breath, in and out. Then I replied: 'One hundred and four. She is very old indeed, but has perfect vision and a clear head. I found her to be wholly credible.'

I hoped that my boss would nod. But instead, he just sat there waiting.

'It is, however, a ripe old age for an eyewitness who has seen something through the window at dusk. The only thing she said that can be checked and that was not reported in the papers, is that Fredriksen was stabbed twice. She might, of course, simply be guessing. That being said, it is unsettling news and could indicate that Fredriksen's murderer is still at large. But it might cause confusion and unfounded speculation if we were to step up the investigation after the prime suspect has committed suicide and left behind a note that was as good as a confession.'

We fell silent. All at once, I found I was not sure of my boss. But I felt that I had to say something, before he asked me to wrap up the investigation as planned.

So I said that the solution would be to announce that the prime suspect had indeed taken his own life and left behind a note that could be interpreted as a confession, but that the police would continue the investigation as a matter of course.

My boss gave a quick nod.

'Yes, let's do that. You follow up things with the family. Question whom you want, call in Danielsen if you need

113

help and let me know immediately of any new developments.'

I promised to do that and stood up to leave. My boss remained sitting. I got the distinct feeling that there was something else, and that he was deliberating whether to bring it up. So I stayed where I was.

He coughed and then said: 'If we follow it through and remain open to the possibility that someone other than the late young Tor Johansen . . .' he paused. 'It seems more likely that we should look for the clues in Fredriksen's private life and any connection to the old mystery from 1932, rather than his political activities. So perhaps it would be best to start with the friends in the group who are still alive?'

Further investigation into the mystery from 1932 was at the top of my list of priorities. So I agreed without hesitation, but added that we should in principle be open to all possibilities as the victim had been a senior politician with many strings to his bow.

My boss could hardly disagree with this. So he simply nodded. I got the impression that he had more on his mind than he was willing to say, and left in anticipation of what more I might discover about the murder mystery from 1932.

XIV

Miriam had been given the spare key to my flat and used it well. Supper was already on the table when I got home at twenty-five past six.

I thanked her for her understanding and apologized for being late. She replied merrily that it was important to use time efficiently, as she had a meeting at the party office at eight. She then asked me to tell her without further ado about any developments in the investigation.

She lost her twinkle when I told her about the death earlier in the day and what had happened since then. Miriam looked as though she might burst into tears for a minute or two when she heard the story of the boy and his mother. She sat deep in thought for the latter part of the meal.

'Tell me again what the quote was,' she said, eventually.

I got it out of my bag.

'"Because either it is the world that is turned to slavery, or me . . . and it is more likely to be the latter".'

She nodded mournfully. 'Just as I thought. It's from a book on the Norwegian literature curriculum – at the end of Jonas Lie's *One of Life's Slaves*. The protagonist, Nikolai, is a young man who has grown up in very difficult circumstances and has done his utmost to be a law-abiding pillar of society, but he ends up in prison all the same. In the novel, Nikolai ends up committing murder out of sheer desperation and frustration. So it could be interpreted however you want. But you don't think he committed the murder, do you?'

Her question was unexpected, but I shook my head firmly all the same. 'What about Hauptmann, then?'

Miriam gave this some thought while she ate the rest of her food.

'I'm not sure. It's a new name to me, but there is something familiar about it,' she said. She sat quietly for a while longer. Then suddenly she pointed at me and jumped up from the sofa.

'I think we saw something about him when we went through the history book,' she said.

Four seconds later she was already over by the bookshelf. She leafed with impressive speed to the middle of the book, then exclaimed with satisfaction: 'And here we have Hauptmann! If he is who I think he is. And it has to be, surely?'

I rushed over to her, looked at the picture and said without thinking that I agreed, it had to be him.

The photograph was from 1936. Hauptmann's first name was Bruno. He was a dark, thin and serious young man in the photographs taken during a court case in New Jersey, where he was being tried for the kidnapping and murder of the legendary pilot, Charles Lindbergh's little boy. Hauptmann came from a simple background and the evidence against him was so controversial that he was not executed until a year after the court case. Hauptmann was a German immigrant who could barely make himself understood, but maintained his stammering innocence until his death.

Miriam and I stood there in the middle of the room, with the book between us and read what was written with wide eyes. Then we looked at each other.

'I think he was innocent,' I said.

'Hauptmann or the boy on the red bicycle?' Miriam asked, more than a little pedantically.

'Both,' I said.

She nodded in agreement and we kissed on it.

'Your memory is impressive. I should have called you as soon as he mentioned Hauptmann,' I said.

We both stepped back and fell silent. The thought that the boy on the red bicycle had been innocent and that he might still have been alive if I had realized this sooner, was very unsettling. It seemed Miriam understood.

'But I was in the library, so you would not have been able to get hold of me by phone. And in any case, we will never know whether the outcome might have been different. He certainly didn't make it easy for you. He was clearly a well-read and intelligent boy, despite his handicap. But it does seem strange that he only added to his problems by speaking in riddles in the way that he did,' she said, slowly.

Again, I had to agree. The young Tor Johansen's mental state remained a mystery within the murder mystery, and we might never know the answer. It did not make the investigation any easier, even though we now assumed that he had come to the scene of the crime after the murder, and had not seen who did it.

'Why on earth did he take the knife with him if he wasn't guilty?' I wondered.

Miriam stood thinking. Then she sighed heavily and said: 'I don't know. It's just one of the things we'll have to ponder. But right now I have to leave for the meeting at the party office, if I'm going to be on time. And tomorrow I'm afraid I have a Socialist People's Party regional meeting and an anti-EEC meeting . . .'

She looked rather apologetic when she said this. I said that I would be more than happy to drive her, but she replied that public transport was more environmentally friendly and also more efficient timewise. Then she made a speedy exit. I had to dash after her to say thank you for her input today and that I would phone her at the halls of residence tomorrow before her meetings.

Then once again I stood alone at the window and watched Miriam become smaller and smaller until she was just a smudged shadow in the evening dark. And I thought about the big question we had not had time to discuss today – in other words, Patricia.

I was absolutely convinced that Patricia would get more out of the facts of the case. I thought to myself that no matter how irregular my contact with Patricia was, it was in a way my duty to call her when I thought that her help might be vital to solving the case.

But even after Miriam had disappeared from sight, I felt that it would be too much of a betrayal to phone Patricia behind her back. Also, I still wasn't sure if Patricia would be willing to help me while Miriam was still around.

So I pushed it to one side and sat down on my own to listen to the news. I was somewhat relieved that the only mention of the politician's murder was a brief report to say that the prime suspect had taken his own life in prison.

As was to be expected, the main stories were about the EEC and the demarcation line agreement with the Soviet Union. The first item was just as controversial today as it had been yesterday, whereas it seemed that the demarcation line issue was now close to agreement. The Government had had a draft agreement confirmed and the opposition was largely in favour of it, though it did have some reservations.

Despite this exciting news, my thoughts kept turning back to the murder investigation. When the evening news had finished reporting on my case, I was finished with it. I sat and looked through the papers I had been working on before I left the office.

They were copies of a short press release and two telegrams that had been sent to Oda Fredriksen at Bygdøy and Lene Johansen at Grønland, telling them that the investigation would continue for a few more days. Then there was a note of two telephone numbers, to three people I had not spoken to yet: Hauk Rebne Westgaard, and the couple Kjell Arne and Solveig Ramdal. The investigation was now becoming an obsession. It was increasingly clear to me that I would not be able to wait until tomorrow to pursue it.

XV

Hauk Rebne Westgaard answered the telephone when I rang at twenty-five to nine. 'Westgaard, how can I help?' he said, in a steady and controlled voice, without the slightest hint of joy.

Our conversation was short and to the point. I told him that I was leading the investigation into the murder of Per Johan Fredriksen and therefore had to ask him some routine questions in connection with the events that took place in 1932. He in turn told me that he had heard about the murder on the news and had been expecting the police to contact him. We agreed that it was a little too late to travel either to or from Holmestrand today. He said that he would be more than happy to talk to me, but was in the middle of renovations at the farm and would therefore not be able to come to Oslo until late afternoon the following day. I offered to drive down to Holmestrand and meet him there around ten o'clock in the morning. He said that that would work well for him and that I was very welcome.

My next telephone call was answered by a man who said: 'The Ramdals, you are talking to Director Ramdal himself.'

When he heard who I was, he said that of course he knew what it was about and that they had expected to be contacted. His wife was at present visiting a daughter and would not be home until later, but he himself was there and had time if I wished to meet him now. I thanked him and said that I would.

I got into my car at a quarter to nine and drove to Frogner-kilen. On my way there, I passed within a few hundred yards of Erling Skjalgsson's Street. I wondered how Patricia was. I imagined her sitting there as she always did, in the library with the papers and reports about the case spread out in front of her. But I had made my decision, at least for today. And I did not even consider turning off into Frogner.

The Ramdals' home was a generous detached house in a garden in the best part of Frognerkilen, with a view to the fjord in the background. Both the house and garden were bigger than I had anticipated. On my way up the drive, I found myself wondering whether the Ramdals knew the Borchmanns, and if they also had servants.

The answer to this proved to be no. When I rang the bell, the door was eventually opened by Kjell Arne Ramdal himself. He was a slightly overweight man with grey streaks in his hair and beard, and yet clearly in good health and fit for his sixty-five years.

There were two pairs of skis leaning up against the wall in the hallway, beside a full to bursting cupboard. The photographs of children and grandchildren on the walls all added to the impression of a happy, upper-class home. Ramdal himself was in several of the photographs together with a slim, black-haired woman whom I assumed was his wife. It occurred to me that there was something odd about the pictures, but I could not put my finger on it.

'As I said, my wife is visiting one of the family – our children moved away from home a long time ago. So I am the only one here at the moment. Which is perhaps a good thing, if we are to talk about business or the old case from 1932,' Kjell Arne Ramdal remarked.

I said that I agreed and followed him into the living room. He sat down on a rather majestic brown leather chair and indicated that I should sit on a slightly smaller leather chair on the other side of a mahogany table. The furniture was very elegant and the living room one of the biggest I had seen, though of course it could not be compared with the drawing room of the late Per Johan Fredriksen.

It was as if Kjell Arne Ramdal had read my thoughts as he started by saying: 'If you have been to Fredriksen's home, you will know that mine can in no way compete with his. But fortunately the same is not true of our financial situation.'

'Because in recent years you have been more successful in terms of business. And as I understand it, you have given an offer for more or less all of his companies?

His nod was brisk and almost too keen.

'All his properties in Oslo and Akershus, yes. It will be my largest investment to date if it all goes through, and I believe it will also be my best. The geographical profile of his properties will complement my own and the advantages of having a large company will be even greater. I have always been more strategic and daring than Fredriksen, which is probably why I have been more successful.'

I asked him without further ado what he had to say about the man, both as a businessman and a person.

'Fredriksen could be very different when in different situations. More recently I have known him mostly in his role as a businessman. And as such he was cautious and focused on the short-term gains to be had from his properties, without having any particular strategy or future vision. For the past fifteen years, he has been more interested in politics and less in the markets than before. His business was healthy and robust. But he stagnated while others expanded and was reluctant to make the necessary investments at a time when people expect a higher standard of accommodation than before. He had a very good accountant and office manager who have been with him for years, but they were constantly overworked and he had too few staff. Over the past three or four years he has let some good opportunities go, and the value of his companies has fallen rather than increased.'

'And does your offer to buy the companies still stand, even though he is now dead?'

He nodded slowly and forcefully. 'His son rang me today to check whether the offer still stands and whether it would be possible to extend the deadline. I told him that of course the offer still stands, but that as I have the bank on standby and my administration have been working very hard on it, I could only offer an extra twenty-four hours before I needed a decision. He thanked me for this and as far as I understand, they are likely to accept the offer. What Fredriksen would have done is less clear, and now we will never know. He had acquired larger and smaller properties throughout his adult life and it was not in his nature to sell, even for a good price.'

I noted that Kjell Arne Ramdal still only used Per Johan Fredriksen's surname, despite having known him for more than forty years. And also it seemed that they had been competitors, rather than associates. I asked if I was correct in understanding that they had once worked together?

'The two companies first worked together for a period after the war and then we had some joint ventures between the mid-fifties and the mid-sixties. We were never close friends even though we were in business with one another, and we did not fall out when we stopped working together. Our business assessments were based on different strategies and ambitions, so in the end, we were better off working alone.'

I made a note to the effect that this was more or less in line with what Fredriksen's children had said. But also that the situation regarding the two companies did give Ramdal a possible motive for murder, albeit a fairly weak one. I then asked about the case from 1932.

Kjell Arne Ramdal lost some of his enthusiasm and sat silently for a moment before he answered.

'It is a tragic story that is still a mystery to this day. We had seen Eva, just as beautiful, young and full of life as she always was, only hours before. Then suddenly there she was lying dead and cold in our midst. I think the shock had a lasting effect on us all. We were carefree youths who became serious, responsible adults overnight. I was on my own in my hotel room for the three hours before we found her, and really don't know what more I can say about the case. Paradoxically, the only thing that is certain is that what became the official truth is not the truth at all. It was not epilepsy that killed Eva. She only had petit mal, which is not life-threatening, and she was otherwise in good shape. But whether it was suicide or murder, and if it was murder who was responsible, I would not like to say, not even today.'

As though to underline this, he pursed his lips and promptly fell silent in his leather chair.

Kjell Arne Ramdal was clearly an intelligent man who had more theories and thoughts about what happened in 1932 than he wanted to say. So I decided that first I would ask him straight about what and who he thought had caused Eva Bjølhaugen's death. He replied that he did not want to answer that here and now, as it would be pure speculation.

I got the feeling that it was some kind of accusation against Per Johan Fredriksen that he did not want to verbalize only a few days after Fredriksen himself had been killed, and while he, Ramdal, was still waiting to hear if his offer to buy up the companies had been accepted. But this was, in turn, no more than speculation on my part. I asked him instead about his wife's engagement to Per Johan Fredriksen, and the circumstances surrounding their break-up.

Kjell Arne Ramdal replied that he did not know much about that side of the case, and that it really was up to his wife whether she wanted to say anything about it or not.

As we sat there, it suddenly struck me that Kjell Arne Ramdal never smiled. Not here, nor in the family photographs on the walls, as far as I could see. He was intelligent, correct and in no way unfriendly, but apparently a man with no sense of humour or joy. I was reminded of the title of one of the most popular Norwegian films in recent years, *The Man Who Could Not Laugh*. Then I remembered what Kjell Arne Ramdal had said, and wondered to what extent the events of 1932 were to blame.

I pondered on this and he looked as though he was thinking about something, though I had no idea what and he was not likely to tell me. So we sat in silence for a while.

Then I thought of another question – about the most recent of their five-year-anniversary meals and what had happened there.

He nodded cautiously in acknowledgement. 'I understand that you are already well informed. So no doubt you know that we met every five years on the day that Eva died, and that at the last meeting, only a few weeks ago, Per Johan suddenly made a very unexpected statement. He said that he now finally understood what had happened, and that one of us also knew and should face the consequences. He said nothing more about what he thought had happened, and the rest of the meal was a cold war where none of us said a word. I could only see surprise, not fear or regret in any of the others' faces. If one of the people round that table was responsible for her death, they kept up appearances well. All I know for certain is that if the murderer was sitting at the table, it was not me.'

I promptly asked if he was certain that his wife had not committed the murder.

He answered in a very solemn voice: 'I would never have married her if I thought that was the case. I have always believed that it was one of the others. But in such situations one can only be certain of what one has seen with one's own eyes, wouldn't you say?'

I had to agree with him there. But at the same time, I could not help thinking that it must be very uncomfortable not to be certain whether your spouse had committed murder or not.

'I do know for certain, however, that she did not murder Per Johan. She was at home here with me on Saturday evening,' he added, hastily.

Just then, we heard light footsteps out in the hall.

'And talking of my wife, here comes the sun,' Kjell Arne Ramdal said, without so much as a hint of a smile, or humour in his voice. 'Do you have any more questions for me? If not, I will hand the stage over to my wife before it gets too late.'

Without waiting for an answer, Kjell Arne Ramdal stood up and left the living room. And as he did so, he reminded me of one of Ibsen's serious, patriarchal family men whom Miriam and I had talked about only a couple of weeks ago.

XVI

I was afraid that Kjell Arne Ramdal might come back with his wife. But she came into the room alone and discreetly closed the door behind her.

Whether calling her the sun was accurate or not, I was unable to decide. It certainly seemed true. Following my deadly serious conversation with Kjell Arne Ramdal, the room definitely lit up when his wife came in. Despite her black hair, she seemed to be of a far brighter disposition than him, and her smile was open and friendly. She was slim and moved gracefully across the floor. Her dress was modern and fitted. I would have guessed that she was under fifty rather than her true age of over sixty.

Solveig Ramdal, née Thaulow, was clearly a confident and well-heeled upper-class lady. She had gold around her neck and on both hands, and in her husband's absence she sat down on his throne. Her hand was small, but her handshake firm. Her voice was soft when she said: 'Good evening. And how can I help you?'

My first thought was that she reminded me of a cat. And I sat there wondering if that sweet smile disguised some sharp teeth.

I did not imagine that she would have much to add to her husband's statement regarding the business. So I cut to the chase and asked how she had experienced Eva Bjølhaugen's death in 1932.

Her smile disappeared as soon as I mentioned the name.

'It was terrible,' Solveig Ramdal said, in an intense, hushed voice.

'Terrible situations like that can push some people together and pull others apart,' I said.

Solveig Ramdal was quick to understand my point. 'That is very true, indeed. But in this case, the two who were pulled apart were already drifting in different directions. But one shouldn't really speak ill of the dead . . .' She bit her lip and fell silent.

'Sometimes it is necessary to tell the truth about the dead. Particularly when they have been murdered,' I countered.

She nodded vigorously, and it seemed to me that she was almost grateful. 'You may well be right, inspector. You see, Per Johan was a very complicated man, who was very different in different situations. He could be a happy, charming and extremely kind man. He was my first great love, and we had many good times together. Only a few months before the trip to Oslo I had been madly in love and thought that he would be the only love of my life. But there were others who had experienced less sympathetic, colder sides of Per Johan. Then one day I was contacted by a friend who had overheard him say that he was more attracted to my inheritance than to me. This was perfectly plausible as I was an only child and the sole heir to a considerable fortune. Per Johan denied it, of course, and I so wanted to believe him. But the doubt was there like a wall between us. And then when another wall sprang up after Eva's death, there was just too much doubt and suspicion.'

'So what you are saying is that you suspected that he was in some way connected to Eva's death?'

She gave a careful nod. 'Suspected is perhaps too strong a word, but it was a possibility, and it hung over us like a dark cloud. The friend who told me what Per Johan had apparently said about me, had also heard him say that Eva was an alternative that he had considered more and more. And that was understandable too, because she was far prettier than I was, and heir to an even greater fortune. So it would be easy to imagine it was some kind of jealousy drama, until you see what happened after Eva died, because it wasn't long before Per Johan married her less attractive sister, who had become sole heir in the meantime. So one might even suspect that the motive was purely gain. Perhaps you did not know that Per Johan got most of his property from the marriage? Oda was worth three times more than him when they got married.'

I said that I had not known that. And I thought to myself that it was a very possible murder motive. I first asked myself and then Mrs Ramdal who might have a motive for revenge now, forty years later.

'Certainly not me, and not Kjell Arne. Hauk, on the other hand, would clearly have a motive. It would seem that the loss of his girlfriend had a profound effect on him and he never married or started a family. Oda might also have reason for revenge. Though I must say, I don't think there was any love lost between them in 1932, but she did lose her only sister, after all. And if you were suddenly to discover that, for the past forty years, every day you had lived was a lie and you had been kept in the dark by a husband who had never told you that he had murdered someone close to you – well, I am sure that would be enough to make most people flip.'

That had crossed my mind too. And for the moment, I liked Solveig Ramdal best of the group from 1932, both when she was happy and when she was serious. Because it was definitely her serious face that I saw when asked what she made of the key found lying outside the room in the hotel corridor.

'I still have no plausible explanation. Whatever else one might say about Per Johan, he was a strong and very focused man. It is unthinkable that he would have dropped the room key in the corridor without noticing, especially if he had just committed a crime. He might have put it there himself, as a kind of red herring, or someone else might have put it there, so that people would suspect him or Hank.'

As we were talking so intimately, I swiftly took the opportunity to ask what she thought about Per Johan Fredriksen's statement at the group's last anniversary dinner.

'Much the same, really. He might have said it to deflect any suspicion, he might have been calling our bluff – or he might have found out that it really was one of us. The only thing I know for certain is that it was not me who killed Eva, if it was indeed one of us who did it.'

Without thinking, I lowered my voice and leaned forwards over the table when I asked if she could not even be certain that her husband had not done it. She remained calm and answered in a hushed voice in return: 'Yes, that is correct. As far as Per Johan is concerned, I know that it was not Kjell Arne. He was here with me on Saturday night. We were sitting here together when we heard about the attack on the radio. But as for Eva's death, I have always thought that Kjell Arne seemed a less likely murderer than Per Johan, Hauk and Oda. But no, I don't know for certain.'

And with that, it was as though she had said all there was to say. She pursed her lips and turned her eyes away to gaze out of the window. And when the large wall clock behind us then struck ten, it felt like a natural end to our conversation.

I quickly noted that two of the group from 1932 could provide each other with an alibi for the murder of Per Johan Fredriksen. And that Mr Ramdal spoke of all the others by their surname, whereas Mrs Ramdal used their first names. Then I thanked her for her cooperation so far, and stood up.

XVII

It was twenty-five past ten by the time I parked outside my flat in Hegdehaugen. It had been a long and demanding day which had yielded some important answers, but also raised many new questions. Without being able to put my finger on why, the whole situation felt very unstable. I walked from the car towards the entrance and everything seemed to be as normal, and yet I was annoyingly gripped by a growing urge to look back. The sensation that there was someone behind me whom I had to see became more and more intense.

Reluctantly, I gave in to the fear and turned around without warning just as I reached the front door.

There was nothing to see. But as I went in I found myself wondering if perhaps there had been someone there before I turned around. On my way up the stairs, I chastised myself for not having turned around earlier, and for allowing my uncertainty about the case to tip into fear.

Once inside my flat, I realized that I still wasn't tired. I stood alone by the window and looked out at the night.

The street below was empty. And yet I could see someone down there. Images of the boy on the red bicycle, who, two evenings before, had pedalled so frantically up the hill in front of the house, were still burned in my mind.

Even though there was much that was still unexplained, it now seemed clear that the boy had been innocent of murdering Per Johan Fredriksen and that he had cycled here in desperation because he trusted that I would discover the truth. The boy had wanted to give me his simple statement: that he was innocent, that he had only tried to help, and that Fredriksen had been dead when he went back. And it had all been true.

But there was also a sense that the boy on the red bicycle had in some way let me down, first by his lack of cooperation and then by taking his own life. Although of course, the stronger feeling was that I had let him down and betrayed the trust he had given me by failing to recognize his innocence in time to save his life.

I had a light snack alone at twenty to eleven. I felt pretty miserable and thought about the case as I ate two slices of bread and cheese in the kitchen, but was no closer to solving either the possible murder from 1932 or the murder from 1972.

At five to eleven, I went back into the living room. I sat there for several minutes looking at the telephone. The temptation to call my secret advisor, Patricia, only got stronger the longer I sat there. I was sure that Patricia would immediately make connections in the case that I could not see, if she was willing to help me. However, I wasn't even convinced that she would want to help me. It was as though Patricia's shadow now eclipsed the case for me. It felt like I had to phone her to find out whether she was willing to help, or if I was on my own.

I thought about the boy on the red bicycle and my meeting with his mother, and came to the conclusion that I should ring Patricia for their sakes. I still knew the number to the telephone on her table by heart. I was suddenly absolutely certain that she was still awake, sitting by the telephone in her library.

Twice I reached out to pick up the phone. The first time, I pulled my hand back before it even touched the receiver and the second time, I dialled the first two numbers before I put it down again. A picture of Miriam appeared and stood between me and the telephone. Miriam had not wanted me to contact Patricia this time and had really done her best to help me herself.

It was a horrible feeling; it would seem as if I lacked confidence in my fiancée if I now asked if I could call Patricia. But at the same time it felt like it would be a betrayal, almost treachery, if I were to ring Patricia without having spoken to Miriam about it first. So I sat there stewing over the dilemma. Then I made a decision and reached out to pick up the phone and ring Patricia.

But the telephone beat me to it: it started to ring while my hand was still in the air. As soon as I heard it ring, I knew who it was – and I was right.

Miriam was calling from a telephone box at her student accommodation. Her voice trembled slightly when she spoke: 'I've tried to call you several times this evening without any answer. I'm so glad that you are all right. Is there any news about the case?'

It felt as though she was asking me if I had been to visit Patricia. And I immediately regretted having tried to call her.

So I quickly told her that I had been to see the Ramdals and that there was some new information, but I could tell her more when we next met.

Miriam sounded pleased to hear this and said that she could leave the library a couple of hours earlier tomorrow so that we could have an early supper together before she went to her evening meetings. This was a rare offer coming from her, so I agreed without hesitation. She promised to be here at four and would wait if I was later. I cheerfully asked her to take with her the book on the history of the German language, and she equally cheerfully said that she would never dream of going anywhere without it.

Her coins and our conversation came to an end at twenty-five past eleven. We felt closer again. I was touched by my Miriam's interest and found her curiosity charming. So I stopped debating with myself whether to call Patricia or not. In any case, it was by now far too late for any more phone calls or visits today. I suddenly felt the exhaustion after a long and demanding day overwhelm me.

I was in bed by a quarter to twelve and barely managed to set the alarm before I fell asleep. But the sheet on my own bed reminded me, all the same, of what I had seen at the main police station earlier in the day. And I saw the boy on the red bicycle once again – dead in his cell.

Monday, 20 March 1972 came to a close with me dreaming that Miriam was back in my bed with me, but Patricia was sitting in her wheelchair in the middle of the room, looking at us with a grim and reproachful expression.

DAY FOUR

Some New Faces – and a
Slightly Surreal Situation

I

On Tuesday, 21 March 1972, it was reported in the morning news on the radio that it now looked as though the Barents Sea agreement would get the support of all parties, even though some individuals in the Conservative Party had raised critical questions about the Soviet Union's intentions. These were possibly in response to the fact that surviving members of the Communist Party of Norway had appeared on the barricades to proclaim the agreement was an example of the Soviet Union's good intentions and genuine desire for peace.

Between the headlines and reports about the Barents Sea agreement and the EEC debate in the morning papers, I found some obituaries for Per Johan Fredriksen and several smaller reports about his murder. The two newspapers that I had delivered wrote that the suspect, who had been held in custody after having fled the scene of the crime, was a young man from the east end of Oslo, and he had since committed suicide in prison. From the evidence, it would seem that the murder was motivated by personal tragedy and the case was now considered closed.

The newspapers did not mention the suspect's name, but did name the head of the investigation. Phrases such as 'the young and already well-known Detective Inspector Kolbjørn Kristiansen solved the case in record time' made for pleasant enough reading. But I read them with mixed feelings, knowing as I did only too well that it could quickly backfire on the police in general and myself in particular. Especially if the press got wind of the fact that the arrestee, who had taken his own life in a cell, was innocent. I came to the conclusion that it might have been better if my name had not been mentioned. I quickly folded the papers and hurried to work.

I was in my office by twenty past eight, in other words, ten minutes early. All the incoming messages to do with the case were requests for interviews. I dealt with them swiftly, replying that the investigation was still ongoing and the police were still open to all possibilities.

At half past nine, I was in my car driving out of Oslo, on my way to meet a man who had apparently lived alone in Holmestrand since finding his girlfriend dead in a hotel room in Oslo forty years ago.

II

The farm was easy to find: not only was it the best signposted, but it was also the largest in the area. After seeing a sign for Westgaard on a side road, I drove for a good three minutes before coming to the farmhouse.

The man was not hard to find either. Hauk Rebne Westgaard was standing talking to two other men in front of the house when I drove up. It was very obvious who he was, thanks to his height, profile and clothes. Without reading very much more into it, I could see that he was the only gentleman there.

The description I had been given was very fitting. Hauk Rebne Westgaard was at least six feet tall, with unusually sharp features and a clean-shaven face, raven hair, a slim build and graceful movements; he could as easily have been forty-five as sixty-five. His handshake was strong and his voice was friendly when he said: 'Welcome.' But he did not smile, and walked into the house without saying another word.

Hauk Rebne Westgaard's living room was large and tidy, but in terms of the furnishing and decor, it was like taking a step back in time to the early interwar period. With the possible exception of a couple of guns on the wall and some of the trophies on the top shelves, it looked as though nothing here was from after 1945. I found myself wondering whether my host's internal life had remained equally untouched since 1932.

Out loud, I asked whether he lived alone or had any family. He replied: 'I have three farmhands who live on the farm with their families, but I live on my own in the house. My parents died long ago, and my only sibling is a younger sister who also has her own house on the farm. I have never married and do not have the pleasure of my own children.'

'But you were once in love and had a girlfriend, whom you lost – unexpectedly,' I said.

He gave a strangely determined and abrupt nod. It was as though his sharp chin cleaved the air in two.

'I understand that you are well acquainted with the events of 1932. Yes, I once had a girlfriend whom I loved very much and lost very unexpectedly. I have carried on with my life, done what I should and could on the farm and in the community, and I've managed well. But I still wonder about what happened, and what my life might have been like had it not occurred. And that I will never know. But I would be very grateful if you could solve the mystery.'

His voice was still friendly, but as he spoke his hawk-like eyes bore into me.

I felt the pressure mounting. So I swiftly replied that I would do my best, but that I first needed to hear his version of the events and how he had experienced them.

'Eva and I had not been together for very long, just four months. And we were very different. She was an irrepressible optimist with a lust for life and had grown up without a care in the world. Whereas the situation here at home had left its mark on me and I was far more serious. But we got on very well together all the same, and in the days before the trip to Oslo had even talked about getting engaged. I was never one for parties really and thought I was the luckiest man in the world to have found such a beautiful and charming girlfriend. I could see that other men looked at me with envy. And I thought to myself many a time that it was too good to last, but I had no idea that it would end as tragically as it did.'

'And in addition, she was rich,' I said, tentatively.

Hauk Rebne Westgaard gave another of his sharp nods. 'That was not important to me. I would have wanted Eva even if she was the daughter of a poor farmhand, but of course I knew full well that she was heir to land and property worth millions. I both saw and heard that it was important to other young men, from families that were often far richer than my own. The wealthy farmers down here used to joke that there were no engagements in Vestfold, only mergers.'

He smiled fleetingly when he said this. But the smile disappeared as soon as I asked if he had known that Per Johan Fredriksen had shown some interest in his girlfriend.

'Yes. He paid a lot of attention to my girlfriend, and Kjell Arne Ramdal showed a lot of interest in both my girlfriend and Per Johan's fiancée. So the atmosphere on the way into the capital and at the hotel was rather tense. I could feel that a drama was brewing, but the form it then took came as a shock. On the surface, Eva was the most carefree and relaxed of us all. She lived to be adored. We had discussed it and I was happy for her to be the centre of attention.'

I noted that jealousy could have been a possible motive for Hauk Rebne Westgaard. I then asked him what he believed happened.

'It was not epilepsy that killed Eva, I am almost certain of that. I had been to the doctor with her a few days before. He had assured her that epilepsy was something she would die with, but not from. Otherwise she was as fit as a fiddle with no sign of any illness. It seems just as unlikely to me that she committed suicide. First of all, she had been in a remarkably good mood all spring, and still was only a few hours before. Second, I don't understand how she committed suicide, if she did. I was with her when she packed and did not see medicine of any sort either then or later in the hotel room. I smelt her lips after she had died, and they did not smell of anything. Even though I cannot categorically dismiss the possibility that she committed suicide or died as a result of her illness, I have always believed that she was murdered. But how she was killed, why she was killed and by whom, remains as much of a mystery to me now, forty years on, as then. And I would be so grateful if you could tell me.'

There was a faint spark in the eyes of the man opposite me when he said this. Despite his control, he suddenly scared me a little, with the feeling only enhanced by all the guns and trophies on the wall.

I said that I was not able to tell him now, but that I would do my utmost to find out.

'I thank you for that. It's more than can be said of the police in 1932. They danced to her father's tune. He was a very conservative and powerful old man who was less interested in finding out the truth than in hiding the potential scandal a suicide would have entailed. As her young boyfriend, and with no contacts in Oslo, I had no rights whatsoever and was ignored when I tried to support her sister's demands for an autopsy. And, likewise, when I informed them that it was clear that another person had been in her room in the hour or two before she died, and also in her bed.'

Hauk Rebne Westgaard's hard and defiant eyes pierced

me to the core when he said this. He replied swiftly and without hesitation when I asked him how he could be so sure of that.

'I was the first person into her room when we all went up. I immediately noticed that the bed, which had been made up earlier in the day, was now crumpled. Eva was full of energy and as good as never slept in the afternoons. She may, of course, have done so that day, but there were also three black hairs on her pillow. Eva had blonde hair, so they were clearly not hers. The police said they were unable to establish who the hair came from. They examined the bed as soon as they were told, but found no evidence of sexual activity and suggested that the hairs could have got there by all manner of ways that might not be directly linked to her death. But I can still only think of one plausible explanation, and that is that there was a dark-haired man in her room – and bed – only hours before she died.'

He said this in a very quiet voice, almost a whisper – which I could well understand. If his story was true, Hauk Rebne Westgaard had lived for the past forty years not only with the uncertainty of how his girlfriend had died, but also with the question of who she had been unfaithful with beforehand.

Hauk Rebne Westgaard's still-black hair was right in front of my very eyes as we sat there looking at each other. So I cautiously asked if those black hairs might not be his own. He nodded very firmly to this and then spoke very fast.

'Yes, I understand that you have to ask. I realized that that was what the police suspected. But Eva and I had not shared a bed that day and, in fact, I had been nowhere near the bed in her hotel room. So the hairs had to be from someone else. Per Johan and Kjell Arne both had dark hair at the time, so if it was either of them it would be difficult to say which one. There may of course have been a third man, unknown to me, but it seems much more likely that it was one of those two . . . and, of course, there is nothing to say that whoever was in the bed took Eva's life afterwards, but again, it seems likely.'

I had to agree with both points, and asked him which of the two he suspected.

Hauk Rebne Westgaard gave it some thought, then answered in an even quieter voice. 'I don't know. I have thought about it a thousand times and changed my mind at least five hundred. I knew Per Johan best from childhood and have always liked him best. But from a very young age he was a man with many faces. On the other hand, I had never cared for Kjell Arne, but only ever saw one face. So it has always seemed more likely to me that it was my childhood friend, Per Johan, who took Eva's life and left mine in ruins.'

He said the latter in an almost inaudible voice and with a faint glow in his eyes. I was aware of all the guns and trophies behind him and thought to myself that Hauk Rebne Westgaard was not someone I would like to have as an enemy.

He apparently realized that he had perhaps gone too far.

'You asked, and I am giving you an honest answer. Obviously, I would not have said that if I had killed Per Johan. Which I didn't. I still don't know if I had a reason to hate Per Johan and I don't know who killed him.'

I quickly followed this up by asking what his thoughts were when Per Johan made his unexpected announcement at the memorial dinner a few days earlier.

'Initially I thought that he had found something out that linked Kjell Arne to the murder. Then I looked at Kjell Arne, and his only reaction was to knit his eyebrows and look puzzled. So then I thought perhaps Per Johan was saying it to deflect any suspicion, but it was hard to understand why he would do that now. And then he said nothing more. He raised his glass of water demonstratively and remained silent for the rest of the meal. It was an interesting meal in that respect, but left me none the wiser.'

I thought to myself that Patricia would be able to discern something from this, but I could not see what it might be.

Before I had time to ask another question, Hauk Rebne Westgaard suddenly moved – with unexpected speed and force. As though pulling a gun, he pulled out his wallet and put it down on the table between us. It was made of brown leather and, as far as I could see, was full of notes and coins. He put his fingers into a small side pocket and carefully took out a small white stamp bag.

And hey presto, there we were with three dark hairs from 1932 between us.

I stared intensely at them for a few seconds, but was unable to guess to whom they belonged.

Hauk Rebne Westgaard asked me in a quiet voice if technology was now so advanced that it was possible to establish someone's identity from three forty-year-old strands of hair. I replied in an even softer voice that it was worth a try, but that normally it was not possible.

He said: 'A small chance is still better than no chance at all,' and pushed the bag containing the three hairs over towards me.

I put it carefully in my own wallet and said that I would look after it well. He said that he would like them back afterwards, and I promised him that he would get them.

'And you have never had a girlfriend since?' I asked, with some caution.

It was a somewhat bold question, but Hauk Rebne Westgaard took it well. He sat in silence for a few moments, but then spoke for a long time once he had started.

'No, I never did. The fact that things were the way they were at home also played a part. Father flew into a rage if anyone forgot the double A in Westgaard. It's a very old name and his family have been wealthy farmers here since the Dano-Norwegian Union. But my father drank himself into the ground, and almost did the same with the farm. After Eva's tragic death I came home to another crisis and possible enforced sale of the farm. My mother and I went to court and managed to have Father declared incompetent in the nick of time, so that I could take over the running of the farm before it all collapsed. I was twenty-five years old when I took over a farm on the verge of bankruptcy, and the responsibility for my ten-year-old sister. In the first few years, we could barely pay anyone to help us with the sowing in spring or harvesting in autumn. In the years before and during the war, I was constantly battling against the frost and down payments for me and my mother. While others fought for their country, I had no time to do anything other than fight for my family's farm. Hunting and shooting were my only form of relaxation and apart from that, I used every ounce of energy I had on the farm. So all I had to offer any potential wife was insecurity, and even so I did not have time to find one. But the shock was the hardest thing to bear. If you lose the love of your life at a young age, without being able to say goodbye, it does something to you. And when you don't know what happened, it's even worse.'

He stopped for a moment to draw breath, and then carried on at a slower pace, in a quieter voice.

'It has always been said that there is a curse on the Westgaard men. My father's father had two wives who both died when they were young. My mother told me more than once that marrying my father had been the greatest mistake of her life. As a modern man, I do not believe that the sins of the fathers are visited on their sons. But until the mystery of Eva's death is solved, I will not be able to put my arms around another woman. And so here I am, a wealthy farmer, with no one to take over the family farm when my time comes.'

I now saw Hauk Rebne Westgaard as both a modern man and an old-fashioned farmer. And I could understand his sorrow.

I asked tactfully whether his sister had any children who might inherit the farm.

'No,' he replied, almost too swiftly. Then he continued in a steady voice. 'There is a young widow on the neighbouring farm who has come to visit several times recently. She is very nice. But I cannot decide whether it is a good or a bad sign that she was born in 1932. It would be the last chance for a new generation to grow up here at Westgaard. But every time I see her, it's as though Eva appears and stands between us. I think about the family curse, about the shock I got when I found Eva dead, and I am still unable to touch another woman. So I would be deeply thankful if you and the police could solve the case.'

I promised him that I would do my very best and that I would let him know immediately if there was any news. He spontaneously held out his hand and I took it. His hand was slim, strong and surprisingly warm; it burned in mine.

I dropped his hand and said that he must be completely honest with me. Then I asked if he had anything more of importance to tell me from that fateful day in 1932 when Eva died.

Hauk Rene Westgaard hesitated for a moment – and then a moment more. Then he continued: 'Yes. You seem to be a fine, open-minded man. So I am going to tell you some-thing that I did not tell the police in 1932. I said nothing because I didn't trust them and I didn't see how it could be significant, but also because I feared that others might take the opportunity to direct their suspicion at me. I was in Eva's hotel room that afternoon. But I left at half past five, and she was still very much alive.'

My nod was almost a reflex and I asked him to tell me in as much detail as possible what had happened. He did so immediately.

'I had been worried because Eva, even though she was in a good mood, had seemed distracted and had avoided look-ing at me earlier in the day. So I knocked on her door at a quarter past five and asked if everything was all right. She let me in, but was unusually serious and a bit evasive. Then she told me that she had found herself attracted to someone else, but that it was complicated, that she still loved me and that I had to give her some time to think about what she wanted to do. It felt as though the ground had opened beneath my feet. I could do nothing other than say that I loved her more than anything in the world, beg her to stay with me and that I would give her all the time she needed to think about the situation. I hugged her and could feel her trembling in my arms. Then I went. I left her standing in the middle of her hotel room, unharmed and alive. In fact, it was the last time I saw her alive. And it was exactly five-thirty when I got back to my room.'

He was now speaking faster again, as though fevered.

It was tempting to believe him. But then I thought that Hauk Rebne Westgaard's own explanation still gave him a possible motive of jealousy – and the fact that his girlfriend had been confused and in a difficult situation could have resulted in suicide.

Out loud, I asked whether he was sure that the bed was still made and that he had not seen any pills or other means of suicide in the room. He gave a sharp nod in answer to both.

The only question that remained was a sensitive one. I paused for a beat and spoke slowly when I said that I had to ask everyone, as a matter of procedure, where they were when Per Johan Fredriksen died at half past eight on Saturday evening.

Hauk Rebne Westgaard conceded that he understood why I had to ask. Then he said: 'Well, in my case, I was unfortunately on my own in the car driving back to Holmestrand. I had been at the anti-EEC conference as part of a delegation of Labour Party members who are against membership. It's no coincidence that Kjell Arne ended up in the Conservative Party, Per Johan in the Centre Party and I in the Labour Party. Per Johan and I agreed on the EEC question. Membership would be catastrophic for rural Norway and the beginning of the end for agriculture as we know it. In fact, Per Johan and I met very briefly that day. We exchanged looks and nods, but no words, when he gave a short talk earlier in the day. I am sure we were both thinking what a social hotchpotch it was, the two of us and other veterans from various parties together with long-haired urban radicals of both sexes. The conference closed around half past seven. I got into the car and was back here around nine. I heard that Per Johan had been stabbed on the ten o'clock news.'

Neither of us said anything. Hauk Rebne Westgaard had been in Oslo on the day that Per Johan Fredriksen was murdered. Having left the conference an hour before, Hauk Rebne Westgaard did not have an alibi for the time of the murder, unless anyone could confirm that he was back here in Holmestrand before nine o'clock.

I asked in as friendly a manner as I could, whether his sister or anyone else here could confirm that he had been back by nine.

He shrugged with his palms up.

'No, unfortunately not. The farm hands were finished for the weekend, so I did not see any of them. I did see my sister, but she would not be able to confirm the time.'

I was once again taken aback by the way in which Hauk

Rebne Westgaard spoke about his sister. So I enquired if I could ask her that myself.

He looked at me with a mixture of reproach and bewilderment, as though I had understood nothing. All of a sudden he reminded me of Patricia. Then he said: 'Of course. My sister is at home. Follow me, you can ask her all the questions you like.'

III

Silent and slightly puzzled, I followed Hauk Rebne West-gaard across the farmyard. We approached what from the outside looked like a very ordinary wooden cabin.

I realized that something was amiss when I saw that the door was locked from the outside; my host produced a key and unlocked the padlock before opening the door.

An even greater shock was waiting behind the door.

The wooden cabin was like any other modern home with a bedroom and a bathroom. The four walls were painted in four different colours – one red, one green, one yellow and one blue. There were no bookshelves or anything else on the walls. And on the floor, in the midst of building blocks and toy animals, sat a plump woman in her fifties.

I looked around for a child, but there was no one else in the room. It finally dawned on me when the woman jumped up, clapped her hands and shouted: 'Food! Yum yum!'

I understood the full horror of my mistake when the woman turned towards us. Her face radiated a childlike joy, but her eyes were empty and uncomprehending. Her expression became fearful and her smile disappeared when she saw that her brother did not have food with him, but instead a man she didn't know.

Fortunately, Hauk Rebne Westgaard dealt with the situation very calmly.

'It's too early for your morning snack, but you will get some food soon. In the meantime, this nice man has come to see us and would like to ask you some questions. His name is Kolbjørn,' he said, in a friendly voice.

Her brother's voice seemed to banish the child–woman's fear straightaway. She clapped her hands again and said: 'Visit! Hooray!'

She beamed up at me and held out her hand. Then she stood there looking at me expectantly as she rocked back and forth on her heels.

Having recognized my blunder, all I wanted to do was to turn around and run out. But that was not possible without frightening the fifty-year-old woman who it would seem had the mental capacity of a five-year-old. So I started by asking her what she was called.

She replied, delighted: 'I'm called Inger!'

I thanked her and then asked dutifully if Hauk was a kind big brother.

She answered immediately: 'Yes, Hauk is kind. He brings me yummy food.'

Her mouth smiled when she spoke, but in her eyes I could also see a deep, serious fear and uncertainty. And I thought to myself that this fear and uncertainty had lain hidden there for all these years. It had been there ever since the day in her lost childhood that she discovered that grown-ups she did not know asked questions she could not answer, more and more frequently. The day she understood that she would never be able to understand. As we stood there looking at each other now, she was back there again, the little girl who didn't understand.

I tried to pull myself together and asked her if Hauk had brought her supper to her on Saturday evening, and if so, at what time. But as far as I could see there was no clock in the room, and the woman who lived here was not likely to have any concept of time. And I knew that a court would never place any importance on her testimony even if she could answer. The whole exercise felt pointless.

Suddenly she pointed down at the floor and said: 'Look – I've built a tower of eight blocks!'

Her brother said it was a great tower and looked at me expectantly.

I said that it was very good and that I was grateful that she had been able to answer all my questions so well.

She nodded and waved gratefully as we left. The fear and uncertainty in her eyes had vanished. Once again, it was clear that she lived a good life here, without a care, in her eternal playroom.

Hauk's hand was trembling slightly as he locked the door behind him. We walked together across the yard back to my car, without looking back.

'I apologize for my blunder,' I said, when we got to the car.

'I perfectly understand. You had a duty to ask, and she was having one of her good, happy days,' he said.

After a brief pause, he carried on: 'That was one of the hardest responsibilities in the years that I struggled to save the farm. As I see it, I managed to escape the madness in my father's family and my sister inherited it all. Sweet Inger is as happy as can be here and she must be allowed to stay here until she dies. The thought that she might be forced to leave and hidden away in some asylum cubbyhole was too awful to bear.'

I told him I fully understood. And it struck me that Hauk Rebne Westgaard was the incarnation of a good family man, just without having his own family. Having met him and his sister, I wanted to believe that he was innocent, as regards to both the death of Eva Bjølhaugen in 1932 and the death of Per Johan Fredriksen in 1972. But I was still not certain. It seemed to me that he, too, was a complex man with many faces.

IV

It was already ten past one by the time I got back to Oslo. There was a visitor waiting in my office, who had been sent there by my boss when he had demanded to talk to the head of the investigation. I was at first curious about my guest, only to be disheartened when I met him.

The lawyer Edvard Rønning Junior was sitting comfortably on my visitor's chair, dressed as usual in a black suit, with a lorgnette and his briefcase on the table in front of him. This could have been from the 1950s, but the rest of him looked as though he had stepped straight out of the

1920s. The impression was in no way diminished when he started to talk.

'Ah, there you are, Detective Inspector Kristiansen. And not before time. It is far from satisfactory that I have wasted the past thirty minutes sitting here waiting for you. It is even more unsatisfactory, however, for a defence lawyer not to know the name of his client, who is furthermore a minor, before the said client is dead. And none of this is made any better by the fact that the client died in police custody. Indeed, police scandal might be an appropriate phrase, if it is later proved that he was entirely innocent of the crime for which he stood accused. This would be highly unfortunate for both you and the police in general, and I will be strongly recommending that the deceased's mother seeks compensation.'

I listened to him talk with a rising sense of panic. I had to admit that he had a point – it could be a very difficult case indeed.

Out loud, I simply said that it was hard to protect clients from themselves if they wanted to commit suicide and that we had spent a day and a half trying to identify his client as he refused to give us his name and no one had reported him missing. The question of guilt remained unresolved, but we were currently investigating other possible suspects and hoped that the lawyer would appreciate this.

This helped a little, but not enough. The lawyer looked at me pointedly over the top of his spectacles and answered: 'The latter is, of course, positive, but in the current situation also a given. The investigation and your good self shall be granted sufficient time to establish the facts regarding the matter of his guilt. I do, however, expect to be informed immediately if there is any new evidence relating to the question of guilt that is of significance to my late client's case. Furthermore, I also expect to be contacted in advance should you wish to talk to the deceased's mother again. Her situation is, as I am sure you are aware, extremely difficult.'

I caught a whiff of idealism behind the lawyer's formal language when he mentioned the mother. So I replied that I knew about the mother's difficult situation, and that he would of course be informed as soon as the question of guilt with regard to his late client had been resolved.

The lawyer could not say that he was anything other than happy with that and so, after a brief, formal handshake, he left.

Edvard Rønning Junior's visit lasted no more than five minutes. But it was still an uncomfortable reminder of the seriousness of my situation in terms of the investigation into the murder of Per Johan Fredriksen, and the tragedy of the boy on the red bicycle.

I no longer thought that the boy had committed the murder and did not think that he held the answer. But I was still curious about his role in the story and so decided that I would have a chat with the teacher he had apparently been so fond of. However, that would have to wait until the end of the school day. For now, having tried without success to find answers in Per Johan Fredriksen's close family and his friends involved in the 1932 tragedy who were still alive, I wanted to get to know the businessman and politician.

V

The company, Per Johan Fredriksen A/S, had centrally located premises in an office block on Roald Amundsen's Street, close to the National Theatre, but they were far smaller than I had expected. Three office clerks sat side by side, squeezed between the bookshelves in a room that was smaller than my office. The offices of the office manager and accountant were also surprisingly small and filled to bursting with lever arch files.

The office manager, Odd Jørgensen, was a slightly overweight, thin-haired besuited man with horn-rimmed spectacles, who looked around fifty or so. He was sitting half buried in a pile of rental contracts, but cleared his desk as soon as I arrived. He suggested that we might like to call in the accountant, Erling Svendsen, straightaway.

I agreed that this was a practical idea, even though there would not be much room round the table in Jørgensen's office. Svendsen was a few years younger, had a bit more hair, a bit less girth and smaller glasses, but was otherwise remarkably like Jørgensen.

I started by asking about the company's financial situation. Jørgensen left this to Svendsen, who gave a very sombre account, similar to the one I had heard from Kjell Arne Ramdal. The company was operating with a healthy profit and had a sound property portfolio, but in recent years had lost ground and momentum in a rapidly expanding market. The investments that had been made in the older flats, for which there was falling demand, were not sufficient and the administration was too overworked to keep a full overview of existing properties and possible new acquisitions.

Jørgensen nodded in agreement to this and then took over, having exchanged a glance with Ssvendsen.

'To be frank, even though it is only days since he died, part of the problem was that Fredriksen was too short-sighted and averse to risk as a businessman. He liked to say that his strategy was to go for the best possible gains next month without the risk of losses this month. He was what is called a quarterly capitalist.'

I looked at Svendsen, who nodded vigorously. It was clear that the two men had worked together for a long time and were reading from the same page when it came to their assessment of the situation. Svendsen quickly took over where Jørgensen left off.

'The offer he was given by Ramdal was extremely good and possibly a few million too high, if one was to add up the estimated value of the properties right now. We both recommended that Fredriksen should accept the offer. But he was hesitant, and we almost wondered if he was considering turning it down. Despite all his years in the capital, he was still a farmer at heart and was inherently sceptical about giving away land and property. In many ways, the business was his life's work.'

I asked if they, for their part, were in favour of the possibility of a takeover. They exchanged a quick look and then nodded simultaneously. The office manager was the one who spoke.

'We and the rest of the office staff were all in favour of it.

Ramdal is known to be a demanding but fair boss and open to suggestions from his staff. We hoped that we might get a bit more space, less overtime and, more than anything, slightly more humane working conditions.'

I gave them a puzzled look and said that according to his family, Fredriksen had always been a kind-hearted and generous man.

They exchanged glances again. Jørgensen nodded and Svendsen spoke.

'His son said the same thing when he came here, and we have to admit that it came as a surprise to us. Fredriksen never invited us to his home and until his son came to the office, we had never met any of his children. We only knew the businessman. And the word heartless would be closer to the truth in describing him, I'm afraid. In fact, Odd and I have remarked more than once that the only time we have seen Fredriksen smile is when he was being a politician on television, but never when he was here as a businessman.'

Svendsen suddenly fell silent, as though he felt guilty and ashamed of what he had said. Jørgensen swiftly picked up the thread and continued in the same vein.

'Fredriksen has not been here much in recent years. He concentrated more and more on his role as a politician and only spoke about the office when someone asked him about business. Fredriksen's instructions to us were clear and ruthless: anyone who falls behind with the rent is to be evicted as soon as it is legally possible, and new tenants are to be offered the highest rent permitted by the law and the market. But the rental market is a hard place to be heartless:

plenty of poor and desperate people come to our door, not knowing that we can't help them.'

'And one of the poorest and most desperate came here last Thursday, didn't she?' I said.

They both nodded at the same time. Jørgensen took off his horn-rimmed spectacles and covered his eyes with his hand for a moment or two. Svendsen came to his rescue and carried on talking in a tremulous voice.

'It was the most terrible experience. The woman had obviously done her utmost in a very difficult situation. But the only thing that mattered in terms of our instructions was that she had no money and no means of earning any money. One former tenant shot himself the day after being evicted, but there were no changes to our instructions as a result. And we had to follow the instructions. We feared that it might end in suicide, but obviously had no idea that it would ultimately affect Fredriksen himself – if it was her son who killed Fredriksen.'

I deftly avoided answering that and emphasized that I was in no doubt that they had simply been following instructions. However, Jørgensen hastily came to their defence.

'It was heartbreaking all the same. And what made it worse was that the woman was a former employee. She had worked here as a cleaner in the mid-fifties. It was before Erling's time, but soon after I had started. She only worked for a few hours in the evening. However, I met her in the doorway several times and remember thinking that she was a beautiful and always cheerful woman, despite her simple clothes and poor pay. It was not easy to see her on her knees, so desperate here the other day.'

I immediately latched on to this new loose connection between the two deceased men, but it was hardly conclusive. To begin with, we already had a clear motive for the boy on the red bicycle to kill Per Johan Fredriksen, and what was more, he had in all likelihood not done it. However, there were clearly a puzzling and striking number of knotted threads that criss-crossed this case.

Jørgensen lowered his hand when he stopped talking. I saw two tears before he hastily wiped them away and put on his glasses again. Even though his crying was silent and discreet, it made quite an impression on me to see an office manager in his fifties, dressed in a suit, sit in his office and cry.

I asked them in conclusion if it was only because of the money that they both had continued to work for Fredriksen for so many years, despite the very difficult working conditions and extremely unpleasant brief.

The office manager and accountant were still remarkably synchronized; as was now to be expected, Svendsen answered my question about their finances and Jørgensen nodded in agreement.

'The wages are not particularly high, in fact, they are probably a band or two below what is normal for similar positions in the sector, but we have permanent jobs with a relatively good salary, and we know what needs to be done, and there is a good atmosphere in the office, despite the lack of space. Better the devil you know, as they say, especially in times like these. So we gritted our teeth when tensions ran high and sat tight waiting for better times. Which we hope will finally come now.'

On my way down the stairs, I thought how Per Johan Fredriksen really had been a very complex person with many faces, as his childhood friend Hauk Rebne Westgaard had said. And then I got something else to think about.

VI

It was as I opened the main door and stepped out onto Roald Amundsen's Street that I saw him for the second time.

Just a brief glimpse, and he was doing nothing alarming. But, all the same, I felt a stab of fear when I saw him.

The man in the hat was dressed in a lighter suit and had no tie today. But he was wearing that same hat and he looked straight at me from where he was on the other side of the street.

He was standing still when I opened the door, but started to walk away as soon as he registered that I had seen him. I took three strides out into the road, but then stopped again without making any attempt to catch up with him.

The man in the hat was already about to disappear into the early afternoon crowds on the main street, Karl Johan. Even if I did catch up with him, I had no reason to demand an explanation. He had not done anything wrong, other than be in the same place as me twice within as many days – in two very different parts of town.

It could still be a coincidence, but I no longer thought it

was. So I stayed standing where I was for a couple of minutes and racked my brains as to who the man in the hat might be and why he was interested in me. There was something alarmingly cold and calculating about him.

I wondered whether I should mention the man in the hat to Miriam or whether to spare her this for the moment. And then thought to myself that I would give my eye teeth to know what Patricia would make of this part of the story.

VII

At ten past two, the school bell rang to mark the end of the day at Tøyen School. As I walked through the gates I had to push against a stream of boys aged around fifteen. I wondered if they were the classmates of the dead boy on the red bicycle. If they were, they did not appear to be affected by the news of his death. Most of them had eager bodies and happy faces. Some of them were smiling, others kept their heads down. Some were in groups, others in twos and only a few alone.

The boy on the red bicycle would almost certainly have been one of those walking alone. I imagined that when the bell rang last Friday, he had walked by himself at the back of the crowd, with his worn satchel and limp. And now, on Tuesday, he was gone forever. There would be an empty desk in a classroom somewhere in this four-storey brick building.

According to a plaque by the entrance, Tøyen School had celebrated its ninetieth anniversary this year. And I thought about all the young people who had burst out through the gates over the years – many to a better life, and many to various forms of human tragedy.

I met her leaving the staffroom on the first floor. She was a blonde woman of around thirty, about five foot two, and was hurrying towards the exit.

'How can I help you?' she said with a curious smile when I stopped her. I asked if Eveline Kolberg was around.

'Yes, I'm Eveline Kolberg. But I have to collect my one-year-old from the babysitter before three,' she added quickly, before I had a chance to say anything.

When I explained that I was a detective and that I wanted to ask her some questions about her now dead pupil, Tor Johansen, her immediate response was: 'Well, the babysitter will have to wait a few minutes, then.'

She led me down the corridor and opened the door to a big classroom.

'We have plenty of space now as the number of pupils has fallen,' Eveline Kolberg commented with a wry smile as we sat down on either side of a brown desk.

The desk resembled its owner: small, tidy and in good condition. Exercise books for social studies lay in a neat, almost perfectly right-angled stack, parallel with the edge of the desk, ready for tomorrow.

'There will always be a number of children with very sad fates in such a big school. But Tor Johansen was one of the saddest.'

She said this before I had even had time to ask a question, and there was a zeal about her that was inspiring. I promptly asked what she meant.

'He was possibly one of the pupils with the least friends. I always feel sorry for those who have learning difficulties, but even more so for those who have difficulties making friends. He and his mother had had to move a number of times, so he only started here last spring. All the other pupils knew each other and he knew no one. He was not able to play football with them in the breaks, and even though he always gave the right answer when I asked him a question, the others inevitably laughed at his speech impediment. Teenagers are heartless. Last year, he would often stand and watch the others playing football in the break and then try to talk to some of them about football afterwards. But then he seemed to give up. He generally stayed at his desk with a book during the breaks. He was the only pupil we ever saw reading in breaks and the only boy who ever took library books to school.'

I asked whether she thought that he suffered because of his physical handicaps, and if he was also retarded in any way. She thought for a moment or two before she shook her head.

'Still waters run deep, as they say. Tor was quiet on the surface, but no one bothered to find out what went on underneath. His written work was consistently some of the best in the class and he nearly always gave the right answer on the rare occasions that he put up his hand. Once when I passed him as he was watching the others play football, I said that he should consider taking the university entrance exam. "It's a long way off. But a nice thought. Thank you," he stammered with a shy smile. I never thought that he had any impediments, other than an inferiority complex driven by poverty. And he was not alone in that, only his complex was perhaps stronger than it is for most.'

Eveline Kolberg was now on a roll. She paused briefly and then carried on.

'I read a biography of the British politician Bevin last week. In the introduction about his childhood, it said that two poorer people than he and his mother have never lived. It made me think of Tor and his mother. His father died long before they moved here, so I never met him. Tor only had his mother and she had practically nothing to give him. He adored his mother – she was his rock and perhaps the only person he believed had ever done anything for him. But he was a teenager now and could also see his mother's weaknesses. "Mum drinks too much and thinks too little," he said once when I asked him how things were at home. So that part of his life was also tragic. He had more reason than most to feel excluded and rail against society. And yet—' She stopped all of a sudden and looked at me intensely.

'And yet – you don't think . . .' I prompted.

She gave me a fleeting, tight-lipped smile and carried on with renewed passion.

'And yet I do not think he murdered anyone, no. It would be so out of character. He always handed things in on time, and never protested if we said he had to go out in the breaks. He would just take his book with him and limp out. If you had come here last Friday and told me that one of our pupils would commit a violent crime over the weekend, he is the last person I would have thought of. It's true, he was very interested in old court cases and the like, but I don't remember him showing any interest in weapons or ever laying a hand on one of his classmates. Physically, he was very reserved. So no, unless you have come to show me photographs and evidence, I do not believe that my pupil killed that politician Fredriksen.'

She said this in a quiet, intense voice. Eveline Kolberg sat fidgeting in her chair, and then leaned forwards over her desk.

I said, as diplomatically and vaguely as I could, that the investigation had to keep all leads open, but that there was an eyewitness whose account gave reasons to doubt that her pupil had been the murderer.

'What kind of eyewitness, what did they see?' she asked, leaning even further forwards over the desk.

It frustrated me that I had to say, for obvious reasons, that I was unfortunately unable to tell her more.

'Of course. I understand. Confidentiality is important,' she said, with palpable disappointment in her voice, and finally leaned back in her chair.

Then she said that she would soon have to relieve the babysitter, if there was nothing more she could help me with.

I replied that there was nothing for the moment, but that I would contact her again if it became necessary. Then I added that I would inform her when the question of Tor's guilt had been clarified.

We left the now empty middle school together. Outside the gates, we stopped at the bus stop. She hesitated at first, but then pointed over the road.

'A couple of times when I came out from evening meetings, I saw Tor cycling past on his way home. I sometimes wondered if I should stop him and ask where he had been and how he was. But, unfortunately, I never did. And now that he's dead, I regret that. I should have done more for him while he was alive. But that's the trouble when you have too many pupils in each class, and a husband and child at home.'

I agreed with her that that was how it was; whether you were a policeman or a teacher, it was not possible to help everyone you met who needed it. She had no reason to reproach herself for the tragedy that had struck one of her pupils. Whether he was guilty or not, she very definitely was not. To the contrary, I had come to see her because his mother had told me how much he appreciated her.

Eveline Kolberg was so happy to hear this that she nearly missed her bus. We separated with a brief hug before I more or less pushed her onto the vehicle.

I stood there and watched the bus drive off. I thought that it had been a rare and inspiring meeting with a rare and idealistic teacher, whom I would gladly meet again under different circumstances. But she had a husband and a child who had to be collected from the babysitter. I had only one hour left before having supper with my fiancée – and more than enough to think about in the meantime.

VIII

It was five to four before I could leave the police station. The day's meeting to report back to my boss was longer than expected.

Based on my description, my boss had no idea who the man in the hat might be, and he thought that it might well just be a coincidence. Otherwise he praised me for having taken the time to interview both Per Johan Fredriksen's employees and Tor Johansen's teacher, but could still not see any clues that might point to another murderer. It all rested on a somewhat unreliable observation by a 104-year-old woman who only contacted the police two days after the murder took place.

My boss was not in the best mood today. He was fortunately more interested in Hauk Rebne Westgaard's story and agreed that after hearing his version, the death from 1932 was even more suspicious. At a quarter to four, we agreed that it was a serious breach of duty that an autopsy had not been carried out at the time. Three minutes later we also agreed that I should keep all possibilities open and carry on with the investigation, but that it still seemed natural to focus on Per Johan Fredriksen's private life, in light of the mysterious death in 1932.

I was very relieved to hand over the hairs from 1932 for technical examination. And then I drove home – pleased that the investigation was to continue, but unsure about how to go about it. Already the case had too many uncertain details that pointed in too many different directions.

Once again I longed for Patricia's clear, sharp voice. As I parked the car, I decided that I would discuss the matter with Miriam over a good meal and then ask for her permission to ring Patricia if we still had not got any further. I suspected that Miriam would not like it, but thought that she would accept that we now had to try every means possible to draw out the truth and prove the innocence of the boy on the red bicycle.

But I did not have the opportunity to discover whether this tactic would work. I did not even have time to say my planned 'sorry I'm a little late' when I got to the flat at five past four.

'There you are, at last. Vera Fredriksen rang for you about half an hour ago. She seemed to be happy and rather excited and said that it was really important that she spoke to you as soon as possible. I said that you were not home yet, and asked if I could give you a message. She asked me to tell you that she was at Haraldsen's Hotel and that she thought she could explain to you what had happened there. I immediately understood what she was talking about, but didn't say anything. I just promised to give you the message as soon as you got in. So you have to go there, straightaway, don't even think about it.'

Miriam was obviously fired up by this unexpected chance of a solution. As was I, of course. So I thanked her and promised to be back as soon as I could.

She said that she would wait until six, but then had to go to her meetings, and would then be back around ten. I gave her a quick kiss on the mouth before running down the stairs and back out to my car.

IX

It was rush hour in Oslo, and I got stuck in traffic twice. So it was twenty to five by the time I got to Haraldsen's Hotel in Ullern. It was a small but reputable old hotel which looked as though nothing had changed since before the war, either inside or out.

And the amount of business now did not bode well for the future. I saw myself reflected in two elegant full-length mirrors on the wall in reception. The only other person I saw was a well-dressed male receptionist, possibly in his sixties, who also looked as though he had been there since before the war. According to his name badge, he was the head of reception and his name was Valdemar Haraldsen.

He looked at me with a friendly smile and asked: 'And what can I do for you? Apologies if I seem a little distracted, but it has been an unexpectedly busy day here today.'

This seemed slightly comical, given that he did not seem to be in the least distracted and it did not look like he had had a busy day.

I introduced myself and said that I had agreed to meet a Miss Vera Fredriksen, who was staying at the hotel.

He squinted at me over his glasses with a smile, then looked down at a good old-fashioned guest book.

'Yes, that is correct. The young lady turned up around midday, without prior warning, and asked if Room 111 was available. It is rather unusual to ask for a specific room, but she paid in cash and made a very favourable impression. Miss Fredriksen asked about the hotel's history and thanked me politely when I could confirm that there has been no major renovation since just after the First World War. Room 111 is as it was then – it had an en suite bathroom even back then.'

The receptionist was obviously a friendly and patient man by nature. I felt a little less patient and a little less friendly right now. So I asked if he could please call Room 111 to let her know that I had arrived.

Valdemar Haraldsen replied in a manner that was just as friendly and patient, that the hotel, true to style and tradition, had not yet installed telephones in the rooms. However, Room 111 was the first room to the left down the corridor upstairs, and he would be happy to go and knock on the door if I so wished.

I assured him that I was perfectly able and happy to do so myself, thanked the head of reception for his help and started up the stairs.

I found the corridor and Room 111 without any difficulty. However, there was not a sound to be heard inside when I knocked on the door. I knocked twice and called out Vera's name once without getting any reaction. The door was locked when I tried it.

The feeling that something was wrong seemed to grow as I stood there in the otherwise empty, dim hotel corridor. And it did not improve when I pressed the light switch.

The light flashed on a small object that was lying on the floor outside Room 114. It was a key. And it said 'Room 111' on the tag.

In a strange way, it felt like I had travelled back to 1932, even when I carefully reached out for the keyring and picked up the key, then put it in the lock of Room 111.

I knocked on the door one last time, without hearing any reaction from within.

Then I turned the key and opened the door.

The situation felt slightly unreal. For a moment I expected to see Eva Bjølhaugen lying there dead on the sofa.

But the woman lying there was, of course, not her.

Vera Fredriksen looked more confident and calmer in death than I had ever seen her in life. All the nervousness had vanished from her face. She was lying with her eyes closed and her face relaxed, and there were no signs of violence or illness. It looked as though she was taking a peaceful afternoon nap on the sofa.

For the second time in two days, I was standing alone in a small room with the body of a young person. The woman on the sofa had been dead slightly longer than the boy on the red bicycle. There was still some warmth in her body, but the skin on her face was cold, and there was no pulse.

I stood there frozen for a few moments, staring at the young, dead Vera Fredriksen, before I managed to pull myself together and look around the room.

There was no sign that anyone else had been there, and there was no sign of a murder weapon or a suicide note of any kind. I sniffed at her mouth, but could not detect anything that smelt like poison. There were no needle marks on her arms either.

I went out into the corridor, which was still empty. Then I went back into Room 111, to make sure that it was not some bizarre dream. But Vera Fredriksen was still lying dead on the sofa. I was in total bewilderment as I walked back down the stairs to reception, in order to ring the station.

X

The head of reception was impressively calm and composed, even when he heard that there had been a suspicious death in the hotel in the past few hours. His statement was clear and to the point, and was taken while I waited for technical assistance from the main police station.

The hotel had very few guests at present, and the head of reception had been the only person on duty since breakfast. Four overnight guests had checked out in the morning and the hotel unfortunately had no further bookings for that night.

However, Vera Fredriksen had shown up without a prior booking around midday. And then at two o'clock or thereabouts, something even more unexpected had happened, when someone telephoned to book a room for the night with a voice that had been distorted. The person who called claimed to be suffering from nerves and was in need of peace and quiet and they were willing to pay for two nights in advance with a tip, if they could come and go without meeting anyone today.

The head of reception was willing to believe this story and agreed to withdraw from the reception area for a couple of minutes so that an envelope with the payment in cash could be left on the counter. The cash was left as agreed, so the head of reception then put out a key and again withdrew for a few minutes. When he came back, the key was gone. He had written the name 'Hansen' down in the guest book for the sake of appearances, but because the voice had been distorted he could not say if it had been a man or a woman who had called.

The head of reception wrung his hands and admitted that it was a deeply unfortunate breach of normal practice, but that the hotel needed more guests, and they had had guests with nerve problems before and there was, at that point, no reason to suspect something criminal.

I said rather impatiently that we would still need to check his story about the mysterious guest and take a statement from him or her.

He immediately agreed to this and took a universal key to Room 112 with him.

We let ourselves in, having knocked twice on the door with no response. The door was unlocked.

The key was lying on the table. It was the only sign that the very mysterious guest had even been in the room.

The head of reception had only seen Vera Fredriksen and myself pass through reception that afternoon. This did not necessarily mean that we two and the mysterious guest were the only people who had been in the hotel. One or more could have passed through in those few minutes when the reception was not manned. There was also a back door at the opposite end of the corridor, by Room 118. The lock meant that it should only be possible to open the door from the inside. However, anyone who was already inside could easily have let others in, and it was not unthinkable that a burglar who came prepared could pick the lock from outside.

Vera Fredriksen had rung my flat from a telephone booth by the hotel reception at around half past three. She had paid for the call in cash at reception, and for two other phone calls she had made earlier in the day – the first around one o'clock and the second around three. Both of the earlier phone calls could not have been longer than a few minutes, but the numbers she had called were not registered anywhere.

XI

I was able to give my boss an update from the telephone in my office at half past six. And it did little to lift spirits.

We had another dead person, and, until the results of an autopsy were clear, no idea of the cause of death.

We knew that there had been another guest in the neighbouring room, but had no idea of the person's identity.

We knew that Vera Fredriksen had made two telephone calls a few hours before her death, but had no idea who she had called or what had been said.

My boss took it much better than I did. He remarked that we did not yet even know if something criminal had occurred. According to what I had said myself, Vera Fredriksen suffered from nerves and her father's death may have triggered suicidal thoughts. Young ladies with a nervous disposition had been known to commit suicide in the most spectacular ways at times, so it was not unthinkable that she had chosen a dramatic replay of the tragedy that her parents had experienced in 1932.

He did, however, concede that the situation was highly suspicious, especially as the mysterious guest from Room 112 had disappeared. If there was any connection to Per Johan Fredriksen's death, this only strengthened the assumption that the explanation was to be found in Fredriksen's private life.

I said that I agreed, and in return he accepted that a priest should be allowed to talk to the three remaining members of the family first, before the police contacted them again.

We also agreed that a forensic investigation should be launched, and that we would talk again as soon as the preliminary autopsy report was ready. I immediately said yes when he suggested ten o'clock the following morning.

I put the telephone down at a quarter to seven, and sat there pondering, looking at it for a few minutes more.

I thought that Miriam would by now have gone to her meetings, and would not be back until late this evening. Then I thought that she would surely be happy for me to ring Patricia now, as yet another young person had lost her life. I concluded that the situation was now so critical that I could not *not* phone Patricia, regardless of what Miriam might think.

At ten to seven, I took the plunge. I lifted the receiver and dialled Patricia's number from memory.

The telephone was answered after two rings.

The woman's voice at the other end simply said: 'Yes?' But I recognized it straightaway all the same and felt a surge of relief and hope that the deaths from 1932 and 1972 could all be solved before a scandal ensued. It all depended on whether or not I was now able to persuade Patricia to help me.

'Hello, it's me,' I said.

There was a few seconds' silence on the other end. For the first time, it felt as though Patricia was surprised that I had rung her, and she needed a few seconds to consider the significance of it. But this did not take long.

'I suppose this is about the Fredriksen case, then. I think there are several very good reasons why I should steer clear.'

I was afraid she was going to put the telephone down, but the line was not broken. There was still hope.

She said nothing about what these reasons might be, and I certainly did not feel like asking. Instead, I tried to tempt her with titbits from the investigation.

'The case is far more interesting than it might at first seem. We now have a statement from an eyewitness that indicates that the young suspect who took his own life did not kill Fredriksen. Though who then might have done still remains a mystery. And then this afternoon, Fredriksen's youngest daughter was found dead in the very hotel room where her mother's sister was found dead in 1932. Fredriksen himself was also there at the time, as one of a group of her friends. So I think I can say that I have never been involved in a more puzzling or tragic case.'

Again, there was a few moments' silence at the other end.

'It certainly sounds that way so far. I am sure that the case is both interesting and important. But for strictly personal reasons I do not think I should get involved in your investigation.'

That was, of course, where the problem lay. But now that it was staring me in the face I could solve it. The telephone line remained open.

I breathed in and out with the utmost control a few times. Then I said: 'I can understand that. Miriam did not want me to contact you about the case either. But I felt that I now owed it to those young people to call you all the same. I believe that only you can help me. So that is why I called, without her knowing.'

I spoke in a hushed voice, even though I knew perfectly well that Miriam was sitting in a meeting a couple of miles away and that no one could hear the conversation.

There was a pause on the other end of the phone. I looked at the clock to keep my mind focused in the pregnant silence and counted to nine before Patricia answered.

'Well, if it is so important to you and for those young people, we will have to see if there is anything I can do to help. If you come here in half an hour, I will see if I can get the servants to whip something up for your dinner by half past seven.'

Patricia said this quickly and with determination. Then she put the receiver down without waiting for an answer.

I sat there with the mute receiver in my hand, and a feeling of enormous relief – tinged with a slight guilt.

XII

The White House at 104–108 Erling Skjalgsson's Street was just as impressive from the outside as I remembered it from previous visits. In the midst of my most complicated and bewildering murder case, there was something enormously calming and reassuring about the very sight of the Borchmanns' monumental family home.

But this time it was tempered by a level of unease. I looked around before I parked the car, before I walked up to the house and before I rang the bell. But no one was following me on the almost empty evening street.

In terms of formality, I was still high and dry: I was officially simply visiting a friend. In reality, though, I would divulge information that could cost me my job if it were ever discovered. But I had done this many times before, and my concern about this side of the matter was minimal. I had known Patricia's late parents since I was a child, and I was absolutely convinced that no information given by me would leak from here. I had successfully convinced myself that I had to do everything within my power to solve the murder case I was investigating.

The door was opened by a maid who looked exactly the same as before, and once again gave me a cautious smile as she welcomed me in. I thought that it was perhaps Benedikte, but still could not be sure that it was not her twin sister Beate. Not that it really mattered. Though she would never admit it herself, Patricia was still in the very best hands and in the safest environment.

The servants had indeed managed to whip up a supper for half past seven. The onion soup starter was already waiting at my usual place at the table when I was ushered into Patricia's library.

Patricia was sitting there herself in her wheelchair on the other side of the table, sovereign of her own small realm. She looked exactly as she had done before. I knew that she had celebrated her twenty-second birthday only a couple of months ago, but could still have mistaken her for a teenager. It struck me that there was something strangely dollish, almost childlike, about Patricia.

I was happy to see her again. So I went around the table and gave her a hug. This seemed to take her by surprise. Her body trembled faintly, but her cheek was warm and her voice a little softer than usual when she said: 'How nice to see you again. I have already eaten. Sit yourself down – eat. And at the same time tell me all that I need to know about Per Johan Fredriksen and his death.'

I sat down, ate, and talked my way through the starter, main course and dessert. Patricia listened with extraordinary concentration as I told her everything about the case so far. She had a large cup of coffee on the table beside her, but did not touch it once. Her hand noted down some names and dates to begin with, without any apparent cooperation with her head. Her eyes were fixed on me the whole time.

When I told her about Eva Bjølhaugen's death in Room 111 in 1932, her eyes sparked for a moment.

'Did the room have an en suite bathroom or not?' she asked quickly.

I told her that the room had an en suite bathroom, which had also been searched without any results. She waved me on, and then sat without moving until I had finished with the story of Vera Fredriksen's death that afternoon. Then she smiled almost merrily for a moment, before once again sitting there gravely in deep concentration.

It was half past eight by the time I had finished my account, put down the almost empty bowl of rice pudding and said: 'So, what do you think? Was it natural causes, suicide or murder, both in 1932 and 1972? As far as 1972 is concerned, we will perhaps get the answer when the preliminary autopsy report comes tomorrow morning.'

And if I had ever thought otherwise, Patricia was no less sharp than she had been before. She sighed in mild exasperation and replied: 'Murder, without a doubt, in both 1932 and 1972. And I am almost certain I know how the murders were committed as well, though one always has to bear in mind poisoning in such situations. It is actually quite obvious, if one just looks beyond the fact that it is a rather unusual way to kill people in a hotel room.'

Patricia fell silent, and took an artful sip of coffee. She immediately started and rang the bell to call the maid.

In the brief minute before the maid knocked on the door, I sat and wondered what Patricia had meant.

'The coffee you served was far too cold, Beate. Pour it out and make some new coffee immediately. And this time make sure the hot plate is on, please!'

Beate rolled her eyes at me and looked like she would love to say that the coffee had been warm when she poured it an hour and a half ago. But all she said was 'Of course, sorry', and then took the coffee cup with her when she left.

The door closed behind the maid and I still did not understand Patricia's meaning. So I had to bite the first bullet and ask how, according to this theory, Eva Bjølhaugen was murdered in 1932 and Vera Fredriksen was murdered in 1972.

Patricia gave a semi-triumphant smile and a swift answer: 'They were drowned. With water from the tap in the bathroom which was poured down their throat as they lay there unconscious. Eva Bjølhaugen fainted after one of her epileptic fits, thus giving the murderer an opportunity that he or she then ruthlessly exploited. Vera Fredriksen could have been knocked unconscious, but as there is no physical evidence of this, it is more likely that she fainted at the sight of an unexpected intruder or something else that frightened her. According to her family she has a tendency to do this when confronted with powerful emotions. In both cases, the murderer then wiped away any spilt water with the towel from the bathroom and left the room.'

It felt slightly absurd when Patricia first said the word drowned. And then utterly logical once she had explained how it happened.

I sat almost thunderstruck, looking at her. She gave a chirpy smile, but was soon serious again.

'So that means that the murderer this afternoon was the same as in 1932?'

Patricia shook her head pensively. 'It is clearly possible that the murderer is one of the group of four friends from

1932 who is still alive. But equally, this is not the only possibility.

'Per Johan Fredriksen had finally understood how the murder was committed when he spoke out at the dinner a few weeks ago. And the reason he raised his water glass was to show the person he believed was the murderer that he knew. The youngest daughter had either heard it from him, or worked it out for herself when she went to the hotel to ask if the room had had an en suite bathroom even in 1932. But that is not to say that the father and daughter actually knew for certain who the murderer was in 1932, nor does it mean that the same person murdered her now. Someone else may have guessed how it was done and used the same method to get rid of Vera, for example, because she now, consciously or unconsciously, had put you onto her father's murderer's trail. Or one of her siblings might have taken the opportunity to get ten million more in inheritance money. There are too many possibilities here. You have given me enough information to work out how Vera Fredriksen died, but not why or who killed her. Her siblings, boyfriend, mother and the others from the 1932 group who are still alive might all have done it, perhaps even someone we are yet to know about. Based on the known facts, it would be pure guesswork to say who she phoned, or who the mysterious guest in the neighbouring room was, and who else might have been in the hotel.'

Patricia had to pause to draw breath, but was obviously in her stride now. She continued a couple of moments later, without waiting for any questions.

'Much the same is true of Eva Bjølhaugen's murder in 1932. We can pretty much say with certainty that she first had a visitor in her bed, that shortly afterwards she had an epileptic fit and then was killed by drowning. We do not, however, know if the person in the bed was the same person who killed her, and again, we do not know who killed her full stop. As things stand, I have possible scenarios that fit for the other five in the group.'

'And what about the murder of Per Johan Fredriksen?' I asked.

Patricia sighed heavily.

Just then we were interrupted by a knock at the door. The maid came in with a fresh, steaming mug of coffee. She seemed to realize that she had come at the wrong time and made a hasty retreat without saying anything.

Patricia sipped her coffee.

'Now it is slightly too hot,' she said, and put the cup down. Then she looked straight at me again.

'The murder of Per Johan Fredriksen is, if possible, even harder to work out. Whereas the murder in 1932 had a limited number of possible killers, the possibilities for the first murder in 1972 are as good as infinite. I have a number of theories, but need more information in order to establish which of them is right. And, what is more, I am not sure that we have a full overview of all the alternatives. There are lots of people with different backgrounds and motives who might want to kill a man like Per Johan Fredriksen. Fredriksen himself was obviously a chameleon man, and I think that the chances are considerable that he was killed by another chameleon person.'

Patricia blew on her coffee, then cautiously took a sip. I had the distinct feeling that she was waiting for me to ask her to explain the concept, and had no alternative but to do just that.

'Goodness, apologies, I was obviously not thinking and used a concept that I made up myself and have since used so much that I forget that it is not generally known. But it is very appropriate and almost self-explanatory. The crime novelist Sven Elvestad based his novel *Chameleon* on the phenomenon in 1912. A chameleon person is someone who can move seamlessly between different circles and switch appearances depending on where they are.'

'Surely that is relatively normal?' I objected.

Patricia wiggled her head from left to right, and carried on speaking.

'Yes and no. Fortunately, most of us behave slightly differently depending on who we are with and which social setting we are in. It is called social skills. But real chameleon people are different: they can change their face, behaviour and even personality within seconds, depending on what they think will serve their interests. Hauk Rebne Westgaard touched on it when he said that, ever since he was a child, Fredriksen had had many different facets and faces. And in more recent years, he had been perceived very differently as a businessman and a family man. His mistress has another impression of him, and people in political circles yet another. I would like to know more about the latter. Even though it may be painful for them, I think you should ask his family what they know about his earlier mistresses. And bear in mind all the time that several people may turn out to have several faces, and that some of those who do not appear to be dangerous on first meeting could be just that. Chameleons are generally thought of as small, innocuous animals, but they can suddenly change face and swallow their prey when least expected.'

I listened to her, fascinated, and promised to bear it in mind.

'The boss is very reluctant to give up on the boy on the red bicycle as a possible perpetrator, but it would seem now that it is just a red herring?' I suggested.

The coffee was no longer steaming. Patricia took another sip and thought for a while before answering.

'We obviously cannot disregard the possibility that the murder may have something to do with Fredriksen's life as a callous businessman and a heartless landlord. I think it is highly likely that what your eyewitness saw is true, despite her age, and that the poor boy was innocent. But we should not take that as a given yet.'

'If the boy was innocent, it seems very odd that he then took the murder weapon with him when he fled to my home,' I remarked.

Patricia shook her head fiercely. 'To the contrary, his behaviour there and then is perfectly logical, if you look at what happened in isolation, in the sequence that he experienced it. Imagine how you would react in that situation. You are out in the street and see a man who has collapsed with a knife in his heart. What would you do?'

'I would run over to see if he was alive. Then I dare say I would pull out the knife,' I said.

Patricia nodded. 'Precisely. Pulling out the knife does not

in any way improve the victim's chances of survival, but it is a natural reaction. Then there is the next stage. Fredriksen is clearly dead. The boy is standing there with the murder weapon in his hand and no other suspect in sight. He realizes in a flash that makes him the prime suspect regardless of whether he is caught at the scene of the crime with his fingerprints on the knife, or leaves the knife with his fingerprints on it behind. His life has never been easy and he does not have much self-esteem or trust in society. He does, on the other hand, have absolute trust in his hero, in other words you, and knows where you live. Given that he is both innocent and intelligent, it is then quite rational that he takes the murder weapon with him, jumps on his bike and cycles to your flat. What is confusing, and what makes me hesitate to dismiss him as the perpetrator—' Patricia stopped in the middle of the sentence and sat there staring into thin air.

'Once again, you are right. What is confusing is not his behaviour after the murder, but his behaviour after his arrest,' I said.

Patricia nodded. 'Precisely. Though to be fair, he did say specifically that Fredriksen was dead when he went back, and he shook his head when you asked him if he had seen the murder. So perhaps he did not have much more to say. The parallels with Hauptmann and van der Lubbe indicate that he was well aware of the situation, despite his communication problems. But his refusal to give his name or other details is very strange and clearly did not help his already difficult situation. There is something irrational about it which could indicate mental disturbance and thus make it possible that he did commit the offence after all. But it was most probably due to shock or an exaggerated belief that you would quickly be able to uncover the truth. Whatever the case, the story of the boy on the red bicycle is so puzzling that we cannot simply write him off as a tragic red herring. However, the most interesting thing is, in fact, not the boy's reaction, but—'

Patricia stopped speaking and looked very pensive indeed. It was obvious that the cogs in her brain were whirring furiously.

'But the mother's reaction?' I tried tentatively.

Patricia shook her head with what looked like irritation. 'No, no, given that she had been away for the weekend and did not get back until Monday, that part of the story is believable enough. What I find strange is your boss's reaction. In part because he is so keen to close the case and put the young boy down as the perpetrator. And in part because he keeps saying that if the investigation is to continue, the focus should be on Fredriksen's private life and the tragedy in 1932. At the risk of sounding paranoid, I wonder whether Fredriksen's murder might be like an iceberg, and that we still cannot see the bulk of what is hidden under the surface. There is one thing that could point in that direction, and I do not like it one bit.'

Patricia fell silent again. Then suddenly she drank the rest of her coffee in one go. Then she said five words: 'The man in the hat.' She sat deep in thought without saying anything as the seconds ticked by. 'I would very much like to know who the man in the hat is. If he really is just a passer-by whom you happened to meet twice in the same day, it is all far less dramatic and I wouldn't fret. However, I do not think that is the case. If he was following you, he could of course be a friend, relative or private detective who is following you on behalf of someone in the Fredriksen family, his mistress, the Ramdals or Hauk Rebne Westgaard. But it would be fairly risky for any of them to ask someone to follow a police detective like that. And what they stood to gain by knowing where you were going is unclear. So I doubt that that is the explanation. In which case, the man with the hat points to something bigger which is still lurking beneath the surface, in possibly rather icy water. Too much importance should not be placed on his missing finger joint, in isolation, but that detail does not make the case any more pleasant . . .'

Patricia's hands were shaking ever so slightly when she lifted the coffee cup to her mouth. She appeared to be lost deep in her own thoughts and did not notice that the cup was empty.

'No, there are far too many possibilities here for me to be able to give you any more help tonight. I need more facts in order to discard those that don't work. Let me know when you have more. Check the alibis of everyone we have spoken about, ask the family if they know about any of Fredriksen's other mistresses, follow up his political life, be open to the possibility that your boss is not telling you everything he knows about the case – and meanwhile, take good care of yourself.'

The latter was said in a slightly tremulous voice.

I was deeply touched by Patricia's concern in the midst of it all. I told her so, thanked her for her help so far and gave her a hug as I made to leave. Patricia's reply was short: 'Good. We will talk again tomorrow, then.' But her cheek burned hot against mine, and I felt that our meeting had been unexpectedly successful.

It was only when I was at the door that I realized what we had not talked about, and that was Miriam. Patricia had not asked after her and I had not mentioned her.

XIII

Despite the new conclusions and Patricia's warnings, as I drove home I thought less about the investigation and more about the dilemma I now found myself in. The magic and optimism of my renewed contact with Patricia receded as soon as I could no longer see or hear her. It felt almost as though I had been unfaithful to Miriam, simply by visiting Patricia without having asked her first. It reached the point by the end of the journey where, despite the progress we had made on the investigation, I regretted having gone and was more worried about what Miriam's reaction might be were she to find out.

It seemed increasingly to me that the best solution for all parties would be if the case could be solved within a day or two, without Miriam ever needing to know about Patricia's involvement. Patricia appeared to be happy with the situation and her role being kept secret, from Miriam as well, and obviously did not need any form of recognition. Miriam was happy when she could discuss the case with me, without knowing that I was also discussing it with Patricia.

My flat lay in darkness when I parked outside at half past nine. I had by then decided that the solution to my great dilemma would be that I would not tell Miriam about my visit to Patricia unless absolutely necessary, but that I would answer honestly if she asked if I had contacted Patricia.

XIV

The night was dark and there was a fine drizzle in the air. I sat indoors alone and stewed until about half-past ten, but did not manage to pull myself together enough to think systematically in any way about the case.

For the first time I found myself thinking it would perhaps be just as well if Miriam did not come as agreed, so that I could talk to her in the morning when I was rested instead. But I knew she would come: partly because she was curious about the case, but mostly because she had promised she would. And I was right, of course. Two minutes after the half-past-ten bus had passed, a familiar figure in a raincoat with a thick book in her hand emerged from the dark.

Miriam snapped the book shut as soon as I opened the door to the flat. 'Sorry, the last meeting dragged on. Did young Vera Fredriksen bring the investigation any closer to a conclusion?' she asked, before she had even taken off her shoes.

I had to tell her that Vera Fredriksen had unfortunately been killed herself before she had a chance to tell me anything and that the investigation was therefore now even more complex.

To begin with, Miriam was very sad to hear about young Vera's death, but soon became increasingly interested to know what had happened.

I had tried to ease my bad conscience by preparing a late supper with the best food I could find in the fridge, which Miriam seemed to appreciate. She ate more than me, of course; I had already had a three-course meal, and was struggling with my guilt. Otherwise, everything went unexpectedly well. Miriam digested the food and the story of Vera Fredriksen's death at the same time, and did not ask about Patricia. It struck me that the situation was the same as it had been at Patricia's: Miriam did not ask, and I did not divulge.

I did not mention the explanation as to why the boy on the red bicycle had taken the murder weapon with him when he fled the scene of the crime. And I kept my worries about the man in the hat to myself. But I did say that it had struck me, before the results of the autopsy were clear, that one possibility was that both Eva Bjølhaugen and Vera Fredriksen had been drowned, using water from the bathroom.

Miriam was very impressed and said that the idea was a good example of my creative thinking when it came to investigations. There was a slightly awkward atmosphere when she said this, but it was the closest that we got to mentioning Patricia that evening. We quickly changed tack; it felt as though both of us wanted to.

XV

On Tuesday, 21 March, I lay awake tussling with my conscience, long after Miriam had gone to sleep.

Around half past midnight, I changed my mind and came to the conclusion that I should have told Miriam about going to see Patricia as soon as she arrived. But Miriam was already deep in sleep by then. So I kissed her tenderly on the cheek and whispered that we would have to talk about it tomorrow. Shortly after, I fell asleep too, finally at some kind of peace with myself.

I woke once, briefly, during the night, when the man in the hat visited me in my dreams. In my dream, he threw a knife at me on Karl Johan Street. I woke up with a start, but the man in the hat was nowhere to be seen, and the woman I was engaged to was asleep in the bed beside me. That calmed me. For the rest of the night I slept the dreamless sleep of an exhausted man – a deep, contented sleep, without the faintest idea of what dramas tomorrow would bring.

DAY FIVE

A New Dimension – and Some New Leads

I

On Wednesday, 22 March 1972, I woke when the alarm clock went off at half past seven. I was clearly so full of adrenalin from the case that my need for sleep had diminished. I was wide awake and ready to face the new day within seconds of the alarm clock ringing.

Miriam, on the other hand, continued to sleep undisturbed, having cast a quick glance at the clock first. I was about to wake her again, but remembered that she did not have a lecture until a quarter past ten on Wednesdays. And I knew from experience that it was a bad idea to wake her unnecessarily early. Furthermore, I still had a lot to think about and a smidgen of a bad conscience. So I left her to sleep on and tiptoed out into the kitchen.

I ate breakfast alone with the newspapers, which made for less pleasant reading than the day before. The headlines were dominated by a new opinion poll that showed a fall in support for the anti-EEC movement, as well as stories on the Barents Sea agreement. It seemed that the agreement would be passed by a majority in the Storting on Friday afternoon and would be ready for signing by Monday. And in between the articles on the significance of the agreement, the reports about my investigation of the murder were becoming more critical. My name was not mentioned today, but both papers noted that the investigation was still ongoing and that the police would not divulge why.

Aftenposten found it reassuring that the police were taking the time to carry out a thorough investigation, even though a young man 'from the east end, with a difficult background' had been arrested and subsequently had taken his own life. *Arbeiderbladet*, on the other hand, questioned if this meant that the presumed killer had, in fact, proved to be innocent. The answer was that this certainly seemed to be the situation, and as such it was 'a very dramatic development' in the case.

Both papers carried small notices that a young woman had been found dead at Haraldsen's Hotel in mysterious circumstances. Neither of them had as yet discovered her relationship to Fredriksen, or the story from 1932. And there was clearly a risk of longer reports once this became known.

I left home at ten to eight, having set the table for Miriam and written a note which read: 'Did not want to wake you. Enjoy your breakfast and have a good lecture!'

It felt like the pressure was mounting on all sides, and, in a way, it was good that Miriam had slept while I had breakfast. During the night, I had once again abandoned the idea of telling her about my renewed contact with Patricia. If Miriam should hear that I had been in touch with her,

I prayed that it would not coincide with the press discovering that the boy who had taken his own life in prison was in all likelihood innocent.

II

My boss was not in his office when I got there at eight o'clock. Outside my office door, however, hopping around impatiently, was a pathologist I had met in connection with one of my earlier cases a couple of years ago.

'The preliminary autopsy report is ready, and quite sensational . . .' he started.

I waved my hand dismissively. 'I don't think you will manage to surprise me this time either. The cause of death was water in the lungs, is that right?'

He nodded swiftly and rolled his eyes to show he was impressed. 'How on earth . . . ?' he said.

'It is actually quite logical that she was drowned. You just need to let go of the fact that it is not a method normally used for murder in a hotel room. I am more interested in knowing if there were any other signs of violence, but I am assuming there were not?' I said.

A little more colour drained from the pathologist's face, and he shook his head.

'No, or that is to say, she had some light bruising on her neck that may indicate that someone held her down as she was being drowned. But otherwise, we have found no other signs of violence.'

I thanked him for this confirmation. Then I quickly

closed the door on the slightly bewildered and very impressed pathologist.

I sat down and rang the Centre Party office. The party leaders were not available, due to meetings in the Storting. However, the Secretary General, Petter Martin Arvidsen, was there and when I told him that I was calling from the police about the murder of Per Johan Fredriksen, he said that he would be happy to meet me. He told me that he had an important meeting at ten o'clock, but had time available before then. And I replied that I did too. We concluded that I should go to meet him in his office as soon as possible. So I walked the few hundred yards over to the party office in Arbeider Street as quickly as I could.

III

I eventually found the Centre Party office on the fifth floor of 4 Arbeider Street, having first climbed the stairs past four floors occupied by the newspaper, *Nationen*. The Secretary General, Petter Martin Arvidsen, turned out to be a slim, yet very jovial man in his mid-thirties, with remnants of a Trønderlag dialect. He was swift to shake my hand and then pointed to a chair, before closing the door behind me.

He looked at me in expectation. I chose a gentle start and asked him to give me his impression of Per Johan Fredriksen.

'You know, over the past few days, I have reflected on how strange it is that in politics today you can see someone every day for years without ever actually knowing them.

That was certainly the case with Fredriksen. He was always there – at all the important meetings: the parliamentary party group, the representative body, the party conference. He appeared to enjoy all social occasions, with or without his wife. He was well respected and a powerful man within the party and, in recent years, had become even more prominent thanks to his keen interest in foreign policy. But I don't think I could say that I knew him as a person, and I am not sure that anyone else did. He was an extremely good politician. He was knowledgeable, to the point, and at times even humorous, both as a speaker and a debater, and he was always very active and interested in his dealings with voters and members of the public.'

I waited a few seconds for a 'but', which never came. So I asked where the problem lay.

'The problem was that the Centre Party is the most united party on the Right and Per Johan Fredriksen was not really a team player. He was an excellent individualist, but always and only an individualist. To put it another way, Per Johan was a man who was respected by all and trusted by none. He was also a touch too pragmatic at times, even for a result-oriented party like ours. People got the feeling that, for Per Johan, politics was not so much about social engagement as personal gain. And that is also probably why he was never part of the party leadership or government, as he so wanted to be.'

'But he was still ambitious?'

Petter Martin Arvidsen gave an unexpectedly broad grin. 'Goodness yes, the man certainly never suffered from any lack of ambition or belief in his own abilities. He had intimated that he wanted to stand again in the general election next year, and undoubtedly hoped for a ministerial post if the party got back into government. There was even speculation that, despite his age, he rather fancied himself as a new party leader if our current leader stepped down at next year's party conference. And there were those who believed and feared—' All of a sudden he stopped and sat in silence for a few moments. Then he said: 'Please understand that I will do whatever I can to help the police, but that my position in the party might make it difficult to talk openly about a late party member like Fredriksen. Will this meeting be minuted in any way?'

I considered this for a moment or two, then said that as this was not yet a formal statement of any kind; he could talk openly without worrying that it might be recorded in the minutes. I could contact him again later if I needed confirmation of anything.

It was a practical compromise that I felt was acceptable in order to move on with the investigation. To my relief, he readily accepted what was basically a horse-trade.

'Very good. I appreciate that. So, there are also those who believed and feared that Per Johan Fredriksen was about to betray the party. He was from good old-fashioned farming stock, but had been living in the city for a long time. With his wealth in properties in the city, he had always belonged to the side of the party that was closest to the Conservatives. His seat in Vestfold was no longer secure, and there was speculation that the Conservatives might offer him a senior position as part of their offensive in rural constituencies. And that would seriously damage the

Centre Party in terms of next year's election. And even more sensational than that . . .'

Petter Martin Arvidsen paused, his face blanched, and when he continued speaking it was in a hushed voice.

'There has also been speculation that he might change sides in the EEC debate and come out in favour of Norway joining! If one of the leading politicians in the party and our representative on the Standing Committee on Foreign Affairs were to change sides, it would have an enormous and devastating impact on both the party and the no campaign. In such a case, it would almost be better if he swapped party.'

I had to ask if anyone in the party might have seen the threat as being so critical that they would commit murder.

Petter Martin Arvidsen sat quietly and looked out of the window briefly before answering. Then he turned to face me.

'I wish that I could answer no, but I don't know that I dare to at the moment. There are powerful emotions at play out there. For some people in our party and in others, this is a religious war. For others it is a fight for their livelihood and to keep the farm that has been in their family for generations. Having said that, I have no one in particular in mind. But I would not like to say that there is no one out there who might be prepared to kill for, or against, the EEC.'

It struck me that Miriam had said more or less the same. And then I thought that I might perhaps have met one such person, when I sat opposite Hauk Rebne Westgaard and heard him say that the EEC would spell the end of agriculture in Norway as we know it.

IV

It was on the way back to the main police station, following my visit to the Centre Party office, that he suddenly appeared for the third time.

When I threw a glance back over my shoulder, there he was on the pavement, moving in the same direction, about four yards behind me.

The man in the hat had changed his suit, and he had his hat discreetly tucked under his left arm. But it was the same hat, and even before I had seen it, I had recognized his walk and expressionless face.

My first thought was to stop and ask him who he was. But I was also afraid of the man, and did not want to confront him. The nightmare where he threw a knife at me on Karl Johan Street had suddenly come back to haunt me in broad daylight.

All I wanted was to get back to the safety of the police station and have some time to think over the situation. So instead of stopping, I carried on walking, speeding up my pace a little.

It felt very uncomfortable to have someone following me so close behind when I had no idea who they were. I tried to pretend I was not concerned, but looked back sooner than I should have.

My encounter with the man in the hat lasted no more than two minutes. We did not exchange a single word; we were never close enough to do so. But it was still a very frightening experience.

As I took those final steps into the main police station, I reflected on what Patricia had said about icebergs, and the fact that the bulk of them lies hidden under the surface. I had not found out who the man in the hat was, but I was certain that he was not a random passer-by. And I was even more certain that he was not good news.

V

I got back just in time for my meeting with the boss at ten o'clock. He was sitting waiting in his office and started to talk as soon as the door closed behind me.

'The pathologist has informed me of his conclusions regarding the most recent murder. He was, with good reason, very impressed that you knew the cause of death before he told you.'

I thanked him with appropriate modesty, and said that when using the process of elimination, it was fairly logical. I added that we were therefore also clearly dealing with murder.

My boss nodded. 'I asked the pathologist if it was possible for Miss Fredriksen to have taken her own life with the help of water. And according to him this was unthinkable, especially as she was lying on the sofa with no trace of water nearby. Someone had poured water down her throat and possibly held her down until she drowned, then dried away any splashes and disappeared. A clear case of murder. And this makes it even more natural to look for the clues in Fredriksen's personal life.'

I chewed on this for a few seconds. Then I said tentatively that there were other possibilities. For example, that the person who killed Fredriksen had also killed his daughter to hide his or her tracks.

He shook his head disapprovingly. 'That seems very unlikely. I think you should focus all your attention on Fredriksen's family and friends; that is where you will find the murderer.'

I thought for a beat, then put my trust in Patricia and took the plunge. 'And with all due respect, I think there is something important that you are not telling me. Something that may not be decisive, but that I should definitely know, as I am investigating the murder of Per Johan Fredriksen.'

My boss started as soon as I spoke. It was a bold shot in the dark: I would have nothing to say if my boss asked what I thought he was hiding. And my boss could be sharp when his authority was challenged. I saw his teeth as he prepared to fire a caustic reply. But instead, when he did finally open his mouth, he spoke in an unexpectedly calm, almost feeble voice.

'I should have known better than to think I could hide something from you, Kristiansen. I apologize as there is, indeed, something important that I've been keeping from you. I thought it was not significant and that it would be best for everyone concerned if you did not know. But it may be important and as head of the investigation you should know what it is, so that you are aware of the possibility. But this must be kept strictly between us – not even Danielsen can know.'

An incredible sense of relief flooded my body. I sent my heartfelt thanks to Patricia – and assured my boss that not even Danielsen would hear a thing about it.

'What I have not told you is that when Fredriksen was killed, he was on the point of being arrested – on suspicion of being a Soviet spy. The police security service had been watching him for some time and believed they had grounds to arrest him. The timing was, as I am sure you can appreciate, highly sensitive in light of the imminent agreement.'

Initially, I was speechless. This was a totally unexpected and dramatic development that added a shocking new dimension to the case.

Then I asked in one and the same sentence if they had planned when they would arrest him, and how many people knew about it.

'I think that only myself and a handful of people at the police security service were involved and knew about this – and now, of course, you do too. The police security service had been following Fredriksen for some months, but the operation was still top secret. I was only informed on Friday, because they had planned to arrest him in connection with a meeting that Fredriksen had arranged with his Soviet contact on Sunday evening.'

I said nothing as my brain worked overtime. Then I asked what the motive was, and my boss promptly carried on.

'His motive is unclear. Politically he was, of course, conservative, and financial gain is not a likely motive for such a wealthy man. But in the past year, Fredriksen has had some suspicious meetings with representatives from the Soviet

Embassy here in Oslo. The police security service believe they have sufficient evidence that he has handed over confidential information, and possibly also secret documents that he had access to through his work with the Standing Committee on Foreign Affairs. The hope was to catch him red-handed with the documents. It would then have been the most notorious Norwegian spy case since the war.'

Coming from my boss, these were strong words. And what was more, they were perhaps not strong enough. I reflected on my meeting with the Centre Party secretary general only an hour before, and tried to imagine what he might have said.

'It would also be one of the greatest political scandals. And it could not only delay, but, in the worst case, sabotage the demarcation agreement with the Soviet Union and that would be a mighty blow for the Centre Party and the anti-EEC campaign. So there are plenty of people who would rather Fredriksen was murdered than arrested.'

My boss nodded. 'I would not like to say whether motives of that sort might have influenced certain parties in the police security service. But the timing was highly controversial, in terms of both the agreement with the Soviets and the EEC referendum. The news that a leading spokesman for the no campaign was guilty of treason in favour of the Soviet Union could have had serious consequences.'

It was all too easy to agree with this. I mentioned the earlier incident outside with the man in the hat. Without mentioning my own fear, obviously, I said that this was now a mystery within the mystery that gave good grounds for concern. Then I said something that I had not thought of before: that it was possible that the man in the hat was working for the police security service.

It looked as though my boss, like me, was not convinced that the answer was no. He stared at me for a few moments. Then he dialled a telephone number from memory, and when the call was answered, he said: 'It's me. There has been a dramatic development in the case we were talking about on Friday. I think that we two and Detective Inspector Kristiansen should perhaps have a chat. You remember DI Kristiansen?'

After a short answer, my boss then said: 'Good, we are on our way', and put down the receiver.

'Asle Bryne remembers you and has asked both of us to go over there as soon as possible,' he said as he stood up.

I got to my feet without protest. I remembered Asle Bryne, the head of the police security service, well from my previous visits to Victoria Terrace, and was grateful that my boss was going to be there. Although it did not make the matter any less serious.

VI

It had been a year and a half since my last visit and the head of the police security service's office had not changed one bit. Asle Bryne was sitting behind his desk with a pipe in his mouth. He gave a brief nod, but made no attempt to shake hands.

'So,' he said, then disappeared behind a small cloud of smoke.

I looked at my boss, who started by saying that this conversation must be kept strictly between us.

I nodded quickly, but did not see any reaction from Asle Bryne.

My boss obviously did not expect to get one. He gave a brief and to-the-point account of the latest developments, including the eyewitness and the murder of Fredriksen's daughter. He concluded diplomatically by saying that there was in all likelihood no link to Fredriksen's contact with the Soviet Embassy, but the possibility could not be ruled out. There was therefore a need now to ask Bryne some questions in connection with the murder investigation.

'I see,' was all Asle Bryne said, and then he looked at me.

I was not sure whether he filled his pipe with more tobacco on purpose or not, but the net result was that it was even harder for me to see his facial expressions through the smoke.

I felt like I had been left out in the thin, cold air. The journey from hearing the sensational news that Fredriksen was suspected of being a spy to the office of the head of the police security service had been so short that I had barely had time to think.

I tried to feel my way forwards and asked if Fredriksen had had direct contact with the Soviet ambassador.

It was a bad start. My boss rolled his eyes, and Bryne looked even less sympathetic when he spoke.

'Obviously the ambassador himself is never directly involved in things like this, that would be far too compromising in the event it was discovered. At various times and places, Fredriksen had contact with three different, lower-ranking diplomats this year. The pattern was suspicious – they met as if by chance at different times and places where they were unlikely to be seen. And we have found information that can only come from closed meetings of the Standing Committee on Foreign Affairs in various Russian sources after these meetings, without me being able to go into any detail. So we know that someone or other, either the Ministry of Foreign Affairs or the Standing Committee, has passed on confidential documents that could threaten national security. We do not know for certain that it was Fredriksen, but it seems natural to assume there is a link.'

I found the answer somewhat vague, but doubted that any question to follow this up would make it any clearer. So I fired a double question instead: if any of Fredriksen's contacts had been younger women, and what they thought might be his motive for espionage.

'No, as far as we know, he has only met with male diplomats. We have of course considered the possibility of sexual liaisons, but have no indication that that was the case. Nor have we seen evidence of any monetary transactions. His motive is one of the mysteries that it may be very hard to establish now that Fredriksen is dead. As the case stands, there seems to be no better solution than to let it die quietly along with the spy, and thank our lucky stars that the leak was stopped before it could cause even greater damage.'

Asle Bryne blew out another little cloud of smoke. He did not look in the slightest bit glad about this or, indeed, anything else. To a certain extent I could understand him.

If Fredriksen really had been a spy, his death had denied the police security service a considerable and much-needed boost.

'Was the arrest imminent at the time of his death?' I asked, trying to be more friendly.

Bryne's clean-shaven chin moved up and down inside the cloud of smoke. 'Within less than twenty-four hours. How we knew that, I cannot say. We knew that Fredriksen was due to meet one of his Soviet contacts on Sunday afternoon. We hoped and believed that he would have documents with him, and were of the view that we had enough on him to make him confess when caught in such a compromising situation.'

I then asked how long they had had Fredriksen under surveillance, and what had made them start in the first place.

The question did not make Bryne any more communicative. He answered curtly it was a matter of two or three months, and he could not say what had triggered it.

I was not very satisfied with the answer. So I threw down my only trump card. 'During my investigation of Fredriksen's murder, I have on several occasions been followed by a man. And I apologize, but I must ask if he is doing so on behalf of the police security service?'

My boss was completely still, whereas Bryne started in his chair. 'That is absolute nonsense, young man. I practically never comment on who we have under surveillance, but will make an exception to say that we do not have any of our highly esteemed colleagues in the Oslo police under surveillance. The incompetent fools at the military intelligence agency might decide to do that, but I can assure you that the police security service never would.'

I felt I was on thin ice, but was still not convinced. 'The man wears a suit and hat, is around five foot nine and has one distinguishing physical feature: the little finger on his right hand is missing the top joint. Are you absolutely sure that you know nothing about him?'

I thought at first that it was a bull's eye and that my theory that the man in the hat was working for the police security service was right after all. A twitch rippled across Bryne's otherwise stony face and with a sudden movement he put down his pipe. Then I realized that something was not right. Bryne knitted his thick brows and looked at me with something akin to paternal sympathy. His voice was far softer and more considerate when he spoke.

'The man you are talking about definitely has no connection whatsoever with the police security service, and is not someone I am acquainted with; I do, however, know who he is. And this strengthens our theory regarding Fredriksen and the seriousness of the matter.'

Both my boss and I stared intently at Bryne, who appeared to have regained his composure. He lit his pipe again and took a couple of thoughtful puffs before opening a drawer in his desk. From it he pulled a photograph and an index card, which he lay down on the desk between us.

'I am guessing that this is him,' Bryne said.

My boss looked at me. I looked at the photograph. And I replied that it was definitely him.

The man in the hat had been photographed, in his suit and hat, from the side, from a street corner. Judging by the signs in the background, the photograph had been taken in London. It was indisputably the same man that I had seen behind me in Aker Street. And it appeared that he really was not good news.

According to the index card, the man in the hat was Alexander Svasnikov, who was also known by a number of aliases. He was forty-two years old, had a PhD in languages from the University of Moscow, but had worked for the KGB since 1965, at least.

'The man with the missing pinky joint normally changes both his first and second name whenever he is posted to a new country. Here in Norway he is called Sergey Klinkalski. Here at the security service we simply call him Doctor Death, after the still-missing Nazi doctor. Svasnikov is, of course, not a medical doctor, but rather a polyglot genius who can learn most languages in no time at all. He has been stationed at embassies in Madrid, London, Bonn and Amsterdam for short periods. And in all cases, these stays have coincided with the unsolved murders of Soviet defectors living in that country. Svasnikov has always had diplomatic immunity and none of the murders can be linked to him in any way. And after a few days he moves on. As far as we know, he has never been to any of the Nordic countries before, so since his arrival we have been wondering what brings such a shark to these cold waters. Svasnikov has never been in a country without someone dying there in the most dramatic way within the space of a few weeks.'

Bryne blew out an unexpected amount of smoke after this tirade and looked even more pensive than usual. There was silence in the room. After a few seconds, I mustered my courage and shared my thoughts.

'If the Soviets are aware that Fredriksen was about to be exposed, it would obviously be in their interests that he die before being arrested. In which case, this Svasnikov might well be Fredriksen's murderer. He has killed before and he has just arrived in Oslo and has an obvious motive. It is almost too incredible to be a coincidence.'

My boss nodded. But Asle Bryne, on the other side of the desk, did not. 'Nothing would make me and the police security service happier than to be able to prove that Fredriksen was a Soviet spy and that he was killed by a Soviet agent. But there are a couple of things that do not add up. First of all, the victim. As far as we know, Svasnikov has only been used to execute Soviet defectors – not to kill Western citizens. And second, the method. A couple of the earlier victims were shot and a couple died in apparent accidents. As far as we know, Svasnikov has never used a knife as a murder weapon before, and it would be rather risky if Fredriksen were to be killed on an open street.'

I suddenly saw a new side of Asle Bryne as he talked. Behind the cloud of smoke and tight-lipped manner, he was clearly still a quick-thinking policeman. When he carried on, he even managed to sound quite considerate.

'As regards your own situation, I appreciate that it might feel rather unnerving. But the danger of an attack on you is probably very small. They have never harmed a policeman on this side of the Iron Curtain, and what is more, you are well known, so killing you would entail a great risk. But you should be armed, and if you would like, we can have some-one tail you.'

I was only partially mollified by the knowledge that killing me would entail a great risk because I was so well known. The fear sparked by the sighting of the man in the hat outside on the street, now flared up again as I sat here inside, in an office, between my own boss and the head of the police security service.

My initial reaction was to say yes please to both a gun and a guard. But then I realized that the possibility of my visits to Patricia being logged in a security service archive would not be particularly smart, either for me or her.

So I said that I was not worried about my personal safety and that I certainly did not want to waste the police security service's resources, but that having a gun did seem like a good idea if that could be arranged.

'Of course it can,' Bryne replied, and my boss hastily agreed.

We could have concluded the meeting there and then, in a congenial atmosphere of agreement. However, I could not help but ask one last question about what significance the imminent agreement with the Soviet Union might have for the situation.

Bryne straightened up in his chair, lit his pipe again and gave me a piercing look. Even through the smoke I could see that his face had hardened and closed once more.

'That depends on what you mean, my young man. The

answer should be obvious anyway. As far as the Soviets are concerned, it was absolutely in their best interest to avoid any spy allegations only days before such an important agreement, especially when they were so pleased with the agreement and worried that their counterparty might regret it later. And as far as the police security service is concerned, it is of course inconceivable that we would allow political considerations to influence the timing of such a situation. The incompetent fools in the military intelligence agency might take account of such short-term factors, but the police security service would never do that.'

I tried to ease the tension by saying that I of course meant how it would affect the situation in terms of the Soviets.

We ended the meeting there. I recognized the old Asle Bryne, but had also seen a better side of him this time. He shook my hand briefly and wished me luck with the investigation. It was an unexpected gesture, but one that I was afraid I would need.

VII

I was back in my office by half past eleven, where I filled in and submitted the necessary form for carrying a service gun.

Then I made the first of several urgent telephone calls. I had not been looking forward to it. It was to a woman who had lost her husband and then her daughter within the space of three days.

The telephone rang and rang, but was eventually answered on the eighth ring. 'Fredriksen', said the voice, very quietly and quickly this time.

Once again I offered my condolences on her family's great loss. Then I assured her that the investigation into the two murders had been given top priority and that there had been some new developments. I did, however, need to ask her some more questions as soon as she felt able to answer them.

There was a few seconds' silence before she answered.

'I have been thinking a lot about something I once read by an American writer. When she lost her husband, she said: the life we shared is over, I walk on alone – but I am still walking. That is what I have to do now. I may be weeping, but I am alive. Otherwise, I am just rattling around in this home of mine and wondering what on earth has happened. So please come whenever you can or like. I had actually thought of calling you about some documents left by my husband.'

I was impressed by the strength of this apparently delicate and slightly theatrical lady. I was also very curious as to what kind of documents she had found. So I said that it was admirable of her and that I would be there as soon as I could.

I picked up my service pistol on the way out. My application had clearly been processed at record speed. I was not entirely sure how reassuring I found that. The situation felt unsafe and what Bryne had said, about Svasnikov never going to a country without someone being killed within the week, was still echoing in my ears.

VIII

The sea of flowers on the drawing-room table in Bygdøy was even bigger today. But the woman on the sofa beside them was, to an impressive extent, the same, only a day after she had been told of her younger daughter's death.

'The children were here all yesterday evening. We agreed to grieve alone today,' she said slowly. It was as if she had read my thoughts and seen my surprise that the family was not together.

'It still feels unreal, that the priest came yesterday. And yet, it was not entirely unexpected that I would outlive my youngest child. Vera has always been too good for this world, really. So small when she arrived, much smaller than the other two. So much more delicate and fragile as a child. Vera was a beautiful, fair little girl as long as the sun shone, but as soon as the clouds gathered she cried or ran and hid. She was always more distant with me and her older brother and sister, but was very close to Per Johan. So, in an odd way, when he died I thought, well, now I am sure to lose Vera as well.'

She did not look at me when she was talking, she gazed out of the window instead. It struck me that she was looking out at the big garden where no doubt Vera had played as a child and cried when it rained.

The situation felt uncomfortable. But I understood her grief and gave her time. It helped. She turned back to me, an odd look in her dark brown eyes: at once focused and distant.

'There were several periods when she was growing up that Vera simply refused to eat food. She tried to take her own life by swallowing a whole lot of pills when she was nineteen and unhappily in love. That is possibly when we all accepted the idea that we might lose her one day. But my little Vera did not take her own life yesterday, did she?'

I shook my head and told her briefly what we knew about the cause of death. Her whole body trembled and she held her hands to her eyes as I spoke.

'My sweet Vera, who was so frightened of water and was thirteen before she even dared to swim – and she drowned in the end. But you are not able to tell me who killed her yet, are you?'

Her voice was weak, yet tense. I had to tell her that I could not at present, but that we were working as fast as we could on the case and that I had some questions to ask her concerning it.

'Yes, of course. Ask away, and I will answer,' she said, and once again she looked at me with oddly ambivalent eyes.

I started by asking when she had last seen or spoken to her daughter. Her face did not relax any for my question.

'Sadly, the truth is that I did not even speak to my daughter on the day she died. I slept late yesterday. She had already gone out when I got up at half past ten. She had left a note on the kitchen table to say that she had gone out and would probably not be home until the evening. I thought she had gone to see a friend or to the university. And I did not hear anything from her until the priest came to tell me she was dead. The last time I saw my younger daughter was the evening before. We sat here in the drawing room, all four of us, talking about the future now that Per Johan had died. Vera thought we should sell the businesses to Ramdal, and came out with a couple of confused sentences about how important art and her boyfriend were to her now. Otherwise she did not say much.'

My next question for Oda Fredriksen was naturally whether she believed that her daughter's boyfriend might have anything to do with the case. This provoked a scornful smile.

'You will have to rule him out, I'm afraid. He travelled to Paris last Thursday to see a friend's exhibition, and is still there. I actually sent him a telegram yesterday to let him know about Vera's death in a respectable manner. Just a moment, I will show you the reply I got today.'

She got up and walked across the floor on light feet, almost without a sound, to the bookshelves. Then she came back with a telegram that she passed to me without even looking at it.

I could understand her irritation when I read the telegram myself. The text was short and still managed to be shocking.

'Devastated by the news and loss of my true love. Hope I will receive inheritance to realize our great dream. Know she would want that.'

'But that is not going to happen, is it?' I said and looked at her.

She shook her head angrily. Her displeasure with her daughter's boyfriend had pulled her back and she was now fully present in the room.

'Absolutely not. They were not even engaged, and Vera

had not written any kind of will. Her share of the inheritance will be divided between her brother and sister, and neither of them will give her charlatan of a boyfriend so much as a krone. We have already discussed this.'

The picture was clear. Vera Fredriksen's boyfriend had not been in the country, and what is more, did not have a motive. His motive for falling in love appeared to have been a financial gain that he would not now get as his girlfriend had died.

I noted down the name so that I could confirm with the French police that he was in France, but did not hope for much help from those quarters.

Then I said, as tactfully as I could, that at this point I had to check the alibis of all the members of the family.

She took this unexpectedly well.

'If you think that I first killed my husband to hide the forty-year-old murder of my sister, and have then murdered my daughter to hide the murder of my husband – well, I hope you understand that that feels rather absurd and unjust. I know that you have to ask, and as far as my husband is concerned, the answer is easy. I was at a party at my cousin's in Holmenkollen when I received the telephone call about his death, and had been there for several hours. As far as my daughter's death is concerned, I was here yesterday. It might not be so easy to prove. It depends on when my daughter died. Can you tell me?'

I of course knew that it must have happened between half past three and half past four, but said that we were still waiting for the final autopsy report to confirm the time of death. In the meantime, I asked her to tell me as precisely as possible the times in the afternoon for which she had an alibi.

'Well, let me see . . . there were several flower deliveries that I had to sign for, the first came around midday and the last was delivered just after three. I rang my eldest daughter at around half past three and then again at five.'

I quickly noted that, based on this, the mother seemed to be an unlikely murderer and that she could not have been the mysterious hotel guest, but that she did still lack an alibi for the time frame in which her youngest daughter was murdered.

I asked if she had also tried to ring her son. She nodded thoughtfully.

'Yes. I rang my son three times – the first time after I had called my eldest daughter at half past three, then around four, and then again at half past four. But there was no answer until around half past five. I can guarantee that he is also innocent. Johan could never do such a thing. But I understand that you are obliged to check his movements too as a matter of procedure.'

I felt a tension rising in my body. There might be many good reasons why Johan Fredriksen had not answered the telephone. But it was certainly worth finding out, especially in a situation where his little sister's death had earned him roughly ten million kroner.

I said to his mother that no doubt there was a natural explanation, but that I was duty-bound to enquire.

I then added quickly that I was also obliged to check out whether any of Per Johan Fredriksen's former mistresses might have anything to do with the case, and so I had to ask if she knew who some of them were.

She let out a heavy sigh. 'Not really. I wanted to know as little as possible about them. My greatest fear has always been that he has an illegitimate child somewhere, but so far there has been no evidence of that. His mistresses were not exactly something we discussed at the dinner table. But I could always see it in my husband. He was more distant and less interested in me for periods. There was a period in the mid-fifties, just after Vera had been born, when he acted this way for a long, long time, and I was worried that I might actually be losing him to another woman. But it passed and faded towards the end of 1956 and the start of 1957. I never found out who it was. But I do have a dreadful suspicion . . .'

She suddenly pursed her lips and sat in silence for a while. I asked her to please finish what she was saying, and to let me decide whether it was of importance to the case or not.

'Well, I would rather not spread rumours about others. My husband was not loose-tongued and wasn't usually a sleep-talker. But one night in the autumn of 1955, when he had a fever, he suddenly started uttering words in his sleep. I couldn't make out much of it, but several times he clearly said my name and the name of a woman I know. It may of course be a coincidence, but it was strange all the same.'

She fell silent again, then took a deep breath. It was clear that it was difficult for her to talk about this. It was while I sat there watching her struggle to find the words that I understood the connection.

'Can I hazard a guess that the name he said was Solveig?'

Oda Fredriksen sighed heavily – grimly, in fact. Suddenly she looked old and bitter.

'Yes, it was. It was as though a ghost from the distant past had appeared in our bedroom. I remember that it felt like the bed under me froze to ice when he said her name, and it was still hard to sit beside her at the dinner nearly two years later. If it really was her he was dreaming about, I never heard anything more. And then things returned to normal a year or so later, and everything was better. Until the one in Majorstuen appeared a couple of years ago, like a snake in paradise, just when I thought my husband was finally done with other women.'

I saw the outline of another face when Oda Fredriksen talked about her late husband's mistresses, even though she remained remarkably controlled.

'You have met my husband's last mistress, haven't you?'

I replied in short that I had gone to see her to get her statement. I gave no more details and Oda Fredriksen did not ask. Instead, she stood up again, walked over to the bookcase and came back with an envelope, on which was written 'strictly confidential'. It had been sealed, but the seal was now broken.

'I went through my husband's office here at home yesterday, and found this in the bottom drawer of his desk. I could not resist opening it, and found three separate documents that might all be of interest to you. One of them is about his mistress.'

I had a quick look and had to agree with her. All three were of interest to me and one was clearly to his mistress.

The first was an undated, typed document, which stated:

'I, Odd Jørgensen, admit that I am guilty of embezzling 30,000 kroner from my employer's company, Per Johan Fredriksen A/S, in the autumn of 1965.'

It was signed by the office manager; I had seen his signature on the notice of termination sent to the mother of the boy on the red bicycle. To see it again here was unexpected, to say the least. I added the office manager's name to the list of people I needed to talk to again, and moved on to the next document.

The second document was in an envelope and I did not recognize the handwriting on the front.

'That is my husband's handwriting,' Oda Fredriksen said, over my shoulder. Judging by the text, that was the case. The letter was dated 18 March 1972 and read as follows:

To my heart's greatest love and my mind's best inspiration,

No one has given me more or greater pleasure than you.
It should have been you and me for the rest of our lives.
But sadly, that cannot be. There is too much left of your life
and too little of mine. And my duties to my children mean
that I can never give you the children you so want. You should
therefore have children with another man before it is too late.
And I must try to live without you. In my heart, I will always
be in your arms and in my mind, always in your bed.

Your ever grieving, Per Johan.

I read the letter twice, thinking how hard it must be for his widow to read this. When Per Johan Fredriksen broke up with his mistress, he mentioned the children, but did not say a word about his wife of nearly forty years.

I looked at Oda Fredriksen. She looked at me, but not the letter. At that moment, it was as if she could read my thoughts.

'It was not easy to read that three days after my husband's death. But regardless of whether the letter was delivered or not, it was a relief all the same to find out that in his final days he had planned to end the relationship with his mistress and come back to me.'

She swallowed deeply a few times as she said this. I had to admire her courage in facing one challenge after another, even after her husband's and daughter's deaths. I felt that I could read her thoughts, too, and that in that moment that she was thinking the same as me; that this gave the mistress the possible motives of jealousy and revenge.

I carried on reading. The third document was written in the same hand as the previous one. It was more keywords than notes, but no less interesting for that. The date was also sensationally recent: 5 March 1972. And I found the rest of the text of even more interest.

Eva's death.

A new thought after all these years: could she have been drowned at some point between six and half past seven?

Met Kjell Arne in the corridor at a quarter past six – with a water glass!

But what about the bang at half past seven? Was that something else? In which case, what? Or did Kjell Arne go back afterwards?

Change of theory: think Eva was drowned by Kjell Arne! But not sure. Will try it out this evening – nothing to lose.

Oda Fredriksen was still standing beside me, and this time she was reading over my shoulder.

I half turned around and asked what she thought about it. Her voice was distant again when she answered.

'Nothing. That is to say, when I read it, I had lots of thoughts, but I know nothing more than I did before. It was just so long ago, and after losing my husband and then my daughter, my sister's death feels even more distant.'

It was hard not to say that I understood. So I did just that. She smiled faintly.

'Thank you for your kind thoughts. I hope you can continue with your investigation without having to worry about me. After forty years of peace, my life has been rocked by two explosions in just four days. But despite now being the widow of a landowner, I still come from farming stock. My great-grandmother's sister survived her three children and her husband, and barely had clothes and food in her old age. I have more than enough of both, and two grown-up children and a grandchild. So don't worry about me. Just do what you can, and let me know as soon as you find out who killed my husband and my child.'

There was a faint glow in her eyes as she spoke. I thought to myself that Oda Fredriksen was to a certain extent what Patricia had in a past investigation called a satellite person. For decades she had circled her husband and children. Now her husband was suddenly gone. She was visibly shaken, but could still stand on her own two feet in the middle of the vast room. And I believed that she would stay standing after I had left, and that with time, she would find herself a new orbit.

So I solemnly thanked her for her help and took the envelope containing the three documents with me out to the car.

I left with three new clues, all of which could lead me to a murderer. I felt an intense need to discuss the case with someone. An image of Patricia in her wheelchair squeezed its way into my mind, between Miriam and my boss, as I sat in the car and flicked back and forth between the three documents. Each time, I stopped at the third document, with the notes about 1932. I was only a couple of miles away from the Ramdals' house in Frognerkilen, so after debating it for a few minutes, I drove straight there.

IX

I stood and looked out over the water at Frognerkilen before I turned and walked to the Ramdals' front door. The view of the fjord below with the sailing boats rocking gently on the waves was idyllic. I had grown up with a father who mockingly called Frognerkilen the Black Sea. By this he was referring to all the black money that he believed the rich upper classes had squirrelled away in the form of unnecessary yachts. I suspected that my father might be exaggerating a little. But as I took the final steps up to the house, I did think that the idyllic scene felt false and could be hiding something darker.

I did not need to ring the bell. Solveig Ramdal saw me from her watch post on the first floor. She waved and then disappeared from the window, clearly with the intention of opening the door. When she did, she said that her husband was unfortunately still at work, but that she would be happy to oblige if there was anything she could help me with.

Solveig Ramdal did not smile today, not when she waved to me from the window, nor when we stood there face to face at the door. I could understand that. There had been another death since we last met. And perhaps she also had a personal reason to be upset. My misgivings followed me into the living room. She sank down into her husband's chair more heavily than the last time, before starting to speak.

'It was so awfully sad to hear about Vera's death. We sent flowers today. These must be terrible days for poor Oda.'

I said there was no doubt about it. I also asked Solveig Ramdal if she had been in direct contact with Vera in the days after her father's death. She looked slightly confused, thought about it, but then shook her head without saying anything.

There was coffee on the table. Solveig Ramdal was still the perfect hostess and she was still youthful and feline in her movements. But as we sat there, I suddenly felt certain that she was hiding something from me. Only I had no idea what.

I started by saying that as a matter of procedure I had to ask for alibis for the previous afternoon.

She nodded pensively. 'I understand. My husband is possibly more fortunate than I am this time. He was at work until he came home at a quarter past five. I was, as usual, at home alone. The only time I went out the gate was when I popped down to the shop around four, half past four. The staff there know me and could probably vouch for that, but it is sadly not possible to prove that I was here the rest of the time.'

The alibi was not as poor as she might think. Given that Miriam had spoken to Vera on the telephone just before half past three, that wouldn't leave much time for Solveig Ramdal to murder her in Ullern and be back at the shop by four. But it was still a possibility.

Solveig Ramdal seemed inexplicably uneasy about her lack of alibi. I felt I was glimpsing a crack in her mask and wanted to know what lay behind it. So I pressed on with a bluff.

'We now have strong indications from, amongst other things, some notes left behind by Per Johan Fredriksen, that your relationship with him in more recent times was far closer than you have previously led me to believe.'

She sat without saying anything, and kept up appearances well. But there was a new uneasy undertone to her voice when she replied.

'I am a little uncertain as to what you mean. Per Johan and I have, for many years now, only met at these dinners every five years. When, roughly, was this and what kind of contact are you talking about?'

Her answer was testing me. She was unsure about how much I knew. And I was unsure if I was on the right track.

'The mid-fifties. And you met – when no one else was present.'

We were beating around the bush, but it was like playing poker. I had no more details and the little I knew that I was now brazenly betting on, was based on Oda Fredriksen's impressions and the fact that her husband had said Solveig's name in his fevered sleep. She, for her part, however, could not know what Per Johan Fredriksen had written.

I was right. Her nod was reluctant and grave.

'It is true that Per Johan and I did meet, one on one, around that time. But it is not true that we had an affair. We only met twice, in 1955, and neither time did we end up in bed.'

She looked at me guardedly. I had nothing up my sleeve which might prove this to be wrong, so I said: 'You should have told me this yesterday, of course, but I am ready to hear it now, too. But you must lay all your cards on the table now and tell me exactly what happened.'

It worked. She nodded several times then carried on swiftly.

'I did think that I should have told you. But it is just such a complex family history. You first have to realize that my marriage of many years has been no more than an empty facade. It started as a marriage of convenience. He was the safe harbour I sought after all the turbulence of Eva's death and my broken engagement with Per Johan. Kjell Arne has been a good provider for me and a good father for my children for nearly forty years. But if I ever had any passionate feelings for him, they were gone by the time our first child was born. He perhaps hoped to develop stronger feelings for me, but, if he ever tried, he never managed it. My husband is a very good and rational businessman, and this carries through to his dealings with his family. If he ever possessed any stronger or more romantic feelings, they were perhaps for another woman. But I have kept my marriage vow and have never been physically unfaithful to him. The only men who have ever been in my bed are Per Johan, back in 1932 and then Kjell Arne ever since.'

She sat staring at the living-room wall. I noticed again that Kjell Arne Randal was not smiling in any of the family photographs that hung there. Solveig Ramdal suddenly reminded me of Nora in Ibsen's *A Doll's House*, a play that I had seen with Miriam last autumn.

'And the woman he loved before you was . . . ?'

She gave a brief nod. I caught a glimpse of two small catlike teeth when she replied.

'Eva, of course. Even a man like him, without a romantic bone in his body, was enthralled by Eva. They all were. She was the most beautiful and sparkling of all the young women in Vestfold, as well as being the only one who knew how to exploit it. She could wrap men round her little finger and would then pull them along behind her to a cliff edge, it was said. Her sister was forgotten the moment Eva came into a room, as was I. So in a strange way, Eva was a symbol of beauty but also a trophy. One that Kjell Arne would have given anything to win. But he never got her – as far as I know. And either way, Eva was gone by the time anything happened between Kjell Arne and me. Although I still had to compete with her for his attention. I have always been second choice and a poor surrogate for something he never even had.'

'I understand. So when Per Johan contacted you one day, you had no misgivings. But what did he want, if not a mistress?'

230

Solveig Ramdal gave me a fleeting, scornful smile before she continued.

'It's almost a bit strange that it did not lead to an affair. His own marriage was like mine; the only difference was that his wife was far more fond of him than I was of my husband. From his perspective, it was a sham. We had both been strongly attracted to each other once upon a time in our youth, but it was impossible to find that magic again. Eva and her death in 1932 was there like a wall between us. And that is what it was all about. Per Johan rang one day while my husband was at work, and asked if we could meet to discuss Eva's death. He said that the case continued to haunt him and that he thought it had been murder. Per Johan said that he was pretty sure that I had not killed Eva, but that it could have been any of the other three. Of course I knew that it was not me, but I also had my suspicions and Per Johan was still a charmer when he wanted to persuade someone. And that's how we ended up one day, sitting in a hotel room, the door locked, discussing whether one of our spouses could have committed murder. It was still all about Eva, more than twenty years after her death.'

'Did you come to any conclusion?'

She shook her head lightly. 'Not really. We just went round and round the possibilities. He did not even rule out the possibility that Oda might have killed her little sister – for the inheritance and finally to be out of her shadow. The sisters did not have a particularly good relationship, but that is not so unusual for sisters at that age. Per Johan was obsessed by the thought of who had been to bed with Eva that day. It was certainly not him, he said several times. So then it must have been Hauk or Kjell Arne. He had seen Kjell Arne in the corridor at around a quarter past six and it looked as though he was heading towards Eva's room. But then –'

She took a short dramatic pause after this piece of information, and looked once again at the family photographs. Her thin, catlike mouth trembled. I thought how her story so far was in line with Per Johan Fredriksen's notes – and that it was pushing her own husband further into the spotlight.

'But then there was the bang that we never managed to work out. I was in the room next to Eva, and had heard a bang or thump around half past seven. Per Johan asked me several times if I was certain that the sound had come from her room. And I was then, and I am now. At the time I thought that perhaps Eva had tripped or dropped something on the floor. Later I figured it must have been when she fell, but then that was always odd as she was on the sofa. I put my ear to the wall in the minutes after the bang, but heard nothing more. The bang in itself does not mean that Eva didn't die earlier, nor that Kjell Arne might have killed her. But it gave rise to doubt, and Per Johan and I could not get past it. Our main theory in the end was that Eva had turned her affections towards Kjell Arne and that it was Hauk who had killed her in a fit of jealousy. Per Johan still had his doubts back then, and what he may or may not have thought about the case in later years, I have no idea.'

Her conclusion was rather abrupt and a bit unexpected. I asked if there was any particular reason for suspecting Hauk.

'It was rather woolly – so woolly, in fact, that we were not really sure of it ourselves. But I had always found Hauk rather distant and a little frightening. So I found it easier to believe that he had committed a murder than my husband or former fiancé. The story of the jilted lover turning to murder is not an unfamiliar one, not then and not now. Per Johan was vague about it, but he implied that Hauk's family situation was very difficult. He also thought that Eva had treated him rather badly. Behind Per Johan's friendly veneer, there were actually very few he respected and even fewer he feared. But when we met in 1955, so many years on, I could tell that he really did both respect and fear Hauk. I got the impression that he thought it was Hauk, but that it was something he could live with. Hauk was stuck down in Vestfold, so was not someone he had to see or deal with often.'

It felt like Solveig Ramdal was starting to open up now. Following a brief pause, she carried on.

'I, for my part, would not completely dismiss the possibility of suicide. I only heard that one single bang between seven and eight – no footsteps. And I *had* heard steps out in the corridor and inside her room an hour earlier. I must say, I thought that some of the footsteps I heard in her room earlier were heavier than hers, which would indicate that at least one or more men had visited her. But anyway, I obviously cannot be certain about the footsteps, and there may have been others that I did not hear. Oh, I really don't know what to believe.'

I could certainly say with a clear conscience that I agreed with the last statement. I had lost count of the number of possible explanations for the death in 1932. I noted down this last theory regarding Hauk and said that I clearly had to talk to Kjell Arne himself.

'Of course you must. Kjell Arne normally works late in the afternoon, so no doubt you will find him in the office at Lysaker. I would also appreciate it if you say as little as possible to my husband about our conversation, but I understand if you must mention it.'

I said that I could not promise anything, but that I would do my best.

She gave a tight-lipped smile, held out her hand and wished me luck with the investigation. She bravely kept up appearances as the stalwart, bourgeois housewife. I understood that Solveig Ramdal had not had an easy life, despite her material comfort. But I did not trust at all that she had told me everything she knew, either about 1932 or 1972. I also noticed on the way out that there were a lady's hat and two men's hats on the rack in the hallway, which made me think. The fact that I was being followed by a Soviet agent did not prove that he had been the shadow with the hat on the night Per Johan Fredriksen was killed.

X

It was half past three by the time I got to Lysaker and found the right building. I met a group of three office workers on their way out. The premises of Kjell Arne Ramdal & Co. were clearly larger than those of Per Johan Fredriksen A/S. They had an entire floor of offices, providing more than enough space for the ten or so employees who were still hard at work.

A receptionist in her early twenties, who resembled an air hostess, smiled broadly at me, but then became more serious when I showed her my police ID. I said that I had to speak to Director Ramdal in person immediately and with a slight tremble in her finger, she pointed me in the direction of the corridor.

I found him at the end of the corridor, in the largest office on the floor, behind what was, no doubt, the largest desk in the office. He was none too pleased to see me, but held his composure even better than his wife.

'So,' he said briskly, as soon as I had settled in the chair in front of his desk and politely declined the offers of coffee and mineral water.

Kjell Arne Ramdal sat with his elbows on his desk like a great shield between us.

I started by asking whether there was any news on the possible acquisition of Fredriksen's companies.

He replied shortly that there was not, but, given developments in the case, he had not expected there to be. He had personally rung Johan Fredriksen earlier in the day to give his condolences on the loss of his sister and had told him that under the circumstances, a twenty-four-hour extension of the deadline was acceptable. It had been a 'constructive' conversation, and he was still of the opinion that the takeover would go ahead.

He spoke confidently and almost enthusiastically about the deal, then stopped abruptly.

I decided to get straight to the point and said that it would appear that Vera Fredriksen had been murdered. As a matter of procedure, I had to ask both the family and others involved of their whereabouts that afternoon.

Kjell Arne Ramdal didn't move a muscle when he answered.

'I was here at the office all day, from nine yesterday morning until I drove home at half past four. Almost all of the staff here attended a conference in the second half of the day, but the office manager and receptionist should be able to confirm that I was here until they left at half past three. Then I was here on my own for the last hour.'

I noted down that Kjell Arne Ramdal's alibi had fallen apart in front of my very eyes. Encouraged by this, I took a leap back to 1932.

'The situation regarding Per Johan Fredriksen's death is still unclear. However, some new information has come to light regarding the death of Eva Bjølhaugen in 1932. We have found some papers that were left by Per Johan Fredriksen and other material that could indicate that he had discovered how she had been murdered and that he suspected that you were behind it.'

Kjell Arne Ramdal raised his eyebrows, but otherwise remained calm. I was not sure whether to be impressed or frightened by his being so calm in the face of such a serious accusation from a dead friend.

'If Per Johan Fredriksen had found out how Eva was murdered, it would be impressive – we have all given it a lot of thought over the years. The fact that he suspected me is less surprising. A distance had grown between us in the last few years. I figured that he was either jealous of my success or thought that I had something to do with Eva's death. He had reason to be jealous, but not to suspect me of murder. If I am to give a more informed answer to the accusation, you might like to tell me how she was murdered and why Per Johan Fredriksen thought that I did it.'

Kjell Arne Ramdal looked at me intensely when he spoke, and it seemed to me that his elbows were weighing more heavily on the desk.

'Fredriksen believed, correctly, that she had been drowned. He suspected you because he had seen you at a quarter past six that day coming out of her room with a glass in your hand.'

Kjell Arne Ramdal sat behind his desk with impressive and irritating composure. There was not so much as a ripple of surprise to be seen on his face. Although it could perhaps be detected in the ten-second pause he took this time before speaking. And then it was only to say: 'Should I perhaps call one of my lawyers at this point?'

I replied that he was more than welcome to do so should he wish, but that there was still no reason to, if he told me the truth and it did not involve a crime.

He nodded, almost gratefully, at that. 'Excellent. Then I will. I did not commit a crime of any sort. And what I did was also morally acceptable, given that I was at the time a young man without obligations. It was before I got involved with my wife, who at that point was engaged to some-one else. It is true that I was in Eva Bjølhaugen's room that afternoon. But nothing dramatic happened there. She was alive and unharmed when I left the room at a quarter past six, and I did not see her again until she was discovered dead two hours later.'

I immediately asked why he had gone to her room and what had happened there.

'It is not a very honourable story. Eva was very beautiful and charming. I was – like all the young men who met her – very attracted to her. I have to admit that I went to Oslo because I hoped a romance might blossom, and I did not want to take the chance that the other two might get in there before me. Earlier in the day, Eva had behaved in a way that gave me reason to believe that this hope might become a reality. She avoided her boyfriend, and was exceedingly friendly towards me. I should have realized that that was just how she was: Eva was a flirt who liked to play different men off against each other. And I made a genuine mistake. I knocked on her door at five past six to offer her my love. I left the room at a quarter past six crestfallen at having been rejected. She turned me down in her characteristically charming way: "Maybe sometime, who knew what the future might hold . . ." but the reality was clear. At one point I tried to put my arm around her and with a scornful smile she shook her head and took a step back. I left without accomplishing my mission. I don't remember the glass, but it is not unthinkable that I took it with me by mistake in my heartbreak. I was truly nervous that day.'

Kjell Arne Ramdal did not, however, look nervous today. He finished there.

I didn't know what more to say. His version was consistent and plausible. And I was not able to check there and then whether it was true.

I asked if the bed was still made when he left the room. He nodded quickly.

'The bed was made up and untouched when I came and when I left. It's fair to say that I had hoped it would not be when I left. But, all the same, it was very definitely made up. I came out with my trousers between my legs, as we say in Vestfold.'

It was the closest thing to humour I had ever heard from Kjell Arne Ramdal. But the mood was too sombre for either of us to smile. We were caught in a frustrating situation. I could not prove that the bed was not still made up when he left the room and he could not prove that it was.

In all honesty, I believed that the bed was still untouched and that Eva Bjølhaugen had been alive when he left. And that left an hour and a half afterwards where anything could have happened. Including the possibility that Kjell Arne Ramdal went back and killed Eva Bjølhaugen having built up a jealous rage; a motive which he had just given me himself.

I said that we also had indications that Per Johan Fredriksen had suspected Hauk Rebne Westgaard, and asked Kjell Arne Ramdal if he knew anything about that.

He nodded quickly and once again spoke briskly. 'The extent to which that is true, I am not able to say, but that suspicion was very definitely the case at one point. There is a bit of a history there that I should probably tell you, though I do not like to spread rumours about other people and things that are none of my business . . .'

He gave me a questioning look. I said that he should certainly tell me everything that might be relevant to the sequence of events and motives.

He nodded again, almost gratefully, and carried on talking with renewed vigour.

'In that case, the situation was that Eva was beautiful, charming, flirtatious and possibly slightly power-crazy. She loved being the centre of attention. Per Johan Fredriksen had had a brief romance with her the year before, which lasted about a month. After a few drinks, he confided in me that he, despite several attempts, had never managed to take off so much as her blouse, let alone her underwear. Behind her flirtatious front, she was pretty demanding and prudish, he said. She was a woman who often said A without wanting to do B. One day she broke it off and told him that he was not going to get what he wanted so badly, at least not for now. It was a humiliating defeat for him and he was visibly jealous of his childhood friend when she started to go out with Hauk Rebne Westgaard instead. But Fredriksen was not convinced that Westgaard had achieved what he so badly wanted either – even after they had been together for a few months. So, between the two of them, there was a lot of competition and a lot of emotion. Westgaard also had a slight inferiority complex in relation to us: his father was half crazy, their farm was smaller than ours and he had less money. So if Eva treated him badly, or if he believed he was about to lose her to one of us, it is easy to imagine that he might have killed her in a fit of rage. Eva was a girl who played with fire. She could have burnt herself on Hauk Rebne Westgaard. But I have absolutely no idea if that is what happened.'

And I certainly did not either. The only thing I felt fairly certain about was that I still had no grounds to arrest any of the suspects for anything.

I said to Kjell Arne Ramdal that it would have made things a little easier if he had told me all this the day before yesterday. He moved his head in a way that, with a bit of goodwill, could be interpreted as a nod. Then I asked if he had anything to add today and he replied succinctly: 'No.'

His answer was the same when I asked if he had been in direct contact with Vera Fredriksen at any point after her father's death. So the question as to who Vera had called remained unanswered.

I thanked him equally succinctly, then, taking these new thoughts with me, I headed for the door.

XI

I had that feeling of general unease when I got back to the station at twenty past four. Things were relatively calm there, though the switchboard had experienced an increase in calls from the media. I prepared a new press release which confirmed that the woman found dead in Ullern was Fredriksen's youngest daughter and that any possible connections were now being investigated, but that no further comment could be made in light of the ongoing investigation.

My boss waved me into his office before I was even at the door. He listened attentively to what I had to tell him, and seemed almost relieved that nothing new had emerged regarding the espionage aspect of the case.

He had given considerable thought to the case and concluded that the investigation should of course continue, but as discreetly as possible for the moment in order not to attract public attention until it was strictly necessary.

In short, the conclusion was that I should continue to work on the case and would get whatever help I needed, but that I should report directly to my boss and not tell Danielsen anything about the possible spy implications.

It seemed that my boss was having second thoughts about our meeting with Asle Bryne at Victoria Terrace. He was unusually sombre and said twice that this was a very sensitive case and that I must not betray his trust, now that it was so important. I promised to do my utmost not to do this.

I made four telephone calls before I left work.

I reached Miriam at the party office and told her that I would have to work late with the murder investigation, but that we could meet around half past eight. She was very understanding and did not ask for any details – even though I could hear in her voice that she was dying to know more.

Then I rang Patricia and asked if we could meet sometime around seven o'clock. She replied positively to this and then hung up without wasting any more of her time or mine.

I still had two hours until I was due to meet Patricia so I called Fredriksen's mistress in Majorstuen, and then his son at Sognsvann.

XII

The door was opened as soon as I rang on the bell at 53B Jacob Aall's Street in Majorstuen. The woman who answered the door no longer had tears in her eyes, but she still had red cheeks and was wearing a black mourning dress. The photograph of Per Johan Fredriksen remained on the coffee table, with a lone candle burning beside it.

The clock on the wall in the hall had stopped at half past eleven, and had not been rewound since, which seemed rather symbolic to me. Time had stopped for the moment for both the flat and the woman who lived in it.

I had some critical questions to ask her and not very much time. But sitting here beside the candle and photograph of Per Johan Fredriksen, I found it hard to get straight to the point.

So I delayed by asking how she was.

'Not good at all, but better than on the evening he died,' she said.

I had to ask her something else, so I asked what her thoughts were about the flat and her future.

'Thank you for asking. I have not been able to face moving the furniture or even a picture yet. It gets harder each day and will no doubt be very painful on Saturday. I just have so many memories of Per Johan here and am constantly finding myself expecting to see him coming round the corner whenever I look out of the window. So I've decided I'm going to go and stay with my mother's family in France for a few months. If I am going to carry on without being weighed down by the past, I have to get away, both from this flat and from Oslo. My current dilemma is whether I should try to sneak into the back of the church for the funeral. It should be possible, as no one in the family has met me.'

I did not want to share my thoughts on whether Fredriksen's mistress should attend the funeral or not. So instead I took the chance to ask her if she had ever been in touch with Vera Fredriksen. She shook her head.

'No. He showed me pictures of his children when I asked, and talked about them a good deal – and particularly about Vera. His paternal urge to care and protect was strongest for her. Probably something to do with the fact that she was the youngest, but also, she had suffered more than the other two. I was not in the slightest bit jealous – in fact, I started to care for them because they meant so much to him. It was obvious that I could not meet them before his wife was either dead or they were divorced. So, sadly, I never saw his daughter except in a photograph, and I never heard her voice.'

I was happy with this answer. It was hard to imagine that Vera Fredriksen would ring her father's mistress, no matter what she thought might have happened in 1932. Furthermore, it was even harder to imagine that his mistress would have gone to Haraldsen's Hotel to murder her late lover's daughter.

I had thought a little about who Per Johan Fredriksen would talk to if he wanted to discuss his Soviet contacts or his future political plans with someone. And I had come to the conclusion that the two most likely people would be his youngest daughter or his mistress. And what his mistress had to say would be even more interesting now that his daughter was dead.

So I asked if she had been aware of any ups and downs in her lover's political life and if he had said anything about his future plans.

To my surprise, she replied without hesitation. 'Yes, of course. I should have mentioned it last time you were here, but it seemed so unlikely that his death had anything to do with that. It was something he had been thinking about for a long time and soon he had to make a decision. He was increasingly unconvinced of his party's scepticism towards membership of the EEC. To begin with, he only said that he could see that there were some advantages to be had with membership, but then through the course of the winter he started to think that there were, in fact, more advantages than disadvantages to joining. He believed that the EEC would grow with or without Norway, and that the terms and conditions would be less favourable if we waited to join. By the new year it was more a question of when, rather than if, he would make it public.'

I thanked her for this interesting piece of information and said that he must have been prepared for strong reactions from his own party. She immediately confirmed that that was the case.

'But of course. He was preparing for death threats and comparisons with the devil. He initially thought about changing party, but then decided that it would be better to just let his new views on the EEC be known. The consequences would probably be that he was squeezed out of the party and into a new party, but he decided that that was a better way to leave.'

It sounded like Per Johan Fredriksen had had a reasonable plan, and some very bad news for his party and the no campaign in general. Something that could indeed be the cause of a politically motivated attack. The question was who else might have known about it.

I asked Harriet Henriksen what she thought about this, and if she had mentioned it to anyone else. She shook her head firmly at the suggestion.

'I knew no one in his party and never discussed what he told me with others. I was happy about it. After all, I am half French and the rest of my family live within the EEC and have always believed in cooperation inside the Western Bloc. So I was pro and liked to think that I had some influence on him there. And in addition, I thought that if he was going to change his stance on the EEC and his party, then perhaps there was a chance that he would change his mind about his wife as well.'

She said this with an almost coy smile.

She was beautiful when she smiled, and despite the fact that I disagreed on the EEC question, I could perfectly well understand that Per Johan Fredriksen had been charmed by her.

The smile disappeared when I asked if there were other aspects of his political life that he had discussed with her. She shook her head and said that he had only talked about the EEC issue and changing party. It seemed reasonable that he had discussed the EEC matter and plans for next year's general election with his mistress, but apparently he had not mentioned his contact with the Soviet Embassy even to her.

It was now half past five and I had run out of my easier questions. So I had no choice but to put the handwritten letter from Per Johan Fredriksen down on the table between us and say that unfortunately I had to ask her to read it.

Harriet Henriksen was a woman whose emotions changed swiftly and easily. Three minutes ago she had been smiling and almost happy at the thought that she may have influenced her lover. Now she was shedding tears as she saw whose handwriting the letter was penned in. Then she flinched as she read what was written. Afterwards, she sat trembling. I hoped that there might be another emotional outburst. But there was not. She just sat there with tears streaming down her cheeks, her fists balling tighter and tighter.

When I realized that she was not going to say anything without help, I asked if she had been given this letter by her lover during his last visit.

She slowly shook her head. Her voice was strained, but still coherent when she started to speak. She began slowly, but then the words just came tumbling out.

'No, I have never seen this letter before. But he did say as much to me as we sat at the table here eating supper on Saturday. It came as quite a blow, but not a shock as such. He had been fretting about it for a long time, that I should find a younger man and have children before it was too late. And he brought it up again then. I said that there wasn't a younger man in the whole wide world I would want more than him, and that I would rather be childless all my life than have children with anyone else. The whole time I was scared that he would simply get up and leave. He was visibly touched by what I said then he turned to me and he said that I was the only person in the world who loved him for who he was and not his money. As usual, we went to bed after the meal. And afterwards any doubt I ever had in him was forgotten. He kissed me before he left and said that we should meet again soon and talk some more. So even though I had had a shock and still had to live with the uncertainty, I continued to be optimistic.'

Harriet Henriksen had slowed down again and seemed distant. Suddenly she reminded me of Oda Fredriksen. It struck me that the two women in Per Johan Fredriksen's life, despite their differences, had both weathered these terrible days and resolutely clung to their love for him.

I thought about how we still only had his mistress's word that Per Johan Fredriksen had not in fact broken up with her on his last visit, as he had intended to do in his letter. And I also only had her word that he had hinted at it but then changed his mind. I had to be open to the possibility that she had run out after him, begged him to come back and then stabbed him when he walked away. The fact that the murder weapon was a kitchen knife fitted well with this theory.

I consequently needed to check Harriet Henriksen's alibi, so I asked tactfully if the last time she saw her beloved it had been through the window.

She understood what I was asking. After a rather tense moment, she replied that she had seen him from the window and that she had not gone out, either with him or after him.

I apologized before asking if there was anyone who could confirm this.

She, for her part, apologized that she could only reply that there was no one. No one had come to see her before I rang the next day. She had no one she could call to talk to about her situation – not after he had gone, nor after she had heard the news that he had been stabbed.

She still just called him 'he' and looked so lonely sitting there on her own. I felt a great deal of sympathy for her. But she did have a motive, and she was the only one of those involved who was still alive and had been in Majorstuen on the evening that Per Johan Fredriksen had died. So when I carried on to Sognsvann, I did not yet dare strike Harriet Henriksen from my list of possible murderers.

XIII

Johan Fredriksen lived in a terraced house a few hundred yards from the lake at Sognsvann. His house was just as I had imagined it would be: larger than was usual for a single lawyer of thirty-five without his own firm, but incomparable to his father's or Kjell Arne Ramdal's in terms of size.

The door was opened no more than ten seconds after I had rung the bell. Seeing him again, I was more struck than ever by how much he resembled me in appearance. And if his sister's death had caused any emotional response, it was not possible to see it on his face or hear it in his voice.

'Welcome,' he said in a staccato tone, and then turned

around. I followed him into the living room. It was also more or less as I had imagined: clean and tidy, but not very exciting. If there had been any photographs of girlfriends, Johan Fredriksen had removed them before I got there. There was not a single picture up on the walls, and as far as I could see, the bookcase only contained books about law and economics.

The only thing lying on the living-room table was a pile of accounts for Per Johan Fredriksen A/S.

I pointed at the accounts and asked if there was any news about the business and the possible takeover.

He told me that the offer was still on the table at a few million more than the actual value, and that the family were inclined to accept the offer and move on. That was what had been agreed at a meeting the evening before last, but they had not managed to talk about it again since Vera's death.

I suddenly thought about what Solveig Ramdal had said about her husband also being a businessman in his private life. The same could be said of Johan Fredriksen. However, when he started to speak again, it was apparent he was a much younger and softer businessman.

'You must excuse me if I appear to be unmoved. My youngest sister's death has affected me deeply. I am just not as good as my father and others at showing my feelings. In fact, I am not as good as my father at anything.'

I asked him how he saw his relationship with his sisters.

'I am not really very close to them in any way, I have to admit. We are different ages, have different personalities and interests. Vera and I never argued, as far as I can remember, but that is perhaps because we did not talk much. Ane Line was closer to her – perhaps because they are both girls. Although I think more recently, they were talking less. As far as I understood it, they had argued about something. Ane Line and I live our own lives and have our own opinions, but we do speak when needs be. We are both pragmatists, in our own way.'

I noted down that I should ask Ane Line Fredriksen what she and her sister had argued about. Otherwise, this was more or less what their mother had said, and I did not think there was much to be garnered here.

So we looked at each other and waited. Then Johan Fredriksen got up, went over to the drinks cabinet and poured himself a glass of wine. He raised the bottle, looking at me questioningly, then nodded with understanding when I said that I could not drink on the job.

'Many gifted young men have bemoaned the fact that they are not the only and eldest son of a rich father. For me it was the opposite. I often thought when I was growing up that it would have been nice to have a brother, who could blaze the trail and relieve some of the pressure and expectation. But I had no older brother, only two younger sisters. My father was kind enough never to complain. But I could tell that he was disappointed, and I heard others say the same. They said that I was doing fine, but that they had expected more of Per Johan Fredriksen's only son. I have always been good, but never great. My sporting achievements were good, my results were good, but I was never the best at anything. I lacked the charisma of which my father had so much. My greatest triumph in life is that I was the fifth best in my year to graduate from law school. The examiner said, "You are not the brightest one here, but you are the one who works hardest to be so." I took that as a compliment and hoped that it heralded my breakthrough.'

He paused briefly and finished his wine. I was glad that he was opening up, and allowed him the time to pour another glass before I said: 'But it was not?'

He grimly shook his head.

'No, it was not. Father congratulated me and smiled, but I could see that coming fifth, which was such an achievement for me, meant nothing to him. He still didn't want to involve me in running the business, and wouldn't give me an advance on my inheritance so I could start my own practice. "You are not robust enough yet to stand on your own two feet as a businessman," he had said to me with this kind but patronizing smile. Apparently I had to get more work experience and preferably also a sensible and helpful wife. So once again, I did what he told me, got a boring job as an associate, while I waited for better times.'

'And now you finally have your chance – because of a tragedy,' I said.

He nodded, but did not smile. 'Not just a tragedy, but a double tragedy. I inherited around twenty million when my father was killed on Saturday, and another ten million yesterday when my little sister died. Suddenly, I have all the opportunities I ever wanted, but this is certainly not how I had wished for it to happen. My little sister was killed, wasn't she? She attempted suicide once a few years ago, but I'm sure that's not what happened this time.'

I confirmed that it did look like his sister had been murdered. In addition, we now also had to keep all possibilities open regarding his father's killer, as a new witness had thrown doubt on whether the boy on the red bicycle had done it.

Johan Fredriksen took this news with unexpected composure. He put his wine glass down and looked at me with a serious, though not unfriendly, expression on his face.

'Then I have a problem, which I am afraid may cause a problem for you too. I was here at home on both Saturday evening and yesterday afternoon, but have no one to confirm that.'

'So you are saying that you were at home alone?' I asked.

He took another sip of wine, then shook his head.

'No. What I am saying – and it is the truth – is that I was here with my girlfriend. But I cannot ask her to confirm that for me. She has made it quite clear that she, for very personal reasons, does not want her name to be public or to be pulled into the investigation in any way. She is the most exciting thing that has happened to me in all my life. I am even more scared of losing her now, having just lost two of my closest family members. I simply cannot burden her with that. So in a situation where I know that I am innocent and did not murder my father and little sister, I choose to respect my girlfriend's wish to remain anonymous, even though I realize that it may not make life any easier for me.'

I could not work Johan Fredriksen out, nor could I decide what I thought of him. On the one hand, I could understand him, even empathize with him, but on the other, it did create a problem for the investigation.

I tried to push him by saying that his mother claimed she had phoned him several times yesterday afternoon without getting an answer. He nodded sharply.

'Yes, I can confirm that, without being able to give you the precise times. I heard the telephone ring out here in the sitting room at least twice. I had a strong suspicion that it was my mother, and indeed, when I then answered the phone at around half past five, I had this confirmed. When she had called earlier, I was in a room with another person, in the middle of things I did not want to interrupt, so I couldn't talk to my mother on the phone.'

He said this somewhat defiantly, and then raised his glass before draining it.

I was still unsure as to how I felt about Johan Fredriksen, but realized that it would be impossible to get anything more out of him now. So I asked him to think hard about the situation. He promised to do that, but said that it was unlikely that anything would change with regards to his alibi and his girlfriend's identity. He added that she had been here with him when both the murders happened, and clearly had no connection to the case. She had never met either his parents or his sisters.

I was increasingly intrigued by Johan Fredriksen's mysterious girlfriend. However, it was perfectly clear that she had no links to the case. And it was not obvious who that young woman might be. I had more than enough parties to juggle with as it was. And what was more, I did not think that Johan Fredriksen would make up a story like that if he had killed his father or sister. His story tallied with what his mother had said and indirectly gave him a kind of alibi. So I dropped it – and left with slightly more respect for Johan Fredriksen than I had arrived with.

XIV

It was after I had got into the car just by Sognsvann at a quarter past seven that I saw him for the fourth time.

The man in the hat was not wearing a hat today, nor was he following me. He was just standing there, casually leaning against a wall on the corner of the street. I started the car.

The encounter lasted no more than a few seconds and felt far less threatening than our previous meetings. I was sitting in a car with a loaded gun in its holster under my jacket. It also helped that I now knew who the man in the hat was, even though I therefore also knew that he was dangerous.

However, seeing him again was an uncomfortable reminder that I was being watched, and that we were still no further forward on the spying aspect of the case.

I drove to Patricia's house and round the block one more time to make sure that no one was following me before I stopped and parked the car a few hundred yards from the house, at twenty past seven. I kept my eyes peeled as I walked from the car to the front door. The man in the hat was nowhere to be seen. And yet still I had the feeling that I had not seen him for the last time.

XV

'Hmm,' Patricia said. She had finished her tomato soup and roast pork with sweet potatoes, but still listened carefully to my account of the day's developments.

I had carried a small dilemma with me as I entered the house that day, but had resolved it by deciding to speak openly about my meeting with the head of the police security service and the suspicions that Per Johan Fredriksen may have been a spy.

I was fully aware that this formally constituted a breach of confidentiality, which could cost me my job if it was ever discovered. What surprised me was that I did not have any particular misgivings about it. I was absolutely certain that Patricia would never tell anyone. And given that, I saw it more or less as my duty to do all that I could to clear up a matter of such national importance. Furthermore, the case had become something of an obsession and the pressure was such that I was willing to go to pretty much whatever lengths necessary to solve it.

Patricia seemed to take it for granted that I told her everything and didn't even look surprised. She had put her soup to one side and given a little nod when I mentioned the suspicions that Fredriksen was a spy, but that was the only reaction I registered.

'So, where shall we begin?' I asked, when the maid had disappeared with the leftovers of supper.

Patricia answered without hesitation: 'At the beginning – in 1932!'

It was eight o'clock already and I was starting to worry that I might be late for my date with Miriam at half past. Patricia did not know about it, of course, and seemed to have all the time in the world. She thought for nearly a full minute before continuing.

'It is possible there are some links here, but they are still so tenuous that it would be best to work with this as three separate murder mysteries. As far as 1932 is concerned, the picture is becoming a bit clearer, but not so clear that we can see the murderer's face. The more we get to know about the great beauty Eva Bjølhaugen, the more she resembles Marilyn Monroe: she liked attention and played with the men who liked to give it to her. All three men desired her, and all three had been to her room. For now, up until a quarter past six, everything is clear . . .'

I was getting lost already. I said that according to Hauk himself, he had been there before half past five and Kjell Arne Ramdal was there between six and a quarter past six, but it was never said that Per Johan Fredriksen had been there.

Patricia gave a contemptuous snort before carrying on. 'Of course he had. He wonders in his note who might have drowned Eva between six and eight. The only logical explanation for the time frame is that he went to see her just before six. So he was there some time before six, presumably with the same mission as Kjell Arne Ramdal, and obviously was equally unsuccessful. Even though both these assumptions are uncertain, we also know that Eva was alive and the bed still made up when Kjell Arne left the room at a quarter past six, and that she was alive until the bang which Solveig maintains she heard at half past seven. In which case, Eva had in the meantime gone to bed with a guest and then been killed either by that person or another guest. Do we agree so far? And in that case, do you have any suggestions as to who it might be?'

Just then there was a knock at the door. Patricia forced a rather tart smile as the maid came in and served us coffee and cakes, before slipping out again. My mind was whirring, but I could not come up with any possible candidates.

'Well?'

Patricia's voice was no less tart than her smile. I had to admit sheepishly that I could not suggest any names.

'I agree with your summary, but cannot see where it goes from here. There is nothing to indicate which of the three was suddenly granted grace and why.'

Patricia nodded quickly, almost appreciatively.

'Precisely. If two of the three enamoured young men had been rejected earlier, it would be natural to suspect the third. But when all three had received a rap on their trouser flies that afternoon, it's apparently not so easy to see who, then, suddenly got their hands on the treat that everyone wanted . . .'

She paused for one of her most unsympathetic girlish titters. Once again, I thought to myself that a contemptuous seventeen-year-old still hid behind her more adult face. However, she quickly returned to her astonishingly mature and highly developed intellectual self once more.

'It may seem strange, but I think I have an answer to the mystery of who went to bed with the beautiful Eva. The problem is: A, it is not entirely certain, and B, it does not necessarily give us the answer as to who killed her.'

Patricia sat lost in thought in her wheelchair, looking out into thin air, not meeting my eye. She moved her lips a couple of times as if to talk, before a sound finally came out.

'No, it is too uncertain to say anything, even though I think I am right. I have to sleep on it. There are a couple of pieces that still need to fall into place. If you have time, confront Hauk with the new information and ask him outright if he had been to bed with Eva. It may be important both for him and the others who were there. And at the same time, ask him if she was religious. And also, even if it is not possible to find out to whom a hair belongs, you can usually tell whereabouts on the body it's from, can't you? In which case, I would like to know where those three hairs in Eva's bed came from.'

I did not understand what she was getting at, but was used to Patricia asking strange questions that later proved to provide decisive answers. So I promised to check both things.

It was now a quarter past eight. I remembered my meeting with Miriam and felt the pressure mounting. So I asked if we could perhaps fast-forward to the present.

Patricia nodded and her face took on a more strained expression.

'Yes, but there is less that is new here, unfortunately. There are still too many possibilities and too many details to verify them in relation to Per Johan Fredriksen's death and that of Vera Fredriksen. And possibly also too many people with hidden faces . . .'

Patricia fell silent again. I remarked that the identification of the man in the hat and the fact that Per Johan Fredriksen was suspected of being a spy were important developments.

'Yes, of course. The identification of the man in the hat is very interesting and rather unsettling. It not only indicates that Per Johan Fredriksen had crossed the line with his Soviet contacts, but also that they knew that he could be exposed. I would certainly like to know what made the police security service start to suspect him, but it would be no easy task to get an answer out of Asle Bryne. The espionage aspect of the case is highly sensitive. So you will just have to keep your ears open and your eyes peeled. In other circumstances, I would have said that it was most likely that Per Johan Fredriksen had been liquidated by a Soviet agent. But the method and place give rise to some questions. If the agent did kill him to avert a very untimely exposure, why did he kill him with a knife, and what did he talk to Fredriksen about before he killed him? If the agent came to Norway to murder Fredriksen, but wanted to avoid a scandal, why is he still here two days later? If it was to kill Fredriksen's daughter, why on earth is he still here today, and how on earth did he find out about the story from 1932?'

Again, Patricia stopped to ponder before she continued. I finished off one of the small cakes and started to get very agitated about the time. As she still had not said anything by twenty past eight, I prompted her.

'The office manager now also has a motive, does he not?'

She nodded. 'Certainly. The office manager cannot explain everything, but he may be able to explain an important part that can unravel the rest. Fredriksen was clearly blackmailing him in some way. But the question is, how much of a motive does that give the office manager? Ask him about it. And ask the accountant at the same time. And when you are talking to them about it, also ask how long the boy on the red bicycle's mother worked in the office and compare that with when her son was born. Ask the mother herself, if their answer is not good enough.'

This was taking a direction I had not even thought about until now. So I tried to follow the thread, though I was still somewhat reluctant to do so.

'But – surely we have established that the mysterious woman in Fredriksen's life in the mid-fifties was Solveig Ramdal. She confirmed it herself!'

Patricia let out a slightly exasperated sigh. 'Nonsense. A chameleon like Fredriksen could quite easily conduct two extra-marital affairs at the same time, particularly if he only wanted to talk about the mysteries from 1932 with one of the women. It may be a coincidence. However, I am not yet willing to conclude that the boy on the red bicycle was simply a red herring in the investigation. The link is too strong, especially given that his mother worked in Fredriksen's office at a time when Fredriksen found himself a new mistress. And given that her marriage had been childless for many years, and she then gave birth to a son around this time. So please do check this in the morning.'

Patricia picked up her first cake and took a bite, but did not seem to be happy with the taste.

'A slightly technical question, which could be very important: were the floors in the hotel carpeted? Both in the hall and in the room?'

I answered straightaway: 'Yes, in both places. I asked the receptionist, and he said there had been no changes there either.'

'Excellent,' Patricia said. She looked a bit happier when she took her second piece of cake. Rather abruptly, she added: 'Another thing – if you are able to, check what is to be found in the archives about the court case against Hauk Rebne Westgaard's father and what happened, before you speak to him. His family history may be relevant here, and there is something about Hauk and the way that the others perceive him that I cannot work out.'

I promised, somewhat distractedly, to do this. Then I asked if there was anything more she would like to discuss today – and stood up a little too fast when she said: 'Sadly, no.'

It was now one minute to half past eight. Patricia still did not know that I had arranged to meet Miriam, but I could see in her eyes when I stood up that she suspected as much and she clearly disliked it intensely. The situation I found myself in was so uncomfortable it almost hurt.

XVI

I was ten minutes late when I opened the door to my flat. I had seen from outside that the light was on. Miriam had, as usual, kept her promise and arrived on time. When I came into the living room, she was sitting on the sofa in her usual reading position – with the big blue book about nineteenth-century Nordic literature. The book looked as though it might be some eight hundred pages long, but she only had about fifty pages left.

I went over to her, said that she was an impressively fast reader, and apologized that I was late, but it had been an unexpectedly busy day. She snapped the book shut, jumped from the sofa and said: 'That's OK. But why was it so long?'

I was not sure if she was actually asking whether I had been to see Patricia or not. As her name was not mentioned, I more than gladly took it to be a question about what had happened in the investigation. So I told her about the day's meetings with the remaining members of the group from 1932, and with Fredriksen's mistress and son.

I gave her a summary of the reasoning and conclusions in the case so far, without of course mentioning where they came from. Miriam got very excited when I explained how Fredriksen's own explanation revealed between the lines that he too had gone to Eva's room before six. She remarked again how well I was doing on my own. And again, we steered clear of mentioning Patricia.

I finished my account of the 1932 case by saying that we had therefore come a bit further, but were yet to identify who had been in Eva's bed – and who had killed her.

Miriam showed a genuine interest in both questions, without being able to suggest any revolutionary solutions.

So far, so good. But all the time, I felt the weight of my spy dilemma. I knew without a doubt that Miriam was trust-worthy through and through, but I still did not trust her in the way that I did Patricia. And I felt horribly guilty that I could show more faith in her than in my fiancée.

But Miriam clearly knew me too well as suddenly she said: 'There's something you are not telling me. Is there something about the investigation that you can't share with me?'

At first I said: 'Yes, I am sorry, but that is unfortunately the case.'

She looked disappointed, but nodded and said: 'You know you can always trust me. But of course I understand if you can't tell me. I just won't be able to help you with it, I suppose.'

It was when I heard her say that, that my bad conscience got the better of me. I assured her that I trusted her whole-heartedly, but that she must never tell another living soul what I was going to tell her now.

She nodded eagerly, raised her chin and said: 'Of course,' then snuggled closer.

I thought to myself that the situation was actually becoming rather alarming, but it was too late now to turn back, and nor did I want to.

So I sat there on the sofa, close to my Miriam, and more or less whispered the story of my visit to the head of the police security service to her, and told her that Per Johan Fredriksen was suspected of being a spy.

I struggled with a horrible mix of feelings as I sat there. One moment I was terrified of the consequences this might have should it ever get out; the next, it felt right to be telling her. Miriam's shoulders were permanently damaged by an injury she had sustained when trying to help me in my last case and her actions had very probably saved the current prime minister's life. She had never let slip a word to anyone about what I had told her then. It did not feel right that I should now hide this from her – especially as it was no more than two hours since I had told another woman.

It made Miriam happy in her own way, without any great display of affection or gushing words. 'Gosh, that really is a dramatic development,' was all she said. Then she sat there deep in thought on the sofa. I could feel her body vibrating with tension.

Then suddenly she stood up and said: 'I have a lecture at eight o'clock tomorrow morning, so I have to get to bed early. But I will think more on this tomorrow.'

I followed her to the door, and offered without success to drive her home. I was not sure whether it was her lecture tomorrow morning or my investigation she was thinking about, but it was obvious that she was mulling something over. Miriam's eyes and voice were both unusually distant. She had the big blue book tucked under her arm. In the doorway on her way out, she said, to my joy, something that Patricia had not said today: 'Good luck with the investigation. Remember to watch out for the man in the hat and any other dangers.'

I kissed her on the mouth, and almost replied that she had to stay; she couldn't possibly leave me in such a frightening and unsafe situation. But I said nothing. Then suddenly she was gone, and I heard her quick steps disappear down the stairs.

I stood by the window and watched her go. I thought

that I had never loved anyone as much as I loved Miriam, but I still felt pulled and stretched in every direction.

For the first time, it was not a disappointment to see Miriam disappear into the night. I had a sudden need to be alone and think about the investigation and my own life, though it could hardly be said that I made much progress with either. I managed to write a list of people I should talk to tomorrow in connection with the investigation. This included Hauk Rebne Westgaard, Ane Line Fredriksen and Lene Johansen, as well as the office manager Odd Jørgensen and the accountant Erling Svendsen. I was impatient to get on, but could not do much more tonight.

Physical exhaustion overwhelmed me without warning. It was eleven o'clock when I set the alarm for a quarter past seven, and went to bed. It was a matter of minutes before I was asleep.

On Wednesday, 22 March 1972, I fell asleep alone, safely locked in my own flat, but with a great deal of uncertainty about what tomorrow would bring. I tried to think about Miriam, but fell asleep with Patricia's sharp, accusing eyes staring me down.

DAY SIX

Some Answers, a Disappearance and a Face in a Car Window

I

The case was becoming more and more of an obsession. On Thursday, 23 March 1972, I leapt out of bed with the first ring of the alarm clock at a quarter past seven and rang Hauk Rebne Westgaard straightaway.

I guessed that he was an early bird, which quickly proved to be true. The telephone in Holmestrand was answered on the third ring.

I apologized for calling so early, then said that there were a number of new things in connection with Eva's death in 1932 that I would like to discuss with him as soon as possible.

He replied that I could call him as early as I liked and could come to see him whenever it suited, if it would help to clarify what had happened when Eva died.

I took him at his word and said that I hoped to be there before ten.

The day's newspapers were a less inspiring read. *Arbeider-bladet* used half the front page to cover the EEC debate and much of the rest was about the Government's plans to establish a state-run oil company. Unfortunately, the murder case had crept onto the remaining space on the front page as it had in *Aftenposten*. *Aftenposten* was still positive about the way in which the police were dealing with the case. The newspaper reported that there might be 'reason to question' whether the investigation had the necessary resources. And if indeed it did not, whether the blame did not lie with 'senior police officers', but instead with the parliamentary majority who had not given the police enough resources.

I heaved a sigh of relief that neither the link to 1932, nor the possible links to the EEC question and espionage, had been discovered. At the same time, I shuddered to think what might happen if they were. It felt like this was the calm before the media storm. Something had to happen today.

All was quiet down at the station when I popped in. I picked up the paper bag with the three hairs in it from my pigeon hole. There was a short statement with it to say that it was head hair, but they could not use them to identify who they came from.

Neither my boss nor Danielsen had arrived yet, which suited me fine. I drove on to Holmestrand without waiting for them.

Today, however, I drove to Westgaard Farm via the sheriff's office in Holmestrand. In the archives, I found a couple of yellowed pages about the transfer of Westgaard to Hauk. Having read them, I drove the last stretch faster than planned.

II

Westgaard looked just as peaceful and idyllic in the Vestfold landscape as it had the last time. And yet it felt like a different place when I got there at a quarter to ten. The weather was more overcast and neither the farmer nor the workers were anywhere to be seen. Not that this meant anything, of course. But it did feel rather ominous, nonetheless.

Hauk Rebne Westgaard had been waiting and opened the door within seconds of me ringing the bell. He was dressed in simple work clothes. His hat lay on the hat rack in the hall. I noted in passing that it was the same shape, if not the same colour, as the one worn by Alexander Svasnikov when he was following me around the streets of Oslo. Svasnikov's hat was brown and this was green, but I thought to myself that on a dark street at night in Oslo, the hats could certainly look the same from a window.

We went into the living room. Almost instinctively, both Hauk Rebne Westgaard and I sat down in the same places as before with about three feet of table between us.

'So, what brings you back to the farm today?' my host asked.

I carefully put the bag with the hairs in it down on the table. He looked at me with bright anticipation, which faded as soon as I said that it was head hair from a person, but they could not establish the identity of the person from the hair. However, he perked up again when I said that we were starting to get an outline of what had happened. Up to the point it certainly seemed that Hauk Rebne Westgaard was genuinely interested in clearing up what had happened when his girlfriend died.

I told him in brief that Eva Bjølhaugen had in all probability been drowned in 1932. We had reason to believe that Per Johan Fredriksen had been in her room soon after Hauk himself, and that Kjell Arne Ramdal had been there after Fredriksen. However, we also had reason to believe that Ramdal left the room at a quarter past six, at which point, Eva had been unharmed and the bed untouched. We were now trying to establish what happened in the next two hours.

Hauk Rebne Westgaard's eyes widened when I mentioned drowning, and he listened to everything that followed intently. When I said that I now had to ask him some personal questions and that the answers could be decisive in solving the case of his girlfriend's murder, he quickly gave me the go-ahead.

'All right, I will answer to the best of my abilities,' he said, sitting up straight in his chair, his face serious in concentration.

I started tactfully by asking if Eva had been religious. He shook his head sharply.

'Not particularly. She went to church at Christmas and Easter and the like, but did not have a strong Christian faith. In fact, her father despaired at her lack of faith. He was a little happier with her sister on that score, although never completely satisfied with either of them.'

This prompted me to ask what kind of relationship Eva had with her sister Oda.

'Well, they were very different – the one blonde and

gregarious, the other dark and taciturn. Eva was someone everyone noticed as soon as she walked into a room, and Oda was often the person you forgot being there at all. Eva dominated, despite being younger. They spent a lot of time together, but were often bickering. But that's not unusual for sisters at that age, so I don't think any of us gave it much thought.'

'Eva liked attention, even after you became a couple.'

He gave an even sharper nod this time. 'Absolutely. Eva got a lot of attention from a lot of men and was a rather self-centred young woman who didn't say no. I took it all with a pinch of salt. I just thought I was lucky to have such a beautiful and attractive girlfriend. And I knew that she was a good girl, proper . . .'

He talked in a low and slightly tense voice. I increasingly got the feeling that this was leading somewhere.

'Almost too proper, in fact,' I pushed, gently.

Hauk Rebne Westgaard looked at me, his eyes still wide, and gave a barely discernible nod. It was the last encouragement I needed to spur me on.

'Because the reason you were so upset and surprised about the hairs in Eva's unmade bed, which you knew were not yours, was because you yourself had never been to bed with her.'

I fixed him with my gaze and thought about Patricia as I said this.

She was right again.

As I watched him, Hauk's mask cracked and another person appeared. A vulnerable, unhappy and uncertain young

271

man. His eyes filled with tears and his hands trembled violently. As did his voice when, eventually, he answered.

'I had been to bed with her, but not like that. Not—' He stopped and sat in silence for a moment, then carried on quickly. 'I had not slept with her, no. And it became an obsession. She was my first girlfriend, the tension and expectations were so great. Day after day passed, week after week and month after month, with ever new excuses. To me, she was the most beautiful woman in the world, and she was so exciting and provocative. I knew that it would be over soon, but was determined that we could not split up before we had—'

He stopped again. I did not push him, but tried instead to coax him on whilst he remained in such an open and emotional mood.

'And your life was not easy. So it felt as though the world was crashing down around you when she told you that she had fallen for someone else and wanted to end the relationship. Because that is what she said, isn't it? She broke up with you and said that you would never get what you wanted most. You desired her and you hated her.'

I stared at him intensely. His nod was almost imperceptible, but his voice was controlled when he spoke.

'Yes. That is what she said. I thought about throwing myself at her, but I didn't. Instead, I turned around and fled. And I thought about knocking on her door later, but I didn't. I hoped and prayed that she would have changed her mind by the time we went down to dinner. But she never came down. When we went up to her room, she was dead.

I still do not know who was in bed with her before she died. And nor do I know who killed her. Please tell me if you know. Please.'

Hauk Rebne Westgaard talked in short bursts and stared straight ahead with a distant look in his eyes as he spoke.

I believed him. And I thought that if what he said was true, here was a man who had dedicated his adult life to his family and their land – without ever experiencing any physical love himself.

I did not think that Hauk Rebne Westgaard had killed his girlfriend in 1932, but could still not tell him who had. So I said that I was working on it and would let him know as soon as I could, and then continued with my questioning.

'Some other things happened in 1932. It was not just your girlfriend who died, but your father as well. You gave me some false information the last time we spoke.'

I took out the Photostat copies of the documents from the sheriff's office and laid them on the table between us.

'Your father was not declared of unsound mind by the court. He died in what the sheriff described, after a short investigation, as an accident, having fallen from a cliff onto the rocks below, here on the property. But it was not an accident, was it?'

It was a challenging question that once again caused an abrupt change in mood. Within seconds, Hauk Rebne Westgaard took on a third face, one without tears or sorrow. It was a ruthless and cynical face. His eyes suddenly ceased to blink. And his voice was hard, almost threatening, when he spoke.

'My father lived on the edge of insanity and was about to

drink away the farm and himself to death. The court would have declared him of unsound mind. However, the hearing was postponed for several weeks as the judge was ill, so a new judge had to be appointed. And in the meantime, the ground was burning beneath our feet. My father was mad and would believe anything. The day before he had given away half an acre for a saucepan. In his confused and drunken state, he would often wander to all kinds of places, in all kinds of weather. It was slippery up there by the cliff, and when the rain had stopped there was no trace that anyone else had been there. So the sheriff quickly concluded that it had been an accident and that he had slipped and lost his footing. Everyone agreed that that must be what had happened.'

The shadow of a crooked smiled slipped over Hauk Rebne Westgaard's lips when he said this. I was sitting out of his reach with a loaded gun and as far as I could see, he was unarmed. And yet I found it alarming to be sitting opposite him.

I remembered what Patricia had said about chameleon people and thought that I had certainly seen Hauk Rebne Westgaard's other faces. It struck me then that I had discovered that one of the five people still alive from 1932 was indeed a murderer, only it was a murder that had nothing to do with my investigation.

I heard myself say: 'But even though everyone agreed that that was how your father died, it was not.'

Hauk Rebne Westgaard stared at me without seeing, without blinking. Again, a hard, almost mocking smile played on his lips before he answered.

'It could well be that you are right. But if anyone pushed my father to his death, it couldn't be proved now. And what is more, the limitation period expired years ago. And it is in no way connected to the murders that you are investigating. For my part, I think about it as little as possible and hope that others do the same.'

This almost sounded like a threat, coming from Hauk Rebne Westgaard's mouth. He realized this himself and raised an apologetic hand to show that it was not meant as such.

So there we sat, with this peculiar balance of power between us. He knew that I knew, and I knew that I could not pursue the case in any way. We were both right. The fact that I knew what had happened, and that he knew what was true, was of no practical importance.

'Your father's death was a saving grace not only for you, but also for your sister,' I said.

He nodded quickly, and blinked his eyes for what felt like the first time since we had started to talk about his father's passing.

'I see my father's death as inevitable, given his state of mind at the time. But I also believe that it was a saving grace for several people – not least Inger.'

I nodded pensively and said that events that were relevant to this year's investigation were of course of more interest right now. Then I asked if he had anything more to add to his statement about Eva's death.

He looked me straight in the eye and said: 'No.'

Without looking away, I said: 'You could still have murdered Per Johan Fredriksen last Saturday – if you had found out that it was he who killed Eva, and perhaps also if you had found out that it was he who had been in her bed.'

He did not flinch, and replied: 'I could have. But I still do not know who killed Eva or who was in her bed. I have no idea who killed Per Johan. I was on my way back here when he was killed.'

That was the last thing that was said. He remained sitting at the table, while I stood up and left.

I had been sitting there face to face with a person who had killed his own father – and never regretted it. It was a frightening experience. Now I understood a little more of what Per Johan Fredriksen had meant, if he really had said that his childhood friend Hauk was a man he both respected and feared.

III

As I was driving out of Holmestrand at around eleven o'clock, I could tell that my working day was going to be long and busy. So I stopped at a telephone box and rang Ane Line Fredriksen at home. She picked up on the second ring.

'Hello, hello. Who is calling me?' said an unexpectedly happy and curious voice at the other end.

It was both calming and refreshing. I quickly expressed my condolences for her sister's death, and said that I had some more questions that I would like to ask her as soon as she had the time and felt able to meet me. I added that I also had some new information that she might be interested to know.

Whether it was the offer of new information that made all the difference was unclear, but the response was certainly very positive. Ane Line Fredriksen said that she had done what she could for the moment, regarding the funeral arrangements, and that right now she was sitting sorting out some party matter. She could come to my office as soon as she managed to find a friend who could babysit. One o'clock should be fine, if that suited?

I had no sooner said that it would be fine, before she replied: 'Great. See you at one, then. Now let me find a babysitter' – and put down the phone. I did not even have time to ask which party she worked for. After the phone call, I sat in the car and speculated for a few minutes, but soon the investigation took hold of my attention again and I carried on to Oslo, driving straight to the offices of Per Johan Fredriksen A/S.

IV

The offices were just as short of space as last time and the faces, as far as I could see, were the same. The office manager was just finishing his lunch, which comprised a cup of coffee, two doughnuts and a piece of cake, but he threw down his serviette as soon as he saw me through the glass door.

The situation was all a bit awkward. The man gave me a friendly smile and made the time to talk to me, even though there was a huge pile of contracts and an even bigger pile of other papers on his desk. And I had a letter in my pocket where the same man confessed to embezzlement. I was here to ask critical questions that might determine whether he was not only a human chameleon, but also a murderer.

So I braced myself, and said that I had a few more questions for him. He said that he was more than happy to answer them, but that we should perhaps call in Svendsen, the accountant, straightaway as well.

I said, in a hushed voice, that I had to ask about something that involved him personally, in connection with a document that had been found in Fredriksen's estate.

The office manager sank a little deeper into his chair. I could see beads of sweat break out on his forehead. But he managed to control himself and replied, in an equally hushed voice, that he would definitely prefer it if Svendsen were part of the conversation.

I said that was fine and let Svendsen in, who just happened to be standing outside the office door.

It was when Svendsen came in and sat down on the chair beside Jørgensen, only to pull it a little closer, that I understood the relationship between them. To be precise, it was when the accountant laid a protective, almost loving hand, on the office manager's shoulder. The contact lasted barely a second, but it was long enough and clear enough for me to understand.

I started by asking a straightforward question as to whether there was any news on the takeover plans.

They both nodded in sync. Nothing had been signed yet, but Johan Fredriksen had called, on behalf of the inheritors, and asked if they could go through the conditions and draw up a contract for signature the next day. The heirs had decided that it would be good to clarify the situation without delay. And the administration was in agreement, Svendsen said. But he didn't smile and Jørgensen looked rather upset.

In anticipation of the change in ownership and new guidelines, any tenants in arrears would now have a further fourteen days, at least, to settle any outstanding payments, the office manager explained tactfully. They would be sending out a letter about it today, but I could certainly mention it to Mrs Lene Johansen, if I happened to talk to her, the accountant added helpfully.

This reminded me of Patricia's question about the relationship between Lene Johansen and Fredriksen. I asked the office manager if he could remember roughly when Lene Johansen had worked there.

He furrowed his brow, pulled a file from one of the shelves, and flicked through it at remarkable speed.

'She started here in May 1954, on ten hours a week. That did not give her much time to clean the whole floor here, but she was so happy to have something permanent. As far as I understood, her husband was not doing very well and money was short. She resigned in September 1956, as she was going to have a child. It was a very pleasant meeting, I remember. I said that it was a shame that she had to resign, but it was for a very good reason. She smiled and said that it was a much-longed-for child and that she had been trying for ten years. Erling and I talked about it on the odd occasion later and hoped that she and the child were well. It was very sad for us to witness their sorry fate.'

Tor Johansen, an only child with a speech impediment and limp, had been born in February 1957. It was rather a striking coincidence that Mrs Johansen, who had been childless for so many years, only became pregnant while she was working here.

I looked directly at Odd Jørgensen and asked if he thought that there might have been some kind of relationship between Fredriksen and Mrs Johansen.

Jørgensen and Svendsen exchanged glances. Then Jørgensen replied: 'I can neither confirm nor deny it, but now that you mention it, I did actually wonder myself at the time. There was one evening in the autumn of 1955 when I had been working late in the office, and was surprised when I left to discover that Fredriksen was still here. He had stopped to chat to Mrs Johansen while she worked. She was young and full of the joys of life back then, and was no doubt an attractive woman. I noticed him smile in a way I had never seen him smile before. But none of us really know the truth of the matter.'

I thanked him for this information. It was not confirmation, but definitely gave grounds for another conversation with Mrs Johansen. There were more and more strange little coincidences springing up in this case.

And now I could not postpone the inevitable. I put Jørgensen's confession down on the desk and asked him to explain.

It was not a pleasant sight. The kind and apparently confident office manager broke down without even looking at the piece of paper. He collapsed forwards onto the desk and sat there with his face buried in his hands. He stayed like this for a minute or so, until the accountant gently put his arm across his rounded shoulders. This helped. The office manager slowly straightened up in his chair again.

I waited with a thumping heart to hear if he would now confess to murder. But he did not. When Odd Jørgensen did eventually speak, he only talked about the document.

'What can I say, other than that I have hoped and prayed in recent days that that piece of paper, which I have lived in fear of for seven years now, had somehow miraculously disappeared. That piece of paper is a reminder of the only mistake I have made in my forty-five years as a law-abiding citizen, and it will now affect the rest of my life.'

I said, carefully, that it would be up to the heirs and possibly the public prosecutor to decide whether it was something they wanted to pursue or not, and that given the type of crime, the limitation period had probably elapsed.

Jørgensen shook his head and pointed out of the window.

'Perhaps the public prosecutor will not bother with it, but the wolves out there will. And neither Ramdal, nor any-one else, will want an office manager who has embezzled funds. The sector has its channels and blacklists. If this got out, I would be lucky to find a job as a clerk. That is what Fredriksen said, that day in 1965. "If this ever leaves these four walls, Jørgensen, you are done for." That is what he said. And he was right, of course.'

Once again, the office manager planted his elbows on the desk and buried his face in his hands. And once again the accountant laid his arm protectively round his shoul-ders. I had understood the secret of the relationship between them now. And they had both understood that I had understood. Certainly, none of us wished to go into any further detail. Instead, we continued to talk about the confession.

I told Jørgensen that it might not be necessary for it to become publicly known, but the best thing he could do now would be to tell me the truth.

'The truth is, in short, that I am a weak person who made a fatal error of judgement and, for very personal reasons, embezzled a large amount of money from the company. It was meant as a loan just for a few weeks while I waited for a bank loan to be sorted out, but I was found out. Fredriksen didn't go to the police. He let me keep my job, but demanded that I pay back the money the same day – and that I sign a confession, in the event that he might have a need for it later.'

I asked why he had done it. The office manager replied that it was highly personal. For once, he was contradicted by the accountant.

'You are too hard on yourself and too kind to others, Odd,' he said, in a quiet voice.

Then he turned to me and spoke normally. 'It was not for Odd, but for my mother. She had been diagnosed with a cancer that could not be treated in Norway. Our only hope was a doctor in a private hospital in the USA, who had saved several patients with the same type of cancer, despite patients being diagnosed as terminal. My mother had no income. I am an only child and as a recent graduate did not have the means to help her. It was a matter of days, and no bank was willing to give us such a big loan in time. Odd desperately wanted to help me save my mother. He asked his employer for a loan – and borrowed the money anyway when Fredriksen, who was a multi-millionaire, said no.'

'Erling never asked me to do it, and did not know about it either. It was my decision and my mistake,' Odd Jørgensen said, with his face hidden in his hands.

'But it was my mother – and for my sake. And you did nothing wrong, Odd. You did what you thought best. It was Fredriksen who not only proved how heartless he was, but also cynically used the opportunity to exploit us.'

'And what about your mother?' I asked, gently.

This gave rise to more tears from the office manager, who was clearly the more emotional of the two. The accountant had kept his composure throughout, but his voice was hard, brusque and angry when he answered.

'Fredriksen demanded to have the money back the same day, and he got it. My mother never got to the doctor in the US. She died in Oslo a few months later.'

'So, the short version is: Fredriksen's heartless exploitation of the situation meant that you, Erling, lost your mother and you, Odd, have lived with the constant threat of scandal and being fired. And you both had to carry on working here year after year for poor pay.'

They both nodded.

'We hated him and hoped that when the day came he would go straight to hell!' the office manager said with unexpected intensity.

The accountant agreed in his concise, controlled manner.

I said that on a human level, I could understand that, but that I was duty-bound to ask them both where they were when Fredriksen was killed last Saturday evening.

They looked at each other – then there was a fleeting smile before they were both serious again.

'We were where we always are on Saturday evenings. Together at Erling's, behind closed doors,' Odd Jørgensen said quietly and discreetly.

I found the situation rather embarrassing and awkward. But I looked at Erling Svendsen and asked where he lived.

'I have a small one-bedroom flat in Eilert Sund's Street,' he replied, and then was suddenly quiet.

A heavy silence sank over the room. I sat and wondered whether it was just a coincidence that Eilert Sund's Street was in Majorstuen, within walking distance of Jacob Aall's Street and the corner of Kirk Road where Fredriksen had been stabbed.

Between the two piles of paper on Jørgensen's desk lay a pipe and a box of matches. I had a sudden impulse to strike a match and burn Jørgensen's confession. But I already had more than enough problems in terms of the investigation and did not need to add burning material evidence to the list. Furthermore, I was no longer sure that one of the two men sitting here, alarmingly close, had not taken the matter into their own hands and killed their much-hated boss. They had already admitted that they despised him. And the visit from the boy on the red bicycle's mother a few days earlier must have been an uncomfortable reminder of just how heartless Per Johan Fredriksen could be when it came to business and other people.

I told them that I had to take the confession with me and that it would be up to the Fredriksen family and the potential new owner to decide what they wanted to do about the matter. I thanked them for their statements and requested that they both stay in town until the investigation into Fredriksen's death had been closed.

They both nodded again. When I looked back from the doorway, Svendsen had put his arm around Jørgensen, which produced a small smile from the office manager. And I thought to myself that in the midst of all this tragedy, it was a touching picture of care and love between two people. I then again thought that one or both of these two hard-pressed men could have committed murder. I closed the door behind me and left without looking back.

V

It was a busy day for both me and the other people involved in the case. At two minutes past one, I was back in my office. Four minutes later, Ane Line Fredriksen came striding in at an admirable pace.

'Sorry, it took a bit longer than expected to find a babysitter. The lack of childcare in this city is a scandal – something needs to be done about it. What have you got to tell me?' she said, without drawing breath. Then she sat down, without me having asked, and leaned across the desk towards me.

Once again, I thought that there was something refreshingly enthusiastic, direct and dynamic about the thirty-year-old redhead. Dressed in jeans and a green hand-knitted sweater, she seemed remarkably unaffected by the fact that she had lost both her father and her sister in the past five days, and as a result was about to inherit a fortune.

I tried to start gently by thanking her for coming at such short notice, and by asking which party she worked for.

She smiled cheerfully, pointed at her red hair and replied: 'The Socialist People's Party. I inherited my political zeal from Father, but not my political views. I doubt that there is anyone in our family who agrees politically, in fact. I'm sure Mother always voted the same as Father, but she is actually totally disinterested in politics. Johan refuses to say who he votes for, but surely it's Conservative, and Vera always leaned towards the Liberals, or something equally tame in the centre.'

I could not help but ask if she knew my fiancée, Miriam Filtvedt Bentsen, through the SPP. She nodded energetically.

'Yes, of course I do. Everyone knows Miriam – she more or less lives in the party office. Oh, so you are the mysterious boyfriend she never wants to talk about? I tried to ask her last year if she had a boyfriend, and she just said yes and stopped there. How exciting. How did you meet?'

I knew that Miriam did not like to talk about her private life either at university or in the party office, and I understood perfectly why she played down her relationship with a well-known policeman in those circles. So I gave her a simple, short answer and said that it had been in connection with an earlier murder investigation, and it was a long story that she would have to hear another time.

Ane Line Fredriksen looked as though she wanted to hear the long story straightaway. But a natural curiosity can quickly be turned in different directions and she listened intently and almost reverently to my account of the investigation into her father's murder. Then all of a sudden her eyes brimmed with tears at the mention of her sister.

'It was of course very sad with Father. But with Vera it is different – tragic. Vera has always been so fragile, physically and mentally. My brother and I had both thought and spoken briefly about the possibility that she would go before us. But then, only a few days after Father . . . No, it was unexpected and just dreadful. It feels terrible to have lost your only sister in that way without the chance to say goodbye.'

I used the opportunity to ask quickly when she had last spoken to her sister.

'The evening before – and then we only spoke about Father's funeral, the inheritance, practical things like that. It was a strange evening. Mother was distant and close to tears every time Father was mentioned. Johan was relatively together, but really only concerned with making a decision about the takeover that was weighing so heavily on him. We did not speak on the day she died. Though I do think she tried to call me.'

I immediately asked how she could know that.

'There was a phone call at home around three, but I did not manage to pick up on time. Of course, I don't know that it was Vera, but it was not Mother, Johan or my ex. If it was anyone else, they didn't call back again later.'

I jumped slightly in my chair. Then I said that the timing fitted well with the phone calls that we knew had been made from the hotel.

This upset Ane Line Fredriksen even more. She had no

idea what her sister might have wanted to say to her – and no explanation as to why her sister appeared to have called her and not her brother or mother.

Ane Line Fredriksen spoke quickly and was visibly upset; it felt possible that she might now give away secrets. So I pushed on.

'The relationship between you and your sister was not the best, was it?'

This worked. She talked even faster and got even more upset. 'Who said that? My mother? My brother? Both of them?'

The way Ane Line Fredriksen looked at me felt almost threatening. I answered with a counter-attack and said that I was unfortunately not at liberty to say, but that I would like to have an answer for the purposes of the investigation.

'My family need to get a grip, they really do. I cared more about Vera and rang her more frequently than they both did. Mother only had eyes for Father, and my brother only had eyes for the mirror. It is true that we have argued a bit recently, yes. Smart girls like Vera have to be braver and stand up for their rights if there is ever going to be any equality in society. I told her as much, and said that she must not give any money to that slippery boyfriend of hers. She was indifferent about the former and vehemently disagreed with the latter. So yes, we had argued a bit recently, but no, we did not hate each other.'

I still liked Ane Line Fredriksen the best of the remaining members of the Fredriksen family. I thought she was a refreshingly engaging and honest person. But I felt less convinced of her honesty right now. Ane Line Fredriksen had just earned roughly thirty million kroner as a result of the deaths this week, she had argued with her sister, she was probably one of the people her sister had tried to contact a few hours before her death, and she clearly had a lively temperament.

So I said that as a matter of procedure I had to ask her if she had an alibi for the time of both her father's and sister's deaths.

She looked as though she was in danger of exploding. She shot forwards in her chair and boomed: 'For goodness' sake, man! Are you accusing me of killing my father and Vera?'

I was slightly taken aback by her reaction, but replied with measured calm: 'For the moment, I am not accusing anyone of having killed either of them. I am trying to find out who did, and it is then a matter of procedure to ask everyone in the victim's closest family for an alibi. It is clearly written in all police rules and guidelines.'

Strictly speaking, the latter was a slight exaggeration, but it did the trick perfectly. Ane Line Fredriksen calmed down in record time. She leaned back in her chair again and answered in a much quieter, slower voice: 'Very well, if it is standard practice and included in the rules. When Father was killed on Saturday evening, I was at home with my daughter. She went to bed at seven, after which I sat alone working on some party matter until the priest came to my door at eleven. When Vera died, I was at home all day with my daughter until I took her to my ex-husband and his parents at around three o'clock. Then I drove home again and was on my own until a friend came to see me at five.'

I had hoped her alibis would be watertight. But they were not. It was becoming frustratingly hard to rule anyone out in this case.

I changed tack and said that there was something in connection with the company that she should perhaps know about. She nodded attentively and listened closely, leaning further across the desk as I told her the story of the office manager and the accountant. Her face was barely a ruler's length from me, so I could see the tears when I told her that the accountant's mother had died.

I put the confession down on the desk and said that it was up to her and her family to decide whether they wanted to report the case or not.

I had made a Photostat of the confession, in case it should prove to be relevant to the murder investigation, and I was glad that I had. Ane Line Fredriksen looked quickly at the confession, shed a couple more tears, then she produced a blue lighter from her pocket and set fire to it.

I did not try to stop her. We sat in silence and watched the confession burn.

I said with due care that the crime had taken place some time ago, but that she should at least discuss it with her brother.

'My brother has so much to think about right now. He can concentrate on the figures and I will look after the people,' she said, and winked almost mischievously at me.

'It really was indecently greedy and heartless of my father. He clearly had many aspects to his personality that we, his family, did not see,' she added quickly, with an angry shake of her head.

I said that there was one thing about her father that perhaps she should know. Again, she nodded attentively – then asked what it was, when I paused for a few seconds.

The suspicions that he was a spy were still strictly confidential. But I thought perhaps it was time to test his daughter's reactions to the possibility that Per Johan Fredriksen had thought about changing party and sides in the EEC debate.

I did not have to wait long for her reaction. She thumped the desk with her fist and the rest of her shot up from the chair before she carried on in a very indignant voice.

'Surely you can't be serious? The Centre Party is one thing. But to change sides in the EEC debate would have been comparable to high treason for all concerned – including me and the rest of the family. That was the only thing we agreed on. Father came from farming stock, and knew what membership of the EEC would mean for lots of farmers. And he had been elected and re-elected to the Storting and as head of the Standing Committee on Foreign Affairs on the promise that he would oppose Norwegian membership.'

I said that all things being equal, it was apparently true. He also feared that if he did not, he would lose his seat in the Storting.

'All the same . . . what an egocentric idiot, liar and political cheat. If you have no more questions for me, I have to get out into the fresh air before I throw up on your desk.'

Without waiting to hear if I had any more questions, she stood up and marched out of my office.

I thought to myself that she would hardly have behaved

like this if she had killed Per Johan Fredriksen, no matter whether it was because of the inheritance or the EEC question. But it had clearly demonstrated to me that the EEC debate really could stir up strong feelings – and that Ane Line Fredriksen was a very complex person.

The day's edition of *Verdens Gang* had arrived and proved to be more critical than the morning papers. 'Despite all the respect that Detective Inspector Kolbjørn "K2" Kristiansen has earned', there was reason to ask if more resources were not needed, as the investigation seemed to be very modest, given that both a leading politician and his daughter had been killed within the space of a few days. According to the newspaper, 'K2's reputation could take a nosedive' if the investigation did not produce any concrete results before the week was out. However, the report did finish with the hope that the investigation was progressing and an expression of deepest sympathy for the victims' family.

VI

I had to make two telephone calls. I made the one I was looking forward to least as soon as the office door had closed behind Ane Line Fredriksen. It was to Edvard Rønning Junior, the lawyer. I got hold of him without trouble at the offices of Rønning, Rønning, Rønning & Rønning. I said that there were some developments in the case that he should be informed of, and as a result of these, some questions that I would like to ask his client, Lene Johansen.

Rønning Junior replied that he had expected to hear from

me sooner, but that of course he appreciated that I had telephoned him now and that he would come in person with his client. There were certain practical problems involved in contacting his client, as she did not have a telephone or work anywhere with access to one. She did, however, ring him at three o'clock every day, and he could ask her then if she would be able come to the station with him at four. I asked him to do that, and he promised with relative goodwill to call me back if it was not possible to meet today.

Then at five to two, I called Patricia. I said that it was rather short notice, but there was a good deal of new information and I would appreciate talking to her as soon as possible.

She said that the maid should be able to rustle up some coffee with fifteen minutes' notice.

I thanked her and said I would be there as soon as possible.

We hung up at the same time without saying any more. I thought that the case, after a hesitant start, now seemed to be of interest to Patricia. So I got up, rushed out to my car and drove to Frogner.

VII

At a quarter past two, I was sitting in my usual place opposite Patricia in her library. Coffee, cakes and biscuits had been put out on the table, but not touched by either of us. Patricia listened in silence for twenty minutes as I told her the most important things from my meetings with

Hauk Rebne Westgaard, the office manager Jørgensen and accountant Svendsen, and Ane Line Fredriksen.

'Good work in such a short time. But for the moment, the result is in fact more potential murderers for this year's killings, rather than fewer,' she said briskly with some frustration.

I had to agree with that.

'What about the hairs from 1932?' Patricia asked.

I told her that they were head hairs, but that it was not possible to establish from whom.

Patricia sighed with frustration. 'There really is not much help coming from anywhere in this case. Which leaves a theoretical doubt. With regards to who was in Eva's bed just before she died, the picture is now so clear that we should confront the person directly. After today's adventures, you no doubt know who it is?'

The challenge was unexpected. I had absolutely no idea who had been in Eva's bed. And I could not understand how I was supposed to know after the day's events.

I thought that it had to be either something Ane Line Fredriksen had said which revealed that it was her father, or something Hauk Rebne Westgaard had said that revealed that it was him. My guess was that it was Per Johan Fredriksen.

Patricia shook her head. It crossed my mind that no one could shake their head with such mild condescension and captivating arrogance as Patricia. She grabbed a pen and wrote something down on her notepad, which she kept hidden behind her coffee cup.

'It is sometimes alarming to discover what conservative

mental barriers even relatively young and enlightened people can set for themselves in this day and age,' she said with a mocking smile as she held up the piece of paper.

I stared at it and immediately forgave Patricia for mocking me. I had to agree that even relatively young and enlightened people in 1972 could still have conservative mental blocks. And that I should have worked this out on the basis of what I had heard earlier, if not before that.

VIII

The wall clock struck three as I stepped into the hall of the Ramdals' house in Frognerkilen. I stood face to face with Kjell Arne Ramdal, who appeared to be on his way out.

As was to be expected, he did not smile, but nor did he express any kind of concern or displeasure at seeing me again. He simply informed me that he had come home for a meal because he had an important business meeting that was starting in half an hour.

I said that it was actually his wife I needed to speak to this time.

He nodded briskly and went on his way without showing any interest whatsoever in what I might want to talk to his wife about.

So there I was in the hallway with Solveig Ramdal. She very definitely did not look happy to see me, but kept up appearances nonetheless and said: 'Welcome back. Let's go into the living room again.' She closed the door, even though we were alone in the house. This little detail reinforced my impression that I was on the right track, and it was a very important one.

'So, what news from the investigation?' she asked as she went over to the leather chair.

I went on the offensive and told her that we now knew who had been in the bed together with Eva just before she died, thanks to, among other things, new analyses of the hairs that had been found there.

'I see,' Solveig Ramdal said, looking straight at me. There was no great change in her demeanour, but a slight tension in her voice galvanized me into making that final leap.

'And so we discovered that you have lied to me in all your previous statements. The mysterious man in Eva's bed was not your husband, or Per Johan Fredriksen or Hauk Rebne Westgaard. It was you.'

I knew before I had even finished that I had hit the bull's eye, with Patricia's good help.

Solveig Ramdal started as if she had received an electric shock. Then suddenly she transformed into a wild cat. She was almost ready to leap from her chair, her fingers curled like claws. And when she replied, she hissed more than spoke.

'You must never tell another living soul – or it could be all the worse for you!'

I was prepared to defend myself physically if she moved in my direction. But she did not; I was at least four stone heavier than her and she was unarmed. But she looked like a wild animal in a cage as she remained seated on her chair, hissing, quivering, and staring at me with pure hatred. I waited a few seconds to reflect before I continued.

'I do not want to create any problems in your private life, only to solve the murders. You have lied to me on several occasions in the course of this investigation, and threatening me now does not make your situation any better. In your own interests, you should just tell me the truth about what happened, immediately.'

Solveig Ramdal sat there fuming for a few seconds more. Suddenly she burst into tears. She sat with her face buried in her hands. After a couple of minutes she regained her composure, lowered her hands and spoke in a weak voice.

'I am so sorry, I was desperate and not thinking clearly. For the past forty years, my worst nightmare has been that my secret would get out one day. My husband and children must never know. Yes, that's right, I was in bed with Eva shortly before she died. She had asked me to come to her room at half past six. It was only a few minutes before we were in bed. We knew only too well that we did not have much time. At ten past seven, I sneaked out of her room and back into my own. She was alive and unharmed when I left her. I got up and dressed, while she lay in the bed naked. She smiled when she said "see you soon". She did not say that she was expecting any more visitors. What happened after I left, I have no idea. What I said about hearing a bang at half past seven is true. I heard a bang and got worried, but hoped that it was nothing dramatic. I was terrified that we would be discovered and didn't dare go into her room again to find out what had happened. It has haunted me ever since. Not knowing if I could have saved Eva if I had gone back. But I did not kill her. On the contrary, I loved her.'

This did not sound entirely implausible.

'So that's the story? Eva liked the attention of men, but in truth loved only women. And that was true of you too?'

She nodded and shook her head at the same time.

'Yes and no. Eva only loved women and the attention, of course – or at least, that is what she told me. I thought at the time that I only loved women, but I realized afterwards that I could love both men and women. My experience with Eva and her death was a shock. I have since only been to bed with two men: my first fiancé and my husband. I tell myself that Solveig Thaulow was attracted to women, whereas Solveig Ramdal is quite normal and only loves men. It was a folly of my youth, but I have lived in fear ever since as a result. My husband and his family are very conservative and have spoken with utter disgust about women who are attracted to women. And the children are more like my husband than me. If this were to get out, I would not only risk divorce and being thrown out of my home, but also losing any contact with my family. So I beg you with all my heart not to let this go any further!'

She said this in an almost breathless whisper. Then she was silent and looked even smaller where she sat hunched up in a chair that was suddenly too big. The wild cat had vanished, and left in its place was a small, trembling kitten. The kitten did not look in the slightest bit dangerous, but I had seen the furious wild cat that also lay hidden in Solveig Ramdal. And I did not doubt that it could kill if it felt threatened and was given the opportunity.

We were caught in an uncomfortable situation, just as I had been with her husband the day before. Solveig Ramdal could not prove to me that Eva Bjølhaugen had been alive when she left the hotel room that day in 1932. I could not prove the opposite. We still only had Solveig Ramdal's word for the bang at half past seven.

The limitation period for the murder in 1932 had long since elapsed and it was really only interesting in terms of the investigation because of its relevance to the murders in 1972. The story that Solveig Ramdal had now told me did not give her a new motive for the murder of Per Johan Fredriksen. On the other hand, it did give her a possible motive for killing Vera Fredriksen, if she had been about to uncover what actually happened in 1932. And that was true regardless of whether she had killed Eva Bjølhaugen, or just gone to bed with her.

I promptly changed tack, looked her straight in the eye and asked if she would now like to change her statement regarding the day Vera Fredriksen died.

And because we were looking straight into each other's eyes, we both knew what happened next. She was confused and hesitated for a few seconds too long to be able to lie afterwards. So she bit her lip and answered.

'Yes, I am afraid that I have to do that as well. Apart from the fact that we both had our clothes on, it is a very similar story forty years on. I was in the hotel room and met Vera, and it must have been shortly before she was killed. But she too was alive and unharmed when I left. And again, it was she who asked me to come, but all we did was talk for a few minutes.'

I asked for more details about what happened. Solveig Ramdal continued without stopping to think. Either she was telling the truth, or her mind worked very quickly.

'I knew Vera a little, but it was still a surprise when she rang me. She said that she had found a document in her father's desk that might shed some light on what had happened in 1932. She had gone to the hotel herself and thought that what her father had written could be true. But she wanted to discuss it with someone who had been there at the time, before going to the police. I didn't know what she knew, but was panicked that she might know my secret and reveal it. So I said that I would get there as quickly as I could. I was beside myself with desperation. Then I put a tea towel over the receiver, rang the hotel and reserved a hotel room, pretending to be a neurotic.'

She stopped for a moment and looked at me expectantly, but carried on hastily when I waved her on.

'The receptionist was not a stickler for rules and regulations, and I managed to get to my room without being seen. I met Vera, who was very agitated indeed. She only talked about the murder and there was nothing to indicate that she knew about my little secret. She had left the document in her father's desk. But she told me that his theory was that Eva had been drowned and that it was my husband who had killed her. Vera said that she wanted to tell me before she went to the police, to tell them about this theory. I said that I appreciated it, and told her the truth – that I was not aware that my husband had committed murder, but could not rule it out either. I said that she should tell the police if she knew anything that might be relevant to her father's death, but said that I would appreciate it if she did not mention our conversation. She promised not to, and we parted as friends around half past three. She was full of life and standing in the middle of the room when I left.'

She was breathing very heavily, but she held my eye as she spoke.

'So what you are saying is that when you went to the hotel, you had planned for a situation where you were willing to kill Vera Fredriksen if she was about to reveal your secret? And you claim that that situation never arose?'

Solveig Ramdal started slightly, but managed to keep impressive control over her voice.

'What I am saying, very clearly, is that no such situation arose and I did not kill Vera Fredriksen. What I thought and imagined about the various situations that never arose is a matter for me, my conscience and God.'

Solveig Ramdal let out a long breath, then looked at me with pleading eyes. She gave a curt 'no' in answer to my question as to whether she had anything to add to her earlier statement about the day on which Per Johan Fredriksen died.

I thought that this made the picture of what happened in 1932 and 1972 clearer, but frustratingly didn't make it any clearer who might have committed the murders. Solveig Ramdal could be lying and she could have carried out one or both of the murders. But I had no proof. If her story was true, it gave me few leads. In fact, Vera Fredriksen's death became even more of a riddle. Given that Solveig Ramdal was the mysterious hotel guest and that the three telephone calls that Vera Fredriksen had made were to her mother, Solveig Ramdal and me, it was even more puzzling how and why the murderer had gone to the hotel. This weakened the credibility of her story, but did not disprove it.

Solveig Ramdal appeared to have fully regained control when she spoke again.

'I understand that my position is pretty weak and I would appear untrustworthy. So I can only hope that you soon find out the truth about all these murders, as it will prove that I did not kill anyone. I have lied to you in our previous conversations, for which I apologize profusely. But there was a danger that I would be accused of a murder I did not commit, or that the secret of a mistake in my youth would be uncovered and ruin my life. In the past few days I have thought a great deal about how people react in different situations. Even though it might take different forms, I believe that most people would, like me, do whatever they could to save their own skins. You can call it egotism, if you wish; I call it self-preservation. It sounds a bit nicer, even though the meaning is much the same.'

I interpreted her concluding words as showing some degree of self-awareness, without feeling any more certain that the rest of what she had told me was therefore true; she had lied to me too much already.

My final words to Solveig Ramdal before I left were that she should stay locally until the investigation was closed, and that I had no need at the moment to tell her husband about her secret. She gave a little nod. She stayed sitting on the chair like a timorous kitten, staring out into thin air.

I found my own way out. It was only when I was in the car that I realized it was now ten to four, and that I had an important meeting back at the station at four. And it was only when I was heading back into the centre of town that I realized that I had not seen even a glimpse of the man in the hat today. Not that I missed the Soviet agent, but it did make me wonder what his sudden disinterest might mean.

IX

I met them on my way into the police station at five past four. They made a very odd couple: he was still a young man, with a lorgnette, suit and hat, and she was an older middle-aged woman with nothing on her head, wearing a worn green winter coat. There was an almost comical performance when both Edvard Rønning Junior and I apologized at the same time for being a few minutes late.

Once we were settled in my office, however, the seriousness of the situation was obvious. To my relief, Lene Johansen was not visibly broken by the events of the past few days. But she was still a tired and sombre woman. Her hair looked a bit greyer than when I had first met her, and I could easily have taken her to be over sixty. There was something heavy and slow about her movements when she sat down.

She looked at me questioningly without saying anything. Her lawyer said: 'Thank you for the invitation to come here. We await with great interest to hear your update and questions.'

I quickly filled them in on developments. I told them that we now had an eyewitness, an old lady who lived in Majorstuen who claimed to have seen the murder, and she was adamant that the perpetrator did not limp. But there was still considerable uncertainty: the eyewitness was over a hundred and had not been able to give a description of the murderer. We had chosen to keep all possibilities open and to continue the investigation. Information had been gathered that could give several people possible motives for killing Fredriksen, but so far we did not have sufficient evidence to arrest anyone. Due to the ongoing investigation I was not able to give them any more details.

Lene Johansen listened attentively. She nodded gratefully when I said that I had been in contact with the company and that she need not worry about being evicted until the case had been solved.

'Well, we will have to accept that as a provisional account and hope to hear better news in the coming days. What are your questions for my client?'

I looked at Lene Johansen and said that as a matter of procedure we now had to follow all leads and all possible links. I therefore had to ask her to explain why she had not previously mentioned that she had any connection with Fredriksen and his company.

The lawyer looked a little taken aback, but his client quickly rose to the challenge.

'Yes, I realized afterwards that I should have mentioned that I cleaned there a couple of evenings a week for two years. But that was ages ago now, and I never really saw much of Fredriksen. It was the office manager I spoke to when I was employed and when I resigned.'

The lawyer looked pointedly at me and asked if the matter was now clarified.

I trusted Patricia and was bolstered by my success with Solveig Ramdal. So I carried on unperturbed.

'I am afraid we can't give up that quickly. It is true that

Fredriksen himself was not often in the office. But you were a beautiful young woman, and according to the staff, he showed great interest in you. Indeed, the staff speculated on whether or not you might be meeting elsewhere as well. Not least when you resigned because you were going to have a child, after having been married for many years without children.'

Rønning dropped his lorgnette and stared aghast at his client, making no attempt to pick it up. And she sat there, frantically shaking her head.

'Are you sitting there saying that Fredriksen and I – that's crazy. We were from completely different worlds. Do you really think that I would let my son live in poverty, as he did, if his father was a multi-millionaire?'

She looked at me indignantly. It was a simple counter-question that I had not considered and I almost found myself blaming Patricia because she had not thought it through.

I was on the defensive now. Lene Johansen looked more and more indignant and then carried on without my asking.

'A poor widow from the east end certainly has to put up with a lot in this town. First I lose my only son, and now you're sitting there saying that he might have killed the rich father he never had. It's all lies, and I can prove it, if you just give me a moment.'

Both Rønning and I sat as if paralysed and stared at her as she quickly pulled from her coat pocket an old purse. I could not see any notes in it, only a few coins. But her trembling fingers fished out an old black-and-white photograph which she held up for me.

'This is my husband,' she said.

I recognized him from the photograph in the flat. And I understood straightaway what she meant to say with it.

The birthmark on her husband's neck was far smaller than the one on the neck of the boy on the red bicycle. But it was on the same side and was the same shape. It could not be a coincidence.

The situation was uncomfortable enough already, before Rønning Junior's voice filled the room.

'We understand that you have to investigate all possible leads in the investigation. However, we hope that you now recognize that this is a wild goose chase and that you will apologize immediately to my client. If you do not have any further questions, we will take our leave and hope that you will be able to give us some better news over the next few days. If not, this could turn into a rather unfortunate matter for both you and the force in general. I had not expected you to stoop so low, Kristiansen.'

Lene Johansen nodded in agreement, put the photograph back in her purse, and stood up abruptly. 'This has been a rather nasty experience. I want to go home,' she said, her voice shaking.

I felt humiliated and in a very vulnerable position. So I did what I could to save the situation, I apologized and told them that I sincerely hoped that I would have better news next time.

I heard Rønning say the words '. . . recommend filing a . . .' to his client as the door slammed behind them.

Another shock followed when my boss knocked on my door and did not wait for an answer before coming in. I was worried that he had come to reprimand me for my unwarranted allegations against one of the parties involved in the case – or for the continued lack of results in the investigation.

But my boss had not come to reprimand me at all. He had come to say that the Soviet Embassy had rather unexpectedly requested a meeting with the head of the investigation. But before that we would need to go to the prime minister's office to give him a report.

X

I had met the leader of the Labour Party, Trond Bratten, a couple of years earlier in connection with another murder investigation, and I had been to the prime minister's office. But I had never met Trond Bratten in the prime minister's office. He had only moved in there the year before, when disagreement about the EEC had ripped apart the blue coalition government, which had been led by the Centre Party's Peder Borgen. In terms of my political preferences, this was an improvement, even though my personal meeting with Peder Borgen here had been very nice.

I was curious to see if Mrs Ragna Bratten had also been included in the move from Young's Square to the prime minister's office. I soon had my answer. She was sitting on a chair in the reception area and jumped up as soon as she saw me. She embraced me and thanked me warmly for all I had done a couple of years earlier. The prime minister's wife assured me that both she and her husband were deeply grateful and that her husband was looking forward to meeting me again. She added hastily that she was here so that she could drive him home after the meeting, but did not know what the meeting was about. So she asked me to look after her husband in the meantime, and then pointed to the door to his office.

My boss and I had been told that it would be a highly confidential briefing. Just how confidential it was became apparent when we entered the prime minister's office and saw that Trond Bratten was there alone, sitting behind a large desk.

If Trond Bratten really had been looking forward to meeting me, it was not clear to see. He said a brisk 'Good afternoon' and shook our hands.

My boss took care to close the door behind us, and then we settled into two chairs that were on the other side of the desk. I noticed that the desk was larger than when I had been here before, and the chairs pulled slightly further back.

Trond Bratten stayed sitting behind the desk and looked at us expectantly.

My boss cleared his throat and said that the prime minster had requested a strictly confidential briefing on the part of the investigation into the murder of Per Johan Fredriksen that might affect the oil agreement and the Soviet Union, as we had now been asked to a meeting at the embassy.

Bratten replied: 'Yes, a short and confidential account.' Then he looked me and said no more.

A short and confidential accounted suited me well. So I reported, without going into any details, that the murder of Per Johan Fredriksen was still unsolved, but that Fredriksen had been suspected of being a spy and was killed, apparently, only a matter of hours before he was due to be arrested. It was not clear whether he was guilty or not, and we had no grounds for claiming that he had been assassinated. The timing was, however, striking, and in the course of the investigation, I had been followed by a man, whom we had now identified as a Soviet agent, who probably had many deaths on his conscience, in a number of countries. He was officially linked to the Soviet Embassy in Oslo and had diplomatic immunity.

'A challenging situation,' was Trond Bratten's succinct comment when I had finished. Then he sat and pondered, without saying any more.

My boss asked carefully if the prime minister had any advice for us with regard to our visit to the Soviet Embassy, in this challenging situation.

'Say as little as possible, without offending them,' Bratten said, in a monotone voice. Then once again, he sat there staring into space, deep in thought.

I noted down the advice and thought to myself that it might be easier said than done.

A few more minutes passed in breathless silence. Finally, I broke it by asking the prime minister what he thought about the situation and how we should go forward.

'Democracy must as far as possible be allowed to take its course, and the agreement that the Storting is due to ratify tomorrow could be of the utmost importance to the nation's future. But it would be both politically and morally impossible for a democratic country to enter into an agreement with a non-democratic country that had just violated the democratic country's sovereignty by carrying out terrorist activities there.'

He spoke without hesitation and the formulation was so precise that I almost broke out into spontaneous applause. Fortunately, I managed to stop myself in time, and instead asked how he would deal with the matter from this point on.

'The ratification procedure must be allowed to run its course, unless there are any dramatic developments in the case. The Government must be informed immediately if there are any such developments, in order to assess the ratification procedure.'

I took the hint and said that the prime minister's office would be told immediately if there was any important news.

My boss and I had barely opened the door before Ragna Bratten slipped in past us. I wondered how much she would be told about this strictly confidential case – and how such different people could function together in a marriage. But then I had more than enough problems of my own to think about.

My boss and I left the prime minister's office in silent thought at five to five. Fifteen minutes later we presented ourselves, still grave and thoughtful, at the reception of the Soviet Embassy in Drammen Road.

XI

The receptionist at the Soviet Embassy was a raven-haired man somewhere between thirty and fifty, who, with his stony face and grey suit, looked just as I had expected a receptionist at the Soviet Embassy to look. His expression did not change in the slightest when we introduced ourselves. He then picked up the internal telephone and relayed a short message in Russian.

We stood waiting for three minutes, until another member of staff, who looked like the first's big brother, appeared. After a brief handshake, he said: 'Please, follow me.'

The atmosphere was not conducive to small talk. We followed him along a dark hallway into a large meeting room with four chairs positioned around a big table set with cake, water and vodka. The member of staff pointed at the two chairs closest to the door, said 'Wait here', and then left the room. So there we sat under a five-foot portrait of the Soviet Union's leader, Leonid Brezhnev. He looked condescendingly down at us, his chest covered in orders and medals.

'Not a promising start,' I said to my boss in a hushed voice, once we were alone in the room. He instantly raised a warning finger to his mouth. I realized my mistake and showed my palms in acknowledgement. There was no reason to believe that the room was not bugged.

Just then, there was a light knock on the door. This preempted a pleasant surprise. In walked a dark-haired, slim and attractive woman in her twenties.

She gave us a timid little smile, shook our hands with an unexpected firmness, and said in perfect Norwegian: 'Welcome. My name is Tatiana Rodionova and I will be the interpreter for your meeting with the vice-ambassador, Igor Sokolov. The vice-ambassador is unfortunately currently caught up in another important meeting, but should be here shortly.'

I was instantly charmed and I remarked that she spoke impressively good Norwegian.

Her smile widened and she replied: 'Thank you, it is a very interesting and beautiful language. I have a PhD from Moscow University. I have only been here for three months, but have given some guest lectures in Russian and been to a few lectures in Norwegian at the university here in Oslo.'

It all started so promisingly. But that all changed when the door opened again, this time without a warning knock. It then slammed closed behind a six-foot-five bald man in his fifties wearing a double-breasted black suit and patent leather shoes. He was the tallest man I had ever met, as far as I could remember, and possibly also one of the heaviest. His build and body language made me feel as though I was standing in front of the great Russian bear, a feeling that was in no way diminished by his unusually powerful handshake.

Vice-Ambassador Igor Sokolov's arrival changed the atmosphere in the room completely. All of a sudden my boss and the interpreter were serious and focused. Sokolov spoke fast and in bursts like a machine gun. The interpreter's voice was flat and serious as she translated.

'The vice-ambassador would like to welcome you and he thanks you for coming at such short notice. The embassy is aware that the investigation into the tragic murder of a leading Norwegian politician, Mr Per Johan Fredriksen, is still ongoing. This is of course an internal, Norwegian case in which the embassy does not wish to become involved.

The embassy is, however, concerned that one of the biggest Norwegian newspapers is planning to make public some unfounded rumours that Fredriksen had improper contact with the embassy here and that this may have been the reason why he was killed.'

This was unexpected. My boss and I exchanged a swift glance, without becoming any the wiser. It was unnerving that the Soviet Embassy had better knowledge than we did of what the Norwegian media planned to write about an ongoing criminal investigation. But more than anything, it would be very uncomfortable for us if such speculations were published in the newspapers.

The vice-ambassador did not give us long to think before unleashing a new volley of verbal gunfire.

'Normally, the ambassador would have taken the matter very seriously, but given the timing, he now finds it particularly pressing. We cannot see any explanation other than that enemies of the Soviet state, by means of these evil rumours, are attempting to block an agreement that is of great national importance to the Norwegian state as well.'

The vice-ambassador's face was grim, the voice of the translator staccato, and I myself thoughtful. I looked over at my boss. He coughed and said: 'We were not aware that some of the press were planning to publish such reports. We have a free press in Norway that cannot be overruled by the police or politicians. What does the embassy wish us to do?'

The response was rapid. 'We want the *Verdens Gang* newspaper to be given the necessary instructions to stop that report being published tomorrow. Alternatively, as soon as the reports are published, the press and politicians could be informed immediately that the reports are completely unfounded. Unless, of course, the police are sitting on evidence that gives grounds for such suspicions. In which case, the embassy should have been contacted long ago in order to clear up any misunderstandings and to disprove such allegations.'

The situation felt more and more tense. We had no evidence to give the embassy, but equally could not rule out any contact. My boss looked at me questioningly. It felt like I was jumping into an ice-cold lake when I took the plunge and started to speak.

'In an open democracy such as Norway, the police cannot instruct the free press on what they can and cannot write. We will of course follow all press coverage closely and assess the need to make a statement, should any of the reports tomorrow be misleading with regard to the situation. We do not believe that the murder of Fredriksen was in any way linked to the Soviet Union. The problem is that in a constitutional state such as Norway it is difficult for the police to make a categorical statement about who has not committed a crime as long as the investigation is ongoing and we have not arrested anyone for the murder.'

I felt my pulse rising as the interpreter translated my answer into Russian, in a slightly less staccato voice. Behind his iron mask, Igor Sokolov was clearly either very well prepared or a very intelligent man. He replied within seconds of the interpreter finishing her translation.

'The vice-ambassador finds it surprising that it is difficult to make such a statement, unless the police themselves also doubt the Soviet state's good intentions. He is also surprised that the investigation has not yet resulted in an arrest almost one week after the murder.'

I looked at my boss, and when he did not answer, did so myself.

'The police do not, of course, doubt the Soviet state's intentions in any way, but the investigation is complex and we are duty-bound to keep all possibilities open. As I said, we will assess the need for a statement as soon as we see what is in the papers tomorrow morning. There are a couple of things that we think may have contributed to these rumours, which, now that we are here, it seems natural to raise. The first is that, on several occasions, Fredriksen was seen having long conversations with representatives from the embassy.'

I looked at my boss as I spoke, and to my huge relief, he nodded in agreement. I hoped, while I waited for the interpreter to finish, that my boss would think the same about my second reason.

Again, we did not have to wait long for the vice-ambassador's reply.

'The vice-ambassador is adamant that there has been no improper contact. Various representatives from the embassy participate, as part of their work to build a friendly relationship between our countries, in a large number of arrangements and talk to various people in this connection. It is perfectly natural that Fredriksen may have spoken to a number of them. To be on the safe side, we have checked with all our employees and can assure you that none of them have had anything other than short, fortuitous meetings with Fredriksen. We are not frightened to call anyone who claims otherwise a liar.'

The vice-ambassador was playing high stakes and spoke even faster than before. I thought I saw a hint of fear in the interpreter's eyes when she said the latter, and hoped that she did not think the same about me. In the midst of it all, I was suddenly very impressed by the interpreter. It could not be easy to interpret such a fast-paced and intense conversation simultaneously – and her Norwegian was almost perfect.

I looked at my boss for a last time, and then turned back to the vice-ambassador. I felt a little frightened, but also rather angry. So I threw caution to the wind and my only trump card down onto the table.

'The other thing that may have given rise to these unfounded suspicions is that a person with connections to the embassy has on several occasions appeared in my vicinity at various places linked to the investigation. This man is called Sergey Klinkalski, but we have reason to believe that his real name is Alexander Svasnikov.'

I quickly glanced sideways at my boss as I spoke. To my relief, he was calm. I did not dare take a breath while I waited for the answer. That was not the only reason the interpreter paused for a beat before she started to translate this time, I thought to myself.

As she spoke, the vice-ambassador's face tightened. For the first time, he was quiet for a few seconds before answering. But his words were all the more rapid and hard as they broke the tense silence.

Then he jumped up and left the room – without shaking

our hands or waiting for the translation. The interpreter held her mask, but there was a tremor in her voice when she relayed the translation after the door had slammed shut behind her.

'The vice-ambassador has every reason to believe that it is purely a matter of unfortunate coincidence. He finds it hard to understand how this should give rise to unfounded suspicions, unless journalists have also been following the head of investigation, or unless the police themselves have informed the press. However, the vice-ambassador takes the matter very seriously and will immediately double-check this new information with Comrade Klinkalski. The vice-ambassador hopes that the investigation will soon have some results and urges the head of investigation to consider measures against the press if unfounded rumours are published in the papers tomorrow. Above all, it is hoped that this does not cause any problems for the pending agreement, and the embassy will do everything in its power to prevent this from happening.'

These final words almost sounded like a threat to me. The interpreter's voice trembled a little as she said them. Then she stood up and closed the meeting by quickly shaking us both by the hand. Her hand was dry and trembled in mine. I smiled at her and got a fleeting smile in return. But before I could say any more than 'goodbye', she had turned and left the room.

My boss and I sat there and looked at each other, without wanting to say anything in the room under the eyes of Brezhnev. We did not have to wait long. Two minutes later the door was opened again.

The interpreter came back in, dressed in a thin red jacket, and said: 'I will show you out.'

We followed her obediently through the corridors. She passed through reception with quick steps and carried on out onto Drammen Road and then a couple of blocks more before turning down a side street. I watched her go. She was dressed in thin clothes and wasn't wearing anything on her head, and looked so small and wet in the early spring evening rain. The interpreter had certainly charmed me and I hoped that she was happy, despite what was obviously a demanding job.

XII

We did not say a word until we were in the car and the engine was running. My boss's first sentence came as a relief: 'The prime minister was right about this being a very difficult situation. You handled it extremely well.'

I exhaled carefully, but felt anything but relaxed.

'Thank you. I don't think there was much more we could do in there. But what do we do now?'

My boss thought for a few seconds, and his voice was just as steady and solid as usual when he replied.

'I will write a strictly confidential memorandum to the prime minister's office about the meeting. Then I will draft a press release that we can send out if the papers print the reports we expect them to. You carry on with the investigation as planned. And we can assess the need for more resources first thing tomorrow morning. The contents of the press release will say something to the effect that while we do not suspect any foreigners to be involved or that the murder is connected to other countries, as the investigation is still ongoing, we have to keep all possibilities open.'

I replied just as we swung into the main police station: 'I agree. But the whole thing does feel a bit like an iceberg: there is still an awful lot of it underwater and we can only guess the size of it.'

'A good image. There is definitely something big and cold just under the surface. And I think it could be dangerous. I only hope that it is not dangerous for you.'

My boss had always shown me great trust in his taciturn and efficient way, and I had always appreciated it. Our drive back from the embassy was short and we only said a few sentences, but it felt somehow as though we were closer. At the same time, it felt as though we had never been faced with a more puzzling case – or a more demanding situation.

XIII

My boss quickly disappeared into his office after we got back. And I was unexpectedly stopped by DI Danielsen just as I was about to go into mine.

'There you are at last, Kristiansen. I won't stick my nose into the investigation by asking where you have been, but I received an urgent telephone call for you half an hour ago, and I promised to give you the message as soon as you were back.'

I was naturally curious to know who had called and for

a moment glimpsed the possibility of a solution. However, the answer was more like a cold shower.

'Miriam Filtvedt Bentsen – who is your fiancée, if I remember rightly. It was a short message: there is something that she has to talk to you about in person as soon as possible. She was clearly frustrated when I told her you were not here and I did not know where you were. She asked me to tell you that she will come to your flat at seven, and it is very important that you are there.'

It was another punch in what was already a difficult situation.

Miriam was very concerned about keeping as low a profile at my workplace as possible and had never left a telephone message before. She was also well aware that I did not particularly like Danielsen and had herself not formed a very good opinion of him when they had met briefly during a previous investigation. So the fact that she had left a message with him was surprising enough in itself. The content of the message made it even more unsettling. The ominous possibility that she might have heard that I had been in contact with Patricia again crossed my mind.

For a few moments, I forgot the murder mysteries, the suspicions of espionage and worry about tomorrow's headlines. My mind and body froze.

Far off in the distance I heard Danielsen's voice say: 'She sounded very agitated. But of course I did not ask what it was about, as I presumed it was of a personal nature.'

The words were friendly, as was the voice, but I detected a forced kindness that left a bad taste in my mouth – which was only made worse by the pat he gave me on the shoulder.

Danielsen worked hard, and as far as anyone in the station knew, had not had a girlfriend since the mid-sixties. He was well known for his quiet schadenfreude when things were not going well in his colleagues' relationships.

I said that it was probably personal, but there was no need to worry. I could tell by Danielsen's smile that he did not believe me, which I could understand, as I did not entirely believe it myself. But whatever the case, I could not bear to see or hear any more of Danielsen right now. So I thanked him for the message, and with a stiff smile, wished him a pleasant evening shift before slipping quickly into my office.

The wall clock showed thirty-three minutes past six. I grabbed the phone and called the halls of residence. But the phone was not answered by Miriam or anyone else. I called the number twice and let it ring for a long time, without it making any difference.

So I rang Patricia instead. She answered on the second ring. It felt good to hear her familiar voice, even though all she said was: 'Yes, it's me.'

So I quickly said that there was a good deal of new information, but we were still not any closer to solving the case. I still had a lot to do, so I did not know when I might be able to call her or drop by.

She said with a degree of tension in her voice that she would try to be available for me for the next couple of hours, wished me luck, and hung up.

It was now nearly twenty to seven. I hurried out of my office and then out of the station. I was very unsure of what was about to happen, but one thing was clear and that was that under no circumstances could I not be home by seven o'clock this evening.

XIV

I opened the door to the flat at five to seven. It was dark, quiet and empty. I was glad to be home first this time, but there was still something unnerving about the darkness.

Without a thought for the electricity bill, I turned on the lights in all the rooms. Then I went and stood by the window and looked down the road.

As I stood there, I did not doubt for a moment that Miriam would come. She was sometimes a couple of minutes later than agreed, when the bus was delayed, or she had missed the one she planned to take. But she had never not come as agreed. And I was convinced that she would come on time today given that she had suggested the time herself.

With every minute that passed I became increasingly worried about what Miriam would have to say when she came. I had only one cause for guilt and one secret from her, but it felt heavier and more treacherous by the second.

It seemed to me that the most likely explanation was that Miriam had somehow found out about my renewed contact with Patricia. In which case, no matter how well I now knew Miriam, I was not sure at all how she would react. Anything seemed possible, from her pulling a face and accepting that it was necessary, to her threatening to break off the engagement. Of course, I hoped that her reaction would be closer to the first, but had a horrible feeling that it might be the latter. I regretted more and more as the minutes passed and Miriam did not appear that I had not told her myself that I had been in touch with Patricia.

The minutes dragged by as I stood there alone with all my doubts and fears. The buses ran more frequently at this time of day, but delays were more often the rule than the exception. Thus it was almost impossible to guess when Miriam would come.

At two minutes to seven, I still believed she would be on time. But the clock crept up to the hour, without her appearing out of the dark.

One and a half minutes later there was a movement down on the street, but to my disappointment, it turned out to be an elderly lady from the neighbourhood walking her dog. My anxiety increased when another movement at three minutes past seven proved to be an old neighbour. I followed him with my eyes until he let himself in the front door. Miriam was still nowhere to be seen when I looked up again. I could feel my pulse racing.

At six minutes past seven, I tried another tactic. I moved away from the window and crossed the room to the telephone. It looked just as it always had and did not make a sound. I thought that it was strange that Miriam had not phoned if she knew she was going to be late, but of course she might have tried before I got home. I went back to my post by the window, with the intense wish that Miriam would now be in view.

She was not. There was not a living soul to be seen on the dark evening street.

Then I started to get annoyed that Miriam, having summoned me for seven o'clock, had not bothered to come on time herself. But this soon spilled over into fear. I felt painfully convinced that Miriam had tried to get here on time, but something out there in the dark had prevented her. The bus could have broken down, or something else equally undramatic, but as the minutes passed, I thought such an everyday occurrence was less and less likely. A numbing fear that something had happened to my fiancée overwhelmed me.

At twelve minutes past seven, I could not bear to stand by the window doing nothing any longer. I had to do something. I went over to the telephone again and with a trembling finger dialled the number of the halls of residence.

The telephone was answered by a happy-sounding voice that I recognized. It belonged to Katrine Rudolfsen, a very nice, if dialectically challenged, friend of Miriam's who had the room next door to hers.

I did not want to worry Katrine unnecessarily, and tried to sound as calm as possible, but I thought I could feel a slight tremor in my voice as I said: 'Hello, this is Kolbjørn Kristiansen. Is Miriam there?'

There was a few seconds' silence before Katrine answered. And when she did, I became absolutely convinced that something serious had happened. It was not only what she said, but her voice as well.

'No, but is she not there? How strange. I met Miriam rushing out when I came back from university about three quarters of an hour ago. I asked where she was going as we passed, and she said she was going to yours and might be out all evening. It's a bit strange that she wouldn't be there yet . . .'

Katrine's voice sounded frightened. I said that she might have got delayed en route to mine, but that it was rather odd. If Miriam had left three quarters of an hour ago, she should have been here by now.

I asked Katrine to stay on the line, put down the receiver and went over to the window again. I thought it looked even darker out there than before, but could still see no one there.

So I went back to the telephone and said to Katrine that I would wait for another five minutes before driving up to the halls of residence.

I waited by the window for three minutes. Then I ran out, crossed the empty square outside the building, and got into my car.

XV

Katrine was waiting and opened the door as soon as I rang the bell, but she shook her head clumsily before I had a chance to ask anything. Miriam had neither come back nor phoned.

I suggested that, given the situation, we should perhaps look in her room to see if we could find any clues. I did not have a key, but knew that Katrine did. She said that she already had, but had not found anything that might help explain. And nor did I when I made a quick inspection.

A pad with notes from her lectures was on the desk, but it only served to confirm that Miriam had been to the morning lecture on Norwegian language history. Beside it was a pile of novels and course books. There was nothing else lying around, and nothing was missing, as far as I could see. Her school satchel, which she had had since primary school and to which she was so charmingly and childishly attached, was standing on the floor by the desk.

It had been cloudy but dry when Miriam had left. According to Katrine she was wearing her green raincoat and was carrying the thick blue book as well as a large white envelope, but no bags or anything to indicate that she was intending to go any further than mine.

I said we should go out and see if we could find any clues on the way to the bus. Katrine nodded silently and turned towards the front door.

There was a light wind outside and it was now drizzling. Katrine's long blonde hair was caught by the wind and her slim body was shaking. We said nothing, just walked in silent concentration along the well-known path to the bus stop, which was about two hundred yards away. Miriam had walked here a thousand times, often reading as she walked. There was no possibility whatsoever that she had got lost, despite her hopeless sense of direction.

Katrine and I walked slowly and kept our eyes open for anything unusual. We got to the main road without seeing anything out of the ordinary. And there was nothing of interest in the first few yards along the pavement.

It was just as we rounded the bend, barely thirty yards

from the bus stop, that Katrine suddenly grabbed my arm and shouted: 'Look! There! In the ditch!'

I felt how violently her hand was shaking on my arm, and wondered if I might see Miriam lying dead in the earth when I turned around. I stood paralysed by fear for a few moments before I could see anything at all.

Miriam was still nowhere to be seen, either alive or dead. But I knew what Katrine meant straightaway. And this confirmed beyond all doubt that something terrible must have happened.

At the bottom of the ditch, between two stones, in a small puddle of water, lay the thick blue book with a library bookshelf reference on the spine.

I stepped down into the ditch and carefully picked up the book. I had recognized it as soon as I saw it. And there was only one possible explanation as to how it had ended up here. It was unthinkable that Miriam had thrown the library book down or dropped it and walked on without noticing.

'Someone has kidnapped Miriam,' I heard myself saying. It sounded so calm and controlled but I felt anything but. In fact, it felt more like I was standing in the middle of an earthquake, my head full of chaos and the ground shaking under my feet.

I heard a faint sobbing beside me and realized that it must be Katrine. Then I heard my own voice saying that I would accompany her back to the halls of residence. I then asked her to stay put and not to panic, and I would inform the police at the station.

XVI

I was back at the station by ten to eight. My boss had been on his way home when I arrived, but immediately turned around without protest when I told him that something very serious had happened.

I stopped and thought for a moment outside my office door. Then without being able to explain why, I went over to Danielsen's office and asked him to come in too. It somehow felt safer to have more people to talk to. Danielsen was the one who had taken the telephone call from Miriam. And as soon as I saw him I realized that he could have been the last person to have spoken to her alive.

Danielsen looked a little surprised, but got up as soon as I said I would like him to come to an important meeting.

We sat round the table in my office and I told them in short what had happened. A heavy silence descended in the room. My boss's face did not so much as twitch.

For the first time, I felt a good deal of support from Danielsen. 'How terrible if criminals have started to kidnap policemen's nearest and dearest,' he said with unexpected feeling.

We both looked at the boss, who hesitated for a while at first and then spoke very slowly and deliberately.

'This is a very difficult situation, for several reasons. Normally, we would not start a search when someone has only been missing for a couple of hours, and it could well provoke unfavourable reactions if it becomes known that we have done so in the case of a leading policeman's fiancée.

But the circumstances undeniably give us reason to fear the worst . . .'

He stopped talking. Then he asked, in a quieter voice: 'Has she shown any signs of depression or other illness recently? I am sorry that I have to ask, but desperate young women have done stranger things than throw away books in a ditch before committing suicide.'

For a moment I wondered if Miriam would really have been that desperate if she had heard that I had been to see Patricia. And if, then, I could live with that. But again I found it unthinkable that she would do anything like that. So I replied, in a firm and controlled manner, that Miriam had not shown any signs of being mentally unbalanced, and had to the contrary been happy and full of life in the past few days. And even though I had been working long hours, we had not had any arguments.

My boss and I now both looked at Danielsen. 'That was more or less how she sounded on the telephone. It was a short conversation and she seemed full of life, if a little agitated, but in no way desperate or depressed,' he said, to the point.

My boss nodded. 'Then we shall consider this to be exceptional circumstances and start an investigation immediately without raising the alarm publicly quite yet. Kristiansen, you continue with your own investigation as before. Danielsen will lead the investigation into Miriam's disappearance. We can discuss the matter again in the morning and update each other as and when necessary.'

I was too exhausted, too scared and too bewildered to

protest. So we both said in short that we agreed. Then my boss stood up and left.

I wrote down the necessary facts, and the names and addresses of family and friends for Danielsen. I said that there was probably not much to be found where the book had fallen or at the halls of residence, but that the places should of course be searched. Then I asked him to pass on my sympathies to Miriam's parents and to be gentle in his dealings with them.

He promised to do this. We shook each other almost warmly by the hand before he left.

Once I was alone in the office, I sat there looking at the telephone for a few seconds. My head was in turmoil. I could only remember two telephone numbers. One was Miriam's number at the halls of residence. The other was Patricia's. And I thought that no matter how strange it felt, there was no one other than Patricia I could turn to for help in finding my Miriam.

She picked up the telephone on the second ring, and with unusual calm, said: 'What has happened? Are you all right?'

Her concern for me was heart-warming in the situation. I quickly replied: 'Someone has kidnapped Miriam.'

There was silence on the other end for a few tense seconds. Then Patricia said: 'Goodness, what on earth do they want with her?'

I felt anger bubbling up, before I realized that the question would actually be decisive in our search for the kidnappers. Patricia also pulled herself together, and hastily added: 'I mean, either it must be because she has discovered something important herself, or to have some kind of leverage over you. I sincerely hope that it is the latter.'

Without thinking, I asked why she hoped this. The answer was like being punched in the stomach.

'Because that would increase the chances that your fiancée is still alive.'

I was completely unable to think clearly about what might be the most likely reasons for the kidnapping. I said to Patricia that I had to see her. She replied that I was welcome any time.

XVII

When I entered Patricia's library, I realized that the table was empty. It was something I had never experienced before. Patricia had a packet of cigarettes in her hand, but there was not even a cup of coffee on the table. She said that if I would like anything to eat or drink, I just had to say, and I told her that I could not even face the thought at the moment.

I sat down and told her about the last few hours and Miriam's disappearance.

Patricia seemed to be unusually unsettled by the situation. She lit a cigarette after only a few minutes and I saw that her hand was shaking. Even though the room was smoky and warm, she was still shivering. This made me even more anxious, but I was also touched by Patricia's concern for Miriam.

'There really are not many leads here,' Patricia said, with a heavy sigh when I had finished.

I had to agree. Practically anyone could, in theory, have driven past and bundled Miriam into a car – especially if she was, as usual, reading as she walked. All that was needed was two people and a car. Another possibility was even more terrible: one person in a car could have stopped, shot her and then taken the body to conceal the crime.

'Unfortunately, I think it is more likely that Miriam has been kidnapped in an attempt to render her harmless because she knows too much, rather than as possible leverage against you,' Patricia then said, gently.

She carried on quickly before I had time to ask why she thought so.

'Partly because kidnapping in order to exert pressure of some kind on a police officer would be tricky and entail a greater risk for the perpetrator. But it is also the matter of the book.'

It was beyond my understanding how she could deduce that from the book, and I was not in the mood to guess. So I asked what she meant. I added that the book was about languages and that Miriam had had it with her the day before as well.

'Exactly. But according to what you said, she only had fifty pages left to read the day before. It would take me no more than half an hour to read them, and I would be surprised if your fiancée was any slower. So if she still had not finished the book, she must have spent a lot of time thinking or doing something else in the meantime. And I would dearly like to know what it was she did instead, as it could be crucial. Do we know anything about her day, before she disappeared?'

I said the same to Patricia that I had to Danielsen: we knew what Miriam had planned to do, but not necessarily what she had actually done. Miriam was going to go to a lecture from a quarter past ten to twelve, as she normally did on a Thursday. She would then go to the library until about three o'clock, before spending a couple of hours at the party office. Danielsen had no doubt started to map out what she had actually done.

'Excellent. Let me know as soon as you have any more information. Otherwise, I wonder what was in the envelope she was carrying. That could also be crucial. There was no sign of that?'

I shook my head. Patricia sighed again.

'Well, it is certainly clear that we cannot expect help from any quarter in this case. Let me know as soon as there is any news on what your fiancée did today or about the envelope. In the meantime, please tell me what you did earlier on this afternoon, as the investigation and kidnapping may well be related.'

It felt good to talk about something else, so I told her without further delay.

Patricia smoked in silence, but nodded with a little smile when I told her about my meeting with Solveig Ramdal. She did not look happy, however, and waved me impatiently on when I told her about my disastrous meeting with the lawyer Rønning and Lene Johansen. Then she listened attentively when I told her about the meetings at the prime minister's office and the Soviet Embassy.

'It could be a coincidence, but has it struck you that one

333

of the key parties in the Fredriksen case lives near Sogn halls of residence?' I asked.

Patricia had clearly thought about this too. She nodded quickly, but opened her hands at the same time.

'Johan Fredriksen lives at Sognsvann, yes. It must be a coincidence. Even though he is about to become a very rich man, following the deaths of his father and sister, it is hard to imagine that he would have a motive for kidnapping your fiancée, and that he would have the resources to do so. Kidnapping for the purposes of extortion would be both complicated and risky for him and anyone else in the family or group of friends from 1932. Most likely they would all need help in order to do it, and they would be in great danger of being caught sooner or later. I think rather that Miriam has been kidnapped because she knew too much, about something significant that has happened or is about to happen. In which case, one might start to think in a different direction . . .'

'To the East, you mean?' I said.

Patricia nodded gravely and stubbed out her cigarette. 'The Soviets have the resources and a possible motive linked to the oil agreement. And even more worryingly, they currently also have a man in Oslo who has killed before. But if it was them, it will not be easy to prove. The big question is how Miriam might have discovered something important in that connection? Did she know about that side of the case?'

My throat tightened, but I managed first to nod, and then to regain my voice. It all fitted uncomfortably well. Miriam had heard about the case from me the evening before – and had been visibly shaken.

Patricia looked as though she wanted to say something. But instead she finished another cigarette, stubbed it out and said: 'I think that is where the answer lies, but we do not have enough information yet to make the connection. Think about it, and get in touch as soon as there is anything new. I will be up first thing and waiting. And in the meantime, know that I am thinking about you. This must be an extremely difficult situation for you.'

I was once again touched by Patricia's concern – and told her so. We hugged each other affectionately and then I left.

XVIII

It was quite a shock to be outside. The rain was heavier and felt cold on my face and head. I thought about how hard it would be to find clues at the spot where Miriam had been taken, if there were any. I suddenly realized how hungry I was.

I could not face going home, and even less making food. So I stopped at a cafe in Frogner that was still open and had a steak alone at a table in one of the darker corners of the cafe. It helped to ease my hunger, but not the feelings of fear and restlessness in the rest of my body.

At ten o'clock I finally went home. There was a brief glimmer of hope when I saw that the light was on in my flat. I ran up the stairs with a thumping heart. But my hope was soon snuffed out. The flat was quiet and empty and there was no sign that Miriam had been there. I had obviously just forgotten to turn off the light when I ran out.

The telephone rang as I sat there, and I answered in the wild hope that I would hear Miriam's voice. But it was her mother's broader Hedemark dialect that I heard at the other end. She asked how I was – and if there was any news of Miriam. I was deeply touched by the fact that she had thought of me in the middle of all this, and said so. But sadly I could not tell her anything about Miriam other than that an investigation had started and we hoped for good news, but everything was very uncertain.

She wondered if they should perhaps come to Oslo. I told her that there was not much they could do here at present, and it was perhaps best to stay where they were – in case Miriam or anyone else contacted her family home. She replied that that was a good idea and that they would hold the fort at home, but added that they were ready to come to the capital straightaway if they could be of any help.

I promised to ring her as soon as there was any news. We quickly agreed that the phone line should be kept open in case Miriam or anyone else tried to call. And then I was alone again in the world.

I stood by the window and looked out at the empty street. I had seen Miriam walking up here in her green raincoat many a time. I could just picture her. But she was not there now. There was no one to be seen at this time of evening.

Having stood there for a few minutes, I suddenly felt absolutely certain that I would never see Miriam walking up towards the house again. At the same time, I felt certain that she was alive, somewhere out in the rain and darkness, only

I did not know who was holding her prisoner, or where – or how to find out.

At ten to eleven, the phone was still silent, the darkness just as dark and I was still just as restless. I did not know what to do with myself. But I knew that I had to do something. So I went out, got into the car and drove back to the station.

XIX

Danielsen was sitting in his office with the door open and jumped up when he saw me.

'Any news?' he asked.

I shook my head and said that I had neither seen nor heard anything from Miriam. I mentioned Patricia's theory about the book, which could indicate that she had been preoccupied, and asked if he had found out what she had done during the day.

He nodded quickly.

'There was not much information to be had from the halls of residence. But I did talk to a librarian on the telephone who knew your fiancée by sight. Miriam had come to the library a bit later than usual after the lecture, around half past twelve or oneish. Then she had sat and read some books that were still lying at her place. But the librarian thought she seemed restless, and thinks she left around half past two. They had not seen her at the SPP party office. So we know where she was until around half past two, but not where she was in those few hours until she called here.'

I thanked him for the information. Then I went to my office to telephone Patricia with the latest news on Miriam's movements.

The telephone at Frogner was not answered. In my nervous state, I was taken aback by this, but then remembered that she had promised to get up early the next day and was probably asleep.

There was no more to be done at the station. I was still agitated and anything but tired, so I drove up to the student halls of residence.

This detour to the halls of residence was basically an emotional whim. I did not believe that I would find any evidence that Danielsen and the others had not found. But I did think that I might find inspiration if I went there again. And that I should talk to Katrine again.

Katrine opened the door as soon as I rang the bell, but only shook her head when she saw me. She had been sitting up and could not think about anything other than Miriam and what might have happened to her.

'But something odd did happen,' she said. 'The phone in the hall rang at around ten o'clock, but I didn't manage to answer in time. And then it rang again, but the voice only said "Miriam" – and then the person hung up when I said she wasn't here. Perhaps I shouldn't have said that, but it was so unexpected.'

I told her that it was fine, especially in a situation where Miriam's disappearance was not yet an official case. The telephone call could of course have nothing to do with her disappearance. I asked Katrine all the same if she could say any more about the voice on the phone. She took her time and then said that it was not easy, as the person had only said one word. But she was fairly sure that it was a woman and someone she did not know.

I thanked her and once more promised to let her know as soon as there was any news of Miriam. Katrine said again how worried she was and assured me that she would stay where she was until the situation was clarified. I could see that she was close to tears and I so desperately wanted to say something that might comfort her, but I had nothing to say.

So I left and walked the route down to the bus stop alone this time. I could imagine Miriam, in her old green raincoat with the thick blue book, as though she was there in front of me. But this inspired no new ideas of what might have happened, even when I passed the spot where we had found the book in the ditch.

It was now nearly half past eleven, the road was dark and there was no one to be seen. I stood there alone at the edge of the road for a couple of minutes and looked up at the stars above. In that moment I wondered if there was a God or anyone else out there somewhere who knew what had happened.

As I stood there, I heard a car coming down the road and turned to look, to make sure that it did not hit me. It was a large car, possibly a van of sorts, but I was not able to see it in detail in the dark. I could make out the shadows of two people in the front and guessed that the large figure behind the wheel was a man and the smaller one in the passenger seat was a woman.

Just as the car passed, I caught a glimpse of the face of

the person in the passenger seat. It was close enough to see, just as I lost my footing and fell into the ditch myself.

The passenger in the car was Patricia.

She was looking straight ahead and did not see me there by the side of the road in the dark. It looked as though she was talking to the person beside her, because her mouth was moving. Her expression was tense and grim, almost angry.

I stood there staring after the car until it disappeared into the dark – in the direction of Frogner. I suddenly felt more alone than I'd ever felt before. Miriam had been kidnapped and I no longer knew if I could trust Patricia.

I stood there for a few minutes more before walking unsteadily back to the car and driving home. It felt like the air was freezing, even though the rain was still pouring down.

XX

As I walked up the stairs, I thought about how happy I would be if Miriam was now sitting in her usual place on the sofa. I would shout with joy, carry her around the flat like a trophy and never let her out of my sight again. But I knew there was no hope. I had seen that the flat was dark. And when I opened the door, I saw straightaway that the sofa was just as empty as when I had left the flat.

Just then the telephone started to ring. I rushed across the room, grabbed the receiver, but all I heard was the dialling tone. Everything felt jinxed that day.

I stood there for a couple of minutes wondering who

might have called, but the possibilities were endless. It struck me as odd that someone had tried to ring me so late, which is perhaps why they did not wait long and I thought in particular of the telephones at the halls of residence. It was probably just a journalist or someone else who knew as little about the kidnapping as I did.

I did not want to sit down on the sofa. So instead I sat down on the chair opposite and reflected on what a terrible day it had been. The night before I had felt stressed enough, but that was nothing compared to the fear I now felt. Yesterday evening Miriam had been sitting here with me, and I had trusted Patricia one hundred per cent. Now I no longer knew what to believe about Patricia and I had no idea where on earth Miriam was – if she was still alive.

I had stood here alone and feared for Miriam's life once before, in connection with an earlier investigation. But then at least I knew where she was, what state she was in, and that she would have the best help she could get at the hospital. And I had known that the situation would be clearer the following day.

Now I did not know where Miriam was or how she was, and had no reason to believe that she was with anyone who wished her well. But the worst thing was the uncertainty. The thought that I might never know what had happened was petrifying.

As I sat there, I understood better than ever before the problems that some people, whom I had met in connection with other murder investigations, had with simply getting on with their lives after a dramatic event. Suddenly I thought of Hauk Rebne Westgaard, who had had to live with the pain of losing his girlfriend, and who had not been able to touch anyone else since. I at least had hope, something that he had never had. Miriam might come back unharmed and healthy. But I had less and less faith in that happening. It felt far more likely that I myself would have to live as a human fly – without Miriam, but with the constant doubt and feelings of guilt.

I went to bed at midnight – not because I was tired, but because I could not stand being awake alone any longer. And I hoped that tomorrow would be a better day – it could hardly be much worse – and that it would come sooner if I went to bed.

I couldn't bring myself to believe that Patricia had anything to do with the kidnapping. But I did not dare to rule it out completely, and came to the conclusion that I would have to confront her with the fact that I had seen her. It did cross my mind that she might have gone there to look at the scene of the crime, even though it would be very unlike her and I could not imagine what she would achieve by doing so. But then the car she was in had passed the scene of the crime at quite a speed and she had not even taken a sideways glance.

It was quite simply a mystery, what Patricia had been doing there and who had been in the car with her. I wondered if she might in fact be a chameleon person herself, with a dangerous side that I had never experienced. I recalled Solveig Ramdal's words about self-preservation being the driving force for all people in critical situations. And I asked myself if Patricia had pointed to the Soviet lead in a bid to divert attention.

I fell asleep eventually around one o'clock in the morning, but the night that followed was as restless and horrible as the day had been. I woke up and fell asleep again three times between nightmares. Each time I woke, it was with the dream of Miriam's sleeping face on the pillow beside me, only then to discover to my distress that the pillow was empty. And each time I fell asleep, it was with the image of Patricia's grim and angry face in the car window in my mind.

Another Death and Some Vital Clarification

I

Friday, 24 March 1972 was one of the rare days when I was woken by the telephone, not the alarm clock. It rang at ten past seven. I was instantly wide awake and ran in my underwear out of the bedroom into the living room. I managed to get to the telephone in time, but this only led to disappointment.

I heard the voice of a *Dagbladet* journalist on the other end, who wondered if I could confirm or preferably deny the headlines in *VG*.

I replied that unfortunately I could not comment in the light of the ongoing investigation. Then I hung up – and told myself that it was going to be another long and demanding day. This feeling was reinforced when *Aftenposten* then called fifteen minutes later, for the same reason as *Dagbladet*.

Verdens Gang was not out yet, but according to its competitors, the whole of the front page was going to be covered by a large photograph of Per Johan Fredriksen under the headline: 'Murdered top politician may have been spy'.

Verdens Gang had somehow found out that Fredriksen was suspected of being a spy. However, the newspaper had no stronger evidence than that he had several times been seen to have 'shady conversations' with representatives from the Soviet Embassy, and that the police security service had shown 'a very strong interest' in him. It was therefore pertinent to question if this was in any way connected to the murder of Per Johan Fredriksen and perhaps to his daughter's mysterious death a few days later.

In the final paragraph, it was asked if it was right for Norway to enter into an important new agreement with a country that may have assassinated one of its leading politicians, though this was as yet unproven. And the final sentence went as far as to say that the answer should be no.

I wondered for a brief moment what Prime Minister Trond Bratten would think when he read this. Then I thought about how it would be for the remaining members of Per Johan Fredriksen's family to wake to this. At which point I realized that I should perhaps have informed them yesterday evening, and that I should certainly do so now.

Two dry and quickly eaten pieces of bread later, I sat down by the telephone. It was twenty to eight and all three were at home. Johan Fredriksen sounded as though he was not an early bird or was just in a bad mood. I said that we were trying to establish what kind of contact Per Johan Fredriksen might have had with the Soviet Embassy. But we currently had no evidence that he had done anything illegal or that it had anything to do with the deaths.

He thanked me for the information and said that his father and all his various activities had not been on his mind of late. The agreement with Ramdal had been signed yesterday afternoon, and Johan Fredriksen wanted to use the weekend to think about what he was going to do with the inheritance and his life now.

I got the impression that perhaps all was not well between him and his girlfriend, but I saw no reason to plague him further by asking.

Ane Line Fredriksen, not unexpectedly, showed more interest in the spy claims against her father. At first she thought that it must be a mistake, but then ten seconds later said she no longer knew what to think about her father. She had never heard mention of this and it felt like yet another betrayal of the family. Otherwise, she could confirm that the contract with Ramdal had been signed without any fuss the day before. It had been a 'good and rather boring meeting' at Kjell Ramdal's office. I did not find that hard to imagine.

It occurred to me that I should perhaps also mention Miriam's disappearance to Ane Line Fredriksen. I thought that she would be interested. But I doubted whether she could tell me anything that I did not know already: there was nothing to indicate that Miriam's disappearance had anything to do with her work for the SPP. But I guessed that Ane Line Fredriksen would have a lot of questions and I did not feel like talking to her about the matter right now. So I finished the call, saying that I also had to inform her mother.

Oda Fredriksen sounded a little stronger and a little sharper today, even though it was still early. She took the news of the *Verdens Gang* headlines unexpectedly well: 'I have heard so many strange allegations about my husband that nothing shocks me any more.' Then she added hastily: 'But this is by far the worst. It is unthinkable that my husband would have betrayed his country in any way – and even more unthinkable that he would have done something that could have such negative consequences for the family, without first discussing it with me.'

I was not entirely convinced of this. It seemed to me that Oda Fredriksen was almost more upset that her husband had been accused of spying than she had been at the news of her daughter's death. But I took it as a good sign, regardless, that she had rallied.

As I spoke to her, I was suddenly overwhelmed by a sense of loss and concern for Miriam, mixed with a guilty conscience because I had not thought of her until now. So I hastily finished the conversation and promised to contact Oda Fredriksen as soon as there was any news. It was now eight o'clock. I was wide awake and keen to know if there was any news down at the station.

II

I was in the office by a quarter past eight. Danielsen had knocked off at around two o'clock in the morning, but had asked a constable to continue following up on Miriam's disappearance as a matter of urgency. There was, however, not much information to follow up, nor many leads. No tips had come in and it was still a mystery what Miriam had done in those final few hours before she disappeared. Her student room had been searched, but no clues had been found.

My boss was sitting in his office, hard at work, when I knocked on his door. Without waiting, I asked if he had seen today's edition of *Verdens Gang*.

'Seen, read, mulled over and called the prime minister's office about it,' he said, with a very serious face.

'And what did the prime minister say?' I asked.

My boss looked even more serious when he replied.

'That democracy should take its course, but that to ratify the agreement now would be bordering on what could and should be justified in a democratic country. The Government is ready to present the agreement to the Storting at three o'clock, but the parties have been called to group meetings and the prime minister is currently assessing the situation. He asked to be informed immediately if there is any news about Fredriksen's murder or the kidnapping of your fiancée. As I understood it, the vote will be postponed if there is a link to either of them.'

This made the situation no less serious. I looked at the clock and calculated that it was six and a half hours until the vote in the Storting. I said that if there was nothing else to report, I should press on with the investigation into Fredriksen's murder.

When I got back to my office and saw my empty desk, my concern for Miriam and uncertainty regarding Patricia overwhelmed me again. I had to admit that I had no new leads to follow in the Fredriksen case, so I pulled over the telephone and dialled Patricia's number.

She answered on the first ring and asked in her usual voice if there was any news. I told her that there was and that I would like to see her as soon as possible.

'Good. Come as soon as you can,' she said and put the phone down.

I sat there for a few seconds and wondered if I could have made a mistake last night. I had never seen Patricia with an expression like that before. But I had been absolutely certain that it was her I saw driving past me last night. And I still was. I got up and walked with heavy steps out to the car on my way to confront Patricia and ask if she was in fact involved in the case.

III

The maid showed me into the library and then made a hasty retreat. It was perhaps just my imagination, but I thought she seemed a little more tense today and that she left in more of a hurry than usual.

Patricia was sitting in her wheelchair with a packet of cigarettes beside her on the table. Fruit, biscuits, cake and coffee had also been put out.

She asked, in an unusually gentle voice, if I had managed to sleep well and if I had had breakfast. Patricia seemed to be genuinely worried about me. It did not make my job any easier.

'So, what have you got to tell me?' Patricia asked.

First of all, I told her what little we knew about Miriam's movements the day before.

'That is not a lot,' she exclaimed.

Was it just my imagination, or did she avoid looking at me when she said this? I gave myself two seconds, then launched into an attack with a hammering heart.

'What is of particular interest is that you know something about the case that you are hiding from me. And in a critical situation where my fiancée has been kidnapped.'

It felt like diving into icy water. My body and head felt cold and stiff within seconds. But it was another bull's eye. For a fraction of a second, Patricia's face froze into a harder and more egotistical expression. I saw that she too had a predator concealed inside.

For a fleeting moment she reminded me of Solveig Ramdal the day before – a cat caught in a corner. Patricia had no means of escape. She sat there in her wheelchair, with her back to the wall. It only took a moment for her face to return to normal, but her eyes slipped away from mine to look at the bookshelf. And as she looked away, she lit a cigarette with a trembling hand.

'I do not know who has taken your fiancée or where she is, if that is what you mean,' she said, finally.

'That is not necessarily what I said. But you are keeping something from me,' I countered, with an edge to my voice.

Patricia sighed. She took a couple of drags on the cigarette, but her breathing was no calmer for it. And she was still looking at the bookshelf.

'I did try to tell you that I should not get involved in the Fredriksen case, in any way. But you insisted,' she said, in an uncharacteristically slow and thin voice. 'How did you find out?' she added, in an even fainter voice.

To tell the truth, I did not know what I had found out, only that I had found something out. And I was becoming increasingly annoyed because on this day of all days, Patricia did not want to tell me what she was hiding.

'I asked you to help me with the Fredriksen case, yes. But I did not ask you to drive past the spot where Miriam disappeared at around half past eleven last night. And now I demand to know why you were there!'

I said Miriam's name on purpose – I had realized that Patricia disliked hearing it intensely. And it worked. She started when I said the name, and her eyes swung back to look at me.

'I see. I sincerely hope that at no point have you suspected me of having anything to do with your girlfriend's disappearance. That is a preposterous idea. I had a very personal reason for driving past there late last night, and hope you will believe that it had nothing whatsoever to do with the kidnapping.'

This was becoming more and more mysterious – and more and more annoying.

I said that my fiancée had been kidnapped, that I wanted to believe that Patricia knew nothing about it, but asked that she now please give me a credible answer as to why she had driven past the scene of the crime last night.

We sat and stared at each other intensely for a few seconds. A bitter expression, similar to the one I had seen through the car window yesterday, passed over Patricia's face. She took a last drag on the cigarette and stubbed it out. Then she put both her elbows on the table and buried her head in her hands for a moment or two.

When she lowered her hands from her face, her expression was one of defiance. 'If you absolutely must know, I was being driven home after having been thoroughly fucked by my, until now, secret boyfriend.'

That was not what I had expected. I sat there like a rabbit in the headlights while she lit another cigarette.

For some reason I had clearly never contemplated the idea that Patricia could have intimate relations with another man. And even now that she had said it, I could not imagine her stretched naked under a man in bed.

And what was worse: I did not like the thought at all. Without having any idea of who her boyfriend was, I immediately felt jealousy, even animosity, towards him. If it was the man who was driving the car yesterday, I had only caught a blurred glimpse of him.

'That is a remarkable coincidence. Where does your secret lover live?'

Patricia sighed and looked at me in exasperation. 'Do you still not understand? It was not a coincidence at all. My until-now-secret boyfriend lives in a terraced house by Sognsvann.'

As soon as she said Sognsvann, I understood. It did not make matters any better. The picture of Patricia in bed with him was even worse than the one of Patricia in bed with some faceless man. And on top of all this confusion was now the fear that someone else might know about my contact with Patricia.

'So the secret boyfriend you have not told me about is Johan Fredriksen?'

She took a long, greedy drag on the cigarette and then stubbed it out, half-smoked.

'Bingo. But Johan of course knows nothing about my contact with you and I have not said a word about what I know about the investigation. I thought, with those parameters, my relationship with him was irrelevant to the case and it would be better for both you and me if you did not know about it.'

I felt paralysed and for a few seconds did not know how to talk or what to say. My mind's eye kept switching between the fully-dressed Patricia sitting in a wheelchair in front of me and the image of a naked Patricia in bed with a naked Johan Fredriksen. And I found this so distasteful that I unsuccessfully tried to shut both images out. But then I only saw the picture I had seen the night before. I was suddenly very curious about Patricia's angry face and what they had been talking about.

Just then, she started to speak again, without waiting for any questions.

'He is not exactly a dream prince, I know. A little too clumsy, a little too dull, and far too interested in figures and material things. But when you can't stand upright, you can't expect to choose from the top shelf. He is clean and good-looking, quite easy to get on with and reasonably educated. He came to Father's funeral and was very considerate, then sent a Christmas card with a long handwritten message last year and the year before that. I answered the one from last Christmas in January. If you can't have the one you love, then try to love the one you have. Other than your extremely sporadic visits, I have been sitting on my own here since I was fourteen. So I thought it was high time to try something new this year.'

That was another slap in the face. As she spoke, I suddenly saw a third Patricia – a sad, lonely young woman, full of longing. I should have realized before that she existed. And I should definitely have remembered to send her a Christmas card.

Then I thought about Patricia's description of him as good-looking, and how I had been taken aback by how similar Johan Fredriksen looked to me. I wondered for a moment if what Patricia was actually saying now was that I was her dream man – and how I should then deal with that.

'He is attentive and gives me presents and the like, he is always on time when we meet, and he has done his best to get me pregnant. I will give him that.'

Another blow. The thought of Patricia with a husband and children was alien and frightening. I had to admit to myself that I was very jealous now. I spontaneously asked, 'But he has not succeeded, has he?'

To my relief, she shook her head straightaway. Her hand trembled as she lit another cigarette and she appeared to have regained her composure when she carried on speaking, but she did meet my eye.

'No danger there. I have no idea if I can even have children after the accident, but I do know that I can't as long as I take the pill. I want interesting company and sex. He wants sex and all my millions, I think. So we each get half of what we want, which seems pretty fair to me.'

I felt reassured and suddenly did not want to know any more details about her contact with Johan Fredriksen. I said that it sounded perfectly fair and then added: 'I would have had a few less worries if I had known this earlier, but I am grateful for your honesty now and believe what you have told me. I think we can see that little mystery as solved now and get on with the investigation.'

Patricia nodded – with unusual swiftness and enthusiasm.

'Yes, let's do that. You fiancée is still missing and two recent murders are still unsolved. But I am afraid that I cannot help you with much more right now. There are still too many possibilities. But you can rule out Johan Fredriksen as far as the murders of his father and sister go. He was at home, and I was with him. And by the way, I have also tried to be the comforting girlfriend in the hope of getting a bit more information about the case, but he does not seem to know any more than what he has told you already. Which is a good thing. Johan may not be very exciting, but he is pretty honest and honourable. I think he just has one face; not a chameleon person in the slightest. I am in more doubt about how many of the others in his family and the group from 1932 you could say that about. I see the outline of several scenarios more and more clearly, but still lack some important details in order to know which ones are right.'

I realized that we would not get any further here and now, so I stood up and said that I would ring or come back as soon as I had more information.

She said that she would wait, and that I was welcome, no matter what time of day it was.

Given the circumstances, my difficult visit ended on

rather a nice note. She had clearly not thought of visiting her lover today, or of him coming to see her.

On my way out, I found my thoughts were not focused on the investigation, only on what Patricia had just told me. I remembered that Johan Fredriksen had seemed a little grumpy this morning and wondered if I had been right when I thought that perhaps things were not going so well with his secret girlfriend. And then I was filled with a sense of almost childish triumph that Patricia had told me about him, but not him about me.

It was only once I was out on the street in the cold air that I realized that I had not thought about my missing fiancée at all during the second half of my visit to Patricia. This prompted another stab of guilt. It felt as though I had let Miriam down by sitting there talking to Patricia, when she had been kidnapped.

The drive back to the station was unexpectedly slow. I felt myself being pulled in all directions, and was certainly no longer giving the road my full attention.

IV

It was ten to ten when I got back to the office. There was one message waiting for me there. And it was both interesting and ominous. Miriam's mother had called and asked me to ring her as soon as I got back.

The fact was that Miriam's mother had not been able to get hold of me because I was sitting with Patricia. This did nothing to salve my conscience.

I dialled the Lillehammer number straightaway and said: 'I am so sorry, I was out in connection with the investigation and rang as soon as I saw your message. Do you have some news?'

Miriam's mother replied in an even thicker dialect than normal: 'Can I trust that we are speaking in confidence and that it will stay between us?'

I quickly said yes. I was calling on a direct line from my office and assured her that I would not pass on anything she told me if she did not want me to.

'I am sorry that I had to ask, but my only daughter's life is at risk. I got a telephone call this morning just after nine from a woman who said that she knew what had happened and that Miriam was still alive. She also thought she knew who had killed Per Johan Fredriksen. She had called you yesterday evening but did not get an answer, and did not want to ring the police station. I promised her I would ring and ask you to go to meet her alone outside the National Theatre at half past eleven. I did not recognize her voice and I am afraid that I couldn't guess her age or anything like that.'

I thanked her for having called and said that I would of course go. Then I started to think about what she had said. In the meantime, she carried on speaking.

'I feel slightly guilty about asking you to do this. It could possibly just be someone playing with us, or worse, there's a danger that someone is planning to harm you. So you must think hard about what you do. But if you think there is any chance that it can help us get Miriam back alive, we obviously hope that you will take the chance.'

I had not thought of my own safety in all of this. I answered that I thought it was far more likely that this would help us get Miriam back alive than that I would be killed, and that I would go no matter what. If anyone wanted to harm me, there were less risky ways of doing that than asking me to meet them at one of the most public places in town.

Miriam's mother said, in a slightly shaky voice, that she was worried that they would lose me too and that I must decide myself whether I told anyone else in the police or went alone.

I said that I would go alone, but asked her to ring the chief constable and tell him what had happened in the unlikely event that I did not come back.

In a tearful voice, she promised to do so.

It was a serious note on which to end the conversation. I said that I would call her later in the day. She replied that she sincerely hoped so, and that she was very fond of me.

It seemed clear to me, while talking to Miriam's mother, that I should go to the National Theatre alone. But I must confess that it felt a little less clear a few minutes after she had put the phone down.

Two people had been killed in the past week. I had stood on my own with the bodies of two young people. Both experiences had made a considerable impression on me. And earlier in the week I had been followed by a man who ostensibly had killed several people. The thought that I might end up dead myself and that this might be my last day on earth was alarming.

But I could feel my adrenalin rising. This all fitted in with the telephone call to the halls of residence yesterday and the voice that had asked for Miriam. And the fact that it was a woman who rang and not a man felt less dangerous. I was now very curious as to who she was. I knew that I would not be able to live with myself if I did not go, and Miriam was later found dead or not found at all. The thought of living with that was worse even than the thought of dying today. Miriam had been injured for life during one of my previous murder investigations, and now apparently had been kidnapped in connection with this one. It was a responsibility that I could not and would not shirk.

I was never in any doubt that I should or would be there at half past eleven. But I was in doubt as to whether I should tell my boss before I went or not. If I did, I was not sure that he would let me go alone, and then I decided that I would not break my promise to Miriam's mother in what was a desperate situation for her.

By half past ten I had come to the conclusion that I should not go to a meeting of this kind without first telling Patricia. It was unlikely that there would be any negative consequences if she knew, and the chances of getting Miriam back alive were far greater if Patricia could glean more from this than I could.

Patricia answered the telephone after one ring. The fact that she was obviously sitting there waiting triggered a burst of joy in all the darkness and confusion.

I told her in short what had happened and said that I had to go.

There was an unusually long silence. I could not remember Patricia ever having thought for so long when I had called her.

Eventually I said that it was interesting to note that there seemed to be a connection between Per Johan Fredriksen's death and the kidnapping of Miriam.

Patricia answered swiftly: 'That is, strictly speaking, only the case if the woman who rang is telling the truth, and is right. But yes, apart from that, it is very interesting.'

Then there was silence again.

'I do understand, and of course agree, that you must go. But I do not like it one bit,' she said eventually.

I felt a kindness in Patricia's concern for me. Out loud I said that if someone wanted to kill me, this was hardly the way to go about it.

'I don't think that the perpetrators want to kill you, and I agree, I don't think they would do it this way if they did. But I still do not like it because everything is so unclear. But there is no option. So good luck and be careful!' Patricia said in a rush.

She did not put the telephone down straightaway. I had time to say that I really appreciated her concern and promised to be careful.

In a strange way it felt as though we both knew that if we were wrong, this might be the last time we spoke.

So I added two more sentences, apologizing for not having trusted her and thanking her for all the help she had given me in this case and previous investigations.

Patricia said she was sorry that she had not been able to

help me enough in time to avoid this dangerous situation. I thought I heard a quiet sob when she said this.

Then we both put down the telephone at the same time.

V

It was now ten to eleven. I realized that it would be impossible to get anything done before half past eleven, and in any case I had no other leads to follow up. I could not bear just sitting here alone with nothing to do, so I decided to have some lunch before I went.

My lunch was not a grand affair. It consisted of a cup of coffee and two Danish pastries that I had bought from the bakers on the way in this morning. The pastries were softer than expected and my appetite really wasn't there. It felt strange to be eating what could be my last meal in this way, on my own.

There was a knock at the door. I jumped up and opened it.

DI Danielsen was standing outside. He raised a hand in apology and said that he hoped he was not disturbing me. Unfortunately he had nothing new to tell me about the case. He just wanted to say that he was back on duty and would carry on working on the kidnapping case. He also hoped that everything was all right and expressed once more that the kidnapping of a policeman's fiancée really was a desperate situation.

I thought to myself that Danielsen was possibly also

someone who had several faces, and that only when it mattered did you get to see the nicer ones. I felt a twinge of guilt at not telling Danielsen about the tip-off I had just received in connection with the case he was investigating.

So I said that I had nothing new to tell either, but would be glad of his company. He came in and sat down. I offered him one of the pastries. We talked for about ten minutes about this and that – the investigation and life in general.

He said that Miriam's mother had made a very personable impression and seemed to be a very nice future mother-in-law.

I said that I would indeed be a very fortunate husband, if only Miriam came back. Then I asked how his parents were keeping.

Danielsen looked rather surprised and very happy when I asked this. He said that his father would soon be eighty, and was slow on his feet, but that his mind was still up to speed. His mother was only seventy-six and still cheerful and in good form, despite having a spot of arthritis. They were both pleased and proud that he had achieved such a high rank at such a young age, but were constantly worried that his job might be dangerous. And they were a little too eager to have grandchildren, but you just had to put up with that.

I knew that Danielsen was an only child, so there was not much more to ask him about. I had a fairly clear picture, though, especially when I calculated that his parents must have been somewhat older when they had him.

Fortunately, in return, he asked how my parents were.

I told him that they were in good health and that they too worried, from time to time, about the dangers inherent in my job, but that fortunately they also had another child and a grandchild to worry about most of the time.

We finished our short lunch at ten past eleven. I said that unfortunately I had to get on with the investigation and he was tactful enough not to ask where I was going.

When Danielsen had left, I got up and checked that my service gun was loaded and in its holster under my jacket. Then I left the station with quick steps and a pounding chest. It was only a quarter past eleven – and already my heart was hammering.

VI

I got to the National Theatre at twenty-six minutes past eleven. It was fairly busy, as it was a Friday and the weather had improved. People hurried by in different directions, on their way to and from work, or to the tram or bus. I stood with my back to the National Theatre and looked down the main thoroughfare, Karl Johan Street.

It was both exciting and frightening to stand there in a crowd of people in a public space, without knowing who I was waiting for. And it was no less exciting and no less frightening that I also had to keep my eyes peeled for a possible attack from any direction. I glanced over my shoulder a couple of times, without seeing anything to alarm me.

I had no idea who the person I was waiting for was, nor

where he or she would come from. My guess was that it was someone I had never seen before, but I kept looking for familiar faces all the same.

I fantasized for a few seconds that Miriam herself would suddenly appear out of the crowd and throw her arms round my neck. And if she did, I told myself, I would throw her up in the air and then carry her in my arms to the Theatre Cafe for a slap-up lunch. But I realized this was nothing more than a dream.

The situation reminded me a little of what I had experienced in my flat last night. The minutes ticked slowly by to three, two, one minute to half past eleven. The difference being that at home I did not fear for my own safety, and that I had known who I was waiting for. Out here, anything was possible and the dangers were unpredictable.

It was half past eleven on the nose when I spotted her. I knew I had seen her before, but it took a couple of seconds to place her. I still could not remember her name, but I remembered very well where I had seen her. Less than twenty-four hours ago.

The interpreter from the Soviet Embassy was walking with quick, neat steps through the people on Karl Johan Street, dressed in a thin jacket, with a handbag in her right hand.

Her face was grave and focused, but she gave a careful smile when she saw me. She was no more than ten yards away, and moved faster to get out of the crowd.

I took three steps forward to meet her.

We were only three or four yards away from each other when I heard the gunshot.

The interpreter gasped and froze mid-step. She stood there swaying on one foot for a moment after the first shot. Then she fell to the ground without a sound after the second shot, which came a mere second later.

And like that, everything had changed and any sense of security was gone. A voice shouted: 'Murder! They're shooting!' and suddenly people were screaming and running in all directions. I threw myself down and pulled out my pistol. I shouted: 'I'm a policeman – who fired the shot?' But even as I shouted I realized it was hopeless. I had not even managed to see where the shots came from. And people were running everywhere in panic and fear of their lives. I saw several hats disappearing into the sea of people, but it was impossible to tell if one of them belonged to the man who had followed me earlier in the week.

In a matter of seconds, there were only two people left who were not fleeing. I lay curled up where I had thrown myself down. The interpreter lay lifeless where she had fallen.

I feared that I would be shot myself any moment, but could not see a potential assailant with anything that resembled a gun within range. It appeared that he had used the chance to be swallowed up by the crowd and escape.

There was suddenly a movement that made me jump. It was the fallen interpreter. Her hand was reaching in my direction. Her fingers had lost hold of her bag, which was now lying beside her hand. My first worry was that it might get lost – and then that she might die.

I was instinctively wary of moving closer to the spot where she had been shot. But then, when there was no perpetrator in sight, I took the few steps needed towards her.

It looked like one bullet had hit her in the back, and the other in her cheek. There was blood in both places. Her left eye had closed, but the right was still open. She was not dead – and she recognized me.

'Bas . . .' she whispered, as soon as she recognized my face. Then her voice stopped. But her eye was still staring at me.

I put my arm around her and said: 'What is it you want to tell me?'

'Ba . . .' she tried again, but her voice gave out. And at the same time, her right eye also slowly closed.

I heard a siren somewhere behind me and hoped that it was an ambulance.

Then I slipped into a peculiar timeless state. I could not say whether five seconds had passed or ten minutes when a man in white suddenly stood there beside me and asked if she was still alive. I did not remember right then that I had touched her. But I heard myself say that she had lost a lot of blood and was not conscious, but that she still had a faint pulse.

Then I took my pistol in one hand and her handbag in the other and withdrew as they lifted her up onto a stretcher and carried her into the ambulance. In my state of shock, I hoped that the interpreter would survive and be able to tell me more. And I hoped that if she did not survive, her bag could tell me something more.

VII

It was ten past twelve. I was sitting in my office with my boss, Danielsen and the handbag.

I had told them the story and criticized myself for not having informed them where I was going. The two others were very understanding. My boss was to the point and said we could talk more about that another day. Danielsen went a bit further and said that, given the situation, he perfectly understood.

Then we looked through the handbag, but all we learned was that there was little there that was of any help. The bag contained her passport, a purse with three ten-krone notes, two one-krone coins and a photograph of an elderly couple we assumed were her parents. That was it. According to her passport, Dr Tatiana Rodionova was twenty-six years old, five foot five, unmarried and childless. She had, if her passport was to be believed, not been abroad before coming to work in Norway.

There was much to indicate that she had intended to tell me the truth about who had killed Per Johan Fredriksen and about what had happened to Miriam – and at the same time, defect. But as yet, no one knew who had shot her. And unless she survived and regained consciousness, no one could know what she had hoped to say to me.

What she had tried to say remained a mystery. The man in the hat had had several names, but as far as we knew, none of them started with 'Bas'. As was the case with the vice-ambassador and any of the names on the embassy list.

All we had was a possible connection to the Soviet Embassy, but no means of proving that it existed or what kind of connection it was. We received a brief message from the University Hospital that the interpreter was being operated on, and was still in a critical and unstable condition.

Naturally, there were a large number of enquiries from the press about what had happened. Eyewitnesses were telling their stories, and their theories, to anyone who wanted to listen.

At twenty past twelve, my boss gave a concise summary of the situation, having first asked if I needed some hours or days off after this shocking experience. Danielsen would contact the embassy about the interpreter and lead the investigation into her attempted murder, which was connected to the abduction of Miriam.

My boss would himself first ring the prime minister's office and then send out a press release to confirm that a Soviet citizen linked to the embassy had been seriously injured when she was shot by an unknown gunman near the National Theatre.

I should stay in the vicinity of the police station for the rest of the day, and continue my investigation into the murders of the Fredriksen father and daughter, should there be any development there.

I said that I hoped this could be an important new lead, but that I needed a bit of time to collect myself. Danielsen and my boss then left, each heading in a different direction.

I sat on my own in the office for a couple of minutes. I tried to pull myself together and reflected on the remarkable contrast between the quiet in here and the cacophony of the world outside.

Then I rang Miriam's mother. I told her in brief what had happened and promised to call her back as soon as there was any other news.

She said she hoped that the interpreter would survive and was relieved to hear that I was unharmed. Then she asked the obvious question: 'So it is obviously the Soviets who have taken Miriam, but who knows where she is and if she is still alive?'

I promised I would do my utmost to find out. Then I finished the call so that I could telephone Patricia.

VIII

Patricia really was sitting guard today. Once again she picked up the receiver on the first ring, and apparently recognized my breathing, because she started to speak before I had said a word.

'So glad that you have not been hurt. I heard on the radio that there had been a shooting and that a foreign woman was the only one injured. I presume that was the interpreter you met yesterday?'

I felt a wave of relief when Patricia said this, but also a hint of irritation that she had not said anything when I called her earlier, if she had known what was coming.

I told her quickly what had happened at the National Theatre.

This was met with silence.

'Some of the connections are becoming clearer now, finally. But there is still more uncertainty than I would like,' Patricia said eventually.

I told her my opinion without beating around the bush – in other words, that I knew she was reluctant to conclude anything until she was absolutely certain, but, in a situation that was critical for both me and the country, I would ask her to be open now about what she thought.

Patricia let out a deep sigh and said: 'I can understand that. Just give me a little time to think about the connections and to check something in a book. Ring me back in ten minutes.'

Then she put the receiver down without waiting for an answer. I sat and wondered what book would be able to say anything about all this.

I rang Patricia back exactly ten minutes later, and she did not make me wait.

'The good news is that I think I can tell you quite a lot about one aspect of the case, and where Miriam is – or at least, where she was yesterday. The problem is that I am not sure how useful it will be.'

This was a sensational, if somewhat confusing, start. I asked her to tell me immediately, and to let me decide whether I could use the information or not.

'Well, let's start at the beginning – in other words, with Per Johan Fredriksen. I think it is overwhelmingly likely that the Soviets wanted him dead to minimize the risk that any spy allegations might upset the agreement, which is very important to them. The man in the hat not only came to Norway to commit murder, he also set out to do so on

Saturday night. But I am far less certain as to whether he actually did or not. I think he was the man who just stood by and watched, and that someone else got there before him. In which case, the man or woman who killed Fredriksen did it for very different reasons.'

Patricia asked if I was following her so far. I said yes, fascinated, and asked her to continue. Which she did, in a low and intense voice.

'The interpreter saw the connection when she heard that the newly arrived agent was out the evening that Fredriksen was killed. She got cold feet after that, possibly after doubting the excellence of the Soviet Union for some time. Coming to Norway could have been quite a shock, particularly if she had never been abroad before. She had got to know your fiancée at the university, and had met up with her at yesterday's lecture. And either then, or at some point later in the day, the interpreter gave your fiancée an envelope with some documents that would prove the connection. It is most likely that they met later on in the day and were seen. Or they may have been seen at the university, if the interpreter was already being followed. Whatever the case, your fiancée was then followed and watched, and they saw her going out, somewhat carelessly, with the envelope in her hand. They struck immediately. I am pretty certain that must be what happened.'

I agreed that it must have been what had happened – although I had not made this connection myself.

'It is worth noting that the interpreter smelt a rat and was nervous. She walked out with you after the meeting and left the embassy. She may have gone to her flat, but it is more likely that she went to a friend's or stayed the night in a hotel. Her experience of the KGB and Soviet police meant that she did not trust the Norwegian police, but she did trust you as she had met you and heard about you from your fiancée. She didn't know if everything had worked out, but tried, without any luck, to ring the halls of residence and then you, when she couldn't get hold of your fiancée. In the end, she called your fiancée's mother, whom she knew of by name, and asked her to give you a message about where and when to meet her. Either the interpreter was extremely unfortunate, or they were already on her trail, which is more likely. What is certain is that she definitely had someone hot on her heels and was shot just before she could speak to you.'

I was very impressed, and said so. Then I asked the most important and vital question that she still had not answered: 'But WHERE is Miriam?'

'That is of course the most important question now. The book I wanted to check was quite simply a dictionary. I have now gone through all the words that start "bas" and there is only one word that fits here, and that is basement. I would assume that means the embassy basement. It would not be easy for them to find a suitable hiding place in the vicinity at such short notice, and if the basement was anywhere else, the interpreter would be far less likely to know about it. However, it would be risky for them to move Miriam today, as now they must presume that the embassy is being watched.'

'So in other words, it is more likely that they might kill her instead?'

Patricia sighed on the other end.

'Clearly that is a possibility, yes. I think they kidnapped her without knowing who she was, simply because they wanted to get the documents back and they had seen her. They should by now have discovered that she is your fiancée. To kill a Norwegian citizen entails a risk, but to kill the fiancée of one of the country's best-known policemen would be even worse. They probably do not know how much you and the police actually know and can prove. The interpreter's handbag may prove to be crucial here.'

'But there is nothing of interest in the handbag,' I retorted, confused.

Patricia sighed again, but then hurried on with renewed vigour.

'Unfortunately not. But they do not know that, or what she might have told you, and nor do they know if she is alive or not. They are no doubt wondering how much the Norwegian police know, how much you can prove, and how to deal with the situation. The chances are that Miriam is still being held somewhere in the basement. But it is impossible to prove it and to get her out of there will therefore not be easy. It quickly becomes a matter of how much you believe what I say is right, and if you are willing to risk your career to save your fiancée. A police raid against the embassy would cause a scandal, and if no hostage was found, heads would roll and tensions between the two countries would escalate. On the other hand, it would also be a scandal if a hostage was found in their embassy, and that could quite literally cause heads to roll in the Soviet Union.'

There was a heavy knock at the door as I was listening. I hastily whispered: 'Thank you for all your help – I will think about it,' and then put the phone down.

IX

Danielsen and my boss were already on their way in as I put down the receiver. They both looked very serious indeed.

'Danielsen has some very bad news, and I have some very onerous information,' my boss told me.

My blood turned to ice and my muscles froze. I sat there, immobile, and stared at Danielsen.

'She is dead,' he said, gravely.

'Who?' I almost shouted.

Danielsen realized his blunder and threw up his hands. 'I am so sorry for putting it so badly. We know nothing more about your fiancée. But unfortunately the interpreter died during the operation at the University Hospital about half an hour ago. She did not regain consciousness. The bullet wounds would have been fatal, no matter how soon she had got to hospital, they said.'

I felt a paradoxical relief as soon as he said that it was the interpreter who had died. I had been terrified that he was talking about Miriam and it was a relief to know that nothing I could have done at the National Theatre would have saved the interpreter's life. But I also felt pained on the part of the interpreter, and realized that this further reduced the chances of getting Miriam back. So I looked back at my boss, without saying anything.

'My news is not necessarily bad, but both pieces of information are onerous. First, on hearing about the shooting at the National Theatre, the Government has postponed the ratification of the Barents Sea agreement in the Storting indefinitely. And second, the Soviet Embassy has just informed us that they take it very seriously indeed that one of their staff has been shot, and have requested a meeting with the head of the investigation as soon as possible.'

'They have got something to hide and are playing with high stakes. I think we should first allow ourselves a couple of hours to think about this, and then all three of us should go,' I said.

They both nodded. But my boss said that we could not delay it too long, with due respect, as he put it, to the embassy, the press, the Government and my fiancée. He suggested that he and I pay another visit to the head of the police security service at two o'clock, and that Danielsen should then come with us to the Soviet Embassy at four.

Danielsen and I quickly agreed. This would give the investigation three hours to produce some evidence – and me three hours to think about the decision I would have to make should no evidence materialize.

X

Nothing more happened between one o'clock and a quarter to two. I sat in my office and waited for a telephone call with good or bad news about Miriam. I had no idea where it would come from though, and, of course, it did not come.

So I sat there alone thinking about what Patricia had said. I found no other explanation that fitted as well as hers, and it seemed more and more likely that she was right. But I could not be sure, and to confront the Soviet Embassy without any evidence was a horrifying prospect.

At the same time it felt like I had a duty to try everything I could to bring Miriam back, without worrying about what the consequences might be for me. She had apparently been kidnapped because of her connection to me, while trying to help me solve the hardest murder case I had ever worked on.

And yet: the thought of being shown to be bluffing, having accused the Soviet Embassy of kidnapping, was terrifying, not least after my last meeting with the vice-ambassador. My career, thus far successful, could crash-land in a scandal if this got out, and result in me being fired. This was a day when I could lose everything: my fiancée, my position and my reputation.

The visit to Victoria Terrace at two o'clock did little to help. Asle Bryne again expressed his guarded sympathy for the situation I found myself in, but could not offer any assistance. He nodded, almost eagerly, to the theory that Soviet agents were behind the kidnapping and today's murder, and believed that the 'communists' were in all likelihood also behind the murders of both Per Johan and Vera Fredriksen. But he had no evidence to substantiate it.

When the question of how the spy allegations had ended up in the press was raised, Asle Bryne again lit his pipe and categorically denied that the leak could have come from the ranks of the police security service. He refused, slightly apologetically and very demonstratively, to give the identity of the police security service's source with regard to the Fredriksen spy claims. However, when I asked him directly, he could confirm that the source had not been the interpreter, whom he maintained was totally unknown to him and the police security service.

I was back in the office by half past two and once again, sat alone with my dilemma. At a quarter to three, I rang Patricia to tell her about the latest development. I could hardly hope that she had any evidence. And indeed, she did not. She did, however, go to unexpected lengths to advise me as to what I should do.

'You have to do it. I am more and more convinced that I am right, and it could save your fiancée's life,' she said.

I said that I had to think about it, and that it felt like leaping into the unknown.

'Remember that you can always rely on my support, even if everything goes wrong,' she said, finishing our telephone call at five to three.

Again I sat there and pondered. To begin with, I was deeply touched by Patricia's care and consideration for both Miriam and myself. Then I thought about what she had said in parting, and again, I wondered what her motive was. It struck me that Patricia, from her perspective, was perhaps manufacturing a win-win situation, where she would either become my hero because she was right, or would be the only person who would still support me if I lost both my fiancée and my job. I could not bring myself to believe that she really would think the latter, but whatever the case, it was a far more painful alternative for me than for her. So in the midst of it all, I harboured a vague doubt as to Patricia's intentions. And in a strange way, I was now fighting with a bad conscience about both Patricia and Miriam.

Two further conversations did not make things any easier or the pressure any less. Miriam's mother rang to ask me if there was any news. I told her that the interpreter had died and that I was going to the embassy in an hour, but there was no news, for better or worse, about Miriam herself. Her mother finished by saying: 'We're losing hope. But we are very grateful for everything you are doing.' There is no doubt that she meant well, but it did not make my situation any easier. I sat with the telephone in my hand, feeling ever gloomier and more and more uncertain.

Two minutes later, a woman from the switchboard knocked on my door. She said that the newspapers had started to ring and asked if it was true that my fiancée had disappeared, and if so, might it have something to do with the Fredriksen case, the day's murder and the oil agreement?

I asked her to come with me to Danielsen's office. We quickly agreed on a two-line standard response: we confirmed that my fiancée was missing and that an investigation was underway, but that it was too early to comment on what had happened.

The switchboard lady then took this back with her. I stood and looked questioningly at Danielsen. He shook his head a fraction.

'Nothing more to report, I'm afraid. We do not know any more about your fiancée, but we do know a bit more about the interpreter. According to the embassy, she lived in a studio flat not far from the embassy itself, but her landlady had not seen her since yesterday morning. A hotel on one of the side streets off Karl Johan called after the announcement of her death to say that they thought she had booked in there overnight. A slightly out-of-breath young woman had suddenly shown up there the evening before, without a reservation and without any luggage. She had paid in cash and seemed very nervous. She said she was called Hanne Hansen and spoke very good Norwegian, but did not have any ID and the receptionist noticed some Russian letters on her jacket. She went down to the reception twice in the evening and once again in the morning to make some short phone calls. Otherwise, as far as the hotel knew, she stayed in her room until she checked out at a quarter past eleven. A man had called in the morning and explained that his mentally unstable wife had run away, but they refused to give out any information about their guests. This enquiry could well have been about the interpreter and would indicate that they were looking for her. But it is still not hard evidence.'

I felt relief surge through my body as I listened to Danielsen. It was clearly the interpreter, and fitted well with the assumption that they were looking for her – and that in turn fitted well with the scenario that Patricia had outlined. When Danielsen stopped talking, I could still hear her voice in my head.

I stood there with Danielsen in front of my eyes and Patricia's voice in my ears, then together we walked pensively over to my boss's office and asked him if we could come in for a minute. I told him the main points of Patricia's reasoning – without of course mentioning her name.

We sat there and looked at each other – and then at the clock on the wall. It was twenty to four. Whereas time had dragged unbearably earlier in the day, it now suddenly seemed to be racing.

'Impressive thinking in such a demanding situation. It may well be the truth, but we still have no evidence,' my boss said, slowly.

Once again, I got unexpected help from Danielsen.

'Good thinking, and I think you are right. But it would be terrible if K2's fiancée is with the communists and we knew and did nothing about it,' he said.

My boss and I suddenly sighed in unison. He spoke first.

'We will have to go soon, if we are going to be on time. We will just have to assess the situation there and then as things unfold,' he said.

Then he stood up without waiting for an answer. Neither Danielsen nor I said anything. We followed him in silence. None of us spoke during the short drive to the embassy.

XI

The table was set with vodka, water and cakes for five, rather than four. Otherwise, everything was the same as it had been the last time we were shown into the meeting room at the embassy. We were met by the same receptionist and shown along the corridor by the same guide. There was still no emotion to be seen on their faces. And again we were shown to places under the huge portrait of Brezhnev. There was no one sitting in the other chairs when we arrived this time, either.

The interpreter and vice-ambassador arrived at the same time. The vice-ambassador was very definitely the same, his handshake if anything a little firmer than before and his voice even louder and faster.

Naturally, the interpreter was new, and I felt sad when I saw her come in. She was not as dark, but all the more serious, and closer to fifty than thirty. She was also twice the size. Her handshake was weak and her voice hesitant when she started to interpret the vice-ambassador's first volley.

'The vice-ambassador welcomes you back and thanks you for making the time on what must be a very busy day for you. This is, of course, a very upsetting time for us at the embassy. One of our dear colleagues has been killed on the street in broad daylight, and wicked rumours published in the press have meant that the agreement, which is so important to both our countries, has not been ratified. We hope that the matter will soon be resolved and that this is no more than a temporary postponement. Otherwise, the good relations enjoyed by the Soviet Union and Norway could be jeopardized.'

The last sentence sounded akin to a threat of war. And in my already fraught frame of mind, I found this very provoking, especially when he spoke of the dead interpreter as a dear colleague. The situation suddenly resembled a game of chess, where the ambassador was playing with the white pieces and had opened with two very aggressive moves.

My boss started tentatively and diplomatically by giving

his condolences for their loss, and assuring the vice-ambassador that the investigation would be given the highest priority. He then asked what measures the embassy would like to see taken.

The answer came fast and hard from the vice-ambassador, and then somewhat more slowly via the interpreter.

'The vice-ambassador thanks you for your sympathies. It is hoped that the press will be reprimanded as soon as possible and that there is an official statement to clarify that there is no suspicion that the crimes committed can in any way be linked to representatives of the Soviet state.'

I looked at my boss, and did not envy him his job.

He replied tersely that in a democracy, the police did not usually reprimand the free press in this way, and as long as the investigation was ongoing, it was problematic to make categorical statements about who had not committed the crimes.

So far, we were covering the same ground as last time. It felt as though the game had stalled. But then the vice-ambassador made another aggressive move.

'The vice-ambassador finds it hard to understand why the police cannot publicly state that there is nothing to indicate that representatives of the Soviet Union are in any way involved in the crimes in question. Unless of course there are grounds for suspicion. And in that case, the vice-ambassador would like to be given the opportunity to clear this up here and now.'

This was a very aggressive move, which made for a moment of drama.

My boss took his time. Danielsen stepped in.

'There is one crime that complicates the situation there, and which could serve to strengthen the press's critical focus. A young female student, who it seems had contact with the deceased interpreter through the university, disappeared last night in uncertain circumstances and has not been seen since. We are concerned that if this remains unresolved, it might draw attention and result in a further postponement and, at worst, a cancellation of the agreement.'

It was a small counter-attack that made our opponent pause and think for a few moments, but no longer. The answer came just as fast and hard.

'The vice-ambassador says that would be a very unfortunate situation indeed, but can only assure you that he and the ambassador know nothing about the woman. He would again like to be given the opportunity to clear up any misunderstandings if the police have grounds not to believe him.'

Yet another fast and aggressive move – as well as a challenging ultimatum.

I looked at Danielsen, who looked back at me. My boss sat quietly between us and said nothing.

Danielsen gave me a quick nod.

It crossed my mind that it was now more like a game of bridge, where no one knew for certain what cards the other players were holding.

I heard the voices of Miriam's mother and Patricia talking over each other in my head. I thought of Miriam as I had last seen her, when she disappeared into the night on her own.

And I told myself that I might lose my job, but I had to do everything I could to save my fiancée – and that I would always have Patricia's support.

So I turned towards the vice-ambassador, hesitated for a brief second, then said: 'The police, of course, are not in a position to say whether this happened with the vice-ambassador's approval or not. But, unfortunately, we have strong indications not only that employees from the embassy have been involved in the kidnapping of the woman in question, but also that she is being held here at the embassy.'

There was silence for a few moments. The interpreter swallowed hard and seemed to struggle to find the right words. The vice-ambassador looked at me, unable to understand, then barked a sharp comment at the interpreter. She answered in Russian – even more slowly, as far as I could make out.

Then time stopped completely – in much the same way that it had during the shooting at the National Theatre earlier in the day. Later I realized that it might only have been five seconds, but it felt like a lifetime that the vice-ambassador and I sat looking at each other.

His face was carved in stone, without a twitch of movement. I did not hear a sound from my boss or Danielsen. And as far as I could tell from my peripheral vision, neither of them nodded or shook their head. They had moved to the sidelines. Suddenly it was a game between the vice-ambassador and me. Which moved on, eventually, after a small eternity, when the vice-ambassador downed half a glass of vodka, and then answered.

'The audacity of this accusation leaves the vice-ambassador speechless and dry-mouthed. He hopes that the police realize that any kind of police operation against the embassy would provoke strong reactions from the Soviet Union and considerable attention in other countries, and that it would have very negative consequences for those responsible on the Norwegian side.'

I worried that my boss would contradict me, but he sat there, calm as ever. So I hurried on.

'That would certainly be the case if the police, after searching the embassy, did not have any evidence of serious criminal activity on the embassy's part. But it would be a very different matter if the police did find evidence that employees of the embassy had committed a serious crime. That would also draw a lot of attention and could have very negative consequences for those responsible on the Soviet side – regardless of whether they knew about the matter or not.'

I was pushing my luck, hinting that we had evidence that we did not have. But I was now totally convinced that it was true. And this was reinforced when the interpreter again hesitated and the vice-ambassador again was silent for a few seconds after listening to the translation.

'The vice-ambassador denies any knowledge of the matter, and stills finds it hard to believe that anything like this could happen without him knowing about it. But given the seriousness of the matter, he will of course investigate. If the police have any evidence of criminal activity, he hopes that the police might be able to tell him where in the embassy the kidnapped person might be hidden.'

'In the basement,' I replied, short and sweet, having first listened to the translation.

I felt an almost wild sense of triumph go to my head. Time stopped again. The vice-ambassador looked straight at me and raised his eyebrows in his otherwise stony face in something that resembled both surprise and fear. He downed the other half of his glass of vodka and when he spoke again, it was more slowly and in a quieter voice. The interpreter also dropped her voice in line with his.

'The vice-ambassador hopes that it will transpire that no one in the embassy has betrayed its trust and that the young woman will turn up alive and unharmed sometime this evening . . . and, if this was to happen, he hopes that the investigation could soon be closed.'

An enormous cloud of relief enveloped me. Miriam was alive and unharmed. And our game of chess was definitely about to turn in my favour. My opponent on the other side of the table was no longer thinking about how to avoid losing, but instead how he could disguise it.

I turned and looked over at my boss. Luckily, he was on the ball.

'If the missing young lady comes back unharmed this evening, there is every reason to believe that the investigation into that part of the case will be closed.'

Without any hesitation, Danielsen nodded in agreement. As did I.

The vice-ambassador thought about it for a few seconds more, then took two more slugs of vodka from the interpreter's glass. Followed by another short volley.

'As far as the death of our colleague is concerned, the

vice-ambassador is still very saddened. He does, however, fully understand that it can be difficult to solve murders that are committed in public places, and would not criticize the Norwegian police in any way if this should prove to be the case.'

It was a cunning, fast move. The offer of understanding was in practice a suggestion that the investigation would be closed without finding the murderer. But it was hard to give a negative response.

My boss said: 'Thank you.' And we all nodded.

At the same time, I thought about the interpreter who had sat here with us the day before and who had been shot in front of my very eyes this morning. It did not sit comfortably. But we had absolutely no evidence in connection with her death. And my picture of the interpreter, who I had only met briefly and did not know, faded as soon as I thought of my fiancée. Tatiana was a foreigner with no family in Norway, who was now gone forever. Miriam was Norwegian, she had family here – and apparently she was alive.

The vice-ambassador nodded gravely – and then fired another round.

'On another note: the vice-ambassador has the impression that the embassy is now under police surveillance, no doubt with the best intentions after today's murder. However, the vice-ambassador finds this troubling. Would it be possible to have the surveillance lifted from this evening? The vice-ambassador hopes that it might help to resolve the matter in the best way for everyone.'

The message was clear: the embassy wanted to ensure that the coast was clear to remove something or someone from the premises. It could well be that they wished to transport the man who had committed the murder, but it was also likely that they were looking for a way to release Miriam without creating a scandal.

I was not aware that the embassy was under surveillance, and I could not assess the implications of the question.

Danielsen and I both looked at our boss, who once again was quick to respond.

'It is a routine procedure when a foreign national is attacked in this way that extra measures are put in place to safeguard the embassy. If the embassy so wishes, we can certainly lift the measure temporarily – between, say, seven and nine o'clock this evening.'

The ambassador did not say any more after listening to the translation. He just held out his hand – first to me, then to my boss, and then Danielsen. Then he stood up to leave.

I felt intoxicated with relief and perhaps emboldened, given these latest developments. And so I played my final card, with the vice-ambassador towering above me.

'One last thing regarding the murder of Fredriksen, which it is in everyone's interest to wrap up as quickly as possible: if we can arrest the person responsible, we will of course then confirm that the murder is in no way connected to the Soviet Embassy. Sometimes embassy staff at various levels can be ordered abroad at short notice. We have reason to believe that the person we discussed when we were here last, might coincidently have been at the scene of the crime, without necessarily having anything to do with the murder. But we do have reason to believe that he was there, and therefore need a statement from him about what he saw.'

It was a daring move. But before I had a chance to be frightened myself, it proved to be a trump card in every sense. The vice-ambassador stood there without saying a word, swaying unsteadily.

It crossed my mind that he also might be a man of many faces. Perhaps he also had a wife and children, or fiancée, whom he missed. And perhaps the pressure on him had been greater than the pressure on me. If I had just risked my job for the case, it could be that he had risked both his freedom and his life.

I had time to think all this because he hesitated again – and still did not answer. He nodded down at me, shook my hand again and then walked out with quick heavy steps.

We sat in silence even after he had left the room, until the new interpreter stood up and said: 'I can follow you out.'

The glasses and cakes on our side of the table were untouched, and yet it felt like we had had a lot to chew on.

The new interpreter followed us to the main entrance, but remained inside herself. I had barely noticed that she was there. All of a sudden I started to wonder what she made of it all. But as soon as she was out of sight, it left my mind. I had too many other people to worry about – alive and dead, but most of all, one who had disappeared.

XII

We said nothing until we were in the safety of the car. As he turned on the engine, my boss said: 'Congratulations once again, Kristiansen. That was a daring and impressive performance in what was a critical situation. Your theory proved to be right. I think you will have your fiancée back this evening and we got as much as we could have hoped for from the situation. We can get on with our jobs and the investigation, and leave the politicians to assess the consequences for them.'

Danielsen also congratulated me on how I had dealt with it, but was rather curt. Once again, I felt the rivalry between us. But I was happy to forgive him today of all days. Especially when he added his sincere wish that my fiancée would turn up unharmed this evening.

I remarked somewhat sheepishly that my greatest fear now was that if surveillance was lifted, the Soviets could move Miriam from the embassy without releasing her.

My boss somewhat patronizingly shook his head.

'I understand, but I don't think that you need to worry. First of all, they clearly believe that we have some kind of evidence, and second, both the vice-ambassador and I know perfectly well that we will not stop watching the embassy. We will know who leaves the embassy this evening and where they go. Only, we will not use it for anything – as long as your fiancée shows up.'

I felt reassured. And even though the anxiety and uncertainty still lingered in my body, in my head, I was increasingly convinced that Miriam really would come back this evening. For a moment or two, I thought about Patricia and how she would react. Then my thoughts moved on to a third woman – the interpreter who had been shot right in front of me this morning.

'The business with the interpreter is very hard,' I said carefully, as we pulled up in front of the police station.

My boss turned around and looked at me with his most inscrutable expression.

'Yes, but we could not have saved her. There is a cold war going on out there, and it has claimed the lives of many in many different countries. The interpreter was a little foreign bird who landed in the wrong place at the wrong time. Her execution was professional and the result a success. As we were not able to arrest the killer on the spot or get any description of him, we have in practice no means of solving the murder. The newspapers will write about it tomorrow, and maybe at the start of next week, but the interest will die down, certainly if we now manage to solve the other murders soon. The interpreter was Russian, and it would appear that she was killed by another Russian, and the Soviet Embassy is well aware of that. The Soviets are obviously not going to complain if the case is not solved, and it is not likely that anyone in Norway will either. The interpreter's death is a tragedy for her and her family in the Soviet Union, but for us, it is the least important crime in a complex case. The most important thing right now is that you get your fiancée back. The next most important thing is that we find out who killed Per Johan Fredriksen and his daughter.'

And with that, Danielsen stopped the car.

On my way into the station, I thought that my boss was right in many ways. The interpreter could not have been saved, and it was apparently a Soviet crime against a Soviet citizen. And in that sense, it was less our case than the others were. But the woman had been living here. It was here she had first of all tried to help me solve a crime and then tried to save her own life. And it was here, right in front of my very eyes and hundreds of others, that she had been shot. And, I thought to myself, I had seen another side of my boss – a more cynical and less likeable face.

I remembered the photograph of the elderly couple in her wallet, and wondered if the young Tatiana's parents were still alive behind the Iron Curtain. According to her passport, she had been unmarried and did not have children. But there might very well be a boyfriend somewhere who did not yet know that she was dead, and would never know why she died.

It was an uncomfortable thought. But then, a moment later, I looked at my hand and a picture of Miriam and her engagement ring filled my head.

My watch said it was a quarter past five. I had several nerve-wracking hours ahead of me.

XIII

After a few minutes at the station, I ascertained that the hours would be insufferably long if I was to stay there all evening. And I could not bring myself to ring Miriam's mother to tell her the good news. The thought of maybe having to call her again a few hours later to tell her that her daughter had died was simply unbearable.

There was no new information about the Fredriksen case waiting for me. I spent a while pondering over who might be behind those murders if it was not a Soviet agent, but I could not really concentrate.

I asked my boss for permission to take a couple of hours off in lieu to go out and get something to eat. My boss was himself on his way home for supper, and agreed straight-away.

Then I rang Patricia. I told her that after our meeting at the Soviet Embassy, there was hope that Miriam would come back, and that some of the information we got in connection with the Fredriksen case reinforced her theory.

Patricia sounded quite jolly when she replied: 'Well, that might give grounds for a quiet celebration for us both. Come for supper, if you have the time and inclination – before your fiancée can be expected.'

This was said with an almost jokey undertone. I felt so grateful to Patricia, and was extremely curious to hear what she might say about the remaining mysteries. So I said yes.

I was shown into Patricia's library at a quarter to six. The asparagus soup was already on the table. I thought to myself that either the kitchen here worked at record speed, or they had had a three-course meal ready in case I should come. I guessed it was the latter, and after what had been an un-usually demanding Friday, I greatly appreciated it. As soon as I looked at the food, I realized that for the first time today, I was hungry.

We gave each other a warm hug as soon as I came in. Patricia was wearing a green blouse that was very light for the time of year and revealed a fair amount of skin. The thought that another man stood between us hit me hard at that moment.

I quickly retreated and once again felt a stab of guilt in relation to the woman who was sitting opposite and my fiancée. It did not make matters any better that my fiancée first of all was still being held hostage, and second, had no idea that I was here.

After a somewhat hesitant start, we had a very nice meal. I was still tense, but naturally also very relieved, following the afternoon's developments and at the prospect of getting Miriam back alive and unharmed. Patricia quickly regained her usual conceited and self-assured air. But I also noted in her a sense of relief that her theory had proved to be right.

Patricia ate the asparagus soup and beef entrecote with a healthy appetite, but listened intently when I recounted our meeting at the Soviet Embassy. She nodded appreciatively, especially when I mentioned my parting shot to the vice-ambassador.

'Excellent. So, it is very likely that your fiancée will appear again soon, and the murder of the interpreter can be seen as solved, even though no one has been arrested. The man in the hat will soon be out of the country, which is considerably more satisfactory, so long as he did not kill either Per Johan or Vera Fredriksen. Something that I am fairly certain he did not. But he was at the scene of the crime when Fredriksen died and anything he can tell us could be decisive to solving the case.'

I asked how close we were to finding the solution – and without thinking, begged Patricia to tell me what she thought. Just then, the maid came in to clear away the main course and serve the dessert. When we were alone again,

Patricia gave a self-satisfied, teasing smile as she spooned a piece of chocolate cake into her mouth.

'I made an exception earlier on today, as your fiancée's life was at risk. But now that it is simply a matter of solving a murder that has already been committed, you will have to forgive me for not wanting to say anything before I am certain enough of my reasoning not just to be guessing. There are still several candidates from different circles who could have killed Per Johan Fredriksen.'

I picked up on this and asked her which candidates she still had on her list of potential murderers. And to my surprise, she answered.

'The problem is exactly that, that there are still a few too many who cannot be ruled out. Other than the boy on the red bicycle, among the men we have the office manager, Odd Jørgensen, the accountant, Erling Svendsen, Hauk Rebne Westgaard and Kjell Arne Ramdal. And among the women, we have Harriet Henriksen, Ane Line Fredriksen, Vera Fredriksen and Solveig Ramdal. Plus the person who I think it most likely is.'

Patricia said this with a sly smile. But then she was suddenly serious again, and started picking at her chocolate cake.

I assumed that the person Patricia believed to be the most likely was a woman, as I could not think of any other men she had left out. More specifically, I thought of the only one from the 1932 friends that she had not mentioned, namely the widow, Mrs Oda Fredriksen. But Patricia shook her head when I mentioned this possibility.

'No, no. I think you can categorically rule out that Mrs

Fredriksen had anything to do with the death of Per Johan Fredriksen. The money will go to the children, she had been devoted to her husband and her life had revolved around him for nearly forty years, and what is more, it is clear that at the time of his death he was closer to leaving his lover than his wife. And in any case, she has an alibi. On the other hand, I do not think we should rule out—'

She stopped abruptly, with an arch smile – without saying who it was we should not rule out.

'Besides,' she said, teasing me, 'who is a chameleon person, and who is not, is very significant. I think that there are still several chameleon people we have not yet discovered in the circle around the late Per Johan Fredriksen. In fact, I think there is only one person who was there in 1932 who is not a chameleon person. And that might also be very significant. But you will have to wait to find out who that is.'

Patricia looked coy and charming, even seductively secretive when she said this.

I had a sudden impulse to march over to her, pick her up out of the wheelchair, put her down on the table, then look her straight in the eye and demand that she tell me who she thought had committed the other two murders. I was convinced that she had her ideas and that what she believed would be right.

I also got the feeling that were I to do that, Patricia would be more than pleased. But I realized that it would be wrong in every way all the same. The fact that my situation and mood had changed from bleak pessimism yesterday evening to more or less cheerful optimism now, was almost entirely thanks to Patricia. I had no right to ask anything more of her today.

And any more physical contact would feel akin to betrayal. After all, I still had a fiancée who had no idea that I was sitting here with Patricia. And even though I did not like it, and found it hard to understand what she saw in him, I had to respect the fact that Patricia had a boyfriend now – and be grateful for the fact that he knew nothing about my contact with her either.

At a quarter to seven, I said that I should perhaps head back to the station. Patricia raised her hand. She said that it was unlikely that anything would happen before half past seven at the earliest, if the police surveillance was to be lifted at seven.

I found it hard to argue with this logic, and it was without a doubt more tempting to spend the nerve-wracking waiting time with Patricia than on my own at the station. So I stayed where I was for a little while longer.

When the clock struck seven, we raised our glasses to what we hoped would be the beginning of the end of the case. I had water, and Patricia poured herself some white wine.

At five past seven, I looked at the clock again. This time Patricia nodded her agreement.

'It may still take some time before anything happens, but you should go to the station just in case.'

At first I thought her words sounded matter-of-fact – as though we had been married for years and I was about to go to work. But then I caught the nervous undertone in her voice, and it reawakened my own anxiety.

I thought to myself that there was absolutely no reason to be nervous just because Patricia was. I knew from before that she was far more sensitive than she appeared to be. I could feel her nerves spilling over into me – and suddenly I just wanted to get out.

I rounded the table, thanked her again for her help and gave her another hug. This did not make things any better: her frail body trembled against mine. I pulled back a little too fast and headed for the door, but stopped when I unexpectedly heard Patricia's voice again.

'I will stay here, then, and hope for the best, and will be waiting from first thing in the morning. I would appreciate it if you could let me know that all is well with your fiancée. Even though the documents and information she will give you will no doubt be of interest, I doubt that she will have anything conclusive to tell you. The Soviet aspect of the case seems to be closed. But ring me as soon as you hear what and who the man with the hat saw on the evening that Per Johan Fredriksen was killed.'

I promised to do that. Then I left, with my heart hammering in my throat, to wait for Miriam to turn up. And for the first time, I thought that I would actually have liked to stay a bit longer with Patricia.

It was now dark outside and the air felt colder than when I had arrived. It struck me that I still did not know where Miriam was out there in the dark. I did not even know for certain that she was alive and only had the vice-ambassador's word that she would come back, if she was still alive. In fact, I did not even have that, as the whole conversation had been indirect, with no concrete promises.

The anxiety sank deep as I sat all alone in my car, surrounded by darkness. And it was followed by an uncontrollable impatience as I swore at every red light on my way to the station.

XIV

My mood had been ever-changing all through this long day. By the time I got to 19 Møller Street at half past seven, I was full, but my mind was distracted and my nerves were frayed.

I popped my head round the door to Danielsen's office, as he was still on duty, but he just shrugged and held up his hands. So I carried on to my own office – which had now become a waiting room. I tried to pass the time by thinking about the Fredriksen case, but it still just seemed to be a chaotic ocean of possibilities that floated and merged together. I always came back to Miriam – and was constantly changing my mind about the chances of her being released.

By ten to eight, I was seriously worried that she would not be released this evening, and at eight I shed a few tears because suddenly I was sure that she had been killed yesterday. By a quarter past eight, I was optimistic once more, having relived the meeting at the embassy. By twenty-five past, my mood was plummeting again and I found it alarming that so much time had passed without anything happening.

At thirty-two minutes past eight, as I was trying to pull myself back up by thinking about the meeting at the embassy, I jumped when the door to my office was opened without warning.

Danielsen was standing there.

'There is a phone call in my office that I think you should take,' he said.

I ran past him and through his door, lifted the receiver from the desk and with forced calm, said: 'Detective Inspector Kolbjørn Kristiansen, how can I help you?'

I heard a very clear man's voice speaking in a deliberate tone on the other end and I knew straightaway that I had heard it before, but I couldn't remember where.

'I am calling about a very confused young woman who was taken here in an ambulance after she was found wandering around up by the university, in a bewildered state. At first we wondered if she was drunk, but it turned out that she was under the influence of some chemical or other. She was not able to tell us her name. But I recognized her from the time she spent here in 1970, and the contents of her handbag confirmed that she was Miriam Filtvedt Bentsen. So I thought I should let the police know, in case she has been a victim of crime. My name is Berg and I am the senior doctor here at Ullevål Hospital, and if you are Detective Inspector Kristiansen, I believe we have been in contact before, remarkably enough, in connection with the same patient.'

In my overwrought state, I did not recognize the doctor until he said his name. But I was ridiculously relieved and almost cried with joy when he did. Bernt Berg had appeared to be incapable of feeling, but in fact he was a warm-hearted and dedicated doctor, and in the summer of 1970, he had saved Miriam when, in connection with one of my previous cases, she had been shot and had hovered between life and death.

I said that I knew who he was and that it was very nice to be remembered by him, and that he had indeed done the right thing by calling here. As he did not respond to this, I asked how the patient was and when it might be possible to see her.

'The police are welcome to see her whenever they like, if that is of interest. She is asleep right now. She was semi-conscious when she was found and should be left to sleep off the effects of the drug, so it probably will not be possible to talk to her before later on tomorrow morning.'

The senior doctor's voice was like a machine, steady and reassuring – just as I remembered it on the odd occasion that I thought about the drama in 1970 that had brought Miriam and I together. It felt strange, almost moving, that we should now be brought together again by the same doctor. Above all, it was a huge relief that she had been found and was in good hands at Ullevål. My voice was shaky all the same, when I asked Bernt Berg how he assessed the patient's condition this time.

He replied in an equally calm and unruffled voice: 'It would seem that there is no danger at all. A young and healthy person should be able to cope without any permanent damage, and there is nothing to indicate that she has been harmed in any way. There are, however, effusions of blood on her wrists which indicate that her hands have been bound for some time, and that would be particularly uncomfortable for anyone who already has shoulder and neck injuries. She could barely move her arms when we found her. But the mobility will gradually return. We will keep her in hospital over the weekend, as she needs rest and quiet. But as far as I can see, there is no reason to fear any long-term physical harm other than the injuries she already had. And we will have to wait until she wakes up to see how she is mentally. As I said, when she was admitted she was terribly confused and kept repeating the same words over and over again. Though I have to say, I am not sure of their significance.'

My heart felt lighter and lighter – but then sank a little when he said this. I immediately asked what the word was.

His reply was short and deadpan: 'The library book. At first I thought I had misheard, but then she said it again, several times.'

It was impossible not to laugh when he said this. I apologized and explained that I knew the young woman in question rather well, as she was now my fiancée. She had been kidnapped, she loved books, and when she was abducted, she had dropped a library book. The fact that she remembered and was worried about the library book showed that she was pretty much herself.

He said, just as seriously, that there was little need to worry then and that I would be allowed to go in and see her sleeping for a few minutes if I came by the hospital in the next hour or two.

I said that I would do that, and ended the call.

I stood there with my ear to the receiver for a moment. And then a wave of euphoria washed over me that needed physical expression. I leapt up and hit the ceiling with joy.

It was only when I landed that I remembered I was in Danielsen's office and not my own, and that Danielsen was standing right behind me.

He took it with good humour, as did I. We generously and jubilantly congratulated one another.

On my way out of the office, I asked how many of the past twenty-four hours he had been on duty. He smiled briefly and said: 'Fifteen. I think I can perhaps go home with a clear conscience now.'

I thanked him profusely and said that he could certainly stay at home all weekend with a clear conscience. He replied that he would like to go home now, but, if it was all right with me, he would come back again tomorrow to help with the Fredriksen investigation. I told him I appreciated that.

I felt tears of joy flood my eyes when I went back into my own office. And seconds later they were streaming down my cheeks as I spoke to Miriam's mother in Lillehammer and told her and the family that Miriam had been found. She asked when they could visit Miriam in hospital tomorrow. I said that I was about to go up there and they could try later on tomorrow morning. We thanked one another three times before we finally put down the phone.

Then I rang Patricia. It was a shorter and far less emotional telephone call. She thanked me for letting her know that Miriam had turned up and said that she was pleased, but was so casual and swift about it that I started to wonder if her boyfriend was there.

'Well, a summary of today would read: great relief, another death and some useful information. Ring me as soon as you know any more tomorrow,' she said, and put down the telephone.

I sat there and wondered if she had actually invited her boyfriend down, as soon as I had gone – or if she was actually jealous of Miriam. And I have to admit, despite my joy at having Miriam back, I found the latter more appealing than the first.

XV

I felt an almost indescribable joy and relief as I stood by Miriam's hospital bed with the senior doctor, Bernt Berg, at around half past nine.

Miriam was, as far as I could see, whole and there was no sign of any physical harm. She was lying with her bandaged arms by her sides, unmoving, but the effusions round her wrists were not as bad as I had feared. She looked as though she was sleeping as peacefully as she did at home, with her hair spread out over the pillow in the same way.

With the senior doctor's silent consent, I gently stroked Miriam's cheek. After such a dramatic and emotional day, I had to touch her to feel that she really had come back alive. It worked. Her cheek was warm and soft against my finger.

Just then, there was a slight movement in her lips, as though deep in her sleep she knew that I was there, and was trying to smile.

I had a few words with Dr Bernt Berg in a side room. He believed that everything was fine and that the patient should be able to converse by the late morning or afternoon tomorrow and would no doubt enjoy getting visitors.

It was a strange experience to see Miriam in the same hospital with the same senior doctor as two years before. But I was delighted to see her alive. As I walked down the stairs on my way out, I realized that the dominant feeling was one of relief, whereas excitement and fascination had been the stronger two years before.

XVI

I ended my slightly surreal Friday, 24 March 1972 quietly, alone in my flat at Hegdehaugen.

I ate a couple of dry slices of bread as I watched the final news of the day on television at eleven o'clock.

Miriam's disappearance and return, which had been the day's great event for me, had not made it into the news. Another mass demonstration against the EEC in Bergen fortunately dominated the programming. The rest focused on the shooting by the National Theatre and the postponed signing of the Barents Sea agreement.

The prime minister, Trond Bratten, was interviewed. He stated in a characteristically laconic and serious manner that it would be irresponsible of the Norwegian Labour Party to submit such an important agreement to the Storting, when incidents such as the killing of Fredriksen and the shooting at the National Theatre remained unresolved. The police would now be given the time necessary to finish the investigation and only then would the agreement be submitted for debate.

There was broad support for this in the Storting, but

leading members of the Norwegian Communist Party were critical of a postponement in signing the agreement with the Soviet Union. A couple of SPP politicians were critical of the NCP politicians' criticism, and feared that any prospects of cooperation to the left of the Labour Party in connection with the general election in 1973 were now slim.

It struck me as I watched that even though my personal drama was hopefully now over after a nightmarish twenty-four hours, I was still investigating two murder cases that could be of considerable importance both nationally and internationally. And I felt remarkably calm about it. All that remained, now that the part of the case that involved a foreign superpower was resolved and my fiancée had been safely returned, was a classic murder mystery. It was, to be fair, an unusually complicated murder investigation, with several parties involved and more possible sidetracks than in any of my other cases. And yet I felt certain that we would solve it in the course of the weekend. Patricia had been so confident and happy, almost lighthearted, this evening – it could only be a good sign.

A quarter of an hour after I had turned off the television, I found myself worrying largely about Patricia's boyfriend. I accepted that Johan Fredriksen was clearly innocent of both murders, and I respected the fact that he was Patricia's boyfriend. But I reserved the right to dislike him and their relationship. The fact that I was jealous that Patricia had a lover bothered me so much that I had to ask myself if my feelings would have been any stronger if it had been Miriam who had one. I remembered Miriam's little smile in her sleep at Ullevål and felt almost sick at the thought. But I still had to admit that the answer was not a clear-cut yes.

In the end, I had to acknowledge that I found myself caught in a painful and classic dilemma. Regardless of what happened now in the investigation, I still had a fundamental problem, in that I now, in two different ways, was very fond of two different women. Both had sacrificed a lot for me, and I had had different strong and emotional experiences with both of them. Before the start of this murder investigation, I had been certain of which one I could not live without. I was no longer so sure.

Paradoxically, the fact that Patricia now had a boyfriend was apparently what was needed for me to realize how much she meant to me. On a number of previous occasions, after her father's death in particular, I had found myself thinking how much easier it would be if Patricia had more friends than just me. And now that she did, I almost instinctively reacted negatively. And my dilemma as to what I should tell Miriam about my contact with Patricia would once again become pressing the moment Miriam woke up.

So Friday, 24 March 1972 had indeed provided great relief, another death and some useful information. It had been a rollercoaster ride to the very end. I fell asleep just before midnight, alone in my bed, with alternating pictures of Patricia and Miriam in my mind.

The picture that stayed just before I dropped off was of the sleeping Miriam as she tried to smile at me from her deep slumber at Ullevål Hospital. I tossed and turned in bed more than usual before eventually I fell asleep.

DAY EIGHT

Lots of Answers – and an Unbearably Painful Question

I

Saturday, 25 March 1972 started for me at half past seven – and on a low, as anticipated. Two of the morning papers carried short reports that the fiancée of the head of the Fredriksen investigation had been reported missing earlier the day before, but had then been found again in the evening.

The shooting at the National Theatre and the postponed signing of the Barents Sea agreement, on the other hand, were on all the front pages. All the newspapers were careful to point out that the incident was as yet unexplained, but all agreed that the signing of the agreement should be postponed as a result of this uncertainty. Any links to the Fredriksen case were still unclear, though even *Aftenposten* wrote that 'the pressure on the head of investigation Kolbjørn Kristiansen will now be even greater.' I could not even bear to think about what *Verdens Gang* would write.

Reading these reports in the papers felt like a hard start

to the day. But gradually I came round to the idea that, in isolation, it was not such a bad thing. I was very glad that the drama with Miriam had not been picked up by the press. I was not sure that my boss had assessed the mood correctly with regards to the interpreter. I thought that her murder, if it remained unsolved, might be revisited by the press, certainly if the suspicions of a Soviet execution proved to be persistent. But if that was the case, it would be Danielsen's problem and responsibility. My responsibility was limited to the murder of Per Johan Fredriksen and his daughter, which I now had every hope we could solve before Monday.

It suited me very well that the Fredriksen murders had been overshadowed by the shooting at the National Theatre. I could eat my breakfast in peace without the telephone ringing. Though they did call from the main station at a quarter past eight to say that I was invited to another meeting at the Soviet Embassy as soon as possible. I asked them to pass on the message that I would be there at nine.

II

The table was set for three today. It almost felt a little unsafe sitting there under the portrait of Brezhnev alone with two Soviet citizens. However, today's meeting was much shorter and far more relaxed. The vice-ambassador came in with the same interpreter as yesterday and smiled as he shook my hand.

'The vice-ambassador hopes that you are pleased with developments and thanks you for your help in resolving the situation without any unnecessary speculation or scandal,' the interpreter said.

For which I thanked him, with somewhat mixed feelings. Then I asked if the embassy had any new information that might help to solve the murder of Per Johan Fredriksen.

'The embassy would be more than happy to help and the vice-ambassador hopes that we can do so. We can first of all assure you that your meetings with our colleague Sergey Klinkalski in various parts of the city were pure co-incidence. Comrade Klinkalski likes to familiarize himself with the different parts of the town or city where he is working, including the more working-class areas, so he spent a couple of days exploring the city. Unfortunately he could not be here himself today, as he has been transferred to an important position in another embassy at short notice. Klinkalski left Norway late yesterday evening. He asked us to pass on his best wishes and this, his written statement.'

I thanked him somewhat insincerely. The situation felt a little absurd – but at the same time, very exciting. And it was no less absurd or exciting when the vice-ambassador then produced a folded sheet of paper and handed it to me almost ceremoniously.

The folded sheet contained a typed statement in perfect Norwegian with a very elegant signature:

As a result of my wish to familiarize myself with Oslo, I found myself at Majorstuen in the evening on Saturday, 18 March 1972. There were not many people around. One of the men was Per Johan Fredriksen, whom I did not know at the time, but subsequently realized was a leading politician when I saw his photograph in the newspaper.

Fredriksen was first stopped on a street corner by a young boy on a bicycle. They exchanged a few words, then Fredriksen waved him off and carried on walking. The boy stood there for a while, then turned round, got onto his bike, and cycled slowly off in the opposite direction.

Fredriksen walked on to the next corner, where a middle-aged woman waved to him. The woman seemed to be known to Fredriksen, as he went over to her. They exchanged a few words, whereupon the woman drew a knife and stabbed Fredriksen in the chest. Fredriksen shouted, fell to the ground and lay there. The woman stood there for a few seconds, then ran as fast as she could down the street in the direction that Fredriksen had come from.

As I am unfamiliar with Norwegian society and conventions, I stayed where I was to observe, as I was uncertain whether the whole thing might have been staged in order to rob me. A few moments later, the boy on the bicycle came back. He leaned down over Fredriksen, pulled out the knife and then stood there with it in his hand. Then suddenly he hopped on his bike and pedalled off at high speed. Several other passers-by were now gathering around Fredriksen. I understood now that he really had been the victim of a crime, but that I might myself be suspected and so withdrew and went back to the embassy, rather than approaching the scene of the crime.

The woman who stabbed Fredriksen had dark hair and looked as though she could be somewhere between forty and sixty. She was bare-headed and wearing an old green winter coat. Because of the distance and the dark, I am unfortunately unable to give any more details about her features or clothes.

Dr Sergey Klinkalski, Oslo, 24 March 1972.

'The vice-ambassador hopes that the information may be of help to your investigation into the terrible murder of Mr Fredriksen,' the interpreter said.

I said that I hoped so too. Then I thanked the vice-ambassador for his help and cooperation. He left with me this time. We parted at the reception, with a firm and almost friendly handshake.

III

'Exactly. Thank you. That is exactly what I was hoping for,' Patricia said, and put the document down beside her cup of coffee.

I remarked that the document provided new information, but not about who killed Per Johan Fredriksen. I added that we might perhaps want to take what Klinkalski said with a pinch of salt, but that what he had written did fit well with what we already knew.

Patricia nodded. 'Like a glove. All the stuff about him and his intentions is of course nonsense, but his eyewitness account is the truth, I think. There is no reason for him to lie about it. On the contrary, it is not only in his interests, but also in the embassy's that this is cleared up. His statement does not tell us who the murderer is, but it does give important information about who it is not. Enough for me now to tell you who murdered Eva Bjølhaugen in 1932 and who killed Per Johan and Vera Fredriksen in 1972. So, we are talking about three murders and two murderers. But I warn you, evidence may be problematic, so having the murderers' identities will not necessarily mean that the case is closed.'

I quickly agreed with her. I probably would have done that no matter what she said in the end. I felt slightly shellshocked – and intoxicated by the possibility that the case might soon be solved.

'Per Johan Fredriksen's death acted as a catalyst killing, to a certain extent, which dramatically escalated certain processes that triggered the deaths of three other people in only a matter of days. But the statement from Dr Death confirmed something that I have thought for some time now, in other words, that the murder of Per Johan Fredriksen had nothing to do with the deaths of his wife's sister in 1932 and his daughter now in 1972. But shall we begin with 1932?'

I quickly said yes. The murder mystery from 1932 had a strange allure for me.

'The death in 1932 still cannot be explained in isolation. However, there is one interesting detail that I have thought about a lot. Solveig Ramdal heard a thump in the room next door at half past seven. That was because Eva Bjølhaugen fainted as a result of an epileptic seizure. The young Solveig obviously had very good hearing and was on the alert in her room, as only she and no one else heard it. She also heard footsteps in the corridor and neighbouring room earlier. After the bang, she becomes even more attentive and practically stands with her ear to the wall. But she hears nothing – even though a person must have been walking around in the room after Eva fainted. What do you think that means?'

I had never thought about it in that way – and was not sure what to answer when suddenly confronted with it from this angle. So my answer was somewhat noncommittal: 'One possible explanation is that Solveig Ramdal is simply lying, as we only have her word for it.'

Patricia gave a thoughtful nod. 'I have also considered that possibility. Solveig Ramdal had something to hide and she has lied before. She is an egotist and a cold-blooded chameleon, who would, no doubt, be capable of killing if it was in her interest. But she had no motive for the murder, unless Eva had threatened to reveal the secret of Solveig's sexuality, but then Eva had no interest in doing that. So we can assume that Solveig is telling the truth. The key question here is which one of the others had the strongest motive, if you ignore the human considerations that most people would assume?'

'Talking of important questions – have you worked out the significance of the key in the corridor?'

'As far as 1932 is concerned, I have from the start worked on the theory that the key was a spontaneous attempt to point the suspicion at Eva's boyfriend, Hauk Rebne Westgaard. And to give the impression that the position of the key was of real importance. But it was not: the murderer was let in by the victim. And forty years later, it was a premeditated attempt to give the impression that it was an enactment of the same murder. This was done by a murderer who had created a kind of alibi in doing this, who had an alibi for the death of Per Johan Fredriksen, and who at first glance was a highly unlikely candidate.'

As Patricia spoke, it suddenly dawned on me who she was referring to. At first it seemed slightly surreal, but then it seemed all the more strange to me that I had not considered this possibility before.

'The last person that anyone remembers was there,' I said, tentatively.

Patricia nodded.

'The one who walks without a sound, even in shoes. So if she was walking on the carpet in the corridor in her stockinged feet, you would not hear her. She was let in by her sister. She knew about her sister's illness, and understood immediately that she was having an epileptic fit. And she had an obvious motive: with her irritatingly beautiful and popular little sister out of the way, she would become a very attractive heir to a considerable fortune. And even more importantly, I think: she would be rid of a dangerous competitor for the affections of the man she wanted – and later got, with the help of the family fortune.'

So it was as I had thought for the past few minutes, and I still could not believe that I had not seen it until now. I was cheered to an extent when Patricia carried on.

'To begin with, when the main focus was on Per Johan

Fredriksen's death, we almost lost sight of the grieving widow, who had an alibi. She was no doubt constantly worried that her husband would discover the truth of what happened in 1932. But he had not and nothing he said to his wife showed that he had. So she was genuinely surprised, and mourned his death. Paradoxically, it was only after the death of the daughter, who also did not suspect her mother, that I started to suspect Oda Fredriksen. In the case of Vera, it was not just that someone knew she was at the hotel, but also who she would let into the room. When Solveig Ramdal confessed to being the mystery guest in the next room, I focused more and more on the last person that Vera Fredriksen rang.'

'But, she only made two phone calls, other than the call to me. Surely one must have been to her sister and the other to Solveig Ramdal?' I said.

Patricia snorted. 'Nonsense. She paid for two telephone calls earlier in the day. But she would of course not have paid for the call to her sister, as it was never answered. After she had spoken to Solveig Ramdal, the nervous Vera would undoubtedly have consulted with someone in her family before phoning you. First she rang her sister, who did not get to the phone on time. The other two possibilities were then her brother, who I knew had not killed her, and her mother. Vera Fredriksen really was a little naive, and made a fatal mistake when she trusted that her own mother was not the murderer. Solveig Ramdal arrived first, and was also prepared to kill her if her secret was about to be revealed. But she had no murder to hide and was smart enough to find out what Vera Fredriksen knew first.'

Patricia stopped and looked at me. I had no questions, so I gave an impatient wave for her to continue.

'The mother, on the other hand, had a murder to hide and thought she had been discovered. She got straight down to business with almost impressive efficiency. She asked her daughter to sit tight and not open the door to anyone until she got there. Then she made herself a kind of alibi by phoning her other daughter just before she left the house. She also rang her son, but got no answer, which gave her an even better idea for an alibi. On her way to the hotel, she stopped at a telephone box, rang her son again, then hung up without waiting for an answer. She knew from previous visits to the hotel that she could get in without being seen from the reception area. As soon as she had been let into the room, she showed her true face and attacked. Poor fragile Vera fainted, as she so often did in frightening situations. Whereupon Oda Fredriksen drowned her youngest daughter in the same way that she had drowned her younger sister forty years earlier. It is a horrific story for those of us who want to believe in kind mothers and secure families. But that must be what happened, and it is unfortunately not unheard of that people with a strong ego or who are secretly deranged have killed members of their family.'

I had to agree with this.

Patricia had spoken for some time with great passion. Now she looked depressed and her hand was shaking when she lit a cigarette. She smoked half of it in silence, before continuing.

'It is not a happy ending, if that is what you were hoping

for. But it is the truth, and so the only solution I can give you to the two murders.'

The shock was subsiding now. I realized that my failure to react had disappointed Patricia, and felt that it was ungrateful of me. So I slowly clapped my hands – and assured her that I was more than happy to have established the truth about the two murders.

Patricia smiled when I started to clap. But if she really was happy, it did not last long. She stubbed out her cigarette, then leaned across the table towards me. Suddenly her face was inches away from mine. I found myself wondering if it was a coincidence that she was wearing a very loose white blouse and an undoubtedly expensive perfume that I had not smelt before. And suddenly found myself very jealous of Johan Fredriksen.

'It is a little early to applaud, I am afraid. As the case stands, I am not sure that a good lawyer might not get her acquitted on the basis of reasonable doubt, with no witnesses or evidence. I have told you how it happened and the sequence of events, now you have to get her to confess. And at the same time, you might find out whether, behind the facade, she is slightly deranged or just extremely calculating. But the overlap there can be scarily hard to define. Come back when you have done that, and we can then hopefully talk about Per Johan Fredriksen and other things of mutual interest.'

I took the hint. Patricia did not want to tell me who had killed Per Johan Fredriksen yet. She knew, but she wanted me to come back – and she had given me the answer to two of the three murders. That qualified as a very good start to the day. On my way from the house into the centre of town, I pondered on who might have killed Per Johan Fredriksen, and what Patricia had meant by 'other things of mutual interest'.

IV

It was a quarter past eleven by the time I parked outside the Fredriksens' family home on Bygdøy, having first swung by to collect DI Danielsen from the station. Danielsen had been working his way through a pile of papers, but his face lit up and he immediately put on his jacket when I asked if he would like to help me with a final push in the Fredriksen cases.

I did not tell Danielsen how it all fitted together, just that it was an important interview. I felt under a lot of pressure but did not let it show. I did not doubt that Patricia was right with regard to the murder of Vera Fredriksen. But she was unfortunately also right with regard to the lack of evidence. I needed a confession. The chances of getting one would undoubtedly be best if I was alone with Oda Fredriksen in the drawing room. But that might cause problems if she did say something that incriminated her, but then later denied it.

The solution was that I took Danielsen with me, introduced him to the widow, and told her that he was only there as a matter of procedure, and that the two of us could talk together alone first, as it involved some very sensitive information. Danielsen gave his most charming smile and offered to wait outside in the hall.

I walked into the drawing room behind her and made sure not to close the door completely. Then I sat down on the sofa and nodded to the chair opposite. Oda Fredriksen sat down – with her back to the door. She had shoes on, and yet seemed to glide across the carpetless floor without a sound. I hoped that Danielsen would hear most of what was said in the event of a later dispute.

And there we sat, Oda Fredriksen and I, face to face in the drawing room, with all the red velvet furniture and a sea of flowers on the table beside us.

'You wanted to ask me some personal questions?' she said, in her slightly distracted voice.

'I understand that this is still a very difficult time for you, following your husband's death. But we have to go back in time first. To your childhood in Vestfold. Your sister was by all accounts a very beautiful and popular young lady. But from what other people have said, I also understand that she could be quite difficult and that it was not always easy for you, being the big sister.'

Oda Fredriksen frowned for a moment, but responded swiftly.

'I don't know who you have been speaking to, but they are right. Eva was always the most beautiful and brightest of us. And she knew it, and what is more, liked it. She had our parents wrapped around her little finger until she was confirmed. And then she started to wrap men around her fingers. I was always just, well, the ugly stupid little sister, even though I was the eldest.'

She sounded angry and bitter when she said this, with knitted brows. I saw a new Oda Fredriksen emerge in the scowl and unblinking eyes. A bitter, older woman looking back on the frustrations in her life. And I wanted to feed this feeling.

'It must have been very hard for you. Especially when she fell in love with the man you loved.'

She nodded vigorously, almost furiously.

'Not only was it hard, it was unbearable. Eva must have known by then that he was the one I wanted. I lay in bed crying alone for hours, whenever he came to visit her. And the evening that I heard that they had broken up, I stood jubilant in front of my mirror.'

'But your victory was not yet won. Another woman you knew inconveniently took her place.'

Her gaze was fixed on me and she nodded again – a little less vigorously this time.

'Solveig Thaulow, yes. My only friend. Clever Solveig. She was also prettier and smarter than me. That is what they all said. I heard them. If only Oda could be a bit more like Solveig, or like Eva, my mother once said to her parents. Then they all nodded. My father, as well. Solveig was less annoying than my sister. But all the same, the fact that they started going out together was terrible, and then even worse, they got engaged. I did not see anyone for several days. When finally I ventured out, I went down to the jetty and seriously considered throwing myself into the water.'

She did not blink and her face had hardened. A third face now appeared from the past. It was a younger, more self-conscious and dangerous face. I sat there and watched, fascinated, as I carried on talking.

'But you did not jump, and you discovered new hope.

You watched and saw that all was not well between Solveig and Per Johan. And this became even clearer on the trip to Oslo, didn't it?'

'Yes, I kept a close eye on them, and could tell even on the train. They did not sit together and barely spoke. I ingratiated myself with Solveig that evening, said she looked so serious, asked if everything was all right. She told me that things were not going well with Per Johan and that she was considering breaking off the engagement. Then she said that she thought he might be interested in me, and perhaps it might be better if that was the case. It was one of the greatest moments in my life. I had never been together with a man, and I had been unhappily in love with Per Johan for several years.'

'Suddenly your goal and your great love were within reach. But then your sister appeared again, like the serpent in Paradise. She fluttered her greedy eyes at Per Johan once more. That is what you discovered that afternoon when you went to her room, isn't it?'

'Yes. She told me. She was dressed when I got there. But I could see that the sheet was crumpled. When I asked her who had been there, she smiled her meanest and most horrible smile. She told me that Per Johan had been there and that he wanted her back. And she said that she had to think about it, but probably would take him back. It might make me even more jealous and unhappy, but she could not let that stop her. She was so indescribably mean.'

This was said with a hiss. Oda Fredriksen's face was now unrecognizably stiff. I understood better than ever before what Patricia meant when she talked about chameleon people, and instinctively pulled back a little for fear that her tongue might suddenly dart out.

'It certainly sounds like it. You did not go there with the intention to harm her. But then she had one of her epileptic fits and fainted. You might even have helped to get her onto the sofa. Then it struck you just how vile and mean she was, and that her death would solve all your problems. It was actually a very smart idea.'

She nodded, almost without thinking.

'Thank you. Yes, I thought it was quite smart myself. No one would think that she might have drowned. Mother and Father would think it was suicide, and as the good old Christian fools they were, they would refuse permission for an autopsy. And if there was an autopsy, they would discover that she had drowned, but would still not know who had killed her.'

I nodded with encouragement.

'Suspicion was more likely to fall on her boyfriend, whom she was in the process of jilting. Especially if you left the room key on the floor outside his door. That was quick thinking and very smart.'

She nodded again, pleased. 'I was not as stupid as everyone thought. I fooled them all. I got the man I wanted, and I managed to keep him, right until . . .'

Suddenly her face changed completely – to the grieving widow. She covered her eyes with her hands and I saw the tears sliding down her cheeks.

'Right until someone killed him. Which was terrible. But were you not sad about Vera? Your sister was nasty, but Vera was so young and kind.'

It did not take much more for the embittered face to appear again. She carried on talking, fast, and pointed her finger as though accusing me.

'Vera was young and kind, but she was so spineless – weak. I always knew that I would outlive Vera. She somehow did not have any fight of her own. Per Johan loved Vera and looked after her well. And now that he was dead, she would die too. She had tried to take her own life before and would have succeeded in the end, if I had not helped her. Sooner or later she would have poisoned herself or starved to death. And in the meantime she would have squandered all her inheritance on that artist twit of a boyfriend. It was not easy. I saw Per Johan's face in hers as she lay there on the sofa and did think it was terribly sad. But Vera was not worth it, and she was threatening to expose me!'

And with that, everything had been said and explained. And suddenly, as if the trance had been broken, Oda Fredriksen was back in the present again. She recognized me and pressed her hands to her face. Her voice was almost normal again, but the bitter undertone remained, when she carried on talking after a brief pause.

'You have no idea what it is like. To live every minute, every hour and every day for so many years in the constant fear of being caught. I hoped it would get better over the years, particularly once the limitation period had expired. But it didn't get easier. My greatest fear was in fact not that I would be caught by the law, but be exposed by my husband, my children and everyone I knew. Keeping it secret became an eternal obsession. Behind the mask, you become an animal, a predator – your instincts and survival mechanisms kick in, especially when threatened.'

Earlier in the conversation I had experienced a horrified fascination listening to Oda Fredriksen. But now the fascination had gone, and only the horror remained. I was still uncertain as to whether she was in her right mind, but the court would have to decide that. I had all the answers I needed, and suddenly felt a great reluctance to talk any more with this emotionally cold, egotistical person.

'Self-preservation instinct is what some people call it. Well, I guess it's time for us to go back to the station and get you a lawyer.'

Oda Fredriksen nodded curtly and stood up unexpectedly fast. She stood there, still as a statue, while I got up.

The movement was sudden, just as I was about to stand up straight. I caught a glimpse of some long, sharp nails and thought that they reminded me of a lioness's claws, before I felt them scratching just under my eyes. Instinctively, I raised my hands to stop her claws. They disappeared from my eyes and instead I felt a hand fumbling around inside my jacket. The hand was thin and burning hot against my skin and the nails tore at me like claws.

Then I heard a semi-triumphant 'haah' and caught another quick movement as she jumped two steps back.

And, for the second time in my life, I found myself looking down the barrel of a loaded gun.

This time it was my own service gun. The experience was no less frightening because Oda had managed to fumble the safety off, and her finger was now shaking violently on the trigger.

The woman in the black dress was now unrecognizable. Her eyes flashed, and she gasped for breath as she hissed: 'Who else knows that I killed Vera?'

I thought about the only other time I had looked down the barrel of a pistol. It had also been a terrifying experience that hounded me in nightmares for months after. But that time I knew that the person holding the pistol was entirely rational. I thought about what Patricia had said: that the overlap was hard to define. I looked at Oda Fredriksen's wild eyes and feared that she might pull the trigger, intentionally or unintentionally, at any moment.

The question was a rational one from her perspective. She repeated it: 'Who else knows that I killed Vera?'

I answered with the truth: 'Only one other person knows that you killed Vera, but several people know that I am here. The truth will come out, whether you shoot me or not. And if you shoot a policeman, you will get a life sentence.'

As I said this, I noticed Danielsen in the background.

He came in quietly, in his socks, gliding cautiously over the floor. He was unarmed. But he was in the room and it was an enormous relief that I was not alone with a half-mad murderer.

It was not clear to me if Danielsen's arrival increased or diminished the chance that I would be shot within the next few seconds. Oda Fredriksen's finger was still shaking violently – and the pistol was still pointing at my chest.

'If I am caught, I will be sentenced to life regardless, for the murder of my daughter. My only chance is not to get caught, so I have to shoot you first. Shoot you, hide your body and escape in the car – to Sweden or somewhere like that.'

Again she was talking as if in a trance. Danielsen moved soundlessly closer as she spoke. He was only a few feet behind her now. He stopped there and hesitated, as if waiting for a signal from me. I understood his dilemma. Oda Fredriksen had her shaking finger on the trigger. The chances that the gun would go off and that the bullet would hit me if he launched himself at her were considerable. In the midst of all this, I suddenly felt sorry for Danielsen.

I did not dare to stop her talking. So I said that she would be arrested even if she fled to Sweden. The police would find her no matter where she went, and the sentence would be all the more severe if she shot a policeman.

'Is there someone behind me?' she asked in a strained voice. Her finger shook even more violently on the trigger when she said this.

I managed to think that the chances of her shooting me might be less if she knew that she would immediately be arrested by another policeman. And that I would be able to throw myself over her if she turned around to shoot Danielsen.

So, with forced calm, I replied: 'Yes. Detective Inspector Danielsen, who came here with me, is standing right behind you now. You cannot get away, even if you shoot me.'

We stared at each other for a few eternal seconds. She was shaking with emotion – and the pistol was shaking with her.

I saw the flash in her eyes and realized that she was going to shoot a second before she did so.

So I was already moving to the right when she fired; like a football keeper diving for a penalty kick, I found myself thinking, as I sailed through the air and saw the bullet penetrate the velvet sofa behind me.

I hit the floor and at the same time my foot hit the table. All the flowers were knocked off, just as Oda Fredriksen also fell to the floor with Danielsen on her back.

Oda Fredriksen lay there on the floor with Danielsen on top of her, and no means of escape. But she did not let go of my pistol. Her hand gripped it tightly like a claw. From my position by the table leg, I saw Danielsen banging her wrist three times without her letting go of the gun. Only then did I realize that I was alive and unharmed.

I leapt up and ran over to Oda Fredriksen, grabbed hold of her wrist and pulled at it so hard that I was frightened her arm might break. But still she did not let go of the pistol. I had to grip it with both hands and pull with all my might to get it free. There was a faint sob from her as I managed to pull it away. But even without her weapon she was still acting like a desperate wild animal as she fought and struggled on her drawing-room floor. She kept twisting her hands away, refusing to give up. It was only on the third attempt that I managed to get the handcuffs round her right wrist and it took two more to get them locked on her left.

And then finally it was over. Suddenly, almost alarmingly so, she regained her self-control. She panted furiously for a few seconds and then relaxed and accepted her fate.

'I apologize, I did not want to kill you. My self-preservation instinct got the better of me,' she said. Her voice was almost as expressionless as it usually was.

I was unharmed, but still in shock. So I did not answer. Danielsen was also paler than I remembered having ever seen him before, and did not look as though he wanted to say any more to Oda Fredriksen. In silent understanding, we each put a hand on her shoulders and walked out with her between us.

None of us said a word on the way out. I only heard a low, animal snarl from Oda Fredriksen as we got into the police car. I looked up and understood why, when I saw that a passer-by had stopped and was looking at us. For her, it was a taste of the disgrace that would follow when her arrest for murder became public knowledge. So I pushed her into the back of the car and then got into the passenger seat without saying any more.

I was still wound up and shaken by the unexpected drama in the drawing room at Bygdøy. It was only halfway back into Oslo that I discovered blood running from a wound under my right eye.

V

The time was five to one. I had returned to 19 Møller Street and handed over Oda Fredriksen.

I was now back at Patricia's in Frogner, and had told her what had happened out at Bygdøy. She showed unexpected concern about the scratch on my face and expressed relief when I assured her that it was nothing serious. I thought to myself that perhaps Patricia had become more empathetic over the years, and I was now seeing a more humane side of her.

'A family tragedy of devastating proportions. Behind her mask, she must have suffered from serious mental illness for years. I understand that it must have been a very unnerving experience for you. But as you came out of it unscathed, the outcome is good, in that the guilty party has been arrested and the question of guilt is indisputable,' Patricia said firmly.

She finished her coffee, but as yet had not touched the packet of cigarettes on the table. Patricia was solemn and distant. She was in no rush to tell me what she had understood earlier today. At first I wondered if she was thinking about the situation with her boyfriend – and then to what extent I should take that into consideration. I waited a minute before carrying on.

'Well, then, perhaps we should push on and talk about how this all started – in other words, the murder of Per Johan Fredriksen.'

Patricia seemed to wake up and look at me. And at the same time, her hand stretched out towards the cigarette packet.

'Yes, of course. I am sorry, I got lost in my own thoughts. Yes, we should carry on, even though it is in many ways an even sadder story. The statement from Doctor Death confirmed what I already believed, and that is that Fredriksen's murder had nothing to do with the murder in 1932. Nor did it have anything to do with his business. Which rules out all the men, and his wife had an alibi.'

'Solveig Ramdal, then?' I asked.

Patricia smiled. 'Perhaps not so clear. But I think that we can rule her out all the same when it comes to Fredriksen's murder. For a start, she does not really fit the description in terms of physique and clothes. Furthermore, the motive would still be unclear, as she had no murder to hide from 1932. Plus, she also had an alibi of sorts from her husband. One could perhaps construct a motive for Solveig Ramdal or Kjell Arne Ramdal for killing Per Johan Fredriksen, but it is hard to imagine a situation where they would both have a motive for killing him – and what is more, trust each other enough to do it together. So their alibi is better than it may seem.'

I recalled my conversations with the Ramdals and had to concede.

'If we are to believe Doctor Death's statement, we can assume that the description also rules out both the Fredriksen sisters and the boy on the red bicycle,' I added quickly.

'Naturally. But I have never at any point thought that any of those three killed Fredriksen. However, I have suspected throughout that one of them might be of more importance than at first we realized. I just struggled to understand the reasons for, and the significance of, his apparently confused behaviour. But there are no other possibilities now. It was no one from Fredriksen's family, nor from his business contacts, nor any of his fated friends from 1932. We will have to see the spying aspect of the case as solved, even though it is still unclear how far Fredriksen went with his contacts and how the police security service found out. But the solution to his murder does not lie there. So we have dismissed those who did not commit the murder, but still do not know who did it. We are back where we started: at the sad story of the boy on the red bicycle, and the question of whether he was of sound mind and why he behaved so oddly. Oh, this really is a terrible story.'

The last exclamation was said in a very sharp voice. I spotted a tear in Patricia's eye that she hastily wiped away. She shook her head angrily and then sat there with a cigarette in her mouth.

'The boy's confusing behaviour and the question of the knife are what roused my suspicion. There were soon so many who could have had a motive for killing Per Johan Fredriksen. But it remained a mystery why anyone would kill him with a knife. Unless of course it was the only murder weapon the murderer had or could get hold of,' Patricia said, slowly.

I had not thought about this before, but started now to get an inkling of where she was going. And if that was the case, I could only agree that it was a terrible story.

Patricia then asked an unexpected question. 'Did you ever find out more about Hauptmann, whom the boy on the red bicycle referred to the last time you spoke with him?'

Reluctantly, I had to admit that I had not thought about checking it in any more detail.

'Well, I did, and there is more to it than you might think. The parallels are a good clue, as he clearly wanted to talk in riddles. Bruno Hauptmann had a box of money in his garage that was proved to be the ransom money from the Lindbergh kidnapping, but right up until his death, he claimed that he had never been given it. The boy on the red bicycle stood there with a knife that had been used to commit a murder, but he maintained until his death that he had not used it.'

'But he was not Fredriksen's son,' I said.

Patricia nodded and let out the heaviest sigh I had ever heard from her.

'No, I know that theory was wrong. But that does not rule out that his mother had a relationship with Fredriksen before he was born – or that Fredriksen later ruthlessly let her down. Perhaps that was the problem: that Fredriksen could have been the child's father, but was not. You will have to ask his mother for the details. Whatever the case, the picture is not entirely clear: she bore him a grudge, and this turned into pure hate and a desire for revenge when Fredriksen again let her down when she was in such desperate need fifteen years later. It becomes more and more reminiscent of a Greek tragedy. The rich mother kills her own daughter from sheer egotism – to conceal the murder of her own sister. The poor mother kills her former lover out of desperation, and without knowing it, takes the life of her only son at the same time.'

'So, behind his limp, speech defect and class complexes, the boy on the red bicycle was in fact completely rational?'

Patricia nodded. 'Completely. From his perspective, it was completely rational to wait for Fredriksen there, to ask him for mercy for himself and his poor mother. He had his back to the wall and had no other hope, so why should he not try? But Fredriksen waved him off and simply referred him to the office manager, as he always did in those situations. The boy cycled off, but stopped – either because he heard the shout, or because he decided to try talking to Fredriksen one more time. Fredriksen did not come. Instead the boy suddenly saw his mother, who was supposed to be visiting his aunt, come round the corner at high speed and run off down the road. He wondered what had happened, limped around the corner and found the dying Fredriksen. The kitchen knife in Fredriksen's chest was one that the boy on the red bicycle recognized from home. Bruno Hauptmann was, if he was telling the truth, sentenced for a serious crime committed by his best friend. Tor Johansen told the truth and was arrested for a serious crime committed by his best friend.'

Patricia paused and shook her head again furiously. She lit another cigarette, then carried on swiftly.

'I have coincidentally read the biography of the foreign secretary Bevin that the boy's teacher spoke about. In a short retrospective, Bevin commented that his mother was the only person he can remember showing any interest or doing anything good for him in his childhood. With a nod to the teacher, the boy on the red bicycle could probably have said much the same. No one had done anything for him, except his mother. Society had definitely done nothing to help him. He could not hand over his mother to upholders of that society, even though he knew that she had done something dreadfully wrong. So he took the murder weapon with him and fled to the home of a hero he had never spoken to before. He hoped and believed that either his mother would give herself up rather than let him take the blame, or that you would solve the mystery without him having to betray his mother. But he fell into despair on the Sunday when his mother did not give herself up and you had not solved the case. He had tried his very best, but still ended up carrying the blame for something he had not done. On Monday morning he was pushed over the edge and took his own life, tragically only a few hours before he might have been saved.'

Patricia stubbed out her cigarette, then sat there staring out into thin air.

I did not feel particularly buoyant either, despite the fact that the last murder case was now solved. My memory of finding the boy dead in his cell returned – along with my bad conscience. If only I had been able to see the connections earlier, I could truly have lived up to his belief in me and saved his life.

To begin with, I was angry with myself, and then angry with Miriam, who had not let me ring Patricia earlier. It struck me then that this was the first time in hours that I had thought about Miriam, and that she should be awake by now. But the thought was interrupted by Patricia's voice.

'You must not blame yourself. It was not easy to see the links at the time and we will never know what might otherwise have happened. However, there is one thing that struck me as rather odd, as you are otherwise usually quite observant. Danielsen supposedly gave the pad and pencil to the boy the day before. It is rather strange, then, that you did not notice them when you spoke to him for the last time.'

I had to think back to my last meeting with the boy on the red bicycle. It was painful – and also unsettling. I ran through the meeting in my mind, twice, and then I shook my head.

'I had not thought about that, what with everything else. But the pad and pencil were not on the table and there were not many places he could have hidden them.'

Patricia gave a thoughtful nod, and lit another cigarette.

'In that case, you were not the last person to speak to the boy before he took his life after all. You might want to have a word with Danielsen about that,' she said, with another little sigh.

I said that I should probably speak to both him and the boy on the red bicycle's mother as soon as possible.

Patricia nodded and said: 'I do not envy you either of those conversations, so good luck with both of them.'

Then she sat still and stared straight ahead again.

I stopped by the door, turned around and said: 'Thank you so much for all your help. You are incredible.'

Patricia smiled and waved two fingers, but said no more. On the way out, I realized that she had not asked me to come back, or not to come back, later.

VI

By two o'clock I had rung Edvard Rønning Junior, the lawyer, and agreed that he would meet me at his client's home as soon after three as possible. I told him that we had important news in relation to the investigation of Per Johan Fredriksen's murder, and he assured me that he would be more than happy to take a couple of hours out of his Saturday to hear what it was.

I had also informed Fredriksen's remaining children. I

had called Ane Line Fredriksen first. She said that she was shaken by the news of her mother's arrest, but then quickly added: 'But nothing in this family can shock me any more' – and then asked to know the details. I told her, tentatively, that the investigation into the murder of her father would probably be closed in the course of the weekend, and that the guilty party quite clearly had no links to the family. I added that I would have to stop there as I still had to ring her brother. She offered spontaneously to call him herself. 'We have become a bit closer as a result of all this, but have yet to have a proper talk about the situation. He was in a foul mood yesterday, by the way. As I understand it, things are not going well with his love life. Which is not entirely unexpected, but it's sad, especially if I never get the chance to know who this secret girlfriend is.'

I noticed that what Ane Line said about her brother and his secret girlfriend buoyed my mood, even if it wasn't for certain. I definitely had no wish to hear Johan Fredriksen's voice at the moment, even though I did not have to see him. So I thanked her for the offer and said that I would appreciate it if she could inform her brother, and promised to telephone later to give her a full update when her father's murder had been solved.

Miriam should have woken up by now, if all was as it should be at Ulleval Hospital. But there was barely time before what presumably would be the final act of the Fredriksen murder investigation, and I thought it might be better for both of us if I could tell her everything at once and that would give her more time with her parents and brother before I got there.

So I steeled myself for another difficult conversation instead, and went to Danielsen's office.

He looked up, smiled briefly and said: 'Good work this morning. Have you got any more exciting news?'

I closed the door and sat down. Then I told him the truth: that I believed we were nearing the end of the investigation into Per Johan Fredriksen's murder as well, but there was a detail in the story of the boy on the red bicycle that we needed to talk about first, just the two of us, right now.

Danielsen looked at me, on guard. 'Just the two of us right now, I see,' he repeated.

I think he knew that I knew. And it felt awkward.

Only a few days ago, a conversation such as this would not have caused me to lose sleep. But now it did. Danielsen had shown me unexpected understanding and support when Miriam was kidnapped. And he had perhaps saved my life during the drama out at Bygdøy earlier today. But there was no way around it, now that we were here.

'It is true that you were the one who gave him the paper and pencil, which he then used to write a suicide note. But it was not quite as you said, was it? I suddenly realized that I hadn't seen the paper and pencil when I was in his cell on Monday morning. So he must have got it later. You must have gone in to see him just before he died.'

I looked at Danielsen. His face was very grave indeed and frightened in a way I had never seen it before. His face confessed before he said anything. But his voice did come eventually.

'I thought – I thought that you had known that all along but had overlooked it for my sake. I was deeply grateful that you did not add to my burden, as it was heavy enough as it was. No matter where I looked in those first few days afterwards, I saw the boy sitting there as he had been the last time I saw him. I should not have come to work on Monday morning. I had had a sad encounter with the woman I had hoped would become my fiancée on the Sunday, who instead said she no longer wished to be my girlfriend. It would be too hard to live with a policeman, she said. So I was in a terrible mood and convinced that the boy was guilty. I became increasingly annoyed that he refused to answer either you or me. So I went back and banged the table a bit more. He still did not answer. He just sat there, silent, and stared straight ahead, as though I was not there.'

'But you didn't touch him, did you?'

He shook his head vigorously. 'No, no, not at all. He hung himself. But I may have said—' Danielsen stopped abruptly, mid-sentence. I could not remember ever having experienced this before. He would not look at me when eventually he continued.

'When I left the paper and pencil, I may have said – well, that he could now either write a confession about what had happened, or a suicide note. I think I must have said that. Of course, I did not mean it like that. His behaviour was just so strange. I really had no idea that he was innocent.'

I felt relieved as soon as he said that. So it was Danielsen, and not me, who had pushed the boy on the red bicycle over the edge. For my part, I felt easier. But with that came a new dilemma. Because as we sat there, I saw something I definitely had never expected to see: Danielsen crying. I felt a surge of sympathy I would never have believed I could ever feel for him. But in the back of my mind I also saw the boy on the red bicycle, pedalling furiously to get to me in time to be saved.

But Danielsen was there, living and breathing in the room with me right now. The boy on the red bicycle was not. Nothing could bring him back. Danielsen had perhaps saved my life earlier in the day. He had risked his own to do so. I thought about the sorrow it would cause the parents he had talked about if this became a cause for dismissal. And that, no matter what, we would never know what exactly had gone on in the head of the boy on the red bicycle in those final minutes of his life. That part of this murder mystery would never be solved.

So I said that in refusing to answer, the boy had behaved very oddly, no matter what his motives were or whether he was guilty or not, and that I believed that Danielsen had meant well, even though what he had done was wrong. And consequently, I thought it best if this stayed strictly between us.

The end of our meeting was very touching; Danielsen took my hand and assured me that he had meant no wrong. And I absolutely believed him.

All the same, in the minute it took to get back to my office, the thin, dark-haired boy flashed up in my mind several times. He was still cycling after me, even though he was nowhere to be seen. I feared that I would continue to see him for some time to come. At that moment I felt a bit like my boss: sensible, successful and cynical. It did not feel good. And suddenly I wondered what Miriam would have said about it all.

VII

At twenty past two, I was sitting alone in my office – not enjoying the silence there.

And it was then, in a flash, that I realized that there was one person whom Patricia had not included in her calculation who could have killed Per Johan Fredriksen.

The possibility felt more and more real as I thought it over. And it would be slightly less of a tragedy after all, if it were the case. It felt less and less tempting to make new allegations about Lene Johansen without having examined and checked all other alternatives. So at twenty-five past two, I asked Danielsen to meet me just before three at 36 Tøyenbekken in Grønland, and apologized in advance if I happened to be a few minutes late.

Then I got into the car and drove to Majorstuen.

Much to my relief, Harriet Henriksen answered her door straightaway. She was wearing a green dress today, not black. But the photograph of her dead lover was still on the table in the living room and a new candle burned beside it.

I started by saying that the old murder from 1932 and the murder of Vera Fredriksen had now been solved. At first she seemed uninterested, but livened up when I said that Oda Fredriksen had committed both murders. 'I always thought that she couldn't be as wonderful as everyone said. It is just a shame that Per Johan never discovered her true nature while he was alive. Everything would have been different then and he might still be here with me now,' she said in a quiet, intense voice.

'And what is more, we now believe that we are close to solving the murder of Per Johan himself. But that requires that you answer me more truthfully than you have done so far,' I said.

This made her start. She stiffened and sat without moving for a few seconds.

'You betrayed him,' I said, and waited.

She stood there, breathing heavily for a while, but when she spoke, it all came tumbling out.

'Yes, I did betray him. And it will always haunt me as it was the end of our love story. But I did not kill him. And as far as I know, informing the police security service about illegal contact with other countries is not a criminal offence,' she said.

That was when I finally got the picture. I had hit the bull's eye, only the target was not the one I had anticipated.

I told her the truth: that it was not illegal if that was all she had done, and as this was a murder investigation I was now duty-bound to ask her for a full explanation. And it should be credible, I added.

'The truth is hopefully always credible, certainly when it concerns a lonely, middle-aged woman's egotism and dreams. I am an anti-communist through and through, but will not try to make myself sound any better than I am. I had lost all hope that Per Johan would leave his marriage for my sake, as long as he was a leading politician. But I thought that if he got caught up in a scandal and had to resign as a politician, the marriage might fall apart anyway. And then I would be the one who was left and who would give him all the support, and a new family with me would be a new start for him. So I told the police security service about his contacts at the Soviet Embassy – on the promise that they would never reveal their source. And it is very disappointing that they have now broken that promise.'

I assured her that I had not heard it from the police security service, but had worked it out myself. Then I added that, strictly speaking, it was not the main line of inquiry in the murder investigation.

She nodded quickly and smiled in appreciation.

'Very good. Given how things stand now, it would be best for everyone if it never got out. Per Johan was unbelievably naive in his dealings with the Soviets. He thought that as an individual he could play an important role in building a bridge between the East and West. And he thought that he would gain widespread recognition if he succeeded. I tried to tell him it was unrealistic, but he didn't want to listen. I am still glad that he discussed it with me, though.'

I saw no reason to start an unnecessary conflict with Harriet Henriksen, so I said that as far as I knew, she was the only one he had spoken to about this. I did not point out the irony that he was then betrayed by the one person he confided in. She did not appear to have thought along those lines herself.

'Oh, how wonderful. I really was the one whom he trusted and loved,' she exclaimed. She stood there with her hand in front of her mouth for a few seconds, before she added, 'But one thing does bother me, as I start my new life alone: I hope that my contact with the police security service had nothing to do with Per Johan's death?'

I suddenly heard a strong undertow of fear when she

said this. Again I was struck by the paradoxical similarities between her and Oda Fredriksen. Both deified a man, and then continued to orbit around him like satellites even after he was dead, even when they were aware of his less virtuous sides. However, the difference was also clear and important. Oda Fredriksen was a rich woman with a family, who had killed her own daughter and sister. Harriet Henriksen was not rich, she was alone, and she had not done anything criminal. So I told her the truth: that the betrayal of her lover had put him in a very dangerous situation, but as far as we knew, it had not been a factor in his death.

She immediately held out her hand and said that it was an enormous relief to hear that. We parted on good terms. It was now ten to three.

VIII

Danielsen was standing in the hallway with Lene Johansen and Edvard Rønning Junior, the lawyer, when I arrived at five minutes past three. Rønning gave me a stern look over his lorgnette, but let his feathers be smoothed when I apologized for my lateness and then said that all the murders in this case could now be seen as solved.

It apparently dawned on us all at the same time that there were not four chairs anywhere in the flat. I suggested that we could just stay standing where we were, as it would not take more than a few minutes. Everyone nodded. And it suited me well. There was a coat stand beside us that was missing three hooks. The only item of clothing hanging there was an old green winter coat. It was the final proof that I needed.

I told them that Oda Fredriksen had been arrested and had confessed to the murder of Vera Fredriksen. Then I took a dramatic pause.

'That is, of course, very interesting, but what about the murder of Per Johan Fredriksen? My client would very much like to have her son's innocence proved,' Rønning said.

My chance was there, and I grabbed it.

'Your client has known all along that he was innocent. The knife that killed Fredriksen came from this kitchen, and he was not the one who used it,' I said.

It worked. Rønning dropped his lorgnette again and his client lost all self-control at the same time. In a matter of seconds, the colour drained from her face and she swayed as though about to faint before I even had a chance to continue.

'Fredriksen had treated you very badly, so there may well be mitigating circumstances. But your betrayal of your son afterwards, and the attempt to exploit his death for economic gain was heartless,' I said.

It was not a nice thing to say. But when I heard my own words I realized I felt very indignant. And it worked. She gasped loudly for air and leaned heavily against the wall.

'Good gracious!' Rønning exclaimed, having finally regained the power of speech and retrieved his lorgnette. But I was not to be put off my stride by him.

'We have a new statement, from a man with a PhD, no less, who witnessed the murder and has given a description that fits your client perfectly. According to him, the murderer was a dark-haired, middle-aged woman in a green winter coat,' I said, and pointed at the coat stand.

Rønning looked as though he was about to protest. But Lene Johansen looked at me and beat him to it.

'I didn't mean it to end like this. I thought that either we would be allowed to stay here a bit longer, or Tor would be looked after and have the chance of a better life than me. Yes, I ran away from the scene of the crime when I saw there was a chance that I might get away with it. My instincts kicked in. But I had never thought of laying the blame on Tor. I almost fainted in the telephone box when I heard that he'd been arrested. I thought I would confess when you came to speak to me, but then the priest got here first and told me that Tor was dead. And then I had no one to live for except me.'

Lena Johansen looked so tragic standing there, swaying. But she had first of all committed a murder, then not told the truth after her son's death, and threatened to sue me and the police. So I still felt no sympathy and saw no reason to be considerate.

'But the sheer audacity – to claim that you are innocent and demand compensation for your son's death, when you yourself were guilty . . .'

On the far left of my vision, I registered that Danielsen had paled. I looked straight at Lene Johansen, who pointed an almost accusing finger at the lawyer.

'I just wanted to crawl silently into a hole under the ground in the hope that no one would see me for the rest of my life. But then he came to my door and said that I might have rights and could perhaps get fifty or a hundred thousand in compensation. I have never got anything from society, so I felt that I owed no one anything. And fifty thousand is an incredible amount when you only have two kroner to your name and are about to be thrown out onto the street any day.'

I kept looking at Lene Johansen. I vaguely registered that Rønning, to my right, was now even paler than Danielsen. And that he had started to speak.

'I realize now in retrospect that my behaviour then may have seemed odd. However, I did all that I did in the good faith that my client and her dead son were innocent, and given certain terms and conditions, I was obliged to inform her about her rights,' he said.

I continued to ignore the lawyer, and looked straight at his client. She was leaning heavily against the wall, but still looked as though she might collapse at any minute. Her hair was grey, her eyes were red and her expression black.

I saw her other face now. And even though it was a murderer's face, it was still a face I felt sympathy for. So I said, in a slightly more conciliatory tone, 'Fredriksen had exploited you and let you down, that was why you hated him.'

She nodded; suddenly there was a spark in her eyes. 'He was my last hope and then everything fell to pieces. It was the first time for years that anyone had asked me out and given me things. He was so charming and kind then. The fact that I got pregnant was unexpected, but once he got over the surprise he was happy. He talked about getting divorced a couple of times and promised at least to look after me and my son. Everything could have been different if only Tor had not been born with that birthmark. I cried when I saw it and knew that he was my husband's son. Per Johan realized as well as soon as he came to the hospital. He pointed at the birthmark and said: "That child is not mine, so good luck with him." Then he laughed scornfully, and threw a fifty-øre coin onto the bedside table and left. He showed a very different, cruel side of himself that day. And I saw that face again at Majorstuen on Saturday, when I asked for a month's reprieve on the rent, and he laughed that same scornful laugh. It was only when he laughed that I finally decided to kill him. And he deserved no better! I may regret everything else I've done in my life, but not that!'

She almost shouted this and looked so desperately bitter now. After my experience earlier in the day, I discreetly took a couple of steps back. Rønning wiped the sweat from his brow, and also retreated a few steps, and said in a very quiet voice that it was a case of a life that had been very difficult for many years, with several mitigating circumstances.

'Believe me, I'm not a bad person, I've just done a bad thing. That is what poverty and all that comes with it can do to a person,' Lene Johansen said suddenly, with only desperation in her voice now.

I was about to say that, in the end, it was all about self-preservation, both for her and for Oda Fredriksen. But it felt wrong to compare the two, and when I looked around me, I had to acknowledge that there was some truth in what she had said about poverty. I said that it was up to the court to consider the mitigating circumstances, and that we really should go now.

I did not want to put handcuffs on Lene Johansen. And after a brief exchange of glances, nor did Danielsen. He held her by the arm to support her out of the flat, and I took with me the green winter coat. The coat stand with its three missing hooks was left naked and alone in the hall. I left the basement flat without looking back; the air felt stuffy now and a few yards behind us an old school satchel was lying on the floor of a boy's empty room. I could not face seeing it again.

IX

It was ten past four when I was let in to see Miriam at Ullevål Hospital. To my great relief, she was in her room, and was lying flat out on the bed.

I hurried in and shut the door, and as it closed, I said: 'I am so sorry that I was not here when you woke up. I had to wrap up the murder investigation and thought that it might be better if you were able to wake up and spend some time with your family first.'

I went over to the bed, bent down and gave Miriam a gentle hug. It was not the welcome I had hoped for. Her cheek was unusually cold and stiff.

I had not noticed yesterday how small the room was. It was just big enough for a bed and a chair. I sat down on the seat, a few feet away from her head on the pillow. It suddenly felt uncomfortably close, even though I had been much closer to Miriam many times before.

She finally spoke when I sat down. 'That's fine. The investigation has to come first, and I only woke up a couple of hours ago,' she said. But she said it in a serious, monotonous voice, without any trace of joy at seeing me again.

I said that I had spoken to her mother several times over the past couple of days, and asked if it was nice to see her parents and brother again.

'Yes. They were very relieved, and Mum could not praise you enough. But you should have rung Katrine. She only heard that I was all right today and was very upset about it.'

I realized that in the midst of everything else I had completely forgotten Miriam's friend – even though she had helped with the investigation. I apologized profusely, and said that yesterday I had been overcome with fear about her safety and then with relief when she came back.

Miriam's head looked so small and her face so pale against the white pillow. If she nodded, it was impossible to see. She still did not look happy. I still felt pretty miserable myself, despite all the developments in the investigation.

I carried on hastily and said that it was fantastic to have her back, and I asked how the whole experience had been and how she felt now.

She paused, and then spoke for longer than I had expected.

'I am fine now. I don't have much movement in my arms yet, but the doctor says that should be better by tomorrow and with a bit of physiotherapy, they will be as good as new. I can't really tell you much about what happened, unfortunately. I was walking along the road when I was pushed into a car with two men in it and someone put a rag over my mouth and nose, then I blacked out. I woke up with my hands tied behind my back in a basement somewhere and stayed there all day. A man in a mask came in twice. I thought he was going to kill me, but instead he fed me. Then they put a rag over my mouth and nose again, and this time I was certain I was going to die. I have blurred memories of wandering around in a street and talking to some people, but it all feels like a dream. Then I woke up here. I understood while I was sitting there in the basement, wherever it was, that it was the Soviets who had taken me and felt the hand of a dictator touch me personally. But I can't prove anything without the envelope that I got from Tatiana, and I guess that has disappeared?'

I confirmed that it had and asked her what had been in the envelope.

'A copy of the KGB file on Fredriksen, which Tatiana had risked her life to get. And a written statement where she confirmed that the agent who had arrived recently had gone out early last Saturday evening, and seemed inexplicably tense when he came back around ten. It was to be her ticket to a new life and my biggest gift to you. But that is not how it turned out.'

For a few seconds, I thought about the white envelope and what a difference it could have made. An image of Asle Bryne popped up in my mind and I wondered if he would have smiled, if I had been able to give him that evidence. But all I said was that the most important thing for me was that Miriam had survived without being harmed.

She was about to smile, but then paused and asked me to tell her what had happened after she was abducted.

So I sat on the chair by her bed and told her everything that had happened since we last spoke, leaving out Danielsen's last conversation with the boy on the red bicycle and my contact with Patricia. I thought that Miriam would have to know about it at some point, but this was perhaps not the right time.

It helped to tell her. Miriam listened intently and smiled a couple of times. But towards the end she became very serious, almost melancholic.

'The story of the boy on the red bicycle really is tragic. But it is all over and solved now,' I said, gently, at the end.

Miriam sighed. 'So Klinkalski was not the murderer after all, and the spying intrigue in fact had nothing to do with your investigation. But you would not have been able to work all this out in such a short time without the genius of Frogner. When did you contact her?' Miriam asked.

I was tempted to say that it was only in a panic when Miriam had been kidnapped. But I thought the situation was bad enough without me lying. So I told her the truth: that I had contacted her after Vera Fredriksen was murdered on Monday night, and that I had regretted bitterly not telling her then.

'It would have been better if you had told me. Hearing it now is a lot more difficult, but I guess it is something I can live with,' she said.

Everything went quiet. The room felt even smaller now.

'Hopefully there is nothing here that you could not live with?' I said, carefully.

Miriam sighed into the pillow, then took two deep breaths before she spoke.

'There is. My friend Tatiana was killed yesterday and now you tell me that no one is going to do anything about it because she was not Norwegian. I could live with all the rest, but not that.'

I immediately told her that I had questioned that as well. I told her what my boss had said when I raised the issue. I had also been very unhappy about it, but had had to accept that that was the way of the world and the situation we were in.

Miriam sighed again. Then she spoke from the pillow in a very quiet and firm voice.

'Yes, it is the way of the world and the situation we find ourselves in. So I now have to live with the fact that she was killed because of her contact with me and because she tried to help me help you with the investigation. And you have to live without me.'

She said it so calmly and so decisively. I felt as though I had been paralysed. For a moment I thought about how deeply ironic it was that our love story should end in exactly the same place that it had started only two years before: with only the two of us present in a room at Ulleval Hospital, where she was lying injured in a bed because of me.

I sat in silence for a while. Time had stopped once again. I would later find it hard to say whether it was ten seconds, a minute or five minutes. However, I remember only too well the great sorrow that I felt – but also, the relief that grew stronger and stronger.

Eventually, I said that I was incredibly sad to hear that, and that it was, of course, entirely my fault and not hers.

And that she had been caught up in something only because she was trying to help me for a second time.

Then I asked, without knowing how she would respond, if the problem was in fact Patricia more than Tatiana.

I realized my mistake as soon as I had said it. I should not have mentioned Patricia's name. Miriam gave a little jolt, as though she had been given an electric shock. But her voice was still just as controlled when she answered.

'I think that it is more to do with Tatiana, as I said. I will think of her with sorrow and guilt for the rest of my life. But naturally, your contact with the genius of Frogner is hard for me to swallow as well. I have tried so hard to do right, as a former president of the United States once said. I did everything I could to help you. And in the end the only result was that one of my friends was killed and you had to get help from the genius of Frogner to save me. I had hoped that I could be of the same help to you as she was. But I realize now that I could never take her place.'

I hastened to say that there had never been anything physical between Patricia and me – and almost bit my tongue when I realized that I had said her name again. Miriam did not react visibly to the name this time, but her reply was succinct and firm.

'I never thought there was. And I, for my part, have not had a physical relationship with anyone else since we got together. But it is not a good sign that we have to tell each other that.'

I had to admit that she was right.

For a moment I became deeply worried about what

might happen if she were to tell anyone what I had told her. But in the next moment I was certain that she would not pass it on. If I mentioned it now, she would only tell me that all my secrets were safe with her, and that it was sad that I had to ask her. So, despite all that was happening, there was still a strange unspoken trust between us.

I wanted to spare her that. So instead I said that I was very sorry for all of this and for all the terrible things she had experienced because of me. Then I asked her if there was anything more I could say or do to help her.

There was silence in the hospital room for a few seconds. Then she answered, slowly, in a slightly tremulous voice: 'As I am unfortunately unable to move my arms right now, I have to ask if you could please take off my engagement ring?'

I thought how paradoxical it was that a day that had given me so many answers, should end with such a painfully difficult question. But I answered, slowly, in a voice that was in danger of breaking, that of course I could not refuse.

Her arms lay still by her side. But they were unexpectedly tense and her fingers surprisingly warm. My hand was shaking so much that it was embarrassing. It was such a painful moment that I just wanted to throw myself down on the floor and beg not to have to do this, and say that I would give anything for her to forgive me. But I did not. Again I felt the relief when finally the ring slipped off and I no longer had to feel her hand against mine.

I took off my own ring and put it on the bedside table. She thanked me for my help, her chin barely moving on the pillow. She was not crying. But I saw that there were tears in her eyes, and could feel them in my own.

I had to turn around and was on my way out when she said: 'There is just one little thing I would like to ask.'

'What is it?' I stopped in my tracks, without turning around.

'What happened to the library book?' she said.

I told her that I had picked the book up out of the ditch, and that it was in safekeeping at the police station, and that I could either post it to her or come by with it one day.

'Thank you. I think it would be best to post it, if it's not too expensive,' she whispered.

That felt like the final, decisive blow. Suddenly I could not bear to see Miriam any longer, and did not want to hear her voice again. But I could not leave the room and let our final words after two years be about a library book.

So I said, without turning: 'Please give my best wishes to your parents. Thank you for everything. I will never forget you.'

'Thank you. Likewise,' she said, almost inaudibly.

It was only three words, and her voice was barely a whisper, but I could hear that she was crying now. I felt the tears on my own cheeks, but I did not want to see her crying. And I did not want her to see my tears.

So I left, alone, without looking back.

It was no more than ten yards from her room to the stairs. But it felt like I had walked for miles. When I got to the staircase it felt like I tumbled all the way down it, even though I could see my legs moving as normal, taking each step at a time, down the endless stairs.

X

It was raining when I got home. And it continued to rain. From half past five until half past six, I just stood by the window and watched the downpour.

I had several telephone calls to make. I should have rung Ane Line Fredriksen to tell her who had killed her father the Saturday before; I should have rung Hauk Rebne West-gaard to tell him what had happened that spring day in 1932 and to finally give him peace, and I should have rung my parents to tell them about my broken engagement. But even though I did not like the silence, I could not bear to hear another voice at the moment.

I tried instead to put on a record, but it didn't help. The first song was 'Days of My Life' by The Seekers. I stood there until the chorus faded out, turned the record player off when the voice of the female vocalist disappeared, and just stayed standing by the window.

At a quarter past nine that Saturday evening, it would be exactly a week since I had stood here and seen the boy on the red bicycle pedalling furiously up the hill. It felt like an age ago. The boy was dead and would be buried within the next few days. His bicycle was being held in the police stores, and would never go out on the road again. Three other people had lost their lives this week, and my life would never be the same again.

I knew that the rain would stop, and on Monday the papers would be singing my praises louder than ever before. But I was far more miserable now than I had been a week ago. Only three days before, I had stood here and watched Miriam leave in her raincoat, with the library book under her arm, without knowing that it would be the last time I watched her leave. The tears stung in my eyes when I thought that I would never again see her coming up towards the house.

Among all the other happy memories of my two short years with Miriam, I remembered the evening we went to the theatre to see *A Doll's House*. It had been Miriam's suggestion, and I had dutifully said yes after a long working week. But it had been an unusually good Saturday evening. On the way home I had said how glad I was that we had gone, and that we should not wait too long to go to the theatre again. She had not answered, just smiled her charming, happy, lopsided smile. But I had never done anything about it – never suggested another play.

And now it was too late for trips to the theatre. And although it was I who had physically walked away that day, it felt like it was she who had done the walking. I felt that she had left the man she thought she loved, just like Nora, because he still did not understand what was important to her. I felt like Helmer, as I had seen him in that final act. And it was not a nice feeling.

At a quarter to seven, I remembered a quote that the now accused murderer, Oda Fredriksen, had used after her husband had died. 'The life we shared is over, I walk on alone – but I am still walking.'

I stood there and reflected on the quote for a few minutes. Then the silence became unbearable. I grabbed my jacket and went out into the rain.

XI

There were no other cars parked outside.

If I had seen a van there, I would have turned round immediately and fled. But there was no one. So I went up to the door and rang the bell.

The maid answered surprisingly quickly; I had only counted to twelve by the time the door opened.

I said that I did not want to disturb the owner of the house if she had visitors, but that I would be grateful to talk to her if she was alone.

The maid smiled to herself and said that I had been expected. The owner of the house was at home and did not have visitors.

This was encouraging, but even so I could not remember ever having arrived here feeling quite so anxious or with quite such a hammering heart.

She was sitting alone in her wheelchair, and her smile had an air of condescension when I came into the room.

'You are a little later than expected. I guessed half past six to Benedicte,' she said, cheerfully.

The maid nodded to confirm this and then withdrew.

'Sorry that I am a bit late,' I said with an uncertain smile, and put my hands on the table. Patricia looked at them, then nodded briefly without saying anything.

I had no idea what to say. So I told her quickly about my meeting with Lene Johansen. The story upset me and I could see that it upset Patricia too, although there were no cigarettes on the table for her to puff on. I made it as brief as possible and once again thanked her for having seen the solution.

'I never doubted it. But thank you for your thanks all the same,' she said with a coy smile.

This annoyed me and I added that I had discovered, on my own, how the police security service had found out about Fredriksen. And I told her about my visit to Harriet Henriksen.

Patricia looked rather peeved to begin with, but then started to smile towards the end.

'I had not thought about that. You were lucky there, I think. Congratulations all the same!'

I asked in passing if Patricia had ever considered that Harriet Henriksen might be the murderer.

Patricia shook her head. 'And I hope that you didn't either. It would barely have been possible for her to stay where she was when Fredriksen left and then to get past him unseen, and wait for him on a street corner a few hundred yards further on.'

I said that I agreed and moved swiftly on.

'You certainly made a good point about chameleon people. And there were a lot of them involved in this case. When you said that there was only one of the five friends from 1932 who was not a chameleon person, you were thinking of Kjell Arne Ramdal, weren't you?'

Patricia nodded. 'Yes, of course. Some were of course more dangerous, but all the others were chameleons with several faces. But it would seem Kjell Arne Ramdal only has one face and is what he appears to be. He is himself and probably very decent – if not particularly charming or attractive.'

I was not sure whether I dared to say what I was thinking. But it was as if Patricia read my mind and came to my aid.

'Not a very exciting man to be married to, I am sure. But Solveig Ramdal found that out a long time ago.'

I took the plunge and asked if she had ever considered that Johan Fredriksen was in many ways more like Kjell Arne Ramdal than his father.

Patricia smiled cheerfully, and then burst into laughter.

'Yes, it has occurred to me. And that was one of the reasons why I broke up with him on Thursday night. Which is also why I may have looked rather grim when I passed you. The mood in the car had become rather sour.'

The relief went straight to my head when I heard this. And I dared to ask if there were other reasons why she had broken off the relationship.

She nodded and shook her head at the same time. 'The short version is that I had been sitting here alone for far too long, and at the beginning thought that Johan Fredriksen looked like my dream man, but soon discovered that he only looked like him. I do not regret the relationship, but nor do I regret finishing it.'

I put my hands on the table again, to be sure that Patricia had understood. She glanced at them again, and nodded impatiently.

'Kidnappings can be difficult,' I said slowly, testing the water.

Patricia nodded and replied without mirroring my speed and caution.

'No doubt about it. And by the way, I did not want to pick bones when you were in the middle of it, but the police really must learn to use the word abduction. Kidnapping should only be used about children for obvious reasons, and this was your ex-fiancée, although at times she was as naive as a child.'

Miriam was in fact three years older than Patricia. But I took the hint. Patricia did not want to hear her name or to talk any more about my ex-fiancée – at least, not now. I was a little unsure as to whether she wanted to say anything more about her ex, but hoped she would not.

So I said: 'Well, that was quite a case. With our combined efforts, we managed to solve all the murders and both lose our partners along the way.'

Patricia yawned and stretched her arms demonstratively. 'Ah well, the case was exceptionally interesting, if also exceptionally tragic. And as far as partners are concerned, I for my part think that when a relationship cannot weather a stormy week, then it is not going to last in the long run. So better to discover it now than in ten years' time, with two children. So, with a bit of humour, you could say that we have unearthed the truth about four murders and two relationships.'

She looked at me with her head cocked as she said this, her eyes curious.

Miriam's face flashed in front of me, and I was not entirely sure that I saw it in the same way as Patricia did. But I got the point and laughed out loud.

'I could kick the staff into action, if you would like to stay for supper,' Patricia said, happily.

I sat there for a few seconds and wondered if she had used 'kick' figuratively or not. But whatever the case, I had decided.

So I said that I thought that her staff deserved the night off, and we deserved to go out for a meal, having worked our way through four murders and two relationships so far this week. And as I had had so many good meals here, I would be delighted to be able to repay her.

I felt my heart beating even faster when I said this.

'That,' Patricia said with her most provocative smile, 'is the best suggestion you have made for as long as I have known you.'

Afterword

When I first let Detective Inspector Kolbjørn 'K2' Kristiansen meet Patricia Louise I. E. Borchmann, the professor's young daughter, in the novel *The Human Flies* in autumn 2010, I had an inkling that they would meet again during later murder investigations. But I had no clear plans for any other novels in the series, and certainly no hopes that the series would be extended by a further four books in the space of three years. But that is in fact what has happened, as I now send *Chameleon People* to print in June 2013. I look forward to hearing what the critics and readers have to say about it, but whatever it may be, I have been astounded by the interest that has been shown in my attempt to revive the historical and classic crime novel in Norwegian. A total of two hundred thousand copies have been printed of the first four books in the series, and as I write this Afterword, the first novels are being translated into English, Italian and Korean.

Inspired by this unexpected success, the ideas for new novels have so far come very fast and easily. In 2011 and 2012, when the latest book about K2 and Patricia went to print, I was already busy writing the next one. But that is not the case now in 2013. My aim has always been to write exciting crime novels that are not simply thrillers, and as part of this, there is a developing relationship between the two protagonists. This book ends with them solving another murder case, but also with some dramatic events in their personal lives. And it feels like both the protagonists and the author need a rest to think about the way forward.

I believe it is more than likely that I will write more books in the series, but think that it is highly unlikely there will be another book before 2015, at the earliest. The ideas that I have at the moment are still far too unformed to keep the standard that I want for the books in this series. It is now time to find out whether I am only able to write books for this series with plots from the 1960s and 1970s, or if, as a literary author, I can also work with other types of novel from other periods. For some time now, I have had ideas for three other novels, with very different protagonists and set in different times, which I hope to realize within the next couple of years. The first, which is called *The House by the Sea*, is set in contemporary Northern Norway, and is due to be published already in late autumn this year.

As *Chameleon People* may be the last book in the series for a while, it is all the more important to thank all my excellent advisors for their work.

My most important advisor in Cappelen Damm has once again been my ever constructive and dedicated editor, Anne Fløtaker, who has been of invaluable importance to my literary career. I also owe a huge thanks to my critical expert advisor, Nils Nordberg, and my loyal proofreader, Sverre Dalin. Both have been observant and alert to all kinds of historical factual errors.

Amongst my personal advisors, my greatest thanks for this book, and all the others in the series, go to my linguistically gifted and reflective young friend, Mina Finstad Berg. Despite working long days in her new post as general secretary of the Socialist Youth League of Norway, she has found time to give me extensive comments on both the idea and the finished manuscript. I also owe Mina enormous thanks for lending her highly personal traits to the fictional character, Miriam Filtvedt Bentsen, who became a challenging third character in books three, four and five of the series. It remains to be seen whether Miriam's goodbye with K2 at the end of this novel will also be her final farewell in the series. I am so grateful to Mina for letting me use her fictional alter ego in any future novels as well, without demanding that Miriam must appear if she is to continue as my advisor.

I have also received valuable comments on the language and content from my good and ever helpful friends: Ingrid Baukhol, Marit Lang-Ree Finstad and Arne Tjølsen. And I must also thank the following people for longer and shorter comments on the manuscript: Roar Annerløv, Lene Di Dragland, Silje Flesvik, Anne Lise Fredlund, Kristine Amalie Myhre Gjesdal, Gro Helene Gulbrandsen, Else Marit Hatledal, Hanne Isaksen, Kristine Joramo, Eva Kosberg, Bjarte Leer-Salvesen, Torstein Lerhol, Espen Lie, Turid Lilleøren, Katrine Tjølsen and Magnhild K. B. Uglem.

Marit appears in my novel in a minor role as Miriam's mother, and Anne Lise and Eva appear as Ane Line Fredriksen and Eveline Kolberg. On this and a few earlier occasions where I have used my living friends as models for fictional characters, I have been very careful to get permission from my friends first and to ensure that the fictional characters' actions have no parallel to events in real life. My responsibility and challenge has been to imagine how my good friends would react if they were transported forty years back in time, to be then dropped into a fictional murder investigation at an important time in Norway's history.

Nor have the dead people I have taken the liberty to use as models for characters in this novel ever found themselves – as far as I know – in any directly comparable situations. They appear here as figures and personalities typical of the time rather than as historical persons. For people who are familiar with Norwegian history, the prime minister in this novel will hopefully have recognizable traits similar to those of the man who was the prime minister of Norway in the spring of 1972. On the other hand, the head of the police security service in this novel has many more similarities with the man who resigned as Head of the Police Security Services in dramatic circumstances some years earlier, rather than the man who held the position in 1972.

And finally, as international politics, in particular, play a far more important role here than in any of the previous books in the series, it is important to underline that the events in this book are fictitious products of the author's imagination. The Cold War and international politics in general had a far greater impact on Norway in the 1970s than previously. The most dramatic incident perhaps was when another country's security service carried out an execution on a street in my home county of Oppland in 1973, the year that I was born. The action in this book takes place in Oslo in 1972 and is in no way linked to the historical event in Lillehammer in 1973. Nor does it build on authentic events or characters in the foreign embassy written about in this book. In the spring of 1972, oil extraction had just started in Norway and Statoil was in its infancy. However, Norway's negotiations with the Soviet Union regarding the demarcation line in the Barents Sea did not start until later in the 1970s, and the parties never came as close to an agreement as they do in this novel.

Readers who wish to send comments to the author about this book, or any of the previous novels in the series, can send them to my email address: hansolahlum@gmail.com.

Hans Olav Lahlum
Gjøvik, 16 June 2013

Looking back on my afterword from 2013, I have to admit that my planning for the next years turned out to be very unreliable. True enough, I did publish *The House By the Sea* later in 2013, but that teen novel is still the only book I've completed that doesn't feature K2 and Patricia (instead, it stars K2's grandnephew and his girlfriend, trying to understand their relationship while solving a murder mystery in a small village on the coast of northern Norway in 2012). But I then completed a fifth novel about K2 and Patricia in 2014, a sixth in 2015 and a seventh in 2016.

English readers interested to follow K2 and Patricia beyond the end of this novel will get the chance to do so in 2017 and 2018, although in 2017 I will write a different novel from a different era and with very different main characters, and it will be in Norwegian. I am very happy and thankful that Mantle will publish three more novels in the series, and would like to thank everyone at Mantle for their help. I would also like to take this opportunity to thank my English-speaking readers in various countries for all the comments they have sent me.

The first chapters of this novel refers briefly to the fourth, fifth and sixth cases with K2 and Patricia. These are all short stories from my 2012 Norwegian book *De fem fyrstikkene* (*The Five Matches*), which is not available in English. Rest assured that I looked over the text and made sure the reader would have no problems whatsoever jumping over these three stories, from the third novel taking place in 1970 to this fourth one in 1972.

Twice in the text of *Chameleon People*, a biography of the UK's former Foreign Secretary, Ernest Bevin (1881–1951), is mentioned. This is volume one of Alan Bullock's *The Life and Times of Ernest Bevin*, first published in 1960. Also twice mentioned in this novel is a quote from an American writer about continuing with life after the death of her husband. The mystery writer is Mary Roberts Rhinehart (1876–1958), still known worldwide for her legendary (and still very funny) novel *The Circular Staircase* (1908). The exact words from the 1948 edition of her autobiography, *My Story*, are 'The shared life is gone. Hereafter you walk alone, but you do walk.' In her final appearance in this novel, Miriam Filtvedt Bentsen quotes a former US President – 'I have tried so hard to do right'. These were the final words of Grover Cleveland (1837–1908), who was president from 1885–89 and from 1893–97.

Chameleon People makes several references to Dutchman Marinus van der Lubbe (1909–34) and German-American Bruno Richard Hauptmann (1899–1936). The characters in the novel consider both men innocent of the crimes of which they were convicted and were executed for. In the Sixties, Seventies and Eighties, van der Lubbe and Hauptmann were often listed in articles and books about wrongful convictions. Later research has more or less concluded that van der Lubbe *did* start the Reichstag fire in 1933, although his trial was a farce and circumstances (including the possible involvement of Hermann Göring and the Nazi Party) remain somewhat unclear. This is the conclusion drawn in Ian Kershaw's excellent biography *Hitler* (2008). In the case of Bruno Hauptmann, it seems clear that the ladder used for the Lindbergh kidnapping in 1932 came from his garage, but it remains disputed whether Hauptmann himself was guilty of the kidnapping and/or the subsequent murder. For a fairly balanced take on this complex and fascinating case, I recommend Richard T. Cahill's book *Hauptmann's Ladder: A Step-by-Step Analysis of the Lindbergh Kidnapping* (2014).

Hans Olav Lahlum
Gjøvik, 25 June 2016

www.panmacmillan.com